"Maya Banks writes the k___ of books I love to read!"
—Lora Leigh, #1 N___ *York Times* bestselling author
of *Secret Sins*

Praise for the novels of Maya Banks

ECHOES AT DAWN

"Quick-paced, high-stakes action and plenty of smoldering explicit sex deliver a satisfying one-two punch of entertainment that will leave readers eager for the next book."
—*Publishers Weekly*

"Incredible. Just beyond incredible and amazing. That's how I feel about *Echoes at Dawn*." —*Romance Books Forum*

"I loved *Echoes at Dawn*, and yes it is now my new favorite . . . a must-read for romantic suspense fans."
—*Sizzling Hot Books*

WHISPERS IN THE DARK

"A must-read for . . . Christine Feehan and Lora Leigh fans. The nonstop action and sensuality is a treat not to be missed. I can't wait for the next installment of the KGI series."
—*Fresh Fiction*

"A deeply emotional, highly satisfying, edge-of-your-seat read . . . Compelling and cutting-edge romance."
—*Joyfully Reviewed*

"Maya—FREAKING—Banks . . . can do it all. Absolutely nothing is out of this author's reach." —*RT Book Reviews*

continued . . .

"You'll be on the edge of your seat with this one . . . and it's so worth the ride." —*Night Owl Reviews*

HIDDEN AWAY

"If I ever wanted to be adopted into a fictional family, it would be the Kellys . . . I am devoted to the Kelly brothers." —*Fiction Vixen Book Reviews*

"[An] action-packed story." —*The Mystery Gazette*

NO PLACE TO RUN

"Fast action is the name of the game . . . If you're looking for a sexual, sensual, romantic suspense story, look no further." —*Night Owl Reviews*

"Great twists and turns." —*CK²S Kwips and Kritiques*

THE DARKEST HOUR

"An intriguing mix of military action and sizzling romance." —*Publishers Weekly*

"Suspenseful, sinfully sensuous and straight-up awesome." —*Joyfully Reviewed*

"Wrought with a sensual tension." —*Romance Junkies*

AFTER
THE STORM

MAYA BANKS

BERKLEY BOOKS, NEW YORK

THE BERKLEY PUBLISHING GROUP
Published by the Penguin Group
Penguin Group (USA) LLC
375 Hudson Street, New York, New York 10014

USA • Canada • UK • Ireland • Australia • New Zealand • India • South Africa • China

penguin.com

A Penguin Random House Company

AFTER THE STORM

A Berkley Book / published by arrangement with the author

For information, address: The Berkley Publishing Group,
a division of Penguin Group (USA) LLC,
375 Hudson Street, New York, New York 10014.

ISBN: 978-0-425-26377-8

PUBLISHING HISTORY
Berkley mass-market edition / January 2014

PRINTED IN THE UNITED STATES OF AMERICA

10 9 8 7 6 5 4 3 2 1

Cover art by Craig White.
Cover design by Rita Frangie.
Interior text design by Laura K. Corless.

*To everyone who has waited patiently
for Donovan's story to be told.*

*I hope it was everything you hoped for,
and that the wait was worth it.*

CHAPTER 1

RUSTY sighed and wondered again if she'd done the right thing in hiring the kid part time. They didn't need the help in the store. Frank kept busy despite objections from the family about overdoing it after his heart attack a few years earlier. Rusty helped out when she was home from school, and there were any number of Kellys willing to drop everything and help anytime they were needed.

And yet . . . She hadn't been able to refuse the kid. Maybe it was the quiet desperation in his eyes. It was a look—and a feeling—she was well acquainted with.

"But by the grace of God—and the Kellys—go I," she murmured, a half smile curving her lips upward.

There was little doubt she'd still be in a run-down trailer living with her shithead of a stepfather, scratching out a hand-to-mouth existence, if Marlene Kelly hadn't taken Rusty in. Oh, she wouldn't still be with her stepfather. She would have run away. Eventually. And she'd likely be on the streets somewhere. Prostituting herself just to survive.

A shiver overtook her as long-suppressed memories crowded to the surface. Painful, humiliating memories. Marlene Kelly was a saint. An angel's angel. Rusty thanked God for her and Frank every single day.

Because of them, she was in university. She'd graduate in a year's time! With a degree. A life. Prospects! All the things she'd never imagined having. But the best part of it all?

She had a *family*. An honest-to-goodness, huge, loyal, fiercely loving family. She was a Kelly. Marlene and Frank had even hired a lawyer so Rusty could legally change her name. She'd been reissued a birth certificate and social security card and everything. Rusty Kelly.

Oh, her first name sounded corny and awful with the last name of Kelly. But then she'd had a perfectly normal, mundane name of Barnes before it had been legally changed. Marlene had wanted to adopt her, even though Rusty had already been a legal adult. She didn't want anything to make Rusty feel as though she weren't truly a part of the Kelly clan.

But it hadn't been necessary. Just knowing she was loved and accepted by all of the Kellys—big-ass surly, overprotective brothers and all—was enough for Rusty. That she could go to school and be known as Rusty Kelly still overwhelmed her, and, at times, remembering caught her off guard and she verged precariously on tears. And she'd sworn never to cry again. She left that life behind. All the pain and embarrassment that she'd lived with for the first fifteen years of her existence.

Gone the moment Marlene tenderly enfolded her in the blanket of the Kelly name.

Rusty sighed as she glanced down the aisle at Travis Hanson—if that was even his real name—and wondered again what she'd gotten herself into.

He was the same age as Rusty had been when she'd broken into the Kelly house wanting nothing more than something to eat. He had the same darkness in his eyes. Sadness. But worst of all . . . fear.

As if sensing her scrutiny, Travis looked up from where he was stocking shelves, and unease registered. Poor kid was absolutely inept at keeping his emotions from being broadcast all over his face. That told her that he wasn't experienced, and so whatever had brought him into this store and put that fear in his eyes was recent.

"Is there something wrong?" he asked in a quiet voice.

He might be fifteen—that was what he'd told her—but he looked a lifetime older. He was much taller than most fifteen-year-old boys. Muscled. Filled out. Not as gangly as so many other boys his age were. He'd aged fast. Grown up. Was old beyond his years.

It was something Rusty could definitely relate to because she'd been forced to grow up when she was only ten years old. For that matter, when had she ever truly been a child?

"Nothing at all," Rusty said cheerfully, hoping she wasn't being as obvious as the kid was about her uncertainty. "Was just thinking that after you finish that shelf we could have lunch. There's a sandwich shop just a few doors down. You hungry?"

The instant flare in his eyes told her that he was indeed hungry. She wondered when his last good meal had been. But she didn't want to ask because he'd probably just run.

"I, uh, left my wallet at home," he stammered. "But I can pay you back tomorrow. That is, if you want me to come in."

Rusty grimaced. Frank didn't open the hardware store on Sundays. That was church and family day. But Travis didn't need to know that Frank would have a fit if any of his employees worked on Sunday. Rusty had already decided she'd pay the kid cash under the table from her own pocket if she had to.

"We stock on Sundays," she said, hoping God would forgive her for that blatant lie. "Store's not open, but I could definitely use you for a few hours in the morning if you can come in."

Relief washed through his eyes and his shoulders sagged. "Sure. No problem. I can come in at eight and stay as long as you need me."

Rusty took a chance and watched his reaction closely. "Sure your mom won't mind that? I mean, most folks around here go to church and spend time with their family. I'd hate to lose a good employee because your mom was upset over you working."

His expression became tight, his eyes impassive, but they flickered just once as he replied.

"I don't have a mother. My sister takes care of me and my younger sister. I like to help out. Eve—I mean she—works too hard. She won't mind if I work a few hours. We could use the money."

Rusty tucked that bit of info away and quickly moved on. Travis was extremely uncomfortable and she didn't want to risk him bolting. Not that she was sure why it mattered. Hell, it would probably be better if the kid didn't hang around too long because when Frank found out what Rusty had done, he'd probably wonder if she'd lost her mind.

"Okay, then. What would you like to eat? They have a great club sandwich. But they also serve up a pretty mean choke-and-puke burger. A boy your size probably needs the protein."

Travis grinned. Just a brief smile that erased some of the shadows in his eyes. But just as quickly it faded, leaving a much-too-old-for-his-age man staring back at her.

"Choke-and-puke?"

She laughed. "Yeah. It's a good thing, though. It's what my brothers call a really good burger with lots of grease and cheese. Homemade. Not the processed crap you get at fast-food restaurants. Around here, home cooking is a matter of pride. How's a good choke-and-puke bacon cheeseburger grab you? And it's my treat. It's the least I can do to thank you for taking so much work off my shoulders."

"That sounds great," he admitted. "And thanks, Rusty. For everything, I mean. This means a lot to me and my sisters."

It was so tempting to grab him and squeeze. To hug him and tell him everything would be all right. But she resisted because she knew that when she was his age, such a move would spook her. It had taken Rusty a long time to realize that not everyone in the world was out to hurt her. And that love was unconditional and given freely. No strings. No repercussions.

But her heart ached for him. She knew what it was like to be afraid. To go hungry. To have far too much responsibility for someone so young. Thank God for Marlene and Frank Kelly. Thank God for them all.

"Hey, no sweat, kid. Like I said, if it wasn't you stocking all this stuff it would be me. Frank puts in way too many hours as it is. He had a heart attack a few years ago, and his wife stays after him to take it easy. But he's stubborn as a Missouri mule, and so we try to make sure he doesn't overdo it. You're doing me a huge favor."

He grinned and then went back to pulling out tools from the box on the floor, carefully arranging them in their respective places.

With a sigh, Rusty turned away and checked her watch. Frank wasn't due in until two. It had taken a lot of arguing on her part to convince him that she was perfectly capable of managing the store until he came in to work from two to closing time at six. By then she would have fed the kid, paid him cash and sent him on his way, and Frank would be none the wiser. Hopefully.

When she got back up to the front of the store, she went behind the counter to get her purse. If she called in the order ahead of time she wouldn't be gone but a few minutes. She didn't like leaving the kid, but the cash register would be locked and she'd lock the door on her way out and flip up the "Closed" sign. She'd be back in a flash.

After phoning her order in, she hoisted her purse over her shoulder and headed for the door after calling back to Travis that she'd be back in five. She nearly collided with a male body on her way out and pulled up, barely able to stifle the curse that blistered her lips. Marlene was forever trying to make a lady of her.

But when she saw who had nearly run her over, she promptly regretted calling back the obscenities.

Sean Cameron stood in front of her, his gaze narrowed as he stared back at her.

"What now, Sean?" she asked in exasperation. The cop had always rubbed her the wrong way.

"Who's the new employee?" Sean demanded. "Frank didn't say anything about hiring someone new."

Rusty sighed. There was nothing new about Sean breathing down her neck. Life in a small town definitely had its drawbacks. The kid hadn't been here but two hours and already super cop was coming to check on him.

"I didn't realize you moonlighted as Frank's HR manager," she said dryly.

His frown deepened. Not that that was anything new for her. Sean lived in disapproval of her. It was like he was just waiting for her to fuck up so he could run her out of town and out of the Kellys' lives.

"Cut the crap, Rusty."

She scowled at him, her patience snapping. "Really, Sean? Can't you be a little more original with your insults? We've known each other how long now? Five years? And yet that's your standard reply any time we're in hearing distance of one another. 'Cut the crap, Rusty.'"

She shook her head.

"Now if you'll excuse me, I have lunch to pick up and then I have work to do. I'm sure you have something more important to do than to be looking over my shoulder every minute of the day."

Sean scowled back. "Who's the kid, Rusty?"

"If you want to interrogate me, then you'll have to come with me to pick up lunch for me and 'the kid,' as you labeled him." She'd referred to him as "the kid" too, but not as derisively as Sean had put it.

And then another thought occurred to her. One that had her locking the door as she shoved past Sean. She turned the key, ensuring that he wouldn't get in while she was gone, and then she whirled, finger up as she leveled it at Sean.

"And you stay away from the kid. Got it? He's none of your business. You don't speak to him and you damn sure don't interrogate him. I can take your shit. God knows I've been dealing with it for years. But you leave him the fuck alone or I swear to God I'll make your life miserable."

Sean's eyes flickered, and for a moment she thought she saw actual regret.

"What's his story?" Sean asked quietly.

Rusty took off in the direction of the sandwich shop, knowing that Sean would follow along. He was too stubborn to just let stuff go. He'd want to hear the kid's life history before he backed off.

"He's a kid who desperately needs a job and money," she said as they walked down the sidewalk.

"And let me guess. Frank doesn't know you've hired him," Sean said.

Rusty shook her head. Sean cursed beside her.

Rusty paused at the door to the sandwich store and stared hard up at Sean. She always felt smaller around him, but then the beating force of his disapproval could weigh down even the biggest person.

"No, he doesn't. Yet," she amended. "I have no intention of keeping it from him. Contrary to what you may think, I love Frank and Marlene. I'd never do anything to hurt them. He just came in today. He's hungry and broke, and he has sisters to support. And don't worry, Sean. I'm paying him out of my own money. Not that it's much. But I figure anything will be better than nothing and it's a safe job. At least here I can look out for him."

Sean's eyes softened, and for a moment he remained silent.

"Look, Sean," Rusty said, hating how entreating she sounded. Like she needed his goddamn blessing. She sucked in a deep breath before she continued. "He's me when I was that age. He's where I could still be if it weren't for Frank and Marlene and the rest of the Kellys. He needs help and I can give it to him. Just like no one until the Kellys was ever willing to give me. So back off, okay? I know it grates on you for me to ask you to trust me, but do you think you can set aside your personal dislike of me long enough to give me a chance here? I'm not stupid. I can help this kid and I'm going to do it with or without your blessing."

Something that looked remarkably like regret flickered in Sean's steady gaze.

"I don't dislike you," he said softly.

She snorted.

"Just be careful," he warned. "I'm not saying this to piss

you off. But damn it, Rusty. Be careful. What do you even know about him? I don't like you being alone with him in the store. What if he tried to rob you? Or hurt you?"

She laughed. "The day I can't defend myself against a fifteen-year-old kid is the day I go to my grave. I'm tough, Sean. I've had to be, growing up the way I did. The last few years with the Kellys may have softened me, but I'm still on my own at school, and believe me when I say that school is not a cakewalk. I take self-defense classes. I can take care of myself."

Sean's eyes narrowed. "What the fuck does that mean? What happened at school? Did someone mess with you?"

She rolled her eyes. "Nothing I can't take care of myself."

He wiped a hand through his short hair and blew out his breath. "Damn it, Rusty. Would it kill you to ever ask for help? Just once?"

She blinked in surprise. "And what would happen if I were to ever ask you for help?"

"I'd give it," he said quietly. "You think I hate you, but that's not true, Rusty, and if you ever actually lowered your hackles around me you'd realize that I only want to make sure you're safe."

She had no idea what to say to that.

"I'll go," Sean said. "But I'm going to be keeping an eye on the kid. If you have any trouble at all, you call me. If you even *think* there will be trouble, you call me. And if you need anything, let me know. If the kid is into any trouble, let me know. There may be a way to help him."

She was so surprised that she couldn't do anything more than nod.

As Sean stalked away, she stared in bewilderment after him.

He actually acted like he . . . *cared.*

CHAPTER 2

EVE looked up from the tattered, worn couch where Cammie was finally sleeping, sprawled across Eve's lap when Travis walked in the door of the dilapidated one-bedroom trailer they rented.

"Is she any better?" Travis asked anxiously as he walked over to the couch.

Eve ran a hand over Cammie's forehead, a motion she'd repeated several times over the last hours.

"Her fever is down a little," Eve said in a low voice. "I'm so worried. We can't take her to the hospital or even a doctor. It's too risky. But I can't get her fever to break no matter what I do."

Travis's expression darkened with the same worry and fatigue Eve felt herself. Then he reached into his pocket and pulled out three twenty-dollar bills.

"I know it's not much," he said. "But I'm going in tomorrow morning for a few hours too. The lady who hired me is really nice. She even bought me lunch."

Eve took the money, tears burning her eyelids. She swallowed hard, determined to remain strong and not allow Travis to see how scared and worried she was. But he knew.

"I hate that you have to work," she said fiercely. "As soon as Cammie is better, I'll find work. I promise."

Travis's nostrils flared. "No. Cammie needs you. I'll do whatever I can. If I can't get in enough hours at the hardware store, I'll find something else. I don't want you to worry, Evie. I'll take care of us. I swear it."

Eve patted the space on the couch beside her and then wrapped an arm around her younger brother when he sat.

"I love you. We'll get through this, Trav. I promise. We'll find a way to stay together and be safe."

He hugged her back, holding and squeezing, offering her the comfort she offered him.

"We'll make it, Evie. We'll never have to go back to that bastard. I'll protect you and Cammie both. I won't let him hurt you again."

Eve cupped his cheek, feeling the slight bristle of the first growth of beard on his jaw. He was so young. Far too young to be saddled with so much responsibility. It should be her taking care of Travis and Cammie. She should have never left them with their father. It was a decision she'd regret for the rest of her life, even though she'd had no other choice. But thank God, she'd gotten them out when she did. Before Walt Breckenridge could act on his sick fantasies.

It had been bad enough that he'd put the moves on Eve after her mother died, but when he'd turned his attention on Cammie . . . Sweet, darling four-year-old Cammie. Eve shuddered, sick at heart, nausea rolling in her stomach when she imagined Cammie's father trying to molest her.

She wished she had killed him. That she'd found a way to kill him. She would have gladly gone to jail for the rest of her life if it meant Cammie and Travis were safe. They'd been lucky to escape with their own lives. But Eve wasn't a fool. Walt wouldn't give up so easily.

Already she was a wanted woman. Walt had filed kidnapping charges and had painted Eve as an emotionally unstable person who needed constant supervision and psychiatric care.

No one would believe Eve. Because Walt was wealthy. He wielded a lot of power and influence. He had far-reaching connections that ensured he could get away with murder. He *had* gotten away with murder.

Dover, Tennessee, seemed a lifetime away from where they'd fled from the West Coast. It was a small, quiet town nestled close to Kentucky Lake. It was here she'd sought refuge after running for the last several months. She hadn't intended to stay even this long, but Cammie was sick and they needed money. And a plan. Where to go next. What to do. How to survive.

She couldn't afford to let her guard down even for a minute. No matter how safe it seemed here, how secluded and out of the way, she couldn't depend on not being found here. Which meant that she needed to keep moving.

It was no way to live. It wasn't the life she wanted for her siblings. She wanted better for them. Wanted Cammie to have all the things a normal four-year-old should. And Travis . . . He needed to be in school. He excelled. Made good grades. Was a natural-born athlete. He could easily get an academic or athletic scholarship. But that was now impossible. She couldn't put him in school, and she hadn't the tools or the knowledge to homeschool him.

One day. It was a vow she made on a daily basis. One day they'd have a normal existence and Travis would have the education he deserved and Cammie would grow up a happy, secure child not having to worry that her own father would abuse her.

"Evie, are you okay?"

Travis's worried question shook her from her thoughts. She glanced up to see that he was staring intently at her. It was obvious he'd said something to her before that she'd missed, being so deep in her thoughts. She forced a smile and nodded.

"I'm fine, Trav. And the money will help. I need to buy more medicine for Cammie and we need food. As soon as she is better, I'll be more comfortable leaving her with you so I can work. I don't want you working so much. You need to be exposed as little as possible."

"You're the one who's wanted," Travis said fiercely. "It's you who should stay out of sight. They wouldn't arrest me. They'd just try to return me to that asshole. If they catch you, you'll go to jail. I won't let that happen."

She smiled again, stroking a hand over Cammie's hot, dry cheek. Cammie stirred slightly and then opened bleary, fever-dulled eyes.

"Trav?" she asked sleepily.

Travis's entire expression softened. "I'm here. How are you feeling?"

"Better now that you and Evie are both here. I don't like it when you go away."

Eve and Travis exchanged stricken looks. Cammie was deathly afraid of being separated from Eve and Travis. It broke Eve's heart that this child had so much to fear in life. That someone who should have taken absolute care of her had betrayed her in the worst way.

"I had to work," Travis said in a gentle tone. "We need money so we can get you medicine to make you better. And food! How does a hot meal sound to you? Maybe some soup?"

Cammie wrinkled her nose. "I'm tired of soup."

Eve's chest tightened. Soup was all they could afford. They existed on cheap foods. Ramen noodles. Canned soups. Sandwich meat and bread.

"Tell you what," Travis said, leaning over Eve so Cammie could better see him. "I'm working again tomorrow and there's this really great sandwich shop just a few doors down. If you're feeling up to a solid meal, I'll bring you home a burger tomorrow. They're really good. I had one today."

Cammie's face lit up. "That sounds yummy. Thanks, Trav."

"You're welcome. Now I want you to rest and get better, okay?"

Cammie nodded and closed her eyes, snuggling more firmly into Eve's side.

"Do you want me to go out and get her medicine?" Travis asked in a low voice.

"Yes. We need acetaminophen and ibuprofen. I've been alternating between the two. And she needs something for her cough. Maybe some liquid cold medicine. Get the off brand. Whatever is cheapest. We have enough food to last until tomorrow. After you come home from work, I'll run out and get some food while you stay with Cammie. For now, just get the medicine from the pharmacy and come right back."

Travis nodded and then squeezed Eve's hand. "It's going to be okay, Evie."

She squeezed back, praying with her entire heart that she wasn't lying. "I know it will."

CHAPTER 3

DONOVAN Kelly glanced over at his dad's hardware store as he drove by. It was a habit all his brothers had of taking a look when they were in the area just to make sure everything was as it should be.

He braked hard when he saw Rusty's Jeep parked out front. Executing a quick U-turn, he drove back and pulled in beside her vehicle. The "Closed" sign was up but a light was on inside.

Frank Kelly never worked on Sundays. No one who worked for them did either. Why on earth would Rusty be here? She hadn't been in church this morning. Not that he himself went often. But he'd let his mom drag him out since KGI was between missions and things were quiet on the home front.

An unusual occurrence to be sure. There was always something going on. But after completing the last mission two weeks earlier with the new team composed of Nathan, Joe, Swanny, Skylar and Zane—or Edge, as he'd been named back when he was an MMA fighter—nothing new had come up.

The new team was working out really well. Better than Donovan could have hoped for, given the length of time the team had been together. With the other two team leaders now married, thoroughly domesticated and enjoying fatherhood, the new team had taken up a lot of the slack while the other two teams had taken fewer missions.

He got out of his truck, but before he could even walk to the door, Rusty hurried out to meet him. He frowned at her expression. She looked . . . guilty. And while in the beginning he—and his brothers—had reservations about Rusty, she'd proven herself in the years since. She'd become a responsible young lady who was doing well in college and was extremely loyal to his parents. She was, in fact, an absolute member of the Kelly family.

"What's up?" Donovan asked, looking beyond to the door that was ajar. "Dad never opens on Sundays. Is there a problem? Do you need help with something?"

Rusty grimaced, took a deep breath and then glanced back in the direction of the hardware store.

"Look, can we talk a minute out here? Preferably down the street a bit?"

Donovan's brows furrowed at the anxious note in her voice. "Sure."

"Let me tell Travis I'll be right back, okay?"

Donovan's brows shot upward. "Travis? Who the hell is Travis? Is he your boyfriend? And if so, what the hell are y'all doing in Dad's store on a Sunday?"

She sighed and shook her head. "Just give me a sec and I'll explain."

Before he could argue further, she hurried back and disappeared through the door to the store. Barely a few seconds later, she came back out, locked the door behind her and then strode in Donovan's direction.

She motioned him down toward the sandwich store two doors down and he followed, wondering what the hell she was up to now. They hadn't had any trouble from Rusty since high school. She was only a year from graduating college and he couldn't imagine her fucking that all up now.

She stopped and then turned, surveying the area as if worried someone would overhear what she was about to tell him.

She shoved her hands in her pockets and sighed again. "I was going to call Nathan, but you're here now, so maybe . . ."

She trailed off, hesitating. It made sense that if she had a problem she'd call Nathan. Of all the Kelly brothers, she was closest to him because he'd been more accepting of her from the very start. But since then he and all his brothers had made it clear to her that she was family and that they looked out for family. She should be able to call *any* of them. Not just Nathan.

"Rusty, if you need help, you can call any of us. You do know that, right?"

She nodded. "I do. I just wasn't sure how to handle this and Nathan is less likely to freak out on me."

"Shit. What have you done now?"

"I haven't done anything!" she said indignantly. "Well, not exactly."

"What does 'not exactly' mean?" he asked dryly.

She glanced back over her shoulder again and then heaved her shoulders in resignation. "I sort of hired someone to work part time at the hardware store."

"Sort of? Either you did or you didn't. And why didn't I know anything about this? I spoke to Dad earlier and I'm sure he would have mentioned it. So my next question is, does Dad know about this new employee?"

"No," she muttered. "I haven't gotten around to telling him yet. But I wasn't planning to keep it from him! I only just hired the kid yesterday. I'll pay him out of my own pocket if Frank doesn't want to hire him."

Donovan studied Rusty intently. "You said *kid*. And you sound very passionate about this kid. Mind telling me the whole story?"

"I was going to call Nathan. I said that. I want to follow him home after he gets off."

Donovan blinked. "You want to do what?"

"He's in some kind of trouble, Van. I can see it. You don't understand. It's like looking at myself when I was that age. He's scared shitless and he's hungry and needs the money. He says he doesn't have parents. Just two sisters he looks out for. Now that's a hell of a lot of responsibility for a fifteen-year-old kid.

I'm worried about him. I wanted to check this family of his out. Make sure he's not in any danger. But I'm not stupid. I wasn't planning to go alone. I was going to ask Nathan to go with me. And now you're here," she finished lamely.

"And you want me to follow this kid with you to where he lives. What then? Do we just say, 'Oh, hi! Just wanted to make sure you weren't being chained in a basement'?"

She shook her head, but her shoulders had relaxed and a smile flirted with the corners of her lips.

"I hadn't gotten that far in my plan yet. I was hoping Nathan would have an idea. I can't explain it, Van. I hurt for this kid and I only just met him yesterday. You'd like him. He's quiet. Very respectful and he's obviously protective of his sisters. I just want to see if there is anything I can do to help."

Donovan's heart softened at the earnestness in her eyes and her impassioned speech. And the hell of it was, he had a huge soft spot for women and kids. Especially kids. It ate at his gut to think of a fifteen-year-old boy living hand to mouth, working part time in a hardware store to support two sisters. Where the hell were his parents?

"I'll go with you," he finally said. "But, Rusty, you're going to do it my way and you're going to listen to everything I tell you. Got it? Which means you stay behind me at all times, and if I tell you to cut and run or to get down, then you better do exactly that. We have no idea what kind of situation we're walking into, so I expect you to pay attention."

She nodded vigorously. "There's another thing, Van. And I don't know how to do it without being pushy."

"You? Pushy?" he mocked.

She rolled her eyes but laughed. "Okay, yeah, I can be pushy. But this is for a good cause! The kid is hungry. And if he's hungry I can only assume his sisters are as hungry as he is. I bought him a burger for lunch yesterday and he scarfed it down in about three bites. So today I got a burger for him, but he didn't eat it. He didn't want me to know he hadn't eaten it. He hid it and is saving it. My guess is he's bringing it home for his sisters to eat. And that kills me, Van. I was that hungry once. It's why I broke into your parents' house. I was starving and would have risked jail just to have something to eat. I don't want that to be this kid. I want to bring them food. I have to do something. I can't just stand by, knowing what I know and seeing what I see and do nothing."

Donovan slung his arm around her shoulders and pulled her into his chest for a hug. "You're a good kid, Rusty."

She elbowed him. "I'm not a kid anymore!"

He chuckled. "No, you're not. You're a young lady now. I forget that sometimes. Hard to believe so many years have passed since you were adopted into the Kelly clan."

"They've been the best years," she said softly.

"Okay, so here's what I propose. We follow the kid home. See what his situation is. Then we can figure out how to get them what they need. I can do some checking on him and his sisters."

"Thanks, Van. This means a lot to me."

"No problem. Just do me a favor, okay? In the future, call me or call someone *before* you make a decision like this. It may have worked out this time and the kid may not mean any harm, but there's no guarantee the next time won't be different. I don't want you getting hurt, Rusty. You can always call me or anyone else in the family."

She smiled. "Having so many older brothers is kind of cool, you know?"

He rolled his eyes. "And I think having older brothers is a pain in the ass."

"That's because Sam and Garrett *are* pains in the ass," she said with a laugh.

"Very true. Okay, so what time are you setting the kid loose? And I don't see a car so I'm assuming he lives close enough to walk?"

"I have no idea. He didn't exactly fill out an official application, so I don't know his address. And no, he doesn't have a car and no one drops him off or picks him up. Don't know how far he lives, but he's definitely been walking."

"Could be hard to tail him without him knowing it if he's on foot," Donovan said dubiously.

Rusty grimaced. "Yeah, he watches his back. It's why I

know he's scared shitless and is in some kind of trouble. I mean, most kids walk around oblivious. Especially in a small town like this. They walk like they don't have a care in the world. This kid? He walks like he expects someone to jump out at him at every turn. He's very cautious. Constantly looking around."

"You've been watching this kid pretty closely."

She nodded. "Yeah. I've been trying to figure out how to approach him. I've gone back and forth in my mind about how to do this. I would just ask him straight out, but that would spook him. Been there, done that. If anyone had come out like that to me, I'd have been gone in a shot. I didn't trust anyone, and I don't imagine he does either."

"I know you had a rough life," Donovan said softly. "It's pretty damn awesome that you're wanting to help this boy out."

Her cheeks went pink, but her eyes gleamed with happiness over his praise.

"I need to get back so he doesn't get antsy. If you could hang around, I planned to let him work thirty more minutes. I'm paying him in cash and I'm going to intentionally short him a twenty. He won't say anything. I know that much. He'll take whatever I give him and be grateful. But it will give us an excuse to follow him to his house. I can tell him I shorted him and we can check out his living conditions."

Donovan gave her a rueful smile. "You've got a quick mind, kiddo. I swear you could take over the running of KGI and probably rule the world one day."

She grinned cheekily. "I wouldn't turn down a tech geek job with you guys. Then I could play on Hoss."

Donovan scowled. "Hoss is mine. No one touches him but me. Besides, I'm not letting you anywhere near our computers. You'd hack into them in thirty seconds."

"I can't help it if my tech skills are superior to yours," she said loftily.

"Oh, good Lord," he muttered. "That's one hell of an ego you've got. I'm the geek in the Kelly family, thank you very much. The really hot, intelligent geek women are powerless to resist."

Rusty burst into laughter. "And you talk about *my* ego?"

He grinned and then pushed her toward the hardware store. "Go take care of the kid. I'll park a block down and watch when he comes out. If you'll hightail it down to my truck, we can follow him and see what happens."

"Thanks, Van. You're the best!"

"I expect you to remember that," he said dryly.

She hurried off with a wave, and Donovan walked back to his truck to move it farther down the street. He couldn't believe he'd just been roped into this craziness, but he also knew that he couldn't just look the other way and pretend ignorance. If this kid truly was in trouble and needed help, he couldn't ignore that. He hated to think of any child bearing so much responsibility at such a young age and worse, going hungry.

His pet charities were all about helping disadvantaged children, homeless and hungry children, and the majority of his financial support went to shelters for abused women. He'd cofounded a foundation to give support and financial help to women getting out of abusive relationships. His family didn't even know about it. Not that they would object in any way. The Kellys as a whole gave back a lot financially and by taking on missions that aided women and children without receiving a cent in compensation.

He just hadn't wanted to make a big deal of his foundation, so he'd funded and set it up with two women who oversaw day-to-day operations and gave him a heads-up when they ran up against a woman who needed more than just financial help. In those cases, KGI took on the mission whether it was to rescue a kidnapped child or to get a woman out of an unhealthy situation. They funded her new life and gave her the opportunity to start over in a place they felt was safe.

His brothers knew of his weakness when it came to taking missions involving children or women, and they were more than happy to lend assistance in any way they could. They gave him shit about his soft spot, but they were every bit as determined as Donovan was to right wrongs against victims.

Hell, the Kelly wives were survivors in their own right and kick-ass women to boot. His brothers were lucky sons of bitches, as were the team leaders, Rio and Steele. They'd all met their women in less-than-ideal situations, but they'd fallen hard and fast, and Donovan envied their connection to their wives. He wanted that. One day. He wasn't in a hurry. It would happen when it happened. But he wanted a family of his own. A wife. Children. To be a bigger part in a family that was his alone.

For now, he played the doting uncle to Charlotte, his oldest brother's daughter, and to his younger brother Ethan's twin boys. And now Rio had a thirteen-year-old daughter and Steele was the proud new father of a daughter. The world was changing around him, and yet he was seemingly standing still. Same routine. Same job. Every day.

He couldn't complain about his love life. He had sex. But he wasn't into cheap thrills or getting laid just to get a piece of ass. He respected women far too much to indulge in meaningless one-night stands. As a result, his relationships were few and far between, and he hadn't fucked his way through countless women. And he was okay with that. When the day came that he met the one, he wanted to be able to tell her that he hadn't been some man whore. He wanted her to know that she was special. For that matter, he wanted it to be special for him as well.

Maybe that made him old-fashioned or a prude. He didn't really give a damn. His parents had brought him up to be respectful not only of others but most of all himself. If he couldn't respect himself, how could he expect respect from others?

Fifteen minutes after he'd relocated down the street, he saw the kid Rusty had hired walk out of the hardware store. She was not wrong. This kid checked his surroundings. In fact, he brought more attention to himself because he was being so cautious. He walked slowly, his head turning side-to-side and then over his shoulder in a regular rotation.

He was a big kid. Tall and muscular, but thin. He had a look to him that told Donovan he was very likely malnourished. His face was thin and his expression was somber. He picked up speed at the end of the block as he crossed the street.

Damn it. If Rusty didn't hurry her ass up, they were going to lose him.

Just when he'd decided to take off after the kid on his own, Rusty hurried out and ran toward his truck. She slid into the passenger seat and Donovan backed out.

"You're right about him being wary," Donovan muttered as he slowed to a discreet distance behind the kid. "He's too obvious about it, though. If a cop sees him they're going to pick up on the fact that it looks like he has something to hide."

Rusty nodded and frowned. "Yeah, I know. But I can hardly tell him to act more casual, you know?"

"Yeah. I hear you."

They drove slowly for several minutes and Donovan cursed.

"Hell, how far is this kid walking to work anyway?"

Rusty looked as unhappy as Donovan was.

"I don't know, but it's been what, a mile so far?"

"Almost two," Donovan said grimly.

"He's turning onto that gravel road ahead," Rusty said, leaning forward in the seat. "I hope he hasn't made us and is throwing us off."

"We'll drive by like we're going ahead and then circle back," Donovan said.

He accelerated and drove past the road the kid had turned onto. He glanced over to see the kid walking along the side, his back to the highway. Donovan went up a ways and then did a U-turn and drove back to the road.

"Damn it!" Rusty said when they took the turn. "I don't see him now!"

Donovan accelerated down the road, dust kicking up behind them.

"Look! There he is!" Rusty said, pointing to the right.

Donovan continued past the run-down trailer and made another turn around to circle back. When they pulled into the driveway—if you could call the rut in the yard an actual driveway—Rusty tensed, her expression sorrowful as she took in the trailer the kid lived in.

He reached over to squeeze her hand.

"This was me when I was his age," Rusty whispered. "God, it makes me sick to think of him living here with two sisters. It's barely big enough for one person, let alone three."

Donovan grimaced and nodded his agreement.

The yard was overgrown and badly in need of mowing. But that was the least of the issues. There was a blue tarp over one half of the roof of the trailer. There were missing shingles in other places. The skirting was missing. One window was busted out and there was a missing step leading up to the door.

It didn't even look livable. The thing should have already been condemned.

He cut the engine and then looked over at Rusty.

"Remember what I said. You stay behind me until I'm certain this is safe. I'll knock and see what happens. When and only when I tell you it's okay, you can tell your story of shorting him money. I want to get inside so I can assess the situation myself."

Rusty nodded. "Let's go before they get spooked with us just parked out here like this. They're probably scared to death, with the way the kid was acting."

Donovan opened his door and got out. He wasn't carrying a gun, which was unusual for him. But he hadn't counted on needing one today. Now he wished he'd kept one in his truck at all times.

He motioned for Rusty to get behind him as they carefully mounted the rickety steps.

There was no screen door and when he knocked, the door shook as if just that little force could knock it over. Hell, it would be child's play to break into this place.

He waited several long seconds before finally the door cracked the barest inch and he found himself staring into the most startling golden-colored eyes.

"Can I help you?" the woman asked.

He was momentarily speechless. Rusty had mentioned sisters. But this was an adult woman. Not that old. Early twenties was his guess.

But what gutted him was that reflected in those beautiful eyes washed with glints of amber and gold was stark fear.

CHAPTER 4

"MY name is Donovan Kelly, ma'am," Donovan hurried to say, wanting to alleviate the terror in her eyes. Her fear had put knots in his stomach and it was all he could do not to charge in, take control and demand to know what the hell was scaring the holy crap out of her.

He restrained himself—barely. But his radar was beeping like an incessant alarm.

Was she in an abusive relationship? But no, Rusty had said the kid said he only lived with his sisters. Was this woman abusing the kid? His stomach knotted all over again. No, that couldn't be the case. The fear in her eyes wasn't of discovery—of her abuse of others. There was something far darker than that, something his eye was trained to catch from the many years he'd saved just such women from horrific situations.

"What do you want?" she asked in a voice too soft to be called blunt. Her words wavered, like she was barely hanging on to the urge to turn and flee. Her hand gripped the dilapidated door frame until the tips of her fingers and her knuckles were stretched thin and bloodless.

He swallowed because what the hell was he supposed to

say to that? That he wanted to know what the fuck had scared her? What she was hiding from? That he only wanted to help?

Rusty saved him from his grappling decision by pushing forward, inserting herself in front of Donovan—exactly what he'd told her *not* to do.

"We're really sorry to barge in on you," Rusty said, keeping her voice soft and unthreatening. "But I shorted Travis when I paid him for today's work. I felt horrible when I realized it. He's a hard worker and he's been such a blessing to have in the store. I brought the money so he'd have it."

There was a hint of relief that briefly shadowed the young woman's eyes before apprehension crept back in. Almost as if she had reminded herself not to take anything at face value. Those lessons were ones learned the hard way, and Donovan was convinced this was indeed a woman who'd learned hard and fast that the world was not a good place.

And then Travis appeared at the door, all but shoving the woman behind him as he faced Rusty and Donovan. He sent Donovan a wary look but quickly shifted his focus to Rusty, as if he wanted to hurry and get the entire thing over with so he and his sister could retreat behind closed doors.

But Rusty wasn't going to be put off. Donovan had to hand it to her. She was ferocious when she set her mind to something.

"Can we come in?" Rusty asked. "We won't take but a minute. In addition to the money I owe you, I realized we hadn't discussed your work schedule beyond this weekend, and I would like to have you come in a few hours each day if you're interested. If we could come in and talk a few minutes, then we can get it all worked out and we'll be out of your hair."

She smiled as she said it, even nearly fooling Donovan with the innocence of her request.

Travis gave a panicked, deer-in-the-headlights look as he glanced over his shoulder and then back to Rusty and finally letting his gaze flicker warily over Donovan.

Rusty edged forward, even as the kid was obviously racked

with indecision, like she was confident that her normal request would be granted. She was already on her way in before Donovan could make a grab for her. Damn it, they had no idea what was inside this house or why the occupants were scared out of their minds. He didn't want Rusty—or himself—to be caught in the middle of a dangerous situation.

Travis stepped back and sent a look of apology toward the inside. To his sister? Someone else?

But Donovan didn't give him a chance to change his mind. He pressed forward, keeping close on Rusty's heels in case he needed to shove her down quickly and cover her.

The very first thing he saw was a very young child—a girl—huddled on a tattered couch riddled with holes, a take-out box from the sandwich shop down the street from the hardware store perched on her lap.

Her mouth was smeared with ketchup and mayonnaise and her hands full of the burger Travis must have brought home. The one Rusty had bought for him and had told Donovan that he hadn't wanted her to know he hadn't eaten. Now they both knew why. He had brought it home to his sister—just a baby—because she was likely starving.

Donovan was gripped by rage as his gaze swept over the living room—if you could call it that. They were living in absolute squalor. It wasn't that the interior was messy or unkempt, as if they were slobs who discarded trash or food on the floor. In fact, what was there was neat and well ordered. But the condition of the trailer was deplorable.

In at least four places on the floor that he could see sat plastic bowls, presumably to catch leaks from the sagging ceiling. It had rained two nights earlier. He flinched to imagine them living here. No protection from the elements.

It was also then that he realized how warm the interior was. Hot, muggy. No air conditioning. The windows, such as they were, the ones not already broken out, were cracked to allow air to flow inside.

It took every bit of his control and training to keep his expression impassive and not to let free the full force of his reaction to what stared him in the face.

"Is there a problem . . . ," the older sister began, her voice soft but laced with fear and hesitancy.

The minute Rusty had barged into the house, Donovan behind her, Travis's older sister had immediately flown to the couch, placing herself between the young girl—she couldn't be more than three or four—and Rusty and Donovan.

Though she tried to look calm and poised, it was obvious she was prepared to fight or flee at a moment's notice. As if she'd had plenty of experience in . . . both.

"No problem at all," Rusty said cheerfully. "As I said to Travis, I wanted to pay him the cash I accidentally shorted him for the hours he worked today, but I also wanted to check with him so we could work out times for him to come in and work this next week. That is, if he's willing."

Travis and his sister exchanged quick, worried glances.

Donovan cleared his throat, determined to add his own two cents.

"Perhaps it would be best if you introduce yourself—and me—so she knows who her brother is working for," Donovan suggested pointedly.

Rusty's hand fluttered. "Oh, of course. How rude of me!" She strode over to where Travis's sister sat and thrust out her hand. "I'm Rusty Kelly."

The woman tentatively took Rusty's hand but remained silent. Donovan's gaze narrowed.

Rusty turned in Donovan's direction. "That's my older brother, Donovan Kelly. Well, one of them," she added with a grin. "There's a lot of us Kellys! Six older brothers, if you can believe it. Not to mention all the other unofficial family members Mama Kelly has adopted over the years."

Donovan didn't blame the woman's look of utter bewilderment. He drew up short of shaking his own head at Rusty's exuberance. She was overdoing it just a little in the let's-get-nice-and-friendly effort. And it wasn't working to relax any of the occupants of the room. If anything, they looked even more ill at ease.

The child clutched at her older sister's hand and edged

more firmly behind her, her eyes wide as she swiped at her mouth with the back of her other hand.

"Who are they, Evie?" she whispered. "What do they want?"

Evie. Well at least they were getting somewhere.

Donovan took a step forward, risking that "Evie" wouldn't tuck tail and run, the child hauled over her shoulder. He extended his own hand but wasn't as forceful as Rusty had been. He simply held it out and waited for her to take it. If she would.

"Glad to meet you, Evie," he said gently.

After a long moment, she slid slender fingers over his palm, and an electric sensation snaked up his arm and into his shoulder. Her touch was a shock, one he hadn't expected. Neither had she, judging by the way she quickly yanked her hand back, looking up at him with even more confusion clouding those liquid amber eyes.

The woman was beautiful. Scared. Haunted. Shadows hung from her like picture frames. But she was stunning. She was too thin. It was obvious they were struggling to even survive, and yet her fragility only made her more beautiful. He was mesmerized by those eyes. Could simply stand there and stare into them, picking out all the different flecks of gold and chestnut.

"It's Eve," she said huskily. "My name, that is. Cammie and Trav call me Evie. It's their pet name."

Donovan knelt on the threadbare carpet in front of the couch and smiled warmly at the child. "You must be Cammie. Pretty name for a very pretty young lady."

She looked confused and huddled more fiercely behind Eve's back. Eve reached over her shoulder to snag Cammie's hand that had crept up toward Eve's neck.

"It's all right, Cammie," she whispered. "He won't hurt you."

Even as she issued the promise, she turned hastily, staring pleadingly into Donovan's eyes as if begging him not to make a liar out of her. Goddamn, but it sickened him that these two females—and their brother—had been conditioned to expect harm from others. And not just others, but particularly men.

Cammie had been nervous, yes, when Rusty had moved in her direction. But when Donovan had approached, the child had panicked and damn near climbed up her sister's back.

He wanted to demand to know who the hell had hurt them, who had taught them pain and fear and who the hell they were running from. Then he wanted to take apart the son of a bitch with his own hands, and the very next thing he wanted was to ensure that nothing would ever harm this ragtag family again.

How crazy was that?

Five minutes in their presence, and he was ready to rush in, take over their lives and make them promises he had no business making. And no guarantee that he could even keep them since he didn't have a fucking clue what they were up against.

"No, sweetheart," Donovan said gently, it taking absolute concentration not to give in to the fiery rage brewing inside him. "I will never hurt you. Never. You can take that to the bank. I'd like to help you. Your brother and your sister. I'd like to be your friend."

Both Cammie's and Eve's eyes went wide. Cammie looked uncertain, while Eve froze. Not a single tremor went through her body. It was as if she'd turned to ice. He could feel her staring at him, staring holes through him as if trying to figure out who and what he was. If he was a threat. If he was telling the truth.

Goddamn it, but he'd never felt so damn helpless in his life. He was a man of action. He wasn't one to fuck around and play games. He never hesitated when it came to someone needing help. And yet he knew he couldn't do that here. This was a delicate situation that he had to tiptoe through as though walking through a minefield. One that could blow up in his face at any moment.

"We don't have any friends," Cammie mumbled. "Evie says it's not safe."

"Cammie, shhh," Eve said, turning swiftly to silence the child. She turned back to Donovan, a weak smile wavering on her face. "Cammie has a very active imagination. Most four-year-olds do, you know."

She was nearly the same age as his niece, Charlotte. Charlotte, who was surrounded by a huge, loving family. Charlotte, who never had to worry where her next meal came from. Or if it would come. Charlotte, who had doting uncles and aunts. Grandparents to spoil her rotten. And an entire organization of badass military operatives who'd start a fucking war to protect her.

This child was the complete antithesis of his niece and her life, and it broke Donovan's heart.

Rusty cleared her throat and inserted herself to alleviate the sudden awkwardness wrought by Cammie's confession.

"As I was saying, Travis—and Eve—I can work Travis in a few hours every day this week, and of course he's welcome to come in next weekend as well. I'm absolutely flexible, so whatever works for you is fine with me."

Unease crossed Eve's face, and then she glanced down, shame and embarrassment flashing in her eyes before they were hidden from view.

"Thank you," she said quietly. "But I don't intend for him to have to work long. Just until Cammie is better and I can leave her. I don't know if things will work out here, so I'd hate for you to depend on Travis when we only plan for him to have a temporary job."

"And why wouldn't they work out?" Donovan prompted carefully.

Her eyes became shuttered, the golden flecks dimming as her expression became indecipherable. She lifted one shoulder in a careless shrug. "There are no guarantees. Ever. It may or may not work out that we can stay here. I have to prepare for reality."

"And if it doesn't?" Donovan challenged. "What then?"

"We move on," she said simply.

She said it so matter-of-factly that Donovan knew this wasn't new to them. He had no idea for how long they'd been running or how far. But relocating on short notice—and often—was not foreign to them at all.

He thought a whole host of crazy things. Things that would have his brothers thinking he'd lost his goddamn mind. Maybe he had. He had to get a grip. Take a step back, take a deep breath and gain some perspective before he did something really crazy like haul every one of them out of this dump and move them into his brand-new, very empty house, which had finished construction mere weeks before.

It was a house built with a large family in mind. The family he knew one day he wanted to be his. Though he had no immediate plans. No specific woman in mind. No one waiting in the wings. No one he was even considering. He hadn't allowed anyone that close.

But it didn't mean he didn't know what he wanted. Someday. He'd always known. A wife. Children. A house full of children. Noisy, rambunctious. Much like his own upbringing in a house full of brothers, two older and three younger.

He wanted that life for himself. Wanted to carry his childhood into his adult life. Provide that warm, stable, loving home for his own children that Frank and Marlene Kelly had provided him and his brothers. He wanted nothing more than to come home to his own wife after being away on a mission. To be welcomed back with a sweet, loving smile. To be surrounded by his children. His kids. A part of himself. His blood.

But for now the house stood alone. A symbol of his hopes for his future. Apart from the other houses his brothers lived in at the Kelly compound surrounded by a tight security field. A reality of their lives and the career choices they'd made.

Empty except for the bare essentials. He'd always known that whenever he settled down, he wanted his wife to decorate. To put her feminine stamp on the furnishings, the wall decorations. He looked forward to girly, frilly knickknacks and fighting over the bathroom sink and arguing over leaving the toilet seat down.

All the things his brothers good-naturedly bitched about

were the things that Donovan craved. Oh, not that any of his brothers truly bitched about their wives. They were completely over-the-moon, head-over-ass, stick-a-fork-in-them done. They'd met their other halves. The women who completed them. He envied them with every breath in his body, even as he shrugged off the teasing that he and Joe were the only ones not hooked and reeled in yet.

He'd perfected the laid-back, easygoing, laissez-faire attitude. To everyone else, he was content with his life. Not actively looking to change it. But his gut tightened every time he saw his brothers with their wives. Their children. His sisters-in-law and his niece and nephews.

One day . . . One day, he kept saying. It would all be his. Just what his brothers had. But that day *hadn't* come, and years kept passing. Fading into yet another. Children getting older. More children on the way. His family was growing around him in leaps and bounds and he was standing still, the only one unchanged.

Christ, he was well into his thirties. Sam was *forty*! Donovan wasn't *that* far behind!

He shook his head, forcing his thoughts back to the present. The utter gravity of the situation before him. Because he had to do something. There was no way in hell he'd stand by and allow this to go unaddressed.

Once again, Rusty saved the awkward silence that had fallen over the tiny room.

"Well, he's welcome to work as long as he'd like. He's good help, and that's hard to find," Rusty said enthusiastically.

But as she said the words, caution and reserve fixed Eve's eyes into an impenetrable shield. She was already withdrawing, backing away like she wanted Rusty and Donovan both gone this very minute.

Rusty powered on relentlessly as if she took no notice of Eve's silent refusal or the tightening of Travis's lips.

"Just plan to come in tomorrow like usual. We'll just play the rest by ear," Rusty said. "And if there's anything else we can do to help, please let us know. We'd be glad to do whatever you need."

There was warmth in Rusty's voice, and Donovan had to hand it to her. Her seeming oblivion to the tension in the room and the warmness in her voice relaxed Travis and even Eve. To an extent.

Donovan doubted the woman ever fully let her guard down. It was evident she'd had far too much practice perfecting that shield. Which only made him more determined to break through. He wanted to know her secrets. What made her afraid. And he also wanted to know . . . her. On a more intimate level.

That shocked the holy hell out of him. He nearly rocked back on his heels over that revelation.

Women in distress were nothing new to Donovan. There had never been one whose circumstances hadn't enraged him. He felt empathy toward each and every victim KGI had rescued or helped in some fashion.

But he'd never felt . . . this. Whatever the hell this was. His emotions had always been involved. His brothers well knew that. They knew women and children were his Kryptonite. No secret there. But this? This was something else entirely that had nothing to do with Eve being a woman on the run. This was something deeper and he suddenly knew he was in some deep shit.

Because this was not a woman he could simply ask out on a date. Exchange good conversation, good food, maybe a good-night kiss with the hope of a second date and maybe more in the kissing department. Not a woman to be slowly wooed and courted until the moment he took her to bed and made love to her all damn night and woke up to the next morning knowing that he held something special in his arms.

Fuck.

There wasn't another word that more aptly described this entire situation. It was fucked and so was he.

"I wouldn't want to impose," Eve said in a husky voice that sent a jolt down Donovan's spine. "I appreciate your offer. You've been very kind to Travis—to all of us. But we have what we need."

She hadn't said *all we need*. There was a huge distinction between having *what* she needed and *all* she needed.

Rusty grimaced and Donovan saw the realization that they couldn't push more. Not yet. But Donovan wasn't giving up. He was on a mission now, and when he set his focus on a goal, he never backed down. Eve didn't realize it yet, but whether she wanted it or not, he was going to help. He just had to decide how the hell to go about it.

CHAPTER 5

EVE breathed a huge sigh of relief as she watched through the window as Rusty and Donovan pulled away. Then she turned back to Travis, who stood in front of the sofa where Cammie sat, her eyes muddled with confusion—and fear.

God, but Eve hated that fear. It gutted her that her baby sister at such a tender age had learned that the very person she should be able to trust most had proved to be a monster. No child should learn fear at such a young age. It made Eve want to weep, but she couldn't give in to her despair. At least not in front of Cammie and Travis. They depended on her. They needed her. They needed her to be strong. To show no fear or uncertainty. If it killed her, she'd swallow it all back and put up a brave front for her siblings.

"How did they know where we lived?" Eve asked Travis softly.

Guilt surged into Travis's eyes and she hurried forward, touching his shoulder, having to reach up to his greater height. So tall and strong. A man long before his time. Like Cammie, he should still be a child, with a child's innocence, and without the knowledge they now held like poison.

"Trav, it's okay," she reassured.

He shook his head. "No, Evie, it's not. I wasn't careful enough. They must have followed me from the hardware store. I saw a truck following me but I didn't want to draw attention by running. I had . . . I had hoped it was just a local going in the same direction and when I turned down our road, I paused to look back, but they drove on. They must have doubled back. I'm sorry."

She pulled him into a hug. "They seem nice. They came all this way to pay you what she owed you and to work out hours you could go in. I'm sure they mean no harm."

The lie passed easily from her lips. Yes, they seemed nice. Normal. But appearances could be deceiving, as she well knew. Her stepfather was the picture of normal, wholesome. Wealthy. Well connected. A philanthropist. Involved in local politics. Nothing to hint at what lay underneath the smooth, polished exterior. It sickened her.

"Do you want me to quit?" he asked anxiously. "Maybe I should try somewhere else. It just seemed too good to be true. She pays cash. Hasn't asked any questions. She's been really nice and I let my guard down."

"No. I think it would be even more suspicious if you suddenly didn't show up, especially since they came out and were so nice. They'd wonder why you quit. And another employer wouldn't be as accommodating. You got lucky. Most wouldn't pay under the table. And it's only temporary. Just a few more days until Cammie is well enough to stay with you so I can work."

"I don't mind," he said fiercely. "You've done so much for us. This is the least I can do. I won't let you work yourself to death like you've been doing. It's not fair. You're supposed to have a life, Evie. You're young and beautiful and now you're saddled with two kids to take care of when you should have a family of your own."

"You *are* my family," she said just as fiercely. "I love you and Cammie. I wouldn't have it any other way. I hate what we had to do. I hate that we have to hide and move. You and Cammie should have a childhood and not be forced to grow up. You're a teenager, Trav. You should be in school with other kids your age. Playing sports. Having fun. This isn't fair!"

"Evie?"

Cammie's soft whisper had her and Travis both turning, and Eve instantly regretted having this conversation in front of her.

"We'll be okay, won't we?"

Eve rushed to the couch and sat, pulling Cammie into her arms and hugging her tight. She stroked her blond curls and pressed a kiss to her sweet head.

"Of course we will, darling. I don't want you to worry. Promise me."

Cammie pulled away and offered a tentative smile and then glanced over at Travis. "We'll be together always, won't we?"

Travis sat on Cammie's other side and wrapped his arms around both Eve and Cammie.

"You betcha, little sis. We're family. Just like Evie said. We're going to be fine. He'll never find us. No one will ever hurt us again."

Eve's heart ached at the tenderness and determination in Travis's voice. She swallowed back the knot of emotion and blinked at the sudden sting of tears. And savored the feel of her siblings in her arms. As if she could protect them from the world. Damn if she wouldn't do whatever was in her power to ensure their well-being. Whatever she had to do. There were no limits to her love or the sacrifices she'd make to keep them safe.

She turned her face up toward Travis. "Just this week, okay? If you can work this week, then Cammie will be better and I'll find work. Something during the day so I won't be gone in the evenings. We can have dinner together. Just like family."

"I'm feeling better, Evie," Cammie said in a solemn voice.

Eve stroked her hand through Cammie's hair and then kissed her temple, leaving her lips there for a long moment. Against flesh that was still warm with fever.

"I know you are, darling. But you need to rest a few more

days. No reason to rush now, is it? Tomorrow I'll do some grocery shopping and I'll be sure and buy you a special treat."

Cammie's eyes lit up. "A treat? I love treats!"

Eve smiled. What little girl didn't? There was a thrift shop not far from the hardware store where Travis worked. She'd go early, before Travis was due in to work, and see what she could find. Cammie needed a few more shirts and shorts. Something cool since they didn't have air conditioning and the temperatures were already quite warm despite the earliness of summer.

"It will give you something to look forward to," Eve said, squeezing Cammie to her once more.

They'd had little to look forward to in the last few months. At times it seemed they'd been running for years. That this was their life, had always been their life. It was hard for Eve to remember what normal was. When she didn't have the weight of the world on her shoulders and taste fear with every breath.

"I'm sleepy, Evie," Cammie mumbled, stifling a yawn with a still-messy hand from the burger she'd devoured.

Travis smiled. "Come on. I'll carry you to bed and tuck you in. That sound good to you?"

In response, Cammie disentangled herself from Eve's grasp and reached up both arms for Travis to pick her up. He swung her easily into his arms and carried her to the only bedroom, one Cammie and Eve shared, with Travis sleeping on the couch.

When they left the living room, Eve buried her face in her hands, briefly giving in to the crushing despair that hovered over her like the blackest thundercloud.

Oh God, what were they going to do? They couldn't run forever. They couldn't escape the past. And not knowing when or how long was eating a hole in her stomach. She had to stay healthy for Cammie and Travis. They depended on her. She was the sole constant in their lives that had been turned completely upside down.

Betrayal.

Bitterness assailed her. Hatred. She would have never thought herself capable of such intense hatred. But it was there. Alive and insidious. She'd never even contemplated crime. But she knew she could absolutely kill Walt without remorse. She'd happily spend the rest of her life in jail if it meant that Cammie and Travis would be safe and have a life.

But for now they needed her. She couldn't leave them. Whatever she had to do to ensure their well-being, she would do. Even if it meant spending the rest of her life running and forever looking over her shoulder.

CHAPTER 6

DONOVAN drove Rusty back to the hardware store so she could pick up her Jeep. As she got out, he called out to her.

"You heading to Mom's?"

Rusty rolled her eyes. "Of course. Sundays are family dinner days at Mama Kelly's house, but she made this one sound important. I mean more important than usual. She made it very clear that everyone was to be present, no excuses allowed."

Donovan chuckled. "Yeah, no doubt she has something up her sleeve. As to what, who knows. I'll follow you over and we'll arrive together. I'm sure everyone else will already be there."

"I'm going to tell them," Rusty said softly. "I never intended to keep this from them. I hope you know that."

"I know, honey. And don't worry. I've got your back on this one."

Warmth flashed in her eyes and her smile widened, making her pretty features even more gorgeous. She really had turned into a very beautiful young lady. Donovan was proud of her, and he lamented the fact that neither he nor his brothers told her that often enough. Mom and Dad, however, made their pride known on a regular basis.

"I'm proud of you, Rusty. I know I don't tell you as often as I should. But you have a good head on your shoulders. Don't let anyone ever tell you otherwise. And more than that, you have a good heart. You're going to be irresistible to the male population, which sucks because it means me and my brothers will have to kick a lot of asses."

Rusty laughed, but her joy was broadcast all over her face.

"It will suck for me a lot more than it will for you! One badass brother is enough. But six badass brothers breathing down some poor guy's neck? It'll be a miracle if I ever get one to stick around and suffer the scrutiny."

Donovan chuckled. "As if that's going to stop you. I hear about your boyfriends."

She raised her eyebrows in mock horror. "What boyfriends?"

Donovan snorted. "You know damn well Mom regales us all with stories about your dates. Hell, I'm just surprised she hasn't asked us to do background checks on the guys you date at college."

Rusty rolled her eyes. "Oh God, don't plant that suggestion in her head. She'd totally do it!"

"It's not a bad idea. It pays to be careful, Rusty. You're several hours away from your family. A young girl at a big university can't be too careful, you know."

Rusty leaned in, her hand on the door. "I am careful, Van. I've been around y'all enough to know what kind of assholes inhabit the earth. I know y'all try to be careful not to talk too much about your missions, but I've gleaned enough to know what's out there. I'm careful and you've all taught me how to take care of myself. Nathan and Joe took it upon themselves to give me self-defense lessons. Garrett even got involved and wouldn't let up until I could throw him. I hurt for a week!"

"Glad to know my brothers do have a little sense in their hard noggins," he said with a grin. "Now let's get on out of here before we incur the wrath of Mama Kelly. You know how unforgiving she can be when it comes to missing her family meals."

Rusty checked her watch and then squeaked. "Oh my God, we are so late!"

With that she gave a wave and slammed the door, then dashed to her Jeep and got in. Donovan grinned and pulled away, Rusty close on his bumper.

Yeah, family dinners were the best. But tardiness wasn't acceptable in Marlene Kelly's world. She wanted all her chicks present and accounted for, and, well, her chicks toed the line with her.

As Donovan drove toward his parents' house, his humor dimmed as he went back over Eve and her siblings and the squalor they were living in. His hands tightened on the steering wheel as he contemplated what the hell he could do about it. He needed more information. He even wondered if those were their real names, and if they were, they weren't doing a very good job of covering their tracks. And that worried him. Because if they were running—and it was obvious that was what they were doing—then at some point, whatever they were running from would catch up.

If that happened, he hoped like hell it was here and not after they'd moved on and disappeared. If whatever was stalking them was going to catch up, then he wanted it to be here where he could protect them.

He shook his head. Not that rage over any woman or child in such a situation was new to him or even a surprise, but his personal reaction to this woman—Eve—well, he wasn't sure what the hell to make of that.

There's been something about her. Those eyes. The moment she'd cracked the door of the dilapidated trailer and he'd glimpsed those beautiful, expressive golden eyes, it had been like being sucker-punched in the gut. The more he'd seen, the larger the knot had grown in his stomach. He'd never felt so goddamn helpless in his life, and helplessness was not an emotion he was frequently confronted with.

He was a take-charge guy. He took action. He wasn't

a passive observer to any wrongdoing. Especially when it involved children or women. And yet he'd had to play it cool. To stand there and pretend mild interest. Had to force himself to back off and not come on strong and overwhelm and frighten the hell out of her.

Because he knew. He knew if he'd made any such movement, she would have bolted and he'd never see her again.

The more he pondered the situation, the more he knew he had to gather as much information as he could about her, and he was going to have to be damn discreet about it. And that frustrated him to no end. It wasn't what he was accustomed to. He solved problems. He took action. It was who he was. It was who KGI was. It was what they stood for.

And now he was going against every instinct deeply ingrained. To walk away. Pretend what he'd seen didn't matter.

The hell it didn't.

There was a way. There was always a way. He wasn't the geek of this organization for nothing. Sure, he had the brawn, but he also had a brain. He could kick ass with the best of them, but his best talent was his intelligence and problem-solving ability. He could work magic with computers and technology. But none of that was going to do him any damn good if he couldn't get close enough to her to figure her out. And that was going to be the biggest challenge of all.

As he and Rusty had suspected, they were the last of the Kelly clan to roll in. The yard in front of his parents' house looked like a used-car lot with all the vehicles scattered. By the time Rusty got out, Marlene was already on the porch, a look of exasperation on her face.

"You're late," she called out unnecessarily. "I've held lunch for half an hour waiting for you two to make your appearance."

"I know, I know," Rusty said as she hurried toward the steps. "I'm so sorry."

Marlene Kelly eyed Donovan, who approached at a slower pace. He had his best puppy-eyed expression in place because it was one his mother couldn't resist. Judging by the resigned look she gave him, she well knew she was being manipulated.

He dropped a kiss on her cheek after he mounted the steps. "Sorry, Ma. We'll explain later."

Her expression immediately became worried and she glanced rapidly between him and Rusty.

"Is anything wrong? Is everything okay?"

"You worry too much, Ma," Donovan chided. "Everything's fine. We'll explain after we have the dinner you've already held half an hour. No need to make everyone wait to eat when they're probably all frothing at the mouth to taste your cooking."

She glared. "Such a smooth talker you are. You know just how to appeal to my ego to get yourself out of trouble. But all right. Let's go eat. It'll wait, but don't think I'll forget! We'll have that conversation before you leave."

Donovan chuckled. "Of course. Would I hold out on you?"

"Yes!"

Rusty laughed and the three entered the house, and Donovan was immediately assailed with the smell of home. Distant conversation. Laughter. A child's giggle. Coming home never got old. Every time he stepped into his parents' home, he was immediately at peace. Only today, he wasn't quite as appeased as he'd usually be because his thoughts were still occupied by Eve, Travis and Cammie, who didn't have this. Family. That sense of unwavering loyalty and unconditional love.

He was lucky. Damn lucky. And it made his chest tighten to think that only a few miles away was a run-down trailer filled with vulnerable people who were desperately in need.

And indeed, his mother did have something up her sleeve. Something more than the usual family gathering on Sundays, when schedules permitted and none of his brothers were off on missions.

It was evident in the secret smile she threw his dad as they all ate lunch around the huge oak table to which leaves had been added over the years as the family had expanded beyond its original size.

Now with all the wives and grandchildren, the table was massive in length, but his mother had been determined that everyone be able to sit at the table. There was no separation. No kids' table to the side. Everyone had a seat where she could look down the table and see all her children and grandchildren at a glance.

His mother was fairly bristling with anticipation, which meant that she had a surprise for them all. He just wondered what the hell it was.

Excitement was in the air. It permeated the entire lunch. His brothers and their wives smiled and the conversation was animated. Sarah and Garrett were glued solidly to one another, Sarah giving the big man a smile that likely melted Garrett to his toes.

Sophie was glowing as she sat between her husband and their daughter, Charlotte. Sam touched her often. Just a brush with his hand. Or he'd loop his arm around the back of her chair and pull her in close as they ate and laughed.

Joe seemed unaffected by the love and intimacy that was so evident between all their brothers and the women they loved. But Donovan was envious. He wanted that for himself. Joe was younger than Donovan and his older brothers. Though Nathan, his twin, had settled down with Shea, Joe had shown no signs of wanting to do the same. He was in his early thirties now. Nathan had been thirty when he and Shea had met in a very unconventional fashion.

Donovan shook his head. It was still hard to believe that Shea had such extraordinary abilities. That she'd saved his brother. More than that, she'd taken his torture and his pain. Absorbed it and made it her own. Donovan couldn't fathom a woman who would be that selfless for someone she didn't even know. Just a stranger that she'd reached out to over thousands of miles that separated them.

That bond between them had been strong and lasting. It had lasted until Nathan had found her. And it was still present. Unbreakable.

And yet the family treated her just as they did every other daughter- and sister-in-law. Normal. Seemingly oblivious to the fact that she had telepathy and shared a mental pathway with both Nathan and Joe. That they could speak through their minds in a much more intimate fashion.

Donovan envied that too. Wished he shared that kind of bond with a woman he loved and who loved him.

"You seem preoccupied today, man," Ethan murmured at his side.

Ethan and Rachel sat to Donovan's right, while Rusty had taken the spot on Donovan's left. Perhaps because she wanted his support once she announced what she'd done to the family. And there would be a hell of a lot of questions.

The twins were sleeping in their bassinets just a few feet away so that if they awakened, someone would be instantly there. And any one of the family members would swoop in, bottle ready to assist in the feeding. That was what his family was all about. Always there. Unwavering, unconditional love and support.

Donovan shook his head. "We'll get into it later. Ma has something up her sleeve. She's about to come out of her chair. I figure soon she won't be able to stand it another minute, and we'll figure out what she's called everyone together for today."

Ethan grinned. "You noticed too, huh."

"Kind of hard not to," Donovan said dryly. "She's fidgeting with impatience. Lord only knows what she's cooked up now. I figure we should all brace for impact."

Ethan smiled even as he slid his arm around Rachel and pulled her close to his side. Rachel sent a smile in Donovan's direction, and Donovan marveled at the joy in her eyes. Eyes that had once been darkened by permanent shadows. Knowledge of the past. All she'd endured. Finally. Finally, she'd stepped into the light. She was happy. Loved. But most of all whole again.

Donovan smiled back at her, allowing all the love he felt for her fill his heart. Ethan was a lucky son of a bitch to get the second chance he'd gotten. He'd damn near lost Rachel, something that would haunt Ethan—and the entire family—forever.

"You're looking good, sweetheart," he said affectionately. "Hard to believe you gave birth not so long ago."

A blush rose in her cheeks, but she looked back at him with answering love and affection.

"It's been nearly a year! Can you believe it? I swear the twins are growing by leaps and bounds. I can't even keep up with them these days. Mason is doing his best to catch up to Ian in the walking department, and God help me when they both cut loose."

An ache settled into Donovan's chest. Yes, time was flying by. Children getting older. It was hard to savor these moments when they went by so quickly.

"Are you okay today?" Rachel asked in a low voice so she wouldn't be overheard. But then the rest of the conversation was loud and raucous. At least three different conversations were ongoing at the table as everyone bantered, laughed and joked, so it was doubtful anything Rachel said would be heard.

Donovan smiled. "Yeah, sweetheart. I'm good. Just thinking about something. I'll tell you about it later. I may need your help with something."

Concern immediately darkened both Rachel's and Ethan's eyes.

"You know all you have to do is ask," Rachel said.

Ethan nodded his agreement as they both stared intently at Donovan.

"I know. And I appreciate it. It's not me, so don't worry. I'll explain everything after Ma tells us what's on her mind."

On cue, the table quieted and Donovan turned his attention to where his father had held up his hand. He marveled at the fact that his father commanded absolute respect in their family.

His brothers were grown men. Had families of their own. And yet Frank Kelly was still the patriarch. When he had something to say, his children listened. He commanded their absolute respect, and every single Kelly toed the line when it came to their father or their mother.

"Your mother has something she wants to share with you all," he said in his gravelly voice. "It's why she wanted all of you here today. All of you," he said pointedly, looking down the table to where Sean Cameron and Swanny sat. Both adopted by his wife into the Kelly fold. Just as Rusty had been.

All eyes went in their mother's direction, waiting. Some worried, some just curious. It was evident by her expression and the smile bursting at her lips that whatever she was going to share wasn't bad. So there was no need to worry.

Marlene Kelly glanced at her husband and then reached above the table to grasp his hand where it rested by his plate. She squeezed and sent him a loving smile that made Donovan's chest ache. So many years gone by. So many trials endured. And yet their love was solid. Unbending. It was a constant in all their lives and had shaped the lives of every single person Marlene and Frank had ever come in contact with.

"Your father and I wanted to give you the news in person. I know you've all wanted us to move into the compound, and I've resisted. It's just that I love this house. It's where my children were raised. It's where my grandchildren come to visit their grandma and grandpa. We made memories in this house and it's not something I'll ever willingly part with."

She paused as if to let her words settled over the gathered family members.

"But we also know you worry. And with good reason. This family has been through so much over the last years. And your father and I don't want to add to your burden. We don't want you to worry when you need to focus on your own families."

She took a deep breath, and this time Frank squeezed her hand and smiled reassuringly.

"So we've decided to do it. We're going to move into the compound on the plot of land Sam has reserved for us, though Lord knows he's probably already given up on us. But we've been in contact with an architect. He's been to this house and drawn the plans of this one so we can replicate this house inside the compound."

There was an instant barrage of comments from all the gathered family members. Frank raised his hand for quiet and all went immediately silent.

"Let your mother finish. This is important to her."

Marlene smiled. "I want everything exactly the same. And I know it's silly to have such a big house when it's just me and your father. We're getting older and one would think we'd be looking to downsize at our age. But we want this house. We want every single thing to be the same. We want a house our children can come home to. Even just to visit. We're keeping every single bedroom the same. So all you boys will have your rooms. It's important to us both not only that we have a house we made so many memories in, but that you boys have the house you grew up in. A place to gather at Christmas and remember. We want our grandchildren to have those same memories of the place their fathers grew up in. We want you to have your home."

Tears glittered in her eyes, and when Donovan did a quick sweep of the table, he could see that his brothers and their wives were similarly affected. Emotion was a thick cloud over the table, but in every gaze, there was overwhelming relief.

Relief that their parents would be safe. That they would be inside the compound where they would be protected.

An instant furor erupted, and his brothers and their wives all got up to hug Marlene and Frank both. Sam's eyes were suspiciously shiny and his jaw was clenched tight. Of all Donovan's siblings, Sam had been the most worried and the most adamant that their mother and father move into the compound. Relief was stark in all his brothers' eyes.

When things settled and everyone took their seats once more, Marlene looked pointedly at Joe and Swanny. The two men shared the house that Donovan himself had lived in for the last several years. A house he'd once shared with Sam and Garrett before his brothers had met the women they married.

That house was on the lake but outside the compound. Donovan had only just finished his own house inside, but Joe had made no start on his own home. His plot of land lay empty and he was content to live in the cabin vacated by his brothers. Swanny had moved in until he found his own place. He was a member of Joe's and Nathan's team and, like the other members of their team, he had moved closer to the compound and training facilities.

"And when are you planning to start construction on your house, young man?" Marlene asked in a stern voice.

Joe laughed. "Oh come on, Ma. Give me a break. I don't have any need to build a house yet. Swanny and I are cool at the cabin. And don't even get any ideas about hooking me up with some nice girl you want me to marry. I'll build my house. One day. But I'm not ready yet. I'll worry about that if and when I meet Miss Right and want to settle down."

Marlene let out a harrumph, but she smiled. "Well, at least you're finally giving some thought to the future and settling down. This is the first time you've actually acknowledged that there *will* be a someday."

Joe groaned and the others burst out laughing as a round of ribbing immediately ensued.

"We have some news too," Sophie said in a soft voice.

Everyone looked their way, taking in Sophie's soft glow and the joy in her eyes. Marlene caught her breath and put a hand to her mouth in anticipation.

Sam smiled lovingly at his wife and put his arm around her, squeezing her shoulders. There was no mistaking the joy in his brothers' own eyes as he offered encouragement to Sophie.

"We're going to have another baby," Sophie announced. "In seven months."

The room erupted in exclamations and congratulations, and a round of mad hugging ensued. Charlotte clapped her hands together and bounced excitedly in her seat.

"I'm going to have a sister!" she proclaimed.

"Or a brother," Sam corrected, amusement glistening in his eyes.

Charlotte shook her head emphatically. "We already have boys. Aunt Rachel has two! I want a sister."

Sophie laughed and hugged her daughter to her. "No matter what we have, you'll love him or her. I promise."

Charlotte didn't look convinced, but she didn't argue the point.

"Um, guys, there's something Garrett and I want to share with y'all too," Sarah said quietly from her place at the table.

All eyes went in her direction and she blushed madly, nearly diving behind Garrett's broad shoulders. Garrett smiled indulgently and wrapped his arm around her, pulling her into the crook of his shoulder.

"We don't want to steal anyone's thunder," Sarah continued hesitantly. "But in light of everything else, it seemed the perfect time."

"Of course!" Marlene exclaimed.

There was an instant round of encouragement from the rest of the table. The knot in Donovan's stomach increased as he took in the wealth of happiness present at the table. It didn't take a rocket scientist to figure out his other brother's news, and it just solidified the longing in Donovan's soul to have what his brothers had.

"We're going to have a baby too," Sarah said shyly. "Close to when Sophie and Sam have theirs. I went to the doctor Friday and he thinks I'm about six weeks along, so maybe right after Sophie has hers."

"Oh, this is wonderful!" Marlene exclaimed, tears shining in her eyes.

She wiped at them as she rose and hurried around to enfold Sarah into her arms.

"Oh, my dear. You've made an old woman so very happy today. You all have. I can't believe I'm going to be blessed with two more grandchildren!"

Another round of congratulations went up and more mad hugging ensued. Rusty glanced at Donovan, unease present in her eyes. He knew exactly what she was thinking. That she shouldn't say anything to ruin the moment. But he shook his head and looked pointedly at her. His father needed to know. His family needed to know. Then they could brainstorm the situation after they knew everything there was to know. And Donovan could make it clear where he stood. That he planned to do whatever necessary to help Eve and her siblings.

The Kelly family as a united front was a daunting, overwhelming force of nature. One that Eve had no hope of resisting. They'd cover her up with so much love and understanding and support that she'd never have to worry about going hungry again. And in time, she'd know without a doubt that whatever it was she feared, that she didn't have to fear it any longer. The Kellys—Donovan—would protect her. No matter what.

"This is better than Christmas," Joe said with a grin. "Don't think I've seen the family together and this happy since the first Christmas Rachel was back home with us."

There were many responses to his proclamation. Ethan's gaze, though happy, was momentarily shadowed by the reminder of all he'd lost—and miraculously regained. Just a brief shadow, one that had been finally erased with time—and the knowledge that Rachel was back and that he wouldn't lose her again.

"This family has been through a lot," Frank said gravely. "But we're Kellys, and above all Kellys prevail. We overcome. Nothing will ever get us down as long as we remain a strong, family unit."

"Hooyah," Ethan murmured, which immediately precipitated groans and good-natured ribbing from his non-Navy brothers.

"I hate to be the damper on so much good news," Rusty began hesitantly.

The moment she spoke, every head turned her way. Marlene immediately glanced between Donovan and Rusty as if remembering that they'd arrived late, together. And that Donovan had told her they'd let her know what was going on later.

Donovan reached over to squeeze Rusty's hand under the table. Just a reminder that he was here and that he had her back.

She glanced gratefully at him but continued on. She didn't put it off on him. Didn't say that she and Donovan had something to say. She put it out there herself. Took full responsibility. Donovan respected her for that. He was damn proud of her.

"I hired someone part time at the hardware store."

There were raised eyebrows all around, and Frank immediately looked confused. But Donovan had to give his brothers credit. They didn't immediately launch into a thousand questions, nor did they interrogate Rusty or ask her what the hell she'd been thinking.

"When did this happen?" Frank asked in a puzzled tone.

Rusty swallowed and glanced back at Donovan, asking for silent support. He nodded and encouraged her to continue on. He'd step in when the time was right. For now she needed to give the details.

"He's a kid," she said quietly. "Fifteen years old. He's in . . . trouble."

When the table erupted in questions and scowls—the usual Kelly response to anyone in need—she held up her hand, and they quieted.

She took a deep breath. "He's hungry. I know how that feels. As I told Van, he could be me—he *is* me—at that age. Desperate. He's a good kid, though. I know y'all will think I'm crazy. Or naïve. But I know he's a good kid. He's quiet. He's a hard worker. He has two sisters he's trying to support and feed. And oh my God, y'all. What they're living in. It makes me want to cry for them."

Marlene's expression was immediately fierce. "How old are his sisters? Where are his parents? Why didn't you come to us immediately? You have to know we'd be willing to help them."

Rusty nodded. "I do know. I do. It just happened yesterday. He came in and asked if we needed any help. And I know I shouldn't have done it without asking, but I was afraid he'd walk out and never be back if I told him I'd have to see. So I made the decision and put him to work. I paid him in cash out of my own money."

Donovan's brothers scowled. Not in disapproval over Rusty. They'd gotten past that stage. But there was worry in their eyes. Not only of the kid Rusty had helped but over Rusty and the fear that she could be harmed.

"I went by today," Donovan said, speaking up for the first time.

Rusty sent him a grateful look for taking over. The entire table went quiet as they waited for Donovan to continue.

"It's why Rusty and I were late. I drove by the hardware store and saw Rusty's Jeep outside. I knew it was Sunday and so I went in to check and see what she was doing there. The kid was working and Rusty said he was hungry and she wanted to follow him home and check out his situation. See if he was in trouble at home and what kind of living conditions he had."

There was an instant round of objections as his brothers voiced their disapproval over Rusty going into a blind situation. One where she could easily be hurt or killed.

Donovan held up his hand. "I went with her. We followed the kid home. It's bad," he said after a pause. He knew he couldn't keep his emotions from the others. Couldn't keep his expression blank. They saw his reaction and they went silent and thoughtful, frowns creasing their brows.

"He has an older sister. Looks to be early to midtwenties. And a much younger sister. Charlotte's age. They're living hand to mouth in complete squalor. It's awful. I couldn't stomach it. I hated to leave them there."

"Why did you?" Garrett asked curiously.

The same question was in all of his brothers' eyes. They well knew his propensity for going in and doing what needed to be done. His softness for women and children in need. It likely did puzzle them as to why he would have walked away.

"Because they're in trouble," Donovan said quietly. "The bad kind of trouble that has nothing to do with being dirt-poor and having nothing to eat. They're running from something and running hard. They're scared to death, living every moment in fear of discovery."

"Fuck," Sam muttered, earning an instant glare of reprimand from his mother over his language at the dinner table.

"What are you going to do?" Garrett asked quietly.

Because it was a foregone conclusion in his brother's eyes

that Donovan would act. He wouldn't just stand back and allow a situation like this to go unchecked.

"The boy—Travis—is fifteen. The little one—Cammie—has been sick. My guess is that Eve has been staying with her while Travis found work just to put food on the table and buy medicine for her."

"Oh my Lord," Marlene whispered, her voice aching with pity. "We have to do something, Donovan. We can't just stand by and let them go hungry and without."

Donovan smiled at the answering agreement in all his family's faces.

"No, Ma, I don't plan to. But Rusty wanted you to know what she'd done and why. And I support her on this. I'll gladly pay Travis's salary out of my pocket. She's going to let him work this week whenever he wants to come in. They desperately need the money. But we have to be careful how we handle this. If we come on too strong, they'll cut and run. I saw the desperation—and fear—in their eyes. We have to tread very lightly."

"No need for you to pay for his salary," Frank said. "I'll gladly take on the kid. If what Rusty says is true and he's a good worker, I could use him around the shop. I'd gladly hire him on and pay him in cash like she's been doing."

"Just be careful," Rusty warned. "Don't question him. I've been very careful not to pry. He's scared and he'll bolt. I was him once. I know what he's thinking. He doesn't trust anyone. He's been conditioned to expect the worst in people. As Van said, we have to be very careful about anything we do, because they'll run. Eve said as much when we were at their house. I hesitate to call it a house. It's a horrible, run-down, leaking, dilapidated trailer."

"What do you want us to do?" Rachel asked softly.

Donovan's other sisters-in-law all looked to him and Rusty, the same question burning in their eyes. How could they help? He loved that they all had hearts the size of Texas and that they'd do anything at all to help someone in need.

His brothers might run a kick-ass organization devoted to helping those in danger, but his sisters-in-law were warriors in their own right and as formidable as KGI was any day of the week.

"For now, nothing," Donovan said. "I need to find out all I can about them and their situation. Try to figure out what they're running from. Travis will continue to work in the hardware store, and I plan to get out there and bring food and other supplies. Hopefully get to know them more so they'll trust me. If the entire Kelly clan descends on them, it'll just overwhelm them, and as Rusty said, they'll run."

His mom didn't look happy with his dictate, but she nodded her agreement.

"They need our help," Donovan added, his voice grim with resolve. "And I'm going to give it."

His brothers smiled ruefully in his direction.

"We would expect nothing less," Sam said.

CHAPTER 7

DONOVAN knew it wouldn't take long to get cornered by his brothers once the furor of lunch had settled and everyone had gotten up from the table and helped with cleanup. Donovan had purposely slipped out onto the back deck and waited for his brothers to follow. He knew them too well to think they'd just let it go and not question him intensely over Eve and her brother and sister.

He stood on the deck and stared out over the backyard. A place where memories had been built over the decades. He smiled, remembering many a barbecue. Wrestling with his brothers. Rusty's graduation, when Nathan had seemed to come out of his shell after his horrific imprisonment in the Middle East. It still chilled Donovan's blood, how close they had come to losing their younger brother.

If not for Shea . . . Donovan shook his head. At Rusty's barbecue, he and Nathan had wrestled, just like old times, and Donovan had been so relieved that he was seeing the old Nathan and not the shell of his younger brother that had returned, broken and changed. And then Nathan had freaked out. Tucked and ran from his parents' house like the hounds of hell were nipping at his heels. All because Shea had finally made contact again. She was in trouble, and Nathan had moved heaven and earth to get to her.

And now they were both home where they belonged. Married. Happy. In love. Just like all his older—and two younger—brothers.

He smiled ruefully. Ma had ribbed Joe at the table about settling down, but he knew that he was on her list as well. He was older than Joe and in his mother's mind, he should be next.

His thoughts drifted once again to Eve. What was her story? How old was she? She had an ageless look to her. She could be anywhere from twenty to thirty. She looked young, and yet when he looked into her eyes, he saw a much older woman. He saw the knowledge gleaned from years of experience. Of lessons learned the hard way. And he saw fear. He hated that the most. That this woman was struggling to keep it together, that she had so much responsibility. Younger siblings to take care of when she couldn't even take care of herself.

He wanted to barge in and demand answers. He wanted to know everything. What she was running from. And then he wanted to move that same heaven and earth that Nathan had moved in order to help Shea.

He had the house. He had the space for Eve and her brother and sister. He wanted them there. He realized that. As crazy as it sounded, he wanted nothing more than to move them into the compound and under his roof where he knew they would be protected. Where he could gain their trust and hopefully get them to open up about what was scaring them so badly.

And he knew he wouldn't like their answers—provided they ever gave them. He knew it was bad. The fact that a four-year-old baby girl looked at him with terror—and knowledge of all the bad things in the world, something no four-year-old should ever be acquainted with—told him everything he needed to know.

His fingers curled into tight fists. Helpless. He felt so

damn helpless and he hated it. Hated that he knew he couldn't just go in like this was a mission, act, remove the threat and ensure the safety of Eve and those precious children. He had to be very careful and take it slow, and that ate at him.

"You're slipping, old man," Sam said dryly from behind him. "You never even heard us come out."

Donovan turned to see Sam and Garrett standing there studying him. They knew something was on his mind and that this thing with Eve was bothering him. They could read him like a book. Always had been able to. But then Donovan wasn't someone who shielded his thoughts or his emotions. He'd never tried.

"Just thinking," Donovan replied.

Garrett nodded. "Yeah, that much is obvious."

"Hey, congrats to both of you," Donovan said. "Can't believe you two are providing more nieces and nephews. How is Sarah? Is she taking it well?"

Sam and Garrett both softened, their hard faces suddenly filling with love at the mention of their wives and their pregnancies.

"She's happy," Garrett said softly. "We both are. I worried it would be too soon. But she wanted a child, and well, I've always wanted a house full. But I'd wait indefinitely if that was what she wanted."

"I think we all know where I stand," Sam said in amusement. "Sophie and I started trying right after Rachel's babies were born. Not sure if this will be the last or not. I'll leave that up to Sophie. Every child is a blessing, and I'll take as many as she wants to have and be grateful for every one."

Garrett nodded. "Sarah and I have some catching up to do. Sam's on his second. Rachel gave Ethan twins. Hell, I'm surprised Nathan and Shea haven't started thinking about children yet."

Donovan smiled. "They're still young and they've both been through hell. It's probably smart that they're waiting. They still have a lot to work through. And they have all the time in the world. Shea is young. And hell, so is Nathan.

They still have a few years before they get to where Sam was when he had his first."

"Don't remind me of my age," Sam said with a grunt. "Turning forty sucks. I feel like an old fart now."

Garrett and Donovan both laughed.

Sam turned his stern gaze on Donovan as the laughter stopped. "Now, what's this about this kid Rusty hired and his sisters? You said it was bad. You also said they're running from something. What do we need to know here and what can we do to help?"

Donovan sighed and ran his hand raggedly through his short hair. "The hell of it is, I don't know. I've never felt so damn helpless in my life."

Garrett frowned and took a step forward. "I've seen you get worked up over women and children in danger plenty of times, Van. But this is different. *You're* different. What's going on here? We need the full truth. Not the watered-down version you gave Ma and the rest of the family at the table."

"Rusty is right. They're in trouble. I just don't know what they're running from," Donovan replied. "They need the money Travis is bringing in. He walks like he expects someone to jump out and attack him at any moment. He's always looking over his shoulder. He's so obvious about it that it makes me cringe. Someone would make him in a minute."

Sam made a sound of disgust and anger. "What do you plan to do?"

Donovan lifted his shoulders and then let them sag. "That's the problem. I don't know and it pisses me off. I can't treat this like a mission. Go in, kick ass and take names. Put a bow on it and call it good and leave knowing I made a difference and the people go on and live their lives. This woman is scared shitless. Her brother and sister are scared shitless. It was like being punched in the balls to see that four-year-old little girl look at me like I was a monster."

"Damn," Garrett said softly. "That sucks, man. There has to be something we can do."

"Oh, I'm going to do something," Donovan said, his soft vow settling over his brothers. "I have to figure out a way to get close to them. To make them trust me. I'm going to start by bringing them food and evaluating the situation more thoroughly. And then, if Cammie is still sick, I want to bring in Maren so she can check out Cammie."

"Is that the little girl's name?" Sam asked. "Cammie?"

Donovan nodded. "Yeah. She's Charlotte's age. Reminds me a lot of her. But where Charlotte is a happy, normal child without a care in the world and an entire family behind her to love and protect her, Cammie has Travis and Eve and that's *all* she has."

"I'm sure Maren would love to help," Garrett said. "Good idea to call her in and bring her out. Not like she doesn't make house calls now that she's taken over Doc Campbell's practice."

"She's been taking it a lot easier and Doc has stepped back in to take some of the patient load while she's been on maternity leave, but she still sees a few patients. Steele's been breathing down her neck trying to make her take it easier," Sam said, amusement thick in his voice.

Donovan and Garrett both chuckled. It was funny as hell to see the team leader so wrapped up in his wife and daughter. Steele with a baby was a sight no one in KGI ever imagined seeing. But it was hilarious to see the ice man thoroughly wrapped around the finger of Dr. Maren Scofield—now Steele—and their daughter, Olivia.

"Steele won't like letting Maren go in alone," Garrett warned. "If he gets wind of the situation, there's no way in hell he'll let her go in without him, and if Eve and her siblings get sight of Steele, he'll scare the shit out of them even more."

Donovan grimaced. "Yeah, I hear you. I could use your help persuading him to stay his ass at home and let me go in with Maren. I will have been out twice by then, so I think they'd be okay with me and Maren. But if Steele comes, yeah, that's not a good idea."

"I'll put a bug in his ear and assure him that you'll be with her and prepared for anything. But I need the situation, Van. I need to know everything about what she's going into, because Steele is going to want to know and I can't just tell him nothing and to trust us. You know him. He plays by his own damn rules, and he's very protective of Maren and Olivia."

"There's no danger inside that trailer," Donovan murmured. "It's a run-down piece of crap that no human should be living in. Cammie is four. Travis is fifteen, but he's a good kid. Earnest. Determined to provide for his sisters. And Eve . . . I'm guessing midtwenties, but it's hard to know. She has this ageless look to her. Like she could be twenty or thirty or anywhere in between. Beautiful. But scared to death."

Garrett's and Sam's brows furrowed as they stared back at their younger brother. Donovan shifted uncomfortably under their scrutiny, knowing he'd probably said too much. Or perhaps it was his tone or expression that had given him away. Fuck it all. The last thing he needed was a lecture about getting *too* emotionally involved. More so than normal, at least.

"What's this woman mean to you, Van?" Sam asked quietly.

"She's in trouble and she needs help," Donovan said, avoiding the question. "That's what she means to me. Some asshole has made that baby girl afraid of men. A part of me doesn't even want to imagine what they've all been subjected to, and we come across a lot of horrific shit in our line of work. At this point you'd think we'd seen it all, and yet I find myself surprised every time I come across some asshole who abuses women or children."

Garrett winced in sympathy. "I hear you, man. But the day we become immune to it is the day we need to hang up the job. It has to mean something to us or we couldn't do what we do. We aren't fucking robots without empathy or emotions. Every mission means something."

"Every mission is personal," Sam said, echoing a statement he'd made many times in the past. "Just some are more personal than others."

"And this is one of them," Donovan said softly. "I can't explain it, but yeah, this is very personal to me and I'm not going to look the other way."

Sam put his hand on Donovan's shoulder and squeezed. "You know we have your back."

Donovan smiled. "Yeah, never doubted it. Never will. I'll call Maren. You put a call into Steele. Get him to stand down. I know it will kill the control freak in him, but explain the situation. Tell him I'd never put Maren into a dangerous situation and that I'll have her covered every second we're there."

"Will do," Sam said. "But Van? And I'm probably wasting my breath saying this, but don't let your emotions overrule your common sense. If you get in too deep, take a step back and let one of us go in. We'd be more objective and you know we'd get the job done."

"No one is doing this but me," Donovan said, his voice more fierce than he intended. "She's mine. *They're* mine. And I protect what's mine."

CHAPTER 8

EVE stopped by the couch where Cammie lay sleeping and swept her hand lightly over Cammie's forehead, frowning when she still felt the evidence of fever. She closed her eyes as she withdrew her hand, not wanting to wake the sleeping child, and walked toward the tiny kitchen area in the hot, muggy trailer.

She filled a glass of water from the tap, not bothering with the ice from the antiquated ice trays in the freezer. Those were saved for Cammie. Eve used them for the drinks she gave Cammie but also to cool her down when her fever got too high.

If she didn't pay the water and electric bill soon, they'd be without both. Electricity they could do without. It wasn't as if they had air-conditioning for relief. Being in the darkness didn't bother her. The heat did.

And it was hot today. No breeze to filter in through the windows and give any relief. She'd spent precious funds on a box fan from the thrift store and pointed it at the couch so Cammie would have some relief from the heat and maybe aid in lowering her fever, but it was still sweltering, even though it wasn't even noon yet. And if they lost electricity, they'd lose the small measure of relief the fan provided.

Yet one more thing to worry over. As if she didn't have enough already just trying to provide food for them to eat.

She took stock of the meager supplies she'd purchased before Travis had gone in to work at the hardware store. She'd stretched the money as far as she could, buying only what was necessary. Food. The fan for Cammie. And more medication. Even buying the generic, she'd winced at the prices.

While she'd been out, she'd stopped in a small coffee shop not too far from where Travis worked and had spent a few precious minutes on the Internet. Looking for any sign that Walt was close. For any new developments. What the latest accusations were he was flinging her way.

All she'd accomplished was renewing her utter panic as she'd gone over the news stories in the local California papers and seen that even a few larger news outlets in the bigger cities in California had picked up on the "human interest" story of a deranged, emotionally unstable woman who'd kidnapped the two children of a wealthy, respected man.

Eve wanted to put her fist through the computer screen. Lies. All of it lies. But who would believe her? Who would ever believe that Walt was the monster and not her? That he was the sadistic, abusive father instead of the doting, worried, grieving man he portrayed to the rest of the world. He had everyone who mattered fooled. Only she—and Travis and Cammie—knew the truth.

Eve's mother had known the truth, and she'd paid for it with her life. Eve could never prove it, but she knew, she *knew* that Walt had killed her mother. It wasn't a guess. She knew absolutely. And so did Travis. They kept that from Cammie. It was something she never needed to know. She had enough to fear from her father without knowing he'd killed their mother. But Eve and Travis knew and they lived with the knowledge every single day. That if they ever went back, they'd be going back to hell.

Eve would be locked away, if not in jail, in some mental

institution where they'd make a vegetable out of her. And Travis and Cammie would be returned to a man who'd destroy them.

It was only a matter of time before the news carried farther than California. Maybe it already had. Walt had the connections, and it was evident he was doing everything in his power to make the media carry the story far and wide. So there'd be no place for Eve to hide. No hole deep enough. No corner far enough out of the way to escape his reach.

An Amber Alert had already been issued for Travis and Cammie. Eve's face was plastered on many a billboard as the one who'd kidnapped the children. She was listed as highly unstable and to be approached with caution, as she could be armed and dangerous.

That was laughable. She'd never even held a gun in her hands. Wouldn't know how to use it. There was a lot she regretted. One was thinking, as many people did, that she'd never have need of self-defense. That she'd never be touched by situations calling for violence. Or to defend herself *from* violence.

She was a naïve fool, and now Travis and Cammie were paying the price for her ignorance.

Her first instinct was to hide behind blissful ignorance. Not to seek out information or remind herself of what she was running from. But that would be the height of stupidity. She couldn't afford blind ignorance or to ever believe for one minute that she was safe. Hidden. Out of Walt's reach.

And so she needed to keep close watch and monitor the news and any other information about Walt's pursuit, both privately and in the media. It was the private pursuit that scared her the most. Not that both avenues weren't frightening. But it was the lengths to which a man like Walt would go *outside* the law that sent chills snaking down her spine and gripped her throat in a paralyzing hold that took her breath.

She tensed, shaken from her chilling thoughts by the sound of a vehicle just outside the trailer door. Sweat broke out on her forehead, and her gaze flew to Cammie, who was still sleeping on the couch.

Oh God. What if he was here? What if he'd found her? There was nowhere for her to run. No escape. She had no vehicle. The one she'd bought with nearly all of her cash reserves—under a false name—from a seedy car lot that charged her three times what the piece of crap was worth had broken down outside Dover.

She and Travis and Cammie had abandoned it, knowing they had no money or means to repair it, and they'd walked. It was how they'd come to stay in Dover. Necessity. Not choice.

With the last of their available cash, Eve had rented the trailer and paid the necessary deposits to have the utilities turned on.

Until she was able to work and stock up enough money to fund their escape to the next place, they were solidly stuck here.

She rushed to the couch, galvanized into action by the sound of a closing door. She curled her arms underneath Cammie and flew into the bedroom. Cammie stirred, a sleepy protest forming on her lips.

"Shhhh, Cammie," Eve soothed. "Be very quiet, darling. Someone's here."

Cammie went instantly still, rigid in Eve's arms. Eve damned the fact that Cammie was well acquainted with the need to hide. To be quiet. On constant alert.

"Crawl under the bed," Eve whispered, setting her on the floor even as she issued the command. "Don't come out, Cammie. No matter what you may hear. You stay here and hide. Don't make a single sound. Promise me."

"I promise," Cammie whispered back.

Eve all but pushed the small child under the double bed and then arranged the faded, worn bed skirt to hide the evidence that someone was hiding underneath. If anything happened to Eve—if Walt had found her—perhaps she could convince them that Travis and Cammie weren't with her. That she'd left them somewhere else. Separating them so that if Eve was arrested, or worse, discovered by Walt himself, maybe, just maybe, Cammie would remain hidden and undiscovered until Travis arrived.

A knock sounded in the distance and Eve's heart pounded

harder. She whispered an urgent prayer as she shakily rose from her perch. *Please, please don't let it be the police.* Or worse, Walt. It was a testament to just how much she feared her stepfather that she'd actually prefer to be confronted by the police than by Walt himself.

For a moment she considered ignoring the knock. There wasn't a vehicle parked outside to indicate anyone was at home. She knew no one here. It was certainly in the realm of possibility given the time of day that one could assume whoever lived here was at work.

Unless they knew better. Unless they knew very well she was here. That this was where she'd fled and hid even now.

Another knock sounded. Harder this time. A knock that told her whoever it was wasn't going away.

Bracing her shoulders, determined not to let anyone see her fear, she walked slowly to the door. There wasn't a window in the door. She was fortunate to have a door at all with the condition of the rest of the trailer. No way to see who was on the other side without revealing herself by looking out the small window in the living room.

But she peeked anyway, wanting to know at least what she was up against. If there were police cars outside.

Frowning, she took in the same truck that had been there just the day before. Donovan Kelly. He'd come with Rusty Kelly, the young woman who'd hired Travis. What could he want?

Feeling only a margin of relief, she went to the door and cracked it cautiously, even though it was ridiculous, because if the man wanted in, there was little she could do about it. Even *she* could break through this door.

"Eve?"

Donovan's soft inquiry slid over her ears, pricking her nape. Her pulse sped up as she met his gaze.

"It's Donovan Kelly. We met yesterday," he said unnecessarily.

She nodded, not trusting herself to speak. She was still dealing with the overwhelming fear she'd experienced when she'd heard the vehicle drive up. She breathed deeply through her nostrils, willing her pulse to slow from its rapid thudding at her temples. It wouldn't surprise her if he were able to see her heart beat against her thin T-shirt.

"Can I come in?"

She gripped the door harder and stared at him, taking in the plastic grocery bags dangling from both hands.

"Why are you here?" she finally managed to get out. "It's not a good time."

"I brought some things that you, Cammie and Travis needed," he said, dipping his head toward the stuffed bags.

She stared in bewilderment at him, unsettled by the unexpected visit, but more so by the determination she saw in his eyes.

"Eve, I'm here to help you," he said gently. "Let me in so I can unload the groceries."

It was voiced quietly enough, but there was a definite thread of command in his tone. Her grip eased on the door, and then she remembered Cammie. Hiding under the bed in the other room. How would it look if Donovan saw?

"Cammie's sleeping," she blurted. "I don't want to disturb her."

Donovan nodded even as he pushed forward, giving her no choice but to let go of the door. As he walked in, his gaze went to the couch where Cammie had been resting just moments earlier. The fan was still humming and panic scuttled up Eve's spine.

"She must have gone to the bathroom. I'll just go check on her while you . . ." She broke off, gesturing toward the bags he held.

"Take your time," Donovan said in an easy voice. "I can make my way around your kitchen just fine."

Eve bolted toward the bedroom, shutting the door firmly behind her. Just in case he had any crazy ideas of following her. She hurried to the bed and knelt, lifting the tattered bed skirt to peer underneath.

"Cammie," she called softly. "Come out, darling. I need you to hurry."

Cammie immediately scrambled toward Eve, and Eve

enfolded her in her arms, picking her up to hurry in the direction of the bathroom so that at least if Donovan did barge in, it would appear as though Cammie had indeed just gone to the bathroom.

Cammie's eyes were huge in her small face, a face that was frozen with fear.

"It's all right, Cammie. It's just Donovan Kelly. You remember him, don't you? He came with the woman who hired Travis yesterday. He was nice. He said he wanted to be your friend."

Cammie slowly nodded, but she still wore a wary, guarded look that made Eve's chest ache.

Eve carried her into the living room and eased her onto the couch so the fan would blow over her flushed skin. To her surprise, Donovan appeared beside Eve, his expression worried as he took in Cammie's appearance.

Cammie shrank back, her eyes widening in fear. Eve wished she could control it, but what four-year-old could? It was a dead giveaway. Anyone with eyes could see the child had much to be afraid of.

Donovan took a cautious step back but turned to Eve, his expression grave—and determined. She felt as if she'd just stepped into a mire by allowing him access to her trailer, but then could she have really kept him out? He didn't look like a man who took no for an answer. Ever.

"She's not better," he said grimly. "Is she still running a fever?"

Eve nodded, her shoulders sagging. She automatically reached for Cammie, putting a reassuring hand on her shoulder and squeezing as if to tell her it would be okay. That Eve would die before allowing anyone to hurt her.

"She needs a doctor," Donovan said bluntly. "She likely needs to be in the hospital. How long has she been ill?"

Eve hit the panic button again. "I can't afford a doctor. Or a hospital." Not to mention the exposure caused by a hospital stay. "I've been giving her fluids and medication around the clock. She's been keeping it down. Well, after that first day."

"Come into the kitchen with me," Donovan murmured.

"Reassure Cammie you won't be going far. We should discuss this away from her."

Eve's eyes widened at his perception. Then she glanced down at Cammie, racked by indecision.

"Eve," Donovan prompted.

Eve closed her eyes and then leaned down to brush a kiss across Cammie's brow. "I'm just going to the kitchen. Donovan brought food. Wouldn't you like a special treat?"

Slowly Cammie nodded, but she kept casting her gaze sideways at Donovan, shadows haunting her young eyes.

Eve turned and made sure Donovan went ahead of her so that she was between him and Cammie at all times. He'd made quick work of putting away the groceries, though he'd left several items out on the small countertop. Sprite. Soups. A loaf of bread. Acetaminophen and ibuprofen as well as several bottles of Pedialyte, a fluid designed to correct electrolyte imbalance.

It would appear he'd thought of everything.

"I can't afford a doctor," she whispered fiercely. "She'll be okay. I'm staying with her and monitoring her fever at all times."

Donovan put his hand over hers where she'd rested it on the countertop. A warm shock raced up her arm. Soothing. It baffled her, because she had everything to fear from this man, and yet something so simple as his touch calmed some of the rising panic and hysteria rampaging through her mind.

"I have a friend—a very close friend—who is a doctor. You'd like her. Her name is Maren. She's married to another very good friend of mine. She's been on maternity leave and is just now starting to get back into the swing of her practice. She routinely makes house calls, and she also sees disadvantaged patients free of charge. And Eve, you *are* in need. Cammie is in need. I'd like to bring her over tomorrow to check on Cammie. I'm concerned. She appears to be a very sick little girl, and while I'm sure you're doing the absolute best you can, sometimes it's not enough."

She sagged, her head lowering because he was right. It wasn't something she could very well hide. One only had to look at her—at where she lived—to know that she was in desperate need. And Cammie *did* need a doctor. Eve had been up with her all night, worried, sick with indecision over whether she should risk taking her into the emergency room. But how would she have gotten there? She was basically trapped here. No access to anything that wasn't in walking distance.

Donovan lifted her hand, curling his fingers gently around hers. She tried to pull away, but he tightened his grip, giving her hand a gentle squeeze. His grasp wasn't painful. Not at all. He wasn't trying to hurt her, but neither did he let her go.

"We aren't going to harm you, Eve. Nobody is. I'll bring Maren out first thing in the morning so she can do an assessment on Cammie. She likely needs more than the over-the-counter medications you've been giving her."

She closed her eyes, bringing her free hand to her throbbing temple. More medications. Prescription medications. No insurance. No way to pay for them. And antibiotics weren't cheap!

"Eve," Donovan said in a voice barely above a whisper. "Look at me."

Eve lifted her gaze and in his eyes she saw—*felt*—warmth. Kindness. And something else entirely that she couldn't quite figure out. He looked at her oddly. Like she was someone who mattered. To *him*.

"I'm going to get you the help you need. Help that Cammie and Travis need."

Eve's knees went weak and nearly gave out. She stumbled and braced her free hand on the countertop while Donovan's grasp tightened on her other hand as if to steady her.

What if he reported her to child protective services? In his place, Eve certainly would. This was no place for a child, and it was equally obvious that Eve wasn't providing for Cammie. He would be well within his rights to report his findings to the authorities, and then they'd sweep in and take Cammie—and Travis—away from her. And eventually return them to their father when it was discovered who they were. And Eve? She'd be punished for what she'd done. For taking desperate measures to protect her family. She simply couldn't be separated from them and leave them at Walt's mercy. It didn't bear thinking about.

"Whatever the hell you're thinking, stop," Donovan said. "I don't know what's going through your head right now, but Eve, you can trust me. I realize that you don't trust anyone. That much is evident. It's also equally evident that you're in some kind of trouble. You have nothing to fear from me. Or from Maren. We only want to help."

"I don't know what to do," Eve whispered, glancing desperately in Cammie's direction.

It was the wrong thing to do, and she cursed that she'd broadcast her fear for her sister to see.

Cammie immediately started crying. Not loudly. No. Cammie had learned to be quiet at all times. Big, silent tears rolled down her cheeks, and her thin shoulders shook. Tears pricked Eve's eyelids as her heart broke into a thousand pieces.

She broke away from Donovan, and this time he let her go. She flew to the couch and knelt, pulling Cammie into her arms.

"Please don't worry, darling," Eve soothed. "He only wants to help. He wants to bring a doctor to see you and make you all better. Wouldn't that be wonderful?"

Even as she said it, she knew that as soon as Travis got home from work, they'd pack their meager belongings and as much of the food that Donovan had brought as they could carry, and by the time Donovan showed up with his doctor tomorrow, they'd be long gone.

They were far too exposed here. First the woman who had hired Travis and now her brother. He wanted to bring in a doctor and God only knew who else. What if it was all a ruse? What if the cops showed up at her door tomorrow?

They needed anonymity. They needed a place where they would gain no notice. Where they'd be just another poor, struggling family among many.

There were shelters in larger cities. Maybe even Memphis, if they could get that far. There had to be a way for them to get the shelter they needed until Eve could pick up a steady enough job to bolster their finances. She and Trav could tag-team, where one would always be with Cammie while the other worked.

"What did he bring to eat?" Cammie whispered.

Her question nearly undid Eve.

"I brought lots of yummy things that my niece, who is about your age, assures me are the best things ever," Donovan said cheerfully.

Eve yanked her head around to see that Donovan had followed them over.

"But I think perhaps we should take it easy on your stomach. At least until you're feeling a little better. How does a grilled cheese, hot soup and a Sprite sound?"

Cammie's eye brightened. "I love grilled cheese sandwiches."

"Consider it done," Donovan said, performing an exaggerated bow that elicited a giggle from Cammie.

Eve watched in wonder as Cammie relaxed under the force of nature that was Donovan Kelly. The man was too good to be true, and Eve had learned the hard way that what appeared to be too good was precisely that. A facade.

"Mind if I steal Eve a moment so she can help me whip up lunch?" Donovan asked.

Cammie slowly nodded, her hand automatically going to her mouth. She slid her thumb inside, a habit she'd only recently adopted. One that was a result of the stress they were all under.

Donovan nudged Eve's elbow, guiding her away from the couch and back to the tiny kitchenette. He took over as if this were indeed his own kitchen. She stood stiffly, watching as he expertly put together the meal, even including a cupcake on a separate paper plate for Cammie's dessert.

"Why are you doing this?" she asked in a low voice. "You don't know me—us. Why would you go to this much trouble for complete strangers?"

His head whipped up and for the first time she caught a glint of anger in his green eyes.

"What would you have me do, Eve? Turn a blind eye to people who desperately need help? Or ignore the fact that you're scared to death and are running from something or someone? Don't look so stunned. It's not hard to figure out. And if I can see it, don't you think everyone else can? Only those others won't be of no danger to you like I am. I get that you don't trust anyone. Believe me, I get that. But I'm going to do everything in my power to change that. There are good people in the world. I'm trying to convince you that I'm one of them."

"It could be dangerous for you," she blurted.

It was as close to an acknowledgment of what he already knew as she was going to get.

Some of the anger dimmed from his eyes, and once again she saw that glimmer that told her she wasn't just someone in need he was helping. And it befuddled her.

"How about you let me decide what I consider dangerous? You say I know nothing about you, but, Eve, you know nothing about me. Yet. And believe me when I say I am not going to let anything happen to you or Cammie and Travis."

The hell of it was, in that moment, he spoke with so much conviction that she found herself believing him when she should be believing or trusting no one.

"Now here's what I want you to do," Donovan said as he pushed one of the two plates he'd prepared across the counter to her. "I want you to go sit with Cammie and eat. You're as badly in need of a meal as she is."

"And what are you going to do?" she asked quietly.

"I'm going to finish putting away the things I brought and make sure your refrigerator is stocked. And then I'm going to make a list of anything else you need so that when I come with Maren tomorrow, I'll bring whatever then."

CHAPTER 9

IT took everything Donovan had to walk out of Eve's trailer and stroll to his truck like he'd just been on some neighborly errand for his mother. He was seething on the inside, and he couldn't even pinpoint the exact target of his rage.

Seeing Eve—and Cammie—look at him like he was some monster and they were expecting the worst turned his stomach. And Cammie. God. He couldn't picture her without seeing Charlotte and couldn't imagine his niece in the same situation.

He—all of KGI—took a hell of a lot for granted. They shouldn't. Enough had happened over the years for them to know all too well not to take a single moment with their families for granted. And yet it was all too easy to forget the circumstances that others lived in. Despite the fact that they saw the worst in the world on a daily basis.

As he drove away, he picked up his cell to call Sam to see if he'd contacted Maren—and Steele—but mainly Maren. Because Steele could put up a fight all he wanted, but if Maren wanted to do something, Steele didn't have a chance. Steele would just make damn sure she wasn't walking into a dangerous situation, and after what Donovan had witnessed, he knew that there was nothing to fear over Maren going to check on Cammie. Whatever the danger was, it wasn't from Eve. No, whatever the hell it was that had struck terror into Eve and her tiny family's hearts was out there lurking and waiting for an opportunity to strike. An opportunity that, if Donovan had any control over it, would never present itself.

After Sam confirmed that Maren was in and that Steele had been assured all the bases were covered as far as Maren's safety, Donovan rang off and drove toward the compound, Eve squarely on his mind.

He activated the key code to open the gate and waited as it swung open, allowing him entrance. The tight security net around the compound reminded him of the reality of his life. His family's lives. It was a necessary evil, one they were all well aware of. But it brought to the forefront that they would never lead *normal* lives. That theirs came with an awareness that at any time, enemies could strike at them, at their most vulnerable weakness. Their wives, mothers, fathers, brothers, sisters, nieces and nephews.

Donovan had wondered in the past, as he was sure all his brothers had, particularly when their family had been in jeopardy, if it was all worth it. If what they did was worth the risk to their loved ones. But at the end of the day, the answer was always the same. Yes. They might not be able to solve all the ills of the world, but they could damn well make it a better place, one mission at a time. For every criminal they took down, for every child they rescued, for every hostage they freed, they made a difference.

Maybe that answer would change if they ever lost any part of their family to the enemies they'd accumulated over the years since KGI's inception. But for now, they were still absolutely devoted to righting wrongs and taking down the evil in the world.

As he pulled up to his house, he was surprised to see Steele's SUV parked out front. Not that it *should* have come as a shock. Steele would want a firsthand accounting of the situation his wife was walking into.

But then the passenger door opened, and Donovan saw Maren step into the sunshine, a warm smile lighting her features as she stared toward Donovan. A moment later, Steele got out of the driver's side, his expression not as warm as Maren's. Donovan sighed and stepped out of his vehicle. Might as well beard the lion now.

"Hello, Van," Maren called out. And then she opened the passenger door and ducked in, a second later reappearing with her daughter.

Donovan's smile was instantaneous. Okay, so he was a total sucker for babies. Sue him.

"Hey, sweetheart," he said as he walked toward where Maren stood with the baby. "I swear that girl gets bigger every time I see her."

Maren grinned. "That's because I'm a twenty-four-seven fast-food restaurant. Clearly she inherited her father's appetite because I swear I can't ever feed her enough."

Steele grunted and then reached for the baby, expertly cradling her in his arms. Donovan shook his head. He still hadn't gotten used to seeing Steele with an infant. The sight still elicited amusement, and if he was honest, it also inspired envy.

"So what's the situation?" Steele asked bluntly.

"Why don't y'all come in out of the heat?" Donovan offered. "I have some iced tea in the fridge and I can brew Maren up a cup of her favorite hot tea. Then we'll talk."

"Hadn't planned to stay long," Steele replied. "Weather's supposed to get bad tonight, and I don't want to have Maren or Olivia out in it."

Donovan frowned. "Bad weather? What are we talking here?"

Maren rolled her eyes. "Steele has become a regular meteorologist in his spare time. He's convinced a storm is going to take us out."

Steele shot her a glare. "It pays to be aware of potential hazards."

Donovan mounted the steps to his home and swung open the door, gesturing Maren and Steele inside.

"So? The weather report?" Donovan queried.

"Severe thunderstorms. Isolated strong cells. The entire western part of the state is under watch overnight."

Donovan blew out his breath. Damn. All he could picture was that first time he'd walked into Eve's trailer and had seen the bowls scattered over the floor to catch the rain. They'd be miserable tonight and with Cammie sick, the last thing she needed was to get rained on inside her house.

"Have a seat," Donovan murmured. "I'll get Maren's tea brewing. Care if I nuke the water and throw a bag in it?"

Maren smiled. "Nope. With my hands full of a starving infant, I've learned the art of a quick brew."

Donovan shuffled into the kitchen and drew water into a coffee mug before slipping it into the microwave. While he waited for the time to elapse, he filled two glasses with ice and took the pitcher of tea from the fridge.

When the microwave dinged, he pulled the hot mug out and dropped the bag into it. Remembering that she liked sugar, he spooned the right amount and gave it a quick stir. Balancing one of the tea glasses between his arm and chest, he picked up the mug and the other glass and headed back to the living room.

"How have you stayed single this long?" Maren teased as she took the proffered cup. "I love a man who spoils me."

Steele grunted again and shot her a bemused look. Donovan chuckled because it was widely known that Steele absolutely spoiled both wife and daughter.

Steele took the glass from Donovan's hand but didn't drink. He leaned forward, setting the glass on the coffee table, and looked expectantly at Donovan.

"It's bad," Donovan murmured.

Steele's expression immediately blackened. "What the fuck? Sam said it was safe."

Donovan shook his head. "Not what I mean. It's safe for Maren. I wouldn't bring her into a situation that put her at risk. You know that."

"Then what the hell do you mean?" Steele demanded.

"Steele."

Maren's soft voice immediately brought the team leader

to heel. If the situation hadn't been so serious, Donovan would totally have given him shit over it.

"Not very far from here, a young woman is living in a run-down, piece-of-shit trailer with her two younger siblings. Cammie, her four-year-old sister, is sick. Travis, her fifteen-year-old brother, is working part time in the hardware store to put food on their table, and Eve . . . She's trying to keep it together."

Steele frowned.

"They're running from something," Donovan continued. "They're all scared shitless."

"Well, fuck," Steele muttered.

"How sick is Cammie?" Maren asked, her eyes narrowing in concentration.

Steele reached for the baby, deftly taking her from Maren's arms as she sat forward, her gaze trained on Donovan.

"I don't know," Donovan admitted. "That's why I wanted you to go with me to check on her. I'd say she's been sick several days. Their living conditions are deplorable. They don't have enough to eat. I took groceries over today, but their roof—if you can even call it that—leaks in a hundred different places, and with all the rain we had last week, I doubt that helped Cammie's condition any."

Maren grimaced, her eyes shining with sympathy and concern. "Of course I'll go."

"I'll go with you," Steele said.

Donovan shook his head. "No way, Steele. I know it chaps your control-freak ass to stand down on this one, but if you show up, I guarantee we won't get anywhere near them. Not to mention they'll likely bolt. When I say Eve's trying to keep it together, I mean trying, as in barely managing it. She was spooked enough with just me there. You show up?"

"He's right," Maren said, looking pointedly in her husband's direction. "You'll scare the poor woman witless."

Steele scowled.

"Maren is in no danger," Donovan said. "The only people who live there are Eve, Travis and Cammie. Travis is a good kid. Shouldering way too much responsibility, but you have nothing to fear. I'll be with Maren the entire time. No way I would let her go into a situation where I wasn't absolutely certain she'd be safe."

Steele's lips thinned, but he didn't argue the point.

"Besides, I'll need you to keep Olivia," Maren said in amusement.

Steele's gaze automatically fell over his daughter, and his expression softened. His face lost the hard lines that seemed permanently etched in his skin, and his eyes lightened with love.

"I'm trusting you with my life," Steele said as he lifted his gaze back to Donovan.

They were words echoed from months before when Donovan had pulled Maren from the helicopter wreckage while Steele had waited, helplessly pinned.

"I know," Donovan said quietly. "I'll take care of her. I promise."

Steele nodded and then glanced in Maren's direction. "You ready? Little bit is about ready for her nap."

Maren laughed. "Which means she'll eat on the way home first." She shook her head. "I swear this kid eats more than Steele does."

"What time do you want her here tomorrow?" Steele asked as he rose, cradling his daughter in the crook of his arm. "I'll bring her here and wait for y'all to get back."

Maren rolled her eyes. "Because heaven forbid I drive myself."

Steele shrugged. "I need to talk to Sam."

Maren nodded, a quick look exchanged by the couple. Donovan lifted an eyebrow.

"Everything okay?"

"Yeah. I know you've had my team, Van, and they couldn't be in better hands, but I'm ready to get back in. Maren and I have talked about it and it's time. Her practice is established and she's going to be taking the patient load back on, and it's time for me to get back to my team before they forget who they belong to."

Donovan chuckled. "As if that's going to happen. I'll miss

them. It's been great working with them over the past several months. But I know they'll be glad to get their team leader back."

Donovan walked out to Steele's SUV with them. Steele turned back to Donovan, his expression serious.

"Give Sam a heads-up on the weather, okay? It's supposed to get bad. Don't know if he's had an eye to the forecast or not."

Donovan frowned. "Will do. Y'all be careful too."

Maren rolled her eyes. "Oh, we'll be spending the night in the basement, no doubt. After the baby was born, Steele set up a bedroom down there, and if there's so much as a chance of severe storms, that's where we sleep."

Steele grunted. "Can't be too careful. Not much of a duck-and-run kind of guy."

"Got a point," Donovan said. "See y'all in the morning."

Donovan watched as they drove away and then glanced across the way to where his brothers' homes were. They were all separated by several acres and Nathan's was even farther away, nestled on a bluff overlooking the lake. Things were quiet. No current mission. They weren't even training today.

The new team had trained extensively over the last several months and Sam had given them all time off, a precursor to setting them loose on their own.

Skylar and Edge had moved closer to the compound while Swanny still lived with Joe in Sam's old cabin a short distance away. Skylar and Edge spent a lot of time at Joe and Swanny's place. It was good for them to bond. Build camaraderie and form the foundation of a solid team.

Complete immersion. They'd spent every day together for the last few months, but now it was time to give them a break before parceling out missions to the new team and trusting them to get it done.

It was hard for Donovan. He'd admit that. He had complete faith in all the teams, but it didn't mean he didn't worry. Nathan and Joe were his youngest brothers. They'd always be his younger brothers, which meant his instinct was to protect them whether they needed it or not.

And the truth was that Nathan, Joe and Swanny had all

been through hell. Nathan and Swanny more so, but Joe
hadn't had an easy time of it either. Donovan worried from
time to time that they weren't ready.

But he and Sam and Garrett had agreed. They were solid.
It was time.

So the next mission would be drawn by Nathan and Joe,
with Steele's team acting as backup. Now that Steele was
getting back into action, things would get back to normal
and Donovan would step back and not take as active a part
in the missions.

Not that he'd ever just stand back and keep out of action.
Sam and Garrett had taken more of a managerial position
over the last year. They coordinated, did the planning, called
in the teams as needed, but they'd stepped back.

They both had wives—and now both were expecting new
additions to the family. Their loyalty belonged first to their
wives and then KGI. Of all the Kelly brothers, Donovan and
Joe were the most involved, although Nathan had stepped up
as the new team came together.

Things were going . . . well. He winced, not wanting to
jinx them all, but things were definitely quiet on the home
front. Everyone was . . . happy. They'd survived setback
after setback and had come out the stronger for it.

Even the team leaders were settling down. Donovan had
honestly never thought he'd see the day that Rio and Steele
would positively ooze domesticity. And yet both men were
married, had daughters and were no longer eating, sleeping
and drinking all things KGI.

They had all turned their eyes toward him, swearing that
he was next. And it wasn't that he didn't want that. Of all his
brothers, he'd probably been the least resistant to marriage
and family. He just hadn't met the right woman yet.

When he married, he knew that his wife and children
would get a hundred and ten percent of his loyalty. And he
hadn't yet met a woman who made him reorder his priorities.

He studied his cell phone a moment and then shoved it
back into his pocket, deciding to head over to Sam's to give
him the heads-up on the weather and Steele's return.

CHAPTER 10

EVE was waiting anxiously just inside the doorway when Travis walked up to the trailer. As soon as he walked in, his gaze caught Eve's and worry instantly flooded his eyes.

"What's wrong, Evie?"

She put a hand to his arm in an attempt to reassure him, but she couldn't very well do that when she knew they had to run. Again.

"We need to leave," she said in a low voice.

Alarm blazed across his face. "What happened? Did he find us?"

She shook her head. "No. At least I don't think so. It's just that . . ." She blew out her breath and then glanced in Cammie's direction. "We need to go. We've gained the notice of too many people here. Donovan was here today and he plans to bring a doctor over to see Cammie tomorrow. I don't want to risk it."

Regret dulled Travis's eyes. "I liked it here. I had hoped . . ."

"I know," she whispered. "I'd hoped too. It will be better the next place, Trav."

It was what she'd said every time they'd picked up and

fled, and they both knew it was a lie. It would never be better until Walt was no longer a threat.

Travis pulled out several folded bills and handed them over to Eve. "I hope this will help some."

Eve took the money and then hugged Travis, pulling his lanky frame into her arms. "Thank you, Trav. You are an amazing guy. Donovan brought groceries when he came today. We'll pack everything we can carry with us. We can't afford to just leave it behind."

Travis hesitated and then pulled away, his eyes troubled. "Evie, do you think we're doing the right thing by leaving? Maybe . . . Maybe they do just want to help."

"I want to believe that. But I can't risk you and Cammie by trusting the wrong people. And while they may not be any danger themselves, we risk a lot by exposing ourselves to even more people here. The fewer people we gain the notice of, the safer we are."

Travis nodded. "I understand. When do you want to leave?"

Eve glanced again to where Cammie was sleeping on the couch. "After it gets dark, I think."

"There are some pretty dark clouds in the distance," Travis said. "It's completely black to the west. Maybe we should wait until whatever storm passes before we take Cammie out."

Eve nodded her agreement. "Yes. We'll pack what we can and let Cammie rest for as long as she's able. After the storm passes, we'll head out."

"Have you given any thought to where?" Travis asked quietly.

Helplessness gripped Eve as she contemplated Travis's question. "Yes and no," she said honestly. "I thought perhaps we could head south. Or maybe west toward Jackson. With the money you've brought in here, it's possible we could afford bus tickets to the next state at least, but I'll need to see a schedule and prices. We could take the bus into Mississippi, to a larger town. I think that was our mistake here. We stopped in too small a town not to gain notice. In a larger city, we'd blend in better and maybe even be able to get a cheap hotel. I can pick up a waitressing job and you can stay at home with Cammie. Hopefully she'll be better by then."

"And if she's not?" Travis asked fearfully.

Eve inhaled sharply. She wouldn't contemplate that possibility. It did no good to borrow trouble.

"She will be," Eve said in a determined voice.

"Tell me what you want me to do and I'll get started," Travis said.

"Get the two suitcases out of the closet and put in as much food as possible from the pantry, anything that's nonperishable in one and pack what clothing will fit in the other. Cammie doesn't need much. Just her nightclothes and a pair of shorts and a top. I'll get one or two changes of clothing to put with whatever you pack of yours."

Travis nodded and then walked quietly through the living room toward the bedroom where the suitcases were closeted. Eve followed behind and stopped at the rickety dresser and opened the top drawer to where her mother's jewelry rested in a torn box.

Regret and sorrow tugged at her chest as she faced the inevitable. She hadn't wanted to part with the only things she, Travis and Cammie had left of their mother. She'd wanted to keep them for Travis and Cammie to have. But they needed the money more than they needed the reminder. She hadn't wanted to risk pawning it before now, saving it for a last resort. It was too risky. Pawnshops required ID. But time had run out, and this was her only option now.

The jewelry wouldn't bring much, though it was fine quality and expensive when it had been purchased. But pawnshops didn't pay even a fraction of retail value. The few hundred dollars she could hope to get from the sale would have to be stretched to provide a place for them to live. Hopefully the food that Donovan had brought earlier that day would last them for some time if they ate sparingly.

"She would want you to use it, Evie," Travis said.

She turned to see Travis staring at her, at the box in her hand.

"I know," she whispered. "But I had wanted to save this for you and Cammie. It's all we have left of her."

Travis shook his head. "No. We have our memories. Good memories. She was a great mom. You're a lot like her, Evie. You look just like her and you have her same heart. She would be so proud of you for doing what you have to protect me and Cammie."

Eve felt guilty for the brief surge of anger she had to battle back. She was in turns angry and sorrowful over her mother's decision to remain with a husband she knew to be a danger to her children. Her mother knew, and yet she'd never tried to get out. To get Travis and Cammie out of his reach.

Eve had seen the truth about Walt, had known the kind of man he was, and she would have never had contact with her mother or Walt—Walt wouldn't have allowed it—if it hadn't been for Travis's phone call to Eve. His plea for help and his suspicions concerning Walt and his intentions toward Cammie. Suspicions that Eve took very seriously, because she knew.

She should have taken more time to develop a plan, thought out their escape better. But she'd been too desperate to remove Cammie from a dangerous situation to take the time to formulate a better plan. And so they were still running.

"We'll stop in Memphis long enough for me to pawn it," she said. "Then we'll take another bus into Mississippi. We'll need a place to live. Somewhere that Cammie isn't exposed like she is now. She needs to get better. Have good food to eat and a dry place to sleep."

On cue, raindrops sounded on the tin roof and Eve glanced up, grimacing.

"I'll finish packing, Trav. You go make sure Cammie stays dry, okay?"

Travis exited the tiny bedroom and went to see to his sister while Eve finished stuffing their belongings into the suitcase.

When she was done, she dragged the full suitcase into the living room and then took the empty one into the kitchen and began packing the food that Donovan had brought over.

The roof had already started leaking and small puddles were forming on the floor. Hopefully the rain wouldn't last long and they could leave as soon as possible.

A loud boom sounded, shaking the entire trailer. Cammie let out a startled shriek and Eve flinched. Her gaze flew to where Travis was holding Cammie on the couch, his arms wrapped around her to shield her from the leaks. Two more lightning flashes illuminated the dark interior of the trailer before the thunder sounded again, right on their heels.

"I'm scared, Evie," Cammie said in a faltering voice.

Her thumb slid into her mouth as Travis comforted her.

"It will be all right, darling," Eve said with a smile. "Trav won't let anything hurt you."

Thunderstorms certainly weren't anything new. The entire two weeks they'd lived here, they'd had many afternoon storms. By the time the trailer dried out from one storm, another would roll through, making the interior musty and dank from mold and mildew.

They had to find a better place to live. For Cammie's sake. She'd never get well in these living conditions. It only hardened Eve's resolve to pawn her mother's jewelry so they could afford better accommodations. It was what she should have done from the beginning. Only fear of discovery had prevented her from the desperate act.

But now she realized she should have pawned it much earlier. When they were still on the West Coast. That way there would be nothing pointing Walt—or the police—in their direction. Live and learn. It wasn't as if she was an expert on being a fugitive. She'd pawn it in Memphis and then relocate to Mississippi as fast as possible and as far away as possible from Tennessee.

She finished packing the food, cramming everything possible inside the suitcase. Then she took one of the bottles of Pedialyte and one of the snacks she'd left out for Cammie over to the couch.

She sat next to Travis, who had Cammie perched on his lap and nestled against his chest.

"Are you hungry?" Eve asked. "You should probably try

to get some fluids down and maybe something to eat before we leave."

Cammie's thumb slid farther into her mouth and she stared at Eve with wide eyes. "Where are we going, Evie?"

Eve slid a reassuring hand down Cammie's leg as she extended the bottle. Travis snagged it from Eve's grasp and put it to Cammie's lips for her to drink.

"I think toward Jackson. It may take us a few days to get there, but once there, we can buy bus tickets to Memphis. When we get to Memphis, I'll sell Mom's jewelry so we can afford a nicer place to live and bus tickets to the next place. The next few days will be the hardest, but if we stick together, we can do anything."

Travis smiled at Eve's statement, and even Cammie nodded solemnly. Eve smiled back and then extended her hand, palm down, in front of Travis and Cammie. Travis slid his hand over Eve's and then Cammie put her free hand on top. Then Eve put her hand over Cammie's, sandwiching hers and Travis's between Eve's. It was a gesture of solidarity that had become familiar to them over the last while. Eve had begun it as a way to reassure Cammie that they were family and that Eve would never leave them.

"Together," Travis said quietly.

"Together," Cammie said in a fervent voice. "We'll always be together, won't we, Evie?"

Eve reached for Cammie, pulling her warm body into her arms. She hugged her close, giving her a squeeze. "Yes, darling. We'll always be together. I promise you that."

It was hard to promise her younger sister something Eve had no way of controlling. But if intent counted for anything, then they'd be together forever. Safe. Away from their father.

"I want you to promise me something," Eve said in a serious voice. She stared over at Travis and then down at Cammie. "I want you both to promise me."

"Anything," Travis said.

Cammie nodded her agreement.

The words knotted in Eve's throat. She didn't even want to contemplate what she was about to say, but it had to be considered. And she wanted to make certain that Travis and Cammie knew what to do if the worst happened.

"If something happens to me . . ."

Cammie immediately went rigid in Eve's arms, and Eve closed her eyes in regret over upsetting her baby sister. But she couldn't afford not to prepare for the worst-case scenario. Travis's and Cammie's lives depended on it.

"Listen to me, darling. If something happens to me. If the police find me or if your father discovers us, you have to promise me that you'll go with Travis and do what he tells you to."

Her gaze lifted to Travis to see the torment in his eyes. The reality that what she was saying could very well come true.

"If something happens to me, you take Cammie and you run. Stay on the move. Do not worry about me."

"I can't do that, Evie," Travis said hoarsely. "You'd never leave us. We can't leave you."

Eve shook her head emphatically. "*Promise* me, Trav. You *have* to protect Cammie. And yourself. That means you keep her away from Walt. Whatever it takes, you keep her safe and keep running."

Travis closed his eyes and bowed his head in resignation. "I promise."

Feeling only marginally better now that she had his promise, she shifted Cammie in her arms and took the drink from Travis's hand to make Cammie sip more.

"You should eat something too," she said quietly to Travis. "I left enough out on the counter to make sandwiches. There's even pop in the refrigerator, thanks to Donovan. Eat now while we have time. We may not have that luxury over the next few days."

Still, Travis hesitated. It broke Eve's heart that he often went hungry and without because he placed Cammie's—and Eve's—needs above his own. He of all of them needed regular meals. In the last year, he'd hit an enormous growth spurt, going from an average height of five foot six to nearly six feet. And it was obvious that he was undernourished. His tall, lanky frame showed his thinness. With adequate nourishment, he'd be a broad, much thicker . . . man. It was hard to envision him as an adult, but in fact, he'd been forced to grow up and mature much too fast. He had knowledge and experience of the evil in the world that most adults never gained.

If it was the last thing Eve did, she was going to ensure that they had a good place to live, or at least an adequate place, and food so Travis and Cammie ate regularly. Even if it meant going without herself.

"Eat," Eve prompted gently. "There wasn't room to pack it all anyway. No sense in it going to waste. Eat as much as you can stomach because as I said, we're going to be on the move for the next several days, and we'll have to eat when we can and sparingly so we stretch the food as far as possible before we have to buy more."

"Do you want anything?" Travis asked as he rose.

Eve started to shake her head. The thought of food made her nauseated when her thoughts were in turmoil over what they faced for the next days. But she also knew that she couldn't very well convince Travis of his need to eat if she refused to eat herself.

She forced a smile in Travis's direction. "That would be nice. Just make me a sandwich. There are two cans of pop left in the fridge that I couldn't fit in the suitcase. Why don't we drink those before we head out?"

There was still enough of a boy in Travis to be happy over the "treat" offered to him. Her heart ached at the idea that something as simple as a sandwich and a can of soda would be a luxury often denied them.

"What do you want on yours?" Travis asked as he headed toward the kitchen.

"Oh, one of everything," Eve said with a smile. "We may as well splurge tonight since we can't bring the rest of the food with us. Cammie, what about you, darling? Are you feeling up to eating something more than the crackers you've been nibbling on?"

"Can I have another grilled cheese?" Cammie asked around her thumb.

"You betcha," Travis said with an indulgent smile. "I'll heat the pan while I make my and Evie's sandwiches. Then we'll all eat together on the couch and wait for the storm to pass. That sound good?"

Cammie nodded vigorously.

"Trav, make sure you eat plenty," Eve reminded. "Don't waste it, and you need to eat good."

He grinned. "Don't have to persuade me. I'm starving!"

Eve sat back, savoring the brief moment of normalcy. It was easy to pretend that they weren't in a run-down trailer living hand to mouth or in constant fear of discovery. For the space of a few stolen minutes, they could be a typical family enjoying something as simple as a meal together.

Eve committed the moment to memory, knowing that the coming days would bring them uncertainty and upheaval. And she prayed for the strength not only to survive but to be strong for her siblings. They needed her. She was the only constant in their lives and they were the only constants in hers.

CHAPTER 11

EVE roused from sleep and panicked as she realized that they'd all fallen asleep on the couch after eating. Travis was leaned over against the arm, his head lolled to the side. Cammie was nestled in Eve's arms and draped across Eve's body.

She lifted her watch but couldn't see the time in the darkness. At least it was still dark and they hadn't slept through the night. She strained to listen for the sounds of rain, but quiet had descended. It was almost eerily quiet. No sounds of frogs or crickets that usually permeated the night.

The air was thick, the humidity so thick it was hard to breathe. She shifted, trying to get a better look at her watch. Cammie stirred in her arms and Eve carefully laid her to the side before reaching for Travis's arm.

"Trav. Trav," she said a little louder. "We have to get up and get moving. It's stopped raining and I don't know how long we slept."

After eating their meal, they'd relaxed, listening to the rain beat against the tin roof and the wind rattling the windows in the trailer. Realizing the storm wasn't just a brief cloudburst of rain, Eve had suggested they try to get in a little sleep. She hadn't intended to drift off, though. She'd wanted Cammie and Travis to rest for the trip ahead and the long days of walking, but she'd wanted to limit it to an hour at the most.

Travis stirred and then immediately sat up, his hand going to Eve's.

"Sorry, Evie. I shouldn't have fallen asleep like that," he said in a regretful tone.

"Shhh, you needed it," she said. "But if you can help me with Cammie, we can be on our way. She needs her shoes and the shorts and T-shirt you laid out for her."

Travis got up and reached for Cammie, who was still half asleep. She muttered a drowsy protest but clung to Travis's neck as he carried her to the bedroom to get her ready.

Eve stood, pushing away the heavy veil of fatigue as she mentally prepared herself for what lay ahead. No matter that they'd led this life for the past several months, she still wasn't used to it. She still couldn't shake the fear that uncertainty brought. She was in way over her head. She wasn't qualified for this, but then who was?

She stretched and then did a quick check to make sure they weren't forgetting anything important. Her mother's jewelry was secure in the suitcase. Eve's wallet with their precious hoard of cash was on the counter, and she shoved it into the backpack, where she'd also put drinks for Cammie and a few of the individually packaged snacks that Donovan had brought.

Donovan's face flashed in her mind, making her pause. Indecision flickered and she shoved it away. She couldn't afford to second-guess herself. Not now.

But what if he truly only wanted to help? Was she doing Cammie and Travis a huge disservice by not staying and allowing Donovan to bring a doctor in for Cammie?

Those intense green eyes. Eyes that saw far too much. That probed the very inside of her mind. He was a man who made Eve feel safe, and perhaps that was what scared her the most. Because one mistake, just one, and Cammie and Travis would pay the price for her stupidity. It was better to trust no one, a mantra she'd embraced when they'd fled California, than to risk trusting the wrong person.

But still, she couldn't shake Donovan Kelly from her mind. He clung tenaciously, refusing to budge. He was handsome, no doubt about that. But it wasn't his physical attractiveness that intrigued her. Though he definitely had no shortage of physical beauty. The man was built solid from the feet up.

He wasn't overly tall. Certainly taller than her petite frame, but he didn't loom over her either. But what he lacked in height, he certainly made up for in other areas. His chest was massive and his upper arms bulged with muscles. It was evident that he stayed physically fit.

But perhaps what had caught her attention the most was simply the way he looked at her. Like he . . . cared. As though somehow their connection was more personal than one of someone helping another human being in need.

Maybe that was fanciful of her. Okay, so it totally was and it made her a flaming moron to even dwell on that possibility. But once it had taken hold, she couldn't rid herself of that feeling. It was a nice sensation. Warm and soothing. Like he was.

And he'd been wonderful with Cammie. It would have been easy for a man like him to scare the bejeebus out of Cammie, and yet he'd taken great pains not to frighten her. He'd been extremely gentle with her—and Eve for that matter.

In another life, Eve would have had the confidence—and the freedom—to act on such an attraction. She wasn't overly bold, but neither was she a shy woman afraid to speak her mind. She'd never been one to adhere to outdated societal mores. Such as the man being the one to ask out the woman. If she met a man she was interested in, she'd never hesitated to take the initiative. Some men liked that. Others? Not so much. Their loss.

But now? That Eve no longer existed. Maybe one day she'd get her back. But for now, dating and relationships were at the very bottom of Eve's priorities. She had a family to protect and raise. She had to stay one step ahead of Walt. Maybe she'd never have a normal life again, but if by not having one she ensured that Travis and Cammie had a quality life, free of Walt's abuse, then she'd gladly give up any hopes she had of a future of her own.

Besides, what man would be willing to take on a ready-made family like hers? No way she'd ever give Travis or Cammie up. So even if she were in a position to have a normal relationship with a man, it was doubtful that many guys would sign up to raise a teenage boy and a four-year-old girl.

Shaking herself from her ridiculous thoughts—what a monumental waste of time it was to even consider her future when it was absolutely uncertain and changed from day to day—she grabbed the backpack and then pushed the two suitcases to the door so they'd be ready to go when Travis returned with Cammie.

A moment later, Travis came back with Cammie dressed and in her shoes. Eve bent to make sure the laces were secure and that she would be comfortable for the long walk ahead. When Cammie grew tired or didn't feel well enough to walk, Eve and Travis would take turns carrying her on their backs.

Though they were certainly used to walking great distances and to carrying Cammie, the thought still made Eve grimace. But it had to be done, and the longer they stood here delaying the inevitable, the longer it would take to get to that bus station. And maybe they wouldn't need to go all the way to Jackson. Clarksville was closer. The army base was there, so there would certainly be a bus depot.

She sighed, racked by indecision. How was she to know what the right choice was? She hadn't had time to plan this out. Donovan's visit and his proposed return with a doctor had panicked her. Maybe she should have let the doctor come, find out how serious Cammie's illness was and then cut and run.

She raised a trembling hand to her temple and massaged as she tried to sort her scattered thoughts.

"Evie?"

Travis's worried voice broke through her frustration.

"Are you all right?"

Eve nodded and attempted a reassuring smile for him and Cammie both. "I was just thinking. Jackson is so far away.

Maybe it would be better if we went to Clarksville and got a
bus from there. It puts us farther away from Memphis, but it
would cut our walking time down considerably."

She glanced down at Cammie as she spoke, realizing that
it was the right thing to do. Cammie didn't need to be out in
God only knew what kind of weather, in the heat and exposed,
for any longer than absolutely necessary.

"I was looking on the map at work earlier," Travis said. "If
we go to Clarksville, then maybe we should consider going
north into Kentucky instead of south to Mississippi. And you
could pawn the jewelry in Clarksville instead of waiting.
They probably have several pawnshops since it's a military
base town, right?"

Here they stood, poised to leave in the dead of night, and
didn't even have a solid plan of attack. Weariness blew over
Eve, despite the fact she'd just slept for a few hours.

"I think you're right, Trav. What you say makes sense. And
the farther north we go, the cooler it will be at least. Mississippi in the dead of summer can't be all that wonderful."

They weren't used to the heat and humidity in the South.
They were accustomed to a much cooler climate with far less
humidity than here. Cammie had suffered even before falling ill.

"Maybe I can even find work in Clarksville just for a day
or two before we move on," Travis suggested. "It couldn't
hurt to pad our cash a little."

"We'll see," Eve said. "For now, let's just head that way
and we'll cross the other bridges when we get there."

Cammie slipped her hand into Eve's and squeezed. Tears
burned Eve's eyelids as she gazed down at the sweet little girl
who was offering Eve reassurance. It should be Eve comforting her siblings, and instead they were trying to reassure her.

Eve squeezed back and smiled. "Shall we start our next
big adventure?"

Travis took the backpack from Eve and curled his hand
around the handle of one of the suitcases. Eve lifted Cammie's hand and then reached for the other suitcase as they
opened the door and stepped into the night.

A stiff breeze immediately blew over Eve's face, startling her with its ferocity. There were bites of rain mixed in the wind, and it pelted her skin, eliciting a shiver. Damn it. She'd thought the rain was over.

"Should we wait it out?" Travis asked in a concerned voice.

Eve stepped farther out into the yard, turning her face up to look at the sky. There was an eerie howl that unsettled her. The quiet that had bothered her earlier was reinforced.

"No, let's go now," Eve said. "It will be morning soon, and I want to be off the main roadways before it gets light."

Travis nodded and shut the door behind him.

"Ready?" Eve asked Cammie in a light tone.

"Ready," Cammie said resolutely.

They started across the yard toward the road. The deep ditch in front of the trailer gurgled with runoff. Water ran through the big culvert that served as their driveway and swirled its way farther downstream.

They were to the road when the wind suddenly picked up and nearly blew Eve over. Her grip tightened around Cammie's hand just as a roar sounded.

Fear tightened Eve's gut and she hesitated, glancing back at the trailer, which shook with the force of the wind.

"Maybe we should . . ."

She never got to finish the thought.

Debris began pelting them. Dime-sized hail began hitting the ground—and them—and the roaring became so loud that it nearly deafened Eve.

Cammie screamed when the force of the wind nearly tore her hand from Eve's grasp.

"We have to take cover!" Travis yelled. "I think it's a tornado!"

Oh God. Oh God. Oh God. The trailer was no shelter from a tornado. It was the very last place they should be.

"The culvert!" Eve cried. "Get in the culvert and stay down!"

She shoved Cammie forward and reached back for Travis's hand to pull him along. A tree branch blew between them, knocking Travis back several feet.

"Travis!"

Eve stumbled toward him, torn between her need to protect Cammie and her desire to make sure Travis made it. To her horror, the wind tugged mercilessly at Cammie, and it took all of Eve's strength to maintain her grip on her wrist.

"Get Cammie in the culvert!" Travis shouted.

"No! I won't leave you, Trav!"

"Evie, do it! Go!"

Eve stared stricken as yet another limb blew right into Travis's side, sending him sprawling to the ground.

"Trav!" Cammie screamed.

It was Cammie's hysterical cry that galvanized Eve to action. She spun, rapidly hauling Cammie into her arms. Adrenaline gave her strength as she dove for the culvert, bearing Cammie's weight the entire way. They hit the ground just as a limb crashed down on them, hitting Eve squarely in the back.

All her breath was knocked painfully from her lungs, leaving her gasping for air. Her eyes watered and stung as bits of hail and rain hit her face. Cammie squirmed beneath Eve, and she worried that Cammie was being smothered by Eve's weight.

Pushing herself up, impeded by the heavy limb, she crawled toward the ditch, determined to get Cammie to safety so she could return for Travis. As she gained her footing, she heaved Cammie upward once more. She was nearly there when she stepped into a hole.

Her ankle gave out, wrenching painfully, and she went to her knees, gasping in pain. Damn it. She was so close. She wouldn't give up now. They'd survived the worst so far. No way she was going to let a damn tornado take them down now.

Using the last of her flagging strength, she managed to push Cammie into the culvert. Water rushed around them, tugging at their bodies. If it got much deeper, they'd be swept away.

"Listen to me, Cammie," Eve shouted above the roar. The wind whistling through the tunnel along with the rushing water made it almost impossible to be heard. "I'm going to position you in the middle of the culvert. Get a handhold on whatever you can and don't move! I have to go back for Trav."

Cammie whimpered but nodded, her fingers wrapped tightly in Eve's drenched shirt. It took everything Eve had to pry her hands away and leave her alone in that culvert even for a few moments. She was terrified of losing Cammie. She was terrified of losing Travis. Neither was an option. She'd die before letting that happen.

She kissed one of Cammie's hands and then cupped her small face in her hands. "Stay here and don't move," she ordered. "I'll be back in a minute."

Stumbling back, she edged her way out of the culvert, relieved that the water level had remained unchanged. Her entire body was heavy as she slogged her way up the ditch. The wind beat mercilessly at her. She was pelted by rocks, small limbs and other debris. Something slammed into her side, eliciting a cry of pain. She went down hard, getting a face full of mud.

It took a moment for her to realize that what had hit her was the door to the trailer. She glanced up in the direction of the trailer and to her horror saw that it simply wasn't there any longer. No part of it was there. It had simply vanished, blown away by the tornado.

A warm metallic taste filled her mouth. Blood. She wiped at her lips with the back of her hand, removing some of the mud and blood.

"Travis!" she yelled.

A firm hand gripped her wrist, pulling her to her feet.

"I'm here, Evie. Now come on. We have to get into the culvert with Cammie."

She was so relieved she nearly passed out on the spot. Grimacing as she put weight on her twisted ankle, she leaned against Travis and turned back toward the culvert.

The wind whipped viciously around them, turning the most ordinary things into deadly weapons. Her hair snapped violently against her face, cutting into her skin. It was as if the sky had caved in and rained down on them in every conceivable direction. And then to her astonishment, her entire body lifted in the air before being slammed back down, separating her and Travis.

"Evie!" Travis cried.

"Get to Cammie," she bit out. "You have to shield her, Travis. Don't worry about me."

"I'm not leaving you!" he roared.

"Damn it, Trav! You made me leave you. Now do it! I'll make it. You're stronger than I am. You have to get to Cammie and make sure she isn't swept away by the wind or the water. Get in there and do not come out until I come for you. Are we clear?"

With a frustrated growl, Travis crawled toward the culvert and Eve pushed herself up again, fighting the force of the wind and the weight of the debris raining down on her. Just as she got to her feet once more, the wind swept her away, lifting her several feet into the air. It tossed her aside like discarded trash. She landed yards away from the culvert, pain splintering through her body. She was barely conscious, but the one thought that hammered through her every bit as strong as the wind was that she had no hope of making it to the culvert.

The winds were too strong, the force too great. Her strength was gone. She lay there like a broken doll, each breath more painful than the last. She could sense the winds growing weaker. The roar had faded to a dull throb. The tornado had ripped through in a matter of seconds and was even now moving on and spreading its destructive path.

Her last conscious thought was that she had to get to Travis and Cammie. Everything they had was gone. Taken by the storm. Tears of frustration and pain crowded her eyes. She wouldn't give up. Nothing on earth would make her cry defeat.

Her eyelids fluttered sluggishly. She tried to shake off the veil of unconsciousness. She had to get to Cammie and Travis. But blackness overtook her, pulling her into its snug embrace.

CHAPTER 12

DONOVAN stood in the war room on the KGI compound, palms down on the planning surface as he meticulously did a check of all the systems. His first priority had been in making sure his family was safe, but close on the heels of that was ensuring that the generators did what they were supposed to do in case of a power failure.

The sophisticated system had been designed so that when power failed, within a tenth of a second, the generators would kick in and no compromise in security would occur. They'd tested it many times but had never faced a real-time situation. Until now.

The tornado had blown through Dover, knocking down power lines and destroying homes and everything else in its path. His brothers and their wives and children had all taken shelter in their basements, something every single house inside the compound had.

They'd taken great pains in designing a compound that was safe not only from human attack but from the elements as well. They were too far inland to ever worry about hurricanes, but tornadoes were very real threats.

Just a few years earlier, tornadoes had devastated Jackson and Clarksville, and then on the heels of Clarksville's recovery, they'd been struck by yet another one. Even Nashville hadn't proved impervious to the killer storms.

Donovan's main concern had been that a storm would compromise their security measures and make it possible for there to be a breach when they were at their most vulnerable. He was satisfied to see that the costly technology on which he'd spared no expense appeared to be doing its job.

"Everything checking out okay?" Joe asked.

Donovan glanced up at his brother, who stood by Swanny. His first call had been to Joe, since he lived outside the compound. Then he'd called his parents, frantic with worry over whether they'd withstood the tornado. Other than a tree down on their property and a few missing shingles, they were okay. Donovan's brothers would go out as soon as it got light so they could assess any damage his father hadn't been able to see.

One by one, other members of the extended Kelly family had checked in, and all were accounted for. Thank God.

"Yeah, it's all looking good. My babies did their job," he said with a grin.

Joe rolled his eyes. "You need to get out more, man. You're developing far too close a relationship with your technology."

"Pull the weather service map of the storm, Swanny. I want to see the path the tornado took."

Swanny bent over one of the computers and a few moments later, the screens in front of Donovan lit up and showed multiple views of the tornado's trajectory.

Donovan studied it carefully and his breath caught when he saw the exact path the storm had taken. A knot formed in his stomach and his fingers curled into tight fists.

"Fuck," he whispered.

"What is it?" Joe asked sharply.

"We have to go," Donovan bit out. "I need you and Swanny."

"What's going on?" Joe demanded. "Talk to us, man."

"Eve," he said. "God. I didn't even think. I never should

have let them stay there tonight. I knew the fucking weather was going to be bad and I knew that shitty trailer they're living in provided no protection from the elements whatsoever. And Cammie is sick. Goddamn it, I should have hauled them out of there earlier."

"You aren't making any sense," Swanny said in a calm voice.

Donovan's fist came down on the countertop with a rattle. "They were right in the path of the tornado. That trailer would have never survived even the weakest storm, much less an F3 like this one was. We have to get over there. I hope to fuck we aren't too late. If they were killed I'll never forgive myself."

"Shit," Joe muttered. "Let's go. Swanny and I are with you. Should we call out the others?"

Donovan shook his head. "Maybe Sean, though he's probably up to his ears with all the other victims. The others need to stay with their own families. We'll see what we're dealing with when we get there. If we need help, we'll call then. Right now I have to get the hell over there and make sure they're all right."

"Let's roll," Swanny said shortly.

Donovan hurried out to his truck. Joe got in the passenger seat and Swanny hopped into the extra cab. He roared out of the compound, scanning the sky for any sign of impending daybreak. It was lightening toward the east and within thirty minutes they'd have enough light to see what they were dealing with.

"There are flashlights in the back, Swanny. Under the seat. Pull those out and make sure they work. It'll be light soon but we'll be there in ten minutes and we'll need them."

"On it," Swanny said.

There was rustling in the back and a few moments later Swanny said, "Got 'em. Looks like you have four."

He handed two up to Joe and kept the others.

"Careful, man," Joe murmured. "Keep it on the road. We aren't going to be of any help to them if you wrap your truck around a tree."

Donovan eased off on the accelerator, knowing his brother was right. But it didn't quell the urgency he had to get to Eve and her siblings. Damn it, but he should have never walked away. He knew in his gut it was the wrong thing to do, but he'd consoled himself with the fact that he and Maren would be returning the next morning. He just hoped to hell his hesitation hadn't cost them their lives.

"Christ, it's a mess," Donovan said as he dodged a fallen tree.

The entire way, he could see no sign of power in any of the houses they passed. But he hadn't seen complete destruction either, something that bolstered his hopes that the trailer hadn't been demolished.

But as he got closer to the road where Eve's trailer was, the worse the damage was. Treetops torn off. Debris everywhere. As soon as he turned onto the road, he knew it was going to be bad. The very first house, well, it wasn't even a house any longer. Only the foundation remained. And oddly, the furniture still sat where it had been situated inside the house. But the walls and roof were gone. He hoped like hell that no one had been inside when the storm struck or that they at least had a basement to seek shelter in.

"Did the rest of your team check in, Joe?"

Unease gripped him. Skylar and Edge roomed together in a house they shared rent on, but Donovan had no idea if they had a basement. Nathan, Joe and Swanny had helped their teammates move in but Donovan had never been to their house, a fact he now lamented.

"Yeah, they're good. Tornado didn't touch them. They barely even got any rain," Joe said.

"Did Steele check in?" Swanny asked.

"Yeah. He and Maren and the baby are fine. Maren gave him shit about them sleeping in the basement, but I'm guessing she won't be complaining in the future."

Donovan braked hard, swerving into the ditch, curses blistering his lips. Fuck, that was close.

"Holy shit, that was a near miss," Joe breathed.

A huge tree was lying crossways over the road, preventing

a vehicle from passing. No way around it or over it. They were going to have to go the rest of the way on foot.

"Let's go," he said grimly.

Grabbing the flashlight and his medic bag from the seat, he climbed out and set out at a brisk pace, climbing over the downed tree and shining his light down the road.

There was shit everywhere. Limbs, shingles, even a badly misshapen door. And a suitcase?

"Grab that, Joe," Donovan directed.

"It's full," Joe said as he hoisted it up.

"Put it to the side where we can find it. I'm sure it belongs to someone on this road."

Donovan broke into a jog, rounding the corner to where Eve's trailer was located. The sky was starting to lighten just enough that Donovan could see where the trailer was. Or rather used to be.

He sucked in his breath. "Oh no. God no."

It was gone. A depressed area of grass where it had rested was the only indication that it had ever been there at all.

"Eve!" he shouted hoarsely as he ran forward. "Eve! Where are you? Are you here? Are you all right?"

"Holy shit," Swanny said in awe. "It looks like a bomb went off."

"Spread out," Donovan snapped, not wanting to hear the fatalistic tone in Swanny's words. He wouldn't entertain that Eve, Travis and Cammie could be dead. They had to have survived. Donovan couldn't live with himself with their blood on his hands. "Look everywhere, and I mean everywhere. If we don't find them in short order, I'm calling in backup. I'll get everyone out here looking until we find them."

They fanned out, each going in a different direction. The trailer had been surrounded by woods on three sides, and across the dirt and gravel road was another home. Strangely, it appeared to be untouched, but then there was no rhyme or reason to the path of a tornado. Hell, he'd witnessed tornadoes that dipped down, took out one house then lifted and left the others next to it untouched. Discriminating, fickle, unpredictable bastards.

Donovan stumbled over a limb lying across the driveway that went over the culvert and nearly went down on one knee. He was picking himself back up, adjusting the flashlight to shine in the direction of where the trailer used to be when he heard a low sob.

He froze, straining to pick up the sound once more. He hadn't imagined it.

"Eve? Cammie? Travis? It's Donovan Kelly. Can you hear me?"

"You got something, Van?" Swanny asked from several feet away.

Donovan held up a hand to silence Swanny. But he heard nothing further.

"I heard something," Donovan said. "I didn't imagine it."

Joe hurried over and then looked down the ditch to where the water had already mostly drained off. Then his gaze flickered to the culvert they were standing over.

He and Joe must have had the same idea at the same time. They both scrambled down the ditch, Joe holding the flashlight to illuminate Donovan's path.

"Eve?" Donovan shouted. "Where are you? I'm here to help."

He crouched down at the entrance to the culvert and surveyed the interior. Definitely big enough for people to fit into. He grabbed Joe's flashlight since it was the bigger and shined it inside.

The beam caught two pairs of wide eyes. Travis was huddled inside the culvert, his arms wrapped tightly around Cammie. They both stared at Donovan, fear and shock evident in their gazes.

"Travis, are you all right?" Donovan demanded.

He started forward on hands and knees, barking back to Joe to keep the light shining on Travis and Cammie.

He reached them in a matter of seconds, and realization struck that Eve was not with them.

"Where is Eve?" Donovan asked.

Tears glimmered in Travis's eyes. "I don't know," he choked out.

Cammie began to cry, and Travis stroked a hand through her matted, bedraggled hair.

"Come on. We need to get you out of here," Donovan said, his heart pounding as he pondered Eve's fate.

He reached for Cammie, but she didn't relinquish her hold on her brother.

"Let me take you, sweetheart," Donovan said gently. "I know you're scared, but I'm here to help you and your brother."

"I want Evie," she wailed.

Tears shimmered in her eyes and then slid down her dirty cheeks. Her thumb slid between her lips and Donovan carefully pulled it away so she wouldn't get dirt and God only knew what else in her mouth.

"Where is your sister, honey? I need to find her so we can make sure she's okay."

"She was caught in the storm," Travis choked out. "She came back for me after putting Cammie in the culvert. I had been knocked down by a limb and she came back for me, but we got separated. Something hit her and she told me I had to get to Cammie and protect her. Not to leave her alone. But oh God, I left her."

The last came out as a sob, and Donovan's heart went out to the kid. He put his hand on Travis's shoulder and squeezed.

"You did right, son. You had to protect Cammie. She's just a little girl and wouldn't have made it on her own. I know you didn't want to leave Eve, but it's what you had to do. Now let's get you and Cammie out of this ditch and inside my truck where you can get warm and dry out some. I'll look for Eve. I won't give up until I find her. I promise you."

"We're not supposed to trust anyone," Travis whispered.

Even as he said it, Donovan could see the wistful look in the kid's eyes. The desire to, for a few moments at least, lean on someone else.

"Listen to me, Travis," Donovan said in a grave voice. "You and your sisters need help. Cammie is ill. Eve could be hurt. You *are* hurt. I understand you're frightened. And I understand that you don't know me. But I only want to help you and your sisters. I swear it. Now you need to let us get you out of here, and then I need to find Eve."

Donovan reached for Cammie again and this time Travis relinquished her, but his eyes tracked Donovan's every movement. Donovan cradled Cammie in his arms and turned, intending to hand her to Joe. The moment Joe reached for her, Cammie let out a shriek and dove into Donovan's chest, her tiny body shaking as sobs welled in her throat.

"Shhh, sweetheart," Donovan soothed. "I won't let you go. I'm going to get you out of here. Okay?"

"'Kay," she said in a faltering voice.

Joe's face was drawn in compassion, his gaze riveted to the precious little girl in his brother's arms.

"Make sure Travis is okay and that he can even get to his feet," Donovan said as he pushed past his brother.

He nearly slipped trying to right himself while holding Cammie firmly to his chest. The mud and debris made walking precarious. Swanny was there to steady him, though he was careful to not touch Cammie in the process.

Donovan turned, waiting for Travis to pop out of the culvert. He moved slowly, his face drawn into a grimace of pain. He was holding his side and trying not to let the others see his discomfort, but he failed miserably.

"Where are you hurt, son?" Donovan asked when Travis was beside him once more.

"It's not bad," Travis said in a firm voice. "We have to find Evie. She was hurt, and I had to leave her."

Tears choked his voice and threatened to slosh over the rims of his tortured eyes.

Swanny put a hand to Travis's shoulder and the boy glanced warily back at him.

"We'll find her, Travis," Swanny assured. "Now what I want you to do is come back to Donovan's truck with me so you can hold Cammie while we search."

Travis started to protest, but Donovan shut him down.

"Cammie needs you. She's scared out of her mind and she needs a familiar face with her. She doesn't need to be out in this. She's sick. Joe is my brother, and Swanny works with us. They're the best. We'll find Eve. I swear it."

Finally Travis nodded his agreement.

"I'm going to send Swanny with you and Cammie to the truck. Is that all right?" Donovan asked.

Travis nodded, but Cammie stiffened in Donovan's arms and to Donovan's surprise she threw her arms around Donovan's neck and held on for dear life.

"I want you," she said plaintively.

Donovan pressed a kiss to her matted hair. "Don't you want me to find Eve? She doesn't know Joe or Swanny. I don't want her to be frightened. Wouldn't you rather I be the one to find her?"

Cammie seemed to consider this a moment, her thumb sliding firmly back into her mouth. Then she nodded slowly, but her gaze was latched cautiously onto Swanny, taking in the jagged scar that covered half his face.

"I'm not as mean as I look, honey," Swanny said with a half smile. "Some bad people did this to me, which is why we don't want any bad people to get you or your brother and sister. We're going to make sure that doesn't happen, okay?"

"Does it hurt?" Cammie blurted.

Swanny reached tentatively for her, taking her from Donovan. Cammie was shaking, but she didn't utter a protest as she was transferred from Donovan's hold to Swanny's.

"No, sweetheart, it doesn't hurt. Not now. Now come on. Let's get Travis into the truck. He's hurting too. And he'll feel much better once you and he are safe."

"Will Trav be okay?"

Swanny nodded and injected a cheerful note into his voice. "Absolutely. In a day or two he'll be right as rain."

"Can you make it?" Joe asked Travis.

Travis nodded resolutely. "You just find Eve. She's out there somewhere. I won't leave her."

Joe clapped a hand on his shoulder and pushed him in the direction Swanny was heading with Cammie. "We'll find her."

As soon as Swanny disappeared down the road to where Donovan's truck was parked, Donovan turned to Joe. "Spread out. Don't leave an inch of ground uncovered."

"Thank God it's starting to get light," Joe muttered. "We're going to need all the help we can get."

Donovan nodded. "If we don't find her immediately, I'll call in the others."

"We might be recovering a body, Van," Joe said quietly.

"She's alive," Donovan said fiercely. "She's a fighter. I don't see her going down that easily."

Joe looked as though he wanted to argue, but perhaps he saw the resolution in his brother's face. He shrugged and then started in the opposite direction, his flashlight bouncing over every single inch of ground.

"Eve!" Donovan called. "Eve, can you hear me?"

Joe picked up the call, shouting Eve's name as they searched the immediate area around where the trailer used to stand. Donovan picked through rubble from the trailer. Twisted metal from the roof. Pieces of the walls. Glass from shattered windows. Pieces of carpet. Drapes.

His flashlight bounced over the mattress from the bed when he saw one side of it lifted from the ground. It didn't lie flush like the other side did. His pulse kicked up and he dropped to his knees, lifting the corner of the heavy, water-logged mattress.

"Joe!" he shouted. "Over here. I need your help!"

Joe sprinted over and bent down next to his brother. Together they lifted the heavy mattress and tossed it over on its side. There underneath, curled into a protective ball, was Eve.

"Holy shit," Joe murmured.

With shaking hands, Donovan reached to feel for a pulse at her neck. He was so relieved to find the faint, erratic patter that he damn near lost it. He had to get it together. His brother would think he'd lost his mind, but then all his brothers already knew he was in way over his head with Eve and her siblings.

"Eve. Eve," he said in a louder tone. "Wake up, sweetheart. I need to see how badly you're injured."

"I should call an ambulance," Joe said grimly. "Travis is hurt too. Looks like he could have busted some ribs."

Donovan shook his head, and Joe looked at him in surprise.

"No. I can't do that. I won't betray their trust."

"What the fuck, man? They need medical attention!"

Donovan stubbornly resisted as he stroked Eve's cheek, trying to rouse her from unconsciousness. "They have no money, no means to go to a hospital. It was why I was bringing Maren out today to check on Cammie. And they're scared shitless. I don't know of who. Yet. But I'll find out. And when I do, then we can tackle whatever the hell it is that's had them running for God only knows how long."

"So what the hell do we do then?" Joe asked in exasperation.

"We have an infirmary in the compound. Sam just had X-ray equipment set up for Maren last month. It's fully stocked and we can call Maren to come over there and check them all out."

"And what if they need a CT scan or something more involved?" Joe persisted.

"Then we'll cross that bridge when we come to it," Donovan said calmly. "Now help me get Eve up. We need to not jostle her more than necessary. I don't have a C collar with me, so we're going to have to be damn careful in case she has a spinal injury or any internal bleeding."

CHAPTER 13

EVE swam to consciousness, her mind muddled, her thoughts filled with panic and pain. She felt herself being swept upward, and for a moment she thought she was in the grip of the tornado. Again.

"No!" she protested, struggling, though she knew it was useless. She had no power against the force of the storm.

"Shhh, Eve, it's me, Donovan. You'll be all right. I've got you now."

The soothing voice broke through her panic, and calm descended. But then Travis and Cammie came screaming to the surface. Her eyes flew open to see Donovan's face outlined by the pale light of dawn. There was determination—and worry—etched into his handsome features. How had he gotten here? Where was she?

"Travis. Cammie," she choked out. Oh God. Where were they? Had she lost them to the storm?

Donovan's grip tightened around her, and she realized he was carrying her. But where?

"They're fine, Eve. My brother has them in my truck.

We're going to take you somewhere you can all get the care you need."

"No," she whispered. "Please. We can't. Let me go. We have to go. Oh God, my suitcase. Where is it?"

Donovan frowned and stopped walking, still cradling her against his chest. Then with a shake of his head, he resumed again, muttering something underneath his breath she couldn't decipher.

She found herself carefully placed in the extra cab of a truck. To her relief, Travis and Cammie were next to her.

"Lean on me, Evie," Travis said, worry evident in his voice.

She sagged gratefully against her brother's shoulder, and he wrapped his free arm around her. His other was curled securely around Cammie. Eve opened her eyes to see both Travis and Cammie staring anxiously at her.

"I'm okay," she said hastily, not wanting to frighten them even more than they already were. "What about you?"

"Fine," Travis said quickly.

"He's not fine," Donovan said bluntly.

Eve swung her gaze over to see Donovan standing in the doorway. She glanced back at Travis, taking in the pallor of his skin.

"What's wrong?" she demanded.

Travis flushed, not looking happy that Donovan had contradicted him.

"He's hurt," Donovan explained. "May have some broken ribs. I'm going to take you all back to my place. We have an infirmary on site, and the doctor I told you about yesterday will come there to check you all out."

His tone brooked no argument and his features were set in stone.

"My suitcase," she said in a quivery voice. "I need that suitcase. It has everything in it."

Donovan turned to one of the other men standing outside the truck, and a moment later he held up a waterlogged suitcase. "This yours?"

Relief hit her hard. It was the suitcase that had their clothing and her mother's jewelry in it. The food they could do without. But the jewelry represented their only hope of supporting themselves for the coming weeks.

And now that they'd suffered yet another setback, who knew when they'd be able to move on?

"Yes," she murmured.

Donovan didn't look happy over that fact, but he remained silent. He tossed the suitcase into the bed of the truck and then handed his keys to one of the men standing behind him.

"You drive and let Swanny ride shotgun. I'll cram in here with Eve."

The man took the keys with a nod and walked around to the driver's side. The other man got into the passenger seat, and it was then that Eve saw the deep scar that puckered the entire side of one cheek. She winced in sympathy. It had obviously been a serious injury.

"Scoot over as close to Travis as you can sit comfortably," Donovan said in a gentle tone. "Cammie, sweetheart, can you sit on my lap so you don't hurt your brother's ribs?"

"She's fine," Travis said hastily.

"You're hurting," Donovan said quietly. "There's no need. I can hold Cammie."

He reached for her and to Eve's surprise, she went willingly, her legs dragging over Eve's lap as Donovan lifted her. He settled her onto his lap and then reached over to carefully engage Eve's seat belt. Then he secured his own, making certain that Cammie was strapped against his chest.

"Who are they?" Eve asked in a low tone as she gazed up at the driver and passenger.

"The one driving is my brother Joe. Swanny is the other. You can trust them, Eve."

If only it were that easy. She couldn't afford to trust anyone. But she kept silent on that account. No sense arguing. She had to figure a way out of her current mess. Her whole idea of avoiding Donovan and the doctor was one huge epic fail. Now even more people knew of her and her siblings. It was hard to keep her despair from overwhelming her. How long before they were discovered? Being exposed to so many people was like a ticking time bomb. She couldn't stay lucky forever. Sooner or later, Walt would find them.

"Why were you leaving, Eve?" Donovan asked quietly.

She yanked her head toward him, sure that guilt was plastered all over her face. She'd never been adept at hiding her feelings.

"It was time to go," she said simply.

A slight frown thinned his lips. "I was bringing a doctor out to see Cammie. Why would you leave before then?"

Her shoulders sagged and she dropped her gaze, but she could still feel his boring into her. Could feel the weight of his stare and the judgment behind it. He thought she was an idiot. That she hadn't wanted her sister to get help.

"The more people we are exposed to, the greater the risk," she said so she wouldn't be overheard by the occupants of the front seat. "I can't risk Cammie and Travis that way. I *won't*."

Donovan sighed and then surprised her by reaching for her hand. He laced his fingers through hers and squeezed. Warmth traveled all the way up her arm and into her chest. His touch was comforting. Like sunshine on a cold day. He made her think crazy things. Worse, he made her *hope*.

"Listen to me, Eve. And listen well. I'm going to help you. I'm going to protect you and Cammie and Travis. No ifs, ands or buts about it. I realize you don't trust me. Yet. But I'm going to prove to you that not everyone in the world is out to get you."

"You don't understand," Eve said, her voice rising as she grew more upset. "You risk a lot by becoming involved. And I could never forgive myself if helping me caused you trouble. I know you probably think I'm exaggerating, but Donovan, I'm not! You can't fix this for us. *Nobody* can."

Her voice ended in a defeated sob. Just hearing the fatalistic words brought home the hopelessness of her situation. She dragged her hand from Donovan's and buried her face in both palms.

She hated to break down in front of Cammie and Travis. They needed her to be strong, to be their rock. But she'd gone too long without cracking and now every fear, every desolate thought came pouring out.

"Don't cry, Evie."

Cammie's sweet, concerned voice filtered through Eve's quiet sobs. Travis's arm went around Eve, hugging her tightly. Then Cammie pushed forward, wrapping her slender arms around Eve's neck and squeezing.

"I love you," Cammie whispered against her ear.

"Oh darling, I love you too," Eve choked out, ashamed of her outburst.

"He said he'd help us," Travis whispered. "Maybe we should . . ."

He broke off and glanced at Donovan with uncertainty in his eyes.

"Maybe we should let him."

"Your brother is a smart man," Donovan said.

Eve pulled her head up and looked at Cammie's sweet face and then over to her brother to see him staring intently at her, purpose glittering in his brown eyes.

"Listen to him, Eve," Donovan prompted. "The three of you need help. You can't continue to run yourselves ragged. At some point you have to take a stand. Stop running and face whatever it is head on. I'll help you if you let me."

"But you don't know what you're up against," she whispered. "God, don't you think I'd love to have help? Do you think I want this kind of life for Cammie and Trav? I'd do anything in the world to give them the kind of life they're entitled to. They deserve better than this. Better than I can provide."

"You're doing fine," Travis said fiercely. "You've done everything to protect us, Evie. You talk about what our lives should be like, but what about your own? You don't deserve this. You've never deserved this. You should have a life too and not fear going to jail because of me and Cammie."

Eve stared stricken at him, at what he'd said for the others to hear. Regret immediately clouded his eyes and he lowered his gaze.

"I'm sorry, Evie. I shouldn't have said anything."

"Whatever it is, I can help," Donovan said, seemingly unfazed by Travis's admission. "There's a lot you don't understand about me and the connections I have. Helping people is what me and my brothers and our teams do."

Eve stared at him in puzzlement. "You're right, I don't understand."

Donovan touched her cheek, stroking it with gentle fingertips. He traced a line down the curve to her jaw, warmth and compassion in his eyes. "Just give me a chance, Eve. That's all I'm asking. Right now what you need is medical attention. A place to sleep where you don't have to worry about being rained on. Food to eat. And you need to feel safe. I can do all those things for you if you just give me a chance. I don't expect you to believe me overnight. But for now, trust me. Okay?"

Shocked at how simple he made it sound, all she could do was nod wordlessly. Satisfaction simmered in his eyes and he pulled his hand away, leaving her feeling bereft of his touch. As long as he touched her, she did feel safe, as insane as it sounded. But she absolutely believed this man when he told her no one would hurt her or her brother and sister. She just hoped to hell she didn't regret her decision. And that Cammie and Travis didn't pay for her mistakes.

Several minutes later, they pulled up to a huge gate. Joe reached up to push a button and the gate began to swing open. Travis and Cammie both stared in awe as they drove inside the fenced area.

It looked like a combat zone or at the very least a high-security military base. There was a landing strip and a hangar that housed two jets. There was also a helicopter parked on the pad. To the right there was a firing range and to the left a large building with no windows.

Then they got to the houses that dotted the landscape. There were five houses spread out, all lining the cliffs that overlooked the lake. Eve glanced uneasily at Travis as they exchanged wide-eyed stares. Had they jumped from the frying pan straight into the fire? Had she resigned them all to a prison there was no escape from? She couldn't imagine that they could just walk out of such a heavily fortified *fortress*.

"What is this place?" Eve whispered.

"Home," Donovan replied. "It's home."

She sent him a puzzled look. "*Home?* Who in the world lives in a place like this?"

"We do," Joe said with an amused grin.

She looked up to see him watching her in the rearview mirror.

"Well, not me, at least not yet," he continued. "Swanny and I still bunk in my oldest brother's old place, but if my brothers get their way, I'll be building a house here soon."

Donovan grunted his agreement.

"I'm so lost," Eve murmured. "Who *are* you people?"

"We're people who help other people in trouble," Swanny said, swiveling in his seat to look at Eve and her siblings. His expression was serious, but his eyes were soft and friendly, contradicting the harsh look given to him by the scar that raked across one side of his face.

His words should have reassured Eve. Because she and her brother and sister were definitely in trouble and they definitely needed help. But the words *didn't* reassure her. They just made her more nervous about the man in whom she'd placed her and her siblings' trust.

As if sensing her unease, Donovan reached for her hand again, curling his fingers around hers. Familiar warmth spread up her arm. She loved his touch. It was something she could become addicted to. Just a brief moment when she felt that all was well and that Walt didn't exist. It was a stupid thought and one that could get her killed if she didn't snap out of it.

There was no safe harbor from Walt. There never would be. She had to remember that.

"It's going to be okay, Eve. I swear it."

The quiet vow shook her to her core. He sounded absolute. How could anyone make such a promise? Especially when they had no idea what they were up against?

For the first time, Eve's confidence faltered. Her confidence that her situation was hopeless. Donovan made her believe—made her *want* to believe—that he could protect her and keep her brother and sister safe. Was she a fool to get sucked into this? But would she be an even bigger fool to turn away such a huge gift? Was she doing Cammie and Travis a disservice by not at least seeing where this took them?

She glanced anxiously at Travis, looking for any sign that he shared her same fears. But what she saw took her breath away and made the decision for her. Hope. She saw hope in her brother's eyes. Saw the same glimmer in Cammie's. A look of awe, as though Donovan were a knight in shining armor, a savior from the months of desperation and constant worry that their past would catch up to them. And there was the fact that Cammie, who was terrified of *all* men, was curled trustingly against Donovan's chest, her head resting just below his chin.

"Okay," she whispered, the simple word catching in her throat.

Oh God, don't let her be making the wrong decision.

Satisfaction glinted in Donovan's eyes. His fingers tightened around hers as he gave them a squeeze.

The truck pulled up to a large house that looked brand-new. Everything was shiny, the paint fresh, the landscaping immaculate. There was no evidence here that a deadly tornado had ripped through just hours before. The only sign was two fallen tree branches at the corner of the house and a few scattered smaller limbs.

Joe hopped out of the truck, as did Swanny. Donovan handed Cammie out to Swanny after reassuring her that he would take her back as soon as he helped Eve out and then climbed out himself.

The door opened on Travis's side, and Joe made to assist him out of the truck, instructing him to lean on Joe and to take it slow. Then Donovan reached for Eve, carefully helping her to her feet. He kept hold of her arm, his touch achingly gentle, until he was certain she could stand on her own.

Cammie didn't protest Swanny holding her, but the minute Donovan reached for her, she all but jumped into his arms, wrapping her arms around his neck, her fingers digging into his skin with the force of her hold.

Donovan took it in stride, cradling her close. Swanny fell in beside Eve, offering his arm. When she stumbled, more because of bewilderment than not having the ability to walk on her own, Swanny's arm swiftly curled around her, anchoring her to his side.

"Take it nice and slow," Swanny said in a low tone. "We'll get you inside and make you comfortable until Maren gets here."

It took her a moment to remember who Maren was. Donovan had said his doctor friend's name was Maren. The one he'd wanted to bring over and examine Cammie.

Her gait was hesitant and to Swanny's credit he didn't rush her. He stayed with her every step of the way, his pace measured as he helped her toward the house.

Travis and Joe went ahead of her, and it concerned her that pain had creased Travis's face the moment he got out of the truck and began walking. What if he was seriously injured? A hospital was out, but if it was a choice between him getting the care he needed or not, she would have no choice but to risk a trip to the ER and possible hospitalization.

"You're going to pass out if you don't slow your breathing down," Swanny murmured.

She swallowed and gulped in a steadying breath, exhaling through her nose in an effort to get control. It did no good to assume the worst-case scenario. A doctor would examine him. Then they'd go from there.

But still, she whispered an urgent prayer that none of their injuries were severe and that Cammie's illness wasn't bad enough to require hospitalization.

They walked into the foyer and then into a sprawling living room that looked bereft of furniture. There was only a small sofa, a recliner and a huge television on the far wall. No end tables, nothing hanging on the walls. And it smelled of fresh paint.

Donovan put Cammie onto the couch while Joe guided Travis into the recliner. Then Donovan turned to Eve.

"Welcome home," he said softly.

CHAPTER 14

DONOVAN waited until Eve was seated comfortably on the leather couch, and then he bent and deposited Cammie beside her but warned her in low tones not to hurt Eve by climbing onto her lap. Eve looked as though she would protest and even reached for Cammie, but Donovan shook his head.

"She'll be right beside you, Eve. You need to take care of yourself. Leave Travis and Cammie to me and the others. I'll go call Maren right now so she can head over. She was planning to be here this morning anyway, but the storm may have delayed her somewhat. I need to find out if they suffered any damage and if she can still make it over."

"And if she can't?" Eve asked, unable to keep the worry from her voice.

Donovan slipped his hand over hers, squeezing reassuringly. "She'll make it. If she's delayed, then I'll do what I can to make sure you're all comfortable. I act as the team medic when Maren isn't around. I know my way around medical equipment."

She was still bewildered by just what she and her siblings had walked into.

"Are you all in the military or something?"

Donovan grinned while Joe chuckled.

"Not any longer. But we all used to be. I was in the Marines. Joe and Swanny were in the army. My other brothers have served in various branches. The only one we don't have covered is the air force."

"And yet you live on some kind of . . . compound," Eve said.

"It's a necessary evil," Donovan said quietly. "We've made a lot of enemies over the years. We want to make sure our families are protected."

Eve looked up at him in alarm, and Donovan swore under his breath. Now wasn't the best time to tell her about KGI and the dangers of what he and his brothers did. He didn't want to lie to her, but she didn't need any additional stress. Not until she had come to terms with her and her siblings being here. And trusting him.

"Would any of you like something to eat?" Swanny broke in as he looked to where Travis sat in the armchair and then to where Cammie sat huddled against Eve. As he spoke, he bent over Cammie and placed his hand over her forehead and then frowned. "She's running a fever. You got any ibuprofen, Van?"

"They need to eat," Eve interjected, her tone brooking no argument. "We ate last night, but they need to eat again. Especially Cammie. She hasn't been eating well since she's been sick."

"I want a grilled cheese," Cammie mumbled around her thumb. "Donovan fixed me a yummy one before."

Swanny smiled, the scar stretching over his cheek as he glanced affectionately down at the little girl. "I think I can manage that." Then he turned his gaze to Eve, pinning her with his stare. "And what about you? You need to eat too."

"Yes, she does," Travis said firmly. "She didn't eat as much as Cammie and I did last night. She was too busy worrying over where we were going."

Donovan frowned at that, but it was something he'd address later. Right now he wanted them all to feel at ease in his home. Their home. At least for the next while.

"I'll have whatever you fix them," she said quietly. "And Cammie does need more ibuprofen. Her last dose was yesterday before we fell asleep."

"I'll help Swanny rustle up some food in the kitchen and we'll get some medicine," Joe volunteered.

"I have some liquid ibuprofen in the cabinet," Donovan told his brother as Joe and Swanny started for the kitchen. "I keep it on hand for when Charlotte is over."

"Who's Charlotte?" Cammie asked.

Donovan smiled down at her. "She's my niece. She reminds me a lot of you, actually. You're about the same age. You'll meet her. Would you like that?"

Cammie nodded vigorously. "Does she have dolls to play with?"

Donovan's heart ached as he looked at the hopeful look on Cammie's face. The things that Charlotte took for granted were things this child knew nothing of. Something as simple as a doll or toys to play with. Charlotte was spoiled by all her aunts and uncles, not to mention her own mother and father. Who spoiled Cammie? It was obvious that Eve and Travis were too busy trying to keep food on their table to worry over things like toys.

"As a matter of fact, I have a few of Charlotte's toys here for when she visits. I babysit from time to time, so I keep stuff here for her to play with. She won't mind a bit if you play with them too. How about after you eat, I see what I can dig up?"

Cammie nodded solemnly. "I'd like that."

"Now if you'll all excuse me for just a few minutes, I need to call Maren. Joe and Swanny are cooking up something for you to eat and I need to see about getting something for you all to change into. Travis, I have some clothes that will likely fit you okay. They might be a little big on you, but we're about the same height. Will a pair of sweats and a T-shirt be okay?"

Travis nodded.

Then Donovan turned his attention to Eve. "I'll have one of my sisters-in-law bring over something for you to wear, but until then, you can wear a pair of sweats and one of my shirts. You need to get out of those wet things. I have a few changes of Charlotte's clothes and some of her PJs. I'll show you both into the bedroom where you'll be staying so you can get her changed and change yourself."

Eve looked poleaxed, but Donovan didn't give her time to ponder the fact that he had presumed that she would be staying here. If he gave her any time at all, she'd probably bolt like a scared rabbit. And that was not happening. So while it might make him a flaming asshole, he was going to barge forward and keep her off balance.

Acting as though she'd already agreed with his plan, he scooped Cammie up and then extended his free hand down to help Eve to her feet. He watched her closely for signs of pain, frowning when she winced as she struggled up from the couch. He put a hand to her back, steadying her and hovering close as he guided them toward one of the guest rooms.

"The house has five bedrooms," he explained as they entered the room next to his. "But I've only gotten beds in three of them so far. You and Cammie can share this one and Travis can have the one down the hall. Cammie would probably feel better with you anyway."

As he watched Eve take in the bedroom—and the bed— he didn't miss the longing look she cast toward the queen-size bed. What surprised him more was the swift urge that overtook him. The thought that what he really wanted was her in his bed. His bedroom. His space. Her in his arms.

He shook his head in consternation. Where the hell had that come from? She was a mission. Like so many others. Never before had he had such a strong emotional reaction. Yes, his emotions were always involved but not on such a personal level. Maybe he was losing his mind.

But the thought remained. The fantasy of having Eve in his bed, him wrapped solidly around her, a barrier to the outside world and to anything that sought to harm her.

How easy it was to slip into the fantasy that this was his family. That they belonged to him. That Eve belonged to him. His woman.

Whoa. He needed to snap out of it quick and get control over his wayward thoughts. The very last thing Eve needed was to be blindsided by his desire. She was fragile and to her breaking point. Hell, maybe she was already there. She'd been poised to run. From him. And that ate at him. That she didn't trust him. He couldn't take it personally. She didn't trust anyone. And he couldn't fault her for that. She had a brother and sister to protect, and in her shoes, he wouldn't be lining up to trust anyone either.

What made her different from any other woman in need? It was a question he couldn't immediately answer. He knew his emotions always got involved, that he never remained a passive observer in any situation where a woman or child was in danger. But never to this extent. He never had crazy thoughts, like wanting her to move into his house. To become . . . his.

He'd never wanted to put his personal stamp of possession on another woman. And with Eve? And it wasn't just Eve. He already looked at her siblings as . . . his. Just as he already viewed Eve as his.

And God help the man who tried to take them away from Donovan.

None of the retribution they'd taken in the past would even come close to the havoc Donovan would wreak if someone came after what he considered his.

"If you'll wait here, I'll get you and Cammie some clothes. There's a large soaking tub in the bathroom as well as a shower. I thought you and Cammie could get cleaned up and into dry clothes while you wait for Maren to arrive."

"Thank you," Eve said in a soft voice.

Her eyes were still clouded with worry, but she didn't look as panicked as she had earlier. Donovan took that as a positive sign and a step in the right direction at least.

Donovan stroked Eve's cheek, unable to keep himself from touching her.

"It's going to be all right, Eve. You'll see. Now you and

Cammie get changed and into more comfortable clothes. When you get out, Joe and Swanny will have lunch ready. We can eat in the living room. I'm going to go check on Travis and make sure he has what he needs. If you need help, call me, okay? Don't try to do too much yourself."

She flushed but nodded. Then to Donovan's surprise, Cammie launched herself into his arms from where she was kneeling up on the bed. He gathered her in his arms and hugged her back, his heart softening as he held the tiny little girl against his chest.

Finally tearing himself away, he left the bedroom, pulling the door shut behind him. Travis was still in the living room when Donovan reentered and he was pushing himself up from the chair, his face a wreath of pain.

"Whoa there, son," Donovan said as he hurried over. "Don't try to do too much on your own. You likely have some busted ribs. One wrong move and you could puncture a lung."

Travis paled at Donovan's words and sagged against Donovan.

"I can't afford to be hurt, sir. My sisters depend on me."

Donovan tightened his hold around the boy's shoulders. "Listen to me, Travis. You're a kid. And I don't say that to take away from anything you've been doing for your sisters. I admire your guts and determination. But everyone needs help sometime in their life. You can't keep up the pace you're keeping. And I'm going to make sure that ends here. Now I want you to go into the bedroom I'm putting you in. Take a shower, but be careful. I'll lay out clothes on the bed and when you're done, come into the living room so you can eat. The doctor will take a look at you and then we'll go from there. But the thing you need to know is that I'm here now, and I'm not going to let anything happen to you or your sisters. Understand?"

Travis relaxed, fatigue evident in his drawn features. Then he simply nodded and Donovan helped him into the other bedroom, pointing out the bathroom, the towels and where he'd lay out the clothes for Travis to change into.

Donovan left, his hand reaching for his phone as he

walked into the kitchen, where Joe and Swanny were preparing sandwiches and soup.

"You weren't wrong about them," Joe said quietly.

Donovan shook his head. "I know."

"What are you going to do, Van?" Swanny asked.

"Whatever I have to," Donovan said, his voice as grim as his thoughts.

He placed the phone to his ear after he dialed Steele's number and waited.

"You all make it through the storm?" Steele asked by way of greeting.

"Yeah, everything's fine here. You?"

"Yeah. We didn't get too much. Just high winds and a little hail. You still need Maren this morning?"

Donovan hesitated. "Yeah, but there's been a change of plans. The tornado wiped out Eve's trailer. Me, Joe and Swanny ran over because I was scared to death they'd been killed. Found them in a culvert and Eve several feet away trapped under a mattress. They're hurt and Cammie's ill. I'd like Maren to come out to check them all over."

Steele swore. "That sucks, man. Where are y'all now?"

"My place. They're all here. I need Maren as soon as you can get her here. Travis is hurt pretty badly. I'm concerned he has broken ribs. Eve's hurt too, but I'm not sure of the extent. She's in shock and scared out of her mind. And then there's Cammie, who was already sick enough before spending a night in the storm."

"I'll have her over as soon as possible," Steele said shortly.

"Thanks," Donovan murmured, but Steele had already hung up.

"They coming?" Joe asked as he plated another grilled cheese.

"Yeah, on their way now."

"Thought about what you're going to do after Maren checks them over?" Swanny asked. "What if they need to be in a hospital?"

Donovan shook his head. "That's going to be our last option. We have the means to take care of them here. Maren

can render her diagnosis and write any scripts they need and
I'll take care of them here."

"So they're staying," Joe murmured.

Donovan looked up at Joe. "You got a better place for
them to go?"

He shook his head.

"Yeah, they're staying," Donovan said resolutely. "Until I
find out what the hell they're running from and eliminate the
threat to them, they aren't going anywhere."

CHAPTER 15

DONOVAN insisted on holding Cammie while they ate despite the fact that Eve offered. Donovan had shaken his head reproachfully and merely directed her—and Travis— to eat.

Cammie crammed the grilled cheese into her mouth, eating with more appetite than she'd had in days, a fact Eve was grateful for. A quick glance over at Travis told her he was wolfing down his food as well. Swanny had fixed a plateful of sandwiches and given each a bowl of soup and glasses of sweet iced tea.

It was the first time in longer than Eve had remembered that they'd enjoyed something as simple as a meal without worry of imminent discovery. The evening before, when they'd eaten as they prepared to flee—again—was the closest they'd come to a few moments of peace. But weighing heavily on her, despite her attempt at putting up a brave front for Cammie and Travis, was the knowledge that once again they were running into the unknown. Now they were here, wherever here was. As much as she'd feared resigning herself and her brother and sister to the tight security of Donovan's compound, at least no one could get in.

That kind of reassurance was priceless.

"You aren't eating," Swanny said, gentle reproach in his voice.

Eve glanced guiltily up to see the quiet man regarding her thoughtfully. She got the impression he didn't say a whole lot. He was someone who blended into the background even though he looked like a total badass. The scar only added to that appearance. What or who had put that mark there? She shuddered to think of the violence he'd endured in the past. It could be the result of an accident. But something told her that wasn't the case. These men, all of them, were fighters. Ex-military, as Donovan had explained. And now they protected people? What exactly did that mean? It was a question she desperately wanted the answer to, but she wouldn't ask now. Not in front of the others. That question was reserved for when she and Donovan were alone.

"I don't have much of an appetite," she admitted.

"And it's equally clear that you've missed far too many meals already," Joe said pointedly. "Eat, Eve. Nothing will hurt you here. You have to stay strong for yourself and your brother and sister."

Knowing he was right, she made an effort to eat more of the food Swanny had prepared. And it was delicious. It didn't taste like something out of a can. It was rich and flavorful and it warmed her from the inside out. She savored each bite and checked occasionally to see that Travis and Cammie were also eating. They were. Much more than she herself was, so she dug in to catch up. It was important that they all ate and regained their strength, because as soon as they were able, they had to leave. They'd already been here too long and it was making her twitch. Sitting ducks. They couldn't run forever. She acknowledged this. Knew it for the truth it was. But she could at least buy them more time. Running from place to place until she could figure out what to do. How to confront Walt and the future.

The doorbell rang and Eve immediately froze. Travis

dropped his half-eaten sandwich—his third—on his plate and looked uneasily in Eve's direction. Cammie burrowed deeper into Donovan's embrace, ignoring the nearly finished sandwich Donovan had been feeding her, her eyes wide and fearful.

Their reactions didn't go unnoticed by the others. Swanny's lips turned down into a grim frown and Joe looked . . . pissed. Not at them. But he seemed angry over their *fear.* Of *what* they had to fear.

"Get the door, Joe," Donovan said calmly. "That will be Steele and Maren. Show them into the living room. When Eve, Cammie and Travis are finished eating, Maren can examine them."

Though it was said to Joe, Eve knew the last was directed at her and her siblings. A command for them to finish eating and reassurance that there was nothing to fear. If only it were that simple.

Joe got up and returned a moment later with a smiling blond woman, glasses perched on her nose, her hair pulled back in a neat ponytail. On her heels was a tall, completely fierce-looking man holding a . . . baby. Somehow the two seemed incongruous, but then Donovan had told her that Maren had recently had a child and had been cutting back on her patient load while she was on maternity leave. This must be her husband. The man Donovan had said was his friend. But now she realized that this man must work with Donovan—and the others—because he screamed *badass* from head to toe.

Donovan didn't move from his perch on the couch, where Cammie was doing her best to burrow underneath him.

"Thanks for coming, Maren. We could use you," Donovan said by way of greeting.

"Hello," Maren said in a warm voice as she took in the occupants of the room.

She turned to the man holding the baby. "I'm Maren, and this is my husband, Steele, and our daughter, Olivia."

Joe gestured toward Eve. "This is Eve and this is her brother, Travis, and her little sister, Cammie."

"Hello," Eve managed to stammer around the knot in her throat.

"Smile, Steele," Maren admonished. "You're scaring the children!"

Steele rolled his eyes but offered a sincere smile first to Eve and then to Travis. When his gaze lighted on Cammie clinging to Donovan's neck, his expression softened and genuine compassion filled his eyes.

"You're in good hands," he said gruffly. "Van will take good care of you and my wife is a doctor, the best. She'll have you all right as rain in no time."

Maren smiled, her cheeks coloring at her husband's praise. But then her expression turned serious. "Whom shall I start with?"

Donovan rose, lifting Cammie with him and then turning to deposit her on Swanny's lap. Cammie didn't look thrilled, but neither did she protest. But she didn't wrap herself around Swanny as she had with Donovan. She stared up at him from underneath her lashes, watching him cautiously. She seemed fascinated with the scar on his face, and then to Eve's surprise she reached up to touch the puckered skin.

"Did a bad man hurt you?"

Swanny smiled, warmth entering his eyes. "Yes, sweetheart. But you know what? Donovan and KGI took care of it. Those bad men won't ever hurt anyone again."

"My daddy hurt Evie," Cammie said quietly. "Can you make it so he never hurts her again?"

"Cammie!" Eve chastened, shocked at the child's outburst.

But no one in the room missed her comment. Donovan's expression grew fierce, and anger surged in Joe's and Steele's eyes. Even Swanny was scowling now, but as if realizing he would scare Cammie, he worked at controlling his reaction.

"No one will hurt Eve. Or you and Travis," Swanny softly amended. "You have my guarantee, little bit."

"'Kay," Cammie said, leaning in a little closer to Swanny's chest. Swanny seemed delighted that the little girl was warming to him and he wrapped his big arms around her, anchoring her more firmly to his chest. It was a silent message to her—and to Eve and Travis—that he was entirely serious in his commitment to see them safe.

"You need to start with Travis," Donovan said. "You'll need the X-ray equipment in the infirmary. I'm concerned he has broken ribs. We can ride over. I don't want any of them walking after what they've been through. I don't want to risk injuring them further."

Maren nodded her agreement. "What else am I dealing with here? Do you know? Have you made an assessment?"

Eve appreciated Maren's brisk, no-nonsense, all-business approach. She was clearly in doctor mode. Intelligence gleamed in her blue eyes, but what Eve liked the most was her gentle manner. She hadn't come in making demands or barking orders.

"No," Donovan said. "We haven't had time. My priority was getting them here so they could be evaluated. Travis and Cammie were in a culvert when we found them. Eve got caught in the storm trying to save Travis and we found her trapped underneath a mattress."

"The mattress probably saved her life," Maren murmured.

Eve felt the blood drain from her face. She hadn't considered it. She'd been too swept up in the terror of the moment and had been relieved to survive such a deadly storm. But Maren was right. If the mattress hadn't knocked her flat and kept her trapped underneath, she probably *would* have been killed.

"Well, let's get to it then," Maren declared. "I'll examine Travis and take X-rays and then go from there."

Donovan made no move to reclaim Cammie from Swanny's arms. Cammie looked as though she'd protest until Donovan put his hand to her cheek.

"I need you to let Swanny carry you, honey. I need to help your sister. Is that okay?"

Eve would have spoken up but as if sensing she'd do just that, Donovan silenced her with a look.

"'Kay," Cammie said, sliding her thumb back into her mouth.

"I'll take good care of you," Swanny said in a grave tone.

Cammie cracked a half smile and settled back against Swanny's chest. Tears stung Eve's eyes. They were all so . . . nice. So very gentle and understanding with all of them. People just didn't *do* what these people were doing. Going out of their way for complete strangers. Taking such a personal stake in their well-being. It flabbergasted Eve and rendered her unable to comprehend their generosity and kindness.

"Steele, can you help Joe with Travis?" Donovan asked as he bent over the couch where Eve sat. "He's in a lot of pain and it would help if he doesn't further aggravate his injuries."

Handing the baby over to Maren, Steele moved to Travis's other side and he and Joe helped Travis to his feet.

"Lean on me," Joe said kindly. "Steele and I will bear your weight."

Then Donovan turned his focus back to Eve. He extended his hand down but at the same time moved his other arm behind her back and gently eased her forward until she was on the edge of the couch.

"I'm really okay," she said quietly. "My head hurts and I'm sure I have bruises in places I don't even know about yet, but nothing feels broken or too badly hurt."

"You're in shock," Donovan said bluntly. "I'd be more surprised if you *were* feeling it yet. But when the reaction sets in, you're going to know it. Now let me help you and don't argue."

She conceded his point and allowed him to ease her to her feet. His strong arm came around her waist, anchoring her firmly to his side. And God, did it feel good. To lean on this man and his strength. It was like being held up by an immovable boulder. In that moment, she knew nothing could hurt her. That Donovan wouldn't allow it. It was a crazy assumption, but she had no intention of thinking differently. She— they *all*—needed a moment where they felt safe and secure.

They moved slowly toward the door, Swanny leading the way holding Cammie. Travis, with the help of Joe and Steele, filed out after Swanny, and Maren, holding the baby, walked on Eve's other side, hovering as if worried Eve would face-plant. Did she look that bad? She didn't feel so terrible. But maybe Donovan was right. When the adrenaline diminished, maybe she would start screaming for mercy.

She tightened her lips, determined that no matter what happened she'd remain stoic for Travis and Cammie. They were afraid enough without her adding to their worries. And the truth was, she was far more worried about them. Travis was moving slowly, each step making him grimace. And Cammie was still running a fever and it was doubtful a night in the rain helped matters any.

"Will Travis be okay?" Eve whispered as Steele and Joe helped him into the backseat of an SUV she guessed must belong to Maren and Steele.

"He'll be fine, Eve. I'm more worried about you at the moment. You'll see that we have practically a damn mini hospital here on the compound. Sam, my oldest brother, outfitted it from head to toe with everything Maren could possibly need to treat our teams."

Her eyes widened. "Do they get hurt so often?"

Donovan carefully put her into the front seat of his truck while Swanny climbed in back with Cammie. Joe got in with Travis, and Maren and Steele climbed in front, so they were taking two vehicles to the infirmary.

It wasn't until Donovan slid behind the wheel that he answered Eve's question. He regarded her with a serious expression as he cranked the ignition.

"I told you what we do. I realize you don't fully comprehend the scope of what it is I do—that we all do—here, but our job is to help people who need it. To protect people. It's a dangerous job and yes, we incur injuries from time to time. Maren used to have a rural practice in Costa Rica. Before that, she worked in Africa. We used her whenever we were in close proximity, but now that she's moved here and is living here with Steele, we've taken her on as our doctor in addition to the patients she sees in the private sector."

"Have you ever been seriously injured?" she asked in an anxious tone. Granted, she didn't know Donovan, but the thought of him being hurt bothered her. It bothered her a lot.

He grinned. "Nothing too serious. All of us have suffered

a bullet wound or two. Nothing that has ever taken me out of action for a long time. Two of my brothers had more serious gunshot wounds. Took them out of action for a bit and laid them up. They weren't too happy about it either."

She shuddered. "How can you be so nonchalant about it? You make getting shot sound so . . . *normal*."

He shrugged. "Like I said. Hazard of the job. We're all very aware of the risks we take when we go on a mission. If we weren't prepared for that possibility, then we wouldn't be doing our jobs very well."

"Not many people would risk their lives for a stranger," she murmured.

"We do," he said simply.

They drove across the compound back in the direction they'd come and pulled up beside the building Eve had noticed on their way in. The one with no windows that resembled a hulking, concrete block. What she hadn't seen at the time was that there was a smaller building right behind it. This one had windows in the front. Was this the infirmary Donovan had mentioned?

It awed her that they had such a sophisticated, self-sustaining facility. Airfields, hangars, a helicopter, shooting range. And an honest-to-God medical clinic.

"What's that building?" she asked, gesturing toward the one with no windows.

"War room," Donovan said.

She gaped at him. "War room?"

"It's where we plan our missions. It houses our communications, computers, all the technology that plays a part in our business. It—and I—are the brains in this operation," he said with a grin.

"He's our resident geek," Swanny said, speaking up for the first time since they'd left Donovan's home.

"It would seem you do a little bit of everything," Eve murmured. "Medic, geek, badass ex-military guy? Is there anything you can't do?"

He pretended to consider the matter a moment, and then his smile broadened. "Nope."

"Very humble too," Swanny said dryly.

Eve couldn't help the light chuckle that escaped her. Donovan stopped in his tracks as he started to get out of the driver's side.

"You have a beautiful smile, Eve."

She had no idea what to say to that. She immediately sobered, because really, what right did she have to be smiling when her brother and sister were hurt and ill?

"I didn't say that so you'd stop," Donovan said as he appeared at her door.

"I haven't had a lot to smile about," she returned quietly as he helped her from the vehicle.

"And I intend to rectify that."

Her mouth fell open, but he ignored her reaction and began walking her in slow, measured steps to the door where Joe and Steele had already taken Travis. Swanny followed swiftly behind, carrying Cammie.

"I want to be with Travis," Eve said anxiously. "I need to make sure he's okay."

Donovan slid a hand down her arm, spreading warmth in its wake. "He'll be fine, Eve. I'll put you and Cammie in the other exam room so you're with her when Maren checks her over."

"Yes, of course," Eve said hastily. "I didn't mean that I'd be leaving Cammie. I just thought that we could all be in the same room."

Donovan led her into a small exam room and set her down in a chair. Then he turned to Swanny and took Cammie from his arms and perched her on the end of the padded exam table.

"The rooms are small and there are only two. Maren will need the room to get the portable X-ray in. Joe and Steele will be with him, and as soon as she's done with Travis she'll let you know how he is. I promise."

Eve nodded, but anxiety was eating her alive. Travis tried so hard to hide his pain from her. She knew he didn't want her to worry. But she'd seen how difficult it was for him to even walk.

The wait seemed interminable. And then finally Maren walked into the room, a reassuring smile on her face.

Eve surged to her feet, earning her a reproving frown from Donovan, who reached to steady her when she wobbled.

"How is he?" she asked anxiously.

"He indeed has some broken ribs, but they're lower and didn't do any damage to his lungs or other internal organs. His pulse is good and he's not exhibiting any signs of internal bleeding, but Donovan will need to keep close watch on him for the next few days. I'll look in on him daily until I'm satisfied that he's recovering well."

"Is that all?" Eve asked, afraid that there was more.

"Just a few bumps, bruises and scrapes. He's very lucky. You all are. A tornado is nothing to sneeze at. You did right by getting them inside that culvert, but you should have been there yourself," Maren chided.

"They're more important," Eve said fiercely.

Donovan touched her arm, rubbing his finger lightly up her skin to her shoulder.

"You're important too, Eve."

"Now how about I have a look at you, young lady?" Maren said in a cheerful tone to Cammie.

Cammie looked shyly up at Maren and then over to Donovan for reassurance. How quickly Donovan had gained Cammie's trust. It was something that still shocked Eve. Cammie had even warmed to Swanny. She was grateful to Swanny and Donovan, and, well, all of them for proving to Cammie that all men weren't to be feared. She just prayed that faith hadn't been misplaced. It would crush Cammie and cement her fear of all men.

"I'll be right here, sweetheart. So will Eve. Maren won't hurt you. She just wants to help you feel better."

Cammie nodded slowly and turned wide eyes to Maren. Maren smiled warmly at her and then began her examination. At times Maren frowned as she listened to Cammie's breath sounds. Then she took her pulse and temperature and looked at her throat and palpated her lymph nodes.

When she was finished, Eve sat forward eagerly, looking to Maren for her diagnosis.

"She's a sick little girl," Maren said bluntly. "Normally I'd have her in the hospital on IV fluids and antibiotics, but I understand that isn't an option for you. I'm going to start an IV on her here and Donovan can administer her meds at home until I see an improvement in her condition."

"How sick is she?" Eve whispered. "What's wrong with her?"

"She has the beginnings of pneumonia. I want to do a chest X-ray to confirm my suspicion, but her breath sounds are labored and she's rattling when she breathes. Left untreated, she could get very ill."

Though Maren didn't say it in front of Cammie so as not to frighten her, Eve got what she'd left unsaid. Cammie could *die*.

Eve buried her face in her hands as sobs welled from her throat. Donovan's arm went around her, pulling her into his embrace. He squatted on the floor beside Eve's chair and held her, rocking her back and forth.

"I tried," Eve choked out. "I've tried so hard and it's not *enough*. It's *my* fault she's so sick. I should have done more but I *couldn't*. You don't understand. He would have found us and I can't let that happen. I can't let her and Travis go back to him. No matter what happens to me, I can't let them down."

"Shhh, Eve," Donovan said gently. "You've taken far too much on your shoulders. You're only one person. You did the best you could. No one faults you for that. You've taken excellent care of Cammie and Travis, but it's time to let someone take care of you."

She shook her head. "They are what matters. Not me. They have their whole lives ahead of them," she sobbed. "I won't let him ruin it for them."

"Eve, I need to examine you now," Maren said in a gentle tone.

Eve lifted her head. "I'm fine. Really. Travis and Cammie are the ones who needed help."

"I'll be the one to determine that," Maren said firmly. "Your head is still bleeding from a wound, and I need to see what I'm dealing with."

Maren lifted her hand in puzzlement and then stared at her fingers as they came away with blood smeared on the tips. Donovan helped her to her feet and then picked Cammie up so Eve could take her place on the exam table.

"Do you remember what all happened during the storm?" Maren asked as she probed into Eve's hair. "Can you tell me where you hurt?"

Her entire body ached. She felt like one giant bruise. Donovan had been right about one thing. Now that reaction had settled in, she felt every part of her body and it was screaming in protest.

"It was all a blur," Eve said. "I was trying to get Cammie and Travis to safety. Travis was hit by a huge limb and I had to leave him to get Cammie into the culvert. When I came out, I was knocked to the ground and then Travis was there. But the wind just picked me up. And I made Travis leave me to go back to Cammie. I don't remember much else."

"Donovan, can you step out so I can do a more thorough assessment of Eve?" Maren asked calmly. "Why don't you take Cammie down to see Travis? Joe and Steele are with him. I've already bound his ribs and given him something for pain."

"Just make sure you give something to Eve too," Donovan said in a firm voice.

Maren's lips lifted in a half smile. "I've got this, Donovan. Now shoo."

After Donovan left, Maren turned back to Eve. "Can you undress for me? I want to go over all your extremities and your abdomen as well. Depending on what I find, I may do X-rays on you as well. You've got quite the bump on your head. I'd prefer to be able to do a CAT scan, but I don't have that capability here."

Eve slowly undressed, with Maren holding on to her arm for support. When she was done, she reclined on the exam table and Maren did a brisk assessment, occasionally asking Eve if an area hurt.

After several long minutes, Maren helped Eve sit up and then get back into her clothing.

"My only concern is how serious your head injury is," Maren said. "You've got extensive bruising, but I don't think anything's broken. But you're going to have to take it easy for several days. All of you. And I mean that, Eve. Complete rest. I don't want you so much as lifting a finger."

"But I can't," Eve protested. "We were leaving. I *can't* stay. I've been here too long as it is. I have to keep moving or he'll find us. I know he won't give up until he does. You don't understand what he's capable of. What he's already done and will do again."

Helplessness gripped her, overwhelming her until she wanted to weep in despair. How could anyone understand the enormity of their situation? That if Walt caught up to them, Eve would be put away and then Cammie—and Travis— would be alone, and he'd vent his rage and tighten his control over them.

"You're staying, Eve."

Eve whirled around to see Donovan standing in the now-open door, grim determination locked on his face.

"I have nowhere *to* stay," Eve whispered. "The trailer is gone. We have nothing. Everything I own is in the suitcase you found. It's all I have to support us and it's not enough!"

Donovan's expression was determined, his lips drawn into a tight line as he stared unblinking at her.

"That's not true, Eve. You have me. You have KGI. You and Cammie and Travis will be staying with me."

CHAPTER 16

DONOVAN watched as the color fled from Eve's cheeks. She braced herself on the exam table, panic evident in her eyes.

"We can't," Eve protested. "You don't understand."

Donovan shook his head. "I'm really tired of hearing *you don't understand.* What I understand is that you and your brother and sister need help. You need a place to stay. You need food to eat. But what you need most is the knowledge that you're safe and that no one will harm you. I understand your fears and reservations, Eve. I get it. Believe me. But *your* answer is no real solution to the problem, and if you stopped and thought for a minute you'd know I'm right."

He continued on, talking over the protest already forming on her lips.

"You can't keep running. It's no way for any of you to live. And the next place you land in won't have what you have *here.* People who care about you. People who will protect you."

"You don't know me," Eve whispered. "How could you possibly care about me *or* Cammie and Travis? What you suggest is crazy! People don't just move strangers in with them. Nor do they make promises when they have no idea what they're up against."

"You're right. I don't know. Yet. But you'll tell me. It's a conversation you and I are having soon. But right now, my priority is getting you all the care you need and making sure you all rest and recover from your injuries and getting Cammie over her illness. You can't play around with this, Eve. Cammie is a very sick little girl. You have to think about her and what's best, not only for Cammie, but for yourself and Travis."

"She's *all* I think about," Eve said fiercely. "She's who I think about every minute of the day."

Donovan moved closer to Eve, reaching for her hand, curling his fingers around hers. Her hand trembled in his and he rubbed his thumb over her knuckles, trying to soothe some of the anxiety rolling off her in waves. For a moment she gripped his hand, almost as if she desperately wanted the comfort he offered. He took that as a positive sign that he was finally getting through to her.

"I never thought for a moment that she isn't uppermost in your thoughts or that she wasn't your priority. If I implied that, I apologize. All I'm saying is that you *need* help and I'm going to give it. I won't take no for an answer."

Eve stared at him in bewilderment. Then she glanced at Maren, discomfort in her eyes that Maren was privy to this conversation.

"Eve," Maren began softly. "I don't want to intrude, nor do I want to step on your toes. But I agree with Donovan. As a doctor *and* as someone who has a very close connection to KGI and the Kelly family. Cammie is very ill and she needs to be on IV medication. She's not going to get well overnight. It's going to take time. And Travis is in no condition to go anywhere but to bed where he can rest and recover. I know you've done the best you can, but everyone needs help at some point. I know I certainly did. And KGI came through for me. Just like they can help you. Take it from someone who has been there and done that. On more than one occasion," she

added with a rueful smile. "Donovan—and KGI—is the best.
And you *need* the best. Cammie and Travis deserve the best
as well. I would be terribly negligent as a medical professional
to condone you going anywhere in your current condition."

Donovan sent her a grateful look. What Maren had said
scored points with Eve. Recognition had settled in Eve's
eyes as Maren had bluntly given her opinion. Recognition
that Maren—and Donovan—were right.

Eve's shoulders sagged and she briefly closed her eyes.
When they reopened, they were wet with a sheen of tears.
Donovan's chest tightened. He hated to see any woman in
distress, but Eve wasn't any woman. Not to him. He couldn't
fully explain his reaction to her, but it went a hell of a lot
further than her being a woman in need. He'd come across
many of them through his years running KGI and he'd never
allowed himself this kind of . . . *attraction*. Emotional *and*
physical. It wasn't even that he hadn't allowed it. It simply
hadn't been there. None of the other women had made him
feel what he felt for Eve.

He already considered Eve—and her siblings—his. His . . .
family.

He could already picture what it would be like to have
this precious group of people as his own. He felt a fierce
protectiveness for Cammie and Travis that went above his
usual reaction to children in trouble. Every mission was personal for him, but this one? This was something else entirely
and he refused to let his *family* walk away into the unknown.
Where they could be hurt or killed or God only knew what
else. It wasn't an option.

He'd tie Eve to his bed and sit on her before allowing her
to walk away.

And if that wasn't a hell of a note he didn't know what was.

He'd ragged on his brothers and his team leaders for their
overprotectiveness and fierceness when it came to their
women, but here he was, in the same position, feeling exactly
as they had felt when it came to the women they loved.

Loved?

Hell, he wasn't in love with Eve. It was as she said. Donovan knew nothing about her. But he knew enough to realize that she was *going* to come to mean a hell of a lot to him. She and her siblings already did. But in order for that to happen, she had to remain here. Under his protection so he could see exactly where things would take them.

That wasn't going away. Not tomorrow or next year. Now he just had to convince them of his position in their lives going forward. And that was going to be no easy task. But he wouldn't be deterred by her resistance. He was every bit as stubborn as his brothers when it came to something he wanted. Eve would learn that soon enough.

"I need to get you home," Donovan said gently. "All of you. Travis needs rest. Cammie needs rest and medication. And so do you."

He turned to Maren, not waiting for Eve's agreement. Whether she gave it or not, things were going to be done his way from now own. That likely made him a huge asshole, to press this woman when she was infinitely fragile and on the verge of breaking. But he'd use that to his advantage and not suffer one iota of remorse for making certain they were safe and taken care of. No matter what it took. He'd spare no available resource in his quest to ensure their well-being. And that they stayed right where they belonged. With him.

"Write her a prescription for pain medication. She probably needs an injection but I'd rather wait until I get her settled at the house. I'll have my hands full getting Travis and Cammie to bed as it is."

Maren nodded and pulled out her prescription pad and scribbled several lines on it. Then she handed it to Donovan.

"I wrote them out to you so there's no record of their names at the pharmacy," she said. "There are meds for Travis and Cammie as well. I'll go start her IV now and get the bags of saline and antibiotics for you to take home. If you have any problem at all, don't hesitate to call me. I'll check in on them every afternoon if that's okay with you, but I'll call before I come so you're expecting me."

Donovan pulled Maren into a hug. "Thanks, sweetheart. I really appreciate all you do for us. Don't know if we say it often enough, but I don't know what we'd do without you."

Maren smiled as she pulled away. "You've done far more for me than I can ever repay. I owe my and Olivia's life to KGI. Steele's too. I'll never forget that. You know I'll be happy to help any way I can. All you have to do is call, okay?"

Donovan gave her another affectionate squeeze and then went back to Eve while Maren stepped into the hall to call for Swanny to return with Cammie.

Knowing Eve would want to be right by Cammie's side when Maren inserted the IV, he positioned her at the head of the exam table and then stood next to her, his arm wrapped securely around her slight waist.

He could feel her thinness. She felt precious and breakable in his arms and he tightened his hold on her, more for his own peace of mind than her own, though he wanted her to have no doubts of the support network that was closing ranks around her.

Swanny carried Cammie into the room and her eyes brightened when she saw Donovan and Eve. Relief shadowed the little girl's haunted eyes and she reached eagerly for Donovan. Donovan loosened his hold on Eve long enough to take Cammie from Swanny and lay her on the table so she'd be close to him and Eve.

Eve brushed her palm across Cammie's fevered brow and then leaned down to kiss her forehead.

"It's going to be all right, darling," Eve said in a soothing tone. "Maren is going to insert an IV in your arm. Just a little prick. I'll be here the entire time."

"And Donovan?" Cammie mumbled around her thumb.

Donovan smiled and added his own hand to her arm, squeezing reassuringly. "Me too, sweetheart. Eve and I aren't going anywhere. And after, you're going back to my house so you can get lots of rest and all the grilled cheese sandwiches you can eat."

Cammie smiled and Eve's breath caught and hiccupped. Donovan withdrew from Cammie and slid his arm back around Eve's waist, presenting a united front for Cammie. So she'd know they weren't leaving her alone.

Maren prepared the catheter and the bag of saline and the piggyback of the IV antibiotic. After swabbing Cammie's arm and securing a rubber elastic above the area she planned to stick, she spoke to Cammie in soft, reassuring tones.

"Just a little stick, but I need you to be brave and hold very still, okay, Cammie?"

Cammie nodded solemnly but tensed as Maren set the needle against her flesh. Her eyes widened in fear and panic flooded her face.

"It will be over in just a moment," Eve murmured. "Be a brave little girl. Maren will be easy."

Maren deftly inserted the needle, probing for the vein. Cammie let out a surprised cry, but to her credit she didn't jerk away. Thankfully she got the vein in one stick, and Cammie's expression eased.

Swanny stood on the other side of Cammie, right above where Maren worked, his hand cupping over Cammie's forehead as he stroked her hair.

"You're doing great," Swanny said.

Maren quickly attached the IV line, taped the IV lock so it was secure and then adjusted the flow of fluid. Then she hooked the piggyback so that the medication flowed into the line along with the saline.

"All done," she announced with a smile at Cammie. "You're a champ at this, Cammie."

Cammie beamed at Maren's praise. "It didn't hurt as much as I thought it would."

"That's because Maren is quite good at what she does," Donovan said. "Now you're all done and we can go back home and get you to bed."

Cammie looked delighted at that declaration. Then she looked shyly up at Donovan, clearly wanting to say something, but she was unsure. Her thumb angled further into her mouth.

"What is it, sweetheart?" Donovan asked in a gentle tone. "You can ask me anything at all. I don't mind."

"Could I have a feather pillow?"

Eve looked pained at Cammie's simple request, her eyes closing briefly to mask her upset.

"They're my favorite," Cammie said around her thumb. "Evie said she'd get me one when we had the money."

Donovan's heart tightened. "I don't have any in the guest rooms, but I just happen to love feather pillows myself and I have four on my bed, so I'm pretty sure I can spare one for you. That will tide you over until I get another for you. How's that?"

Cammie nodded, her eyes lighting up with delight.

"Make sure you hold the bags above her head while you ride over and then get her settled into bed. Do you have an IV pole at your house or do I need to send one with Joe and Swanny?" Maren asked, breaking into their conversation.

"I'll grab one," Swanny volunteered. "Joe and Steele will need to help Travis into the truck."

Donovan let go of Eve and bent to scoop Cammie into his arms. He sent Swanny a look that told him to help Eve out while Donovan carried Cammie and the IV bags.

Once they were all out in the vehicles again, Donovan drove quickly to the house. Steele and Joe got Travis into bed in the bedroom Donovan had allocated for his use and then Donovan put Cammie into bed in the room she would share with Eve. Swanny brought in the IV pole for Donovan to hang the bags on and then Donovan thrust the prescriptions at Swanny.

"Go have these filled and wait on them. Tell them we need them to put a rush on it. Jimmy knows me so he'll fill them quickly. But he's also nosy and he'll want to know what's wrong with me since they're all made out in my name. Don't volunteer anything."

Swanny nodded. "Will do. You want me to throw together dinner tonight? I don't mind and getting the meds won't take long. Let me do a quick check of what you have on hand and if I need to pick up anything while I'm out, I'll do it."

"Would appreciate that," Donovan said gratefully.

After Swanny walked away, Donovan turned to Eve.

"My sisters-in-law are getting together clothing for you as well as some for Cammie. Joe will run out and get what Travis needs, but for now, what you all need most is rest. Travis is already sleeping, thanks to the injection Maren gave him for pain, so he's comfortable and you don't need to worry about him. It will take an hour or so for Swanny to get back with the meds Maren prescribed and whatever else he needs to pick up, so I'm going to give you an injection as soon as you've gotten into bed with Cammie and then I don't want to see or hear a word from you until dinnertime."

Eve opened her mouth to protest, but Donovan silenced her.

"Don't argue, Eve. You're all exhausted and hurt. Cammie is already halfway asleep, but she's anxious because she's worried about you. The best thing you can do for the both of you is crawl into bed with her and for you both to get some sleep."

Eve sighed but nodded her agreement.

"I'll give you one of my T-shirts. You can change once I leave and then get into bed. I won't see a thing. No sense wearing sweats. I'll give you five minutes and then I'll be back to give you that injection for pain. It'll help you relax and sleep."

Not waiting to hear if she agreed or not, he strode into his bedroom and pulled out a T-shirt that would likely hit her at the knees. While he wasn't as tall as his brothers, he was broad chested and the shirt would hang loosely on Eve and cover her modestly.

The idea of her in his shirt gave him a ridiculous sense of satisfaction.

He returned and thrust the shirt into Eve's hands. Cammie was struggling to remain awake, and Donovan knew that as soon as Eve crawled in beside her, the little girl would be out like a light.

"Five minutes, Eve. And then I'm coming in to give you an injection."

Not waiting for a response, he strode out of the room to where the others were gathered in the living room.

"Can we do anything?" Joe asked.

Donovan nodded. "After you go out and get clothing for Travis, I need you to stop by Sam's and pick up clothing that Sophie and Shea are getting together for Cammie and Eve. Shea is closest to Eve's size, so she's running some stuff over to Sam's, and Sophie is getting some of Charlotte's clothes for Cammie. I have no idea what their shoe sizes are, but we'll tackle that at a later time. They won't need them anytime soon anyway because they're not leaving the house."

"No problem, man," Joe said. "I'm on it."

Donovan looked toward Steele and Maren and baby Olivia in Steele's arms. "Thank you for coming so quickly, Maren. I really appreciate it."

"Is there anything else I can do?" Steele asked pointedly. And Donovan knew he wasn't referring to medical help.

Donovan shook his head. "After they're all asleep, I'm going to have everyone over so we can discuss a game plan. I'm going to get Sean involved as well. If you want to hang out so you don't have to drive back out to your place and then turn right around again, make yourself at home. Swanny is preparing dinner for everyone when he gets back."

Steele nodded. "Do I need to call up my team for this?"

Donovan thought for a moment and then shook his head. "Not yet. Until we at least know what we're up against. Nathan and Joe's team can handle things for now. It's perfect for them and they're all right here local. No sense pulling in your or Rio's teams until I have to. I'll have to fill my brothers in and I don't intend to tell the same story more than once. So I'll wait for everyone to get over before I say what's on my mind."

Swanny and Joe took off to do their respective tasks, and Donovan excused himself to go tend to Eve. When he entered the bedroom, Eve had already crawled under the covers with Cammie, who was huddled into Eve's body.

It was such an endearing sight that for a moment all Donovan could do was stare. At what could be his. At what he *already* considered his. He was struck by the rightness of it all. But he also knew he couldn't afford to get distracted by the fantasy. Somewhere out there, a monster lurked. Waiting for an opportunity to strike. At his family.

The *hell* that was happening.

He uncapped the syringe Maren had prepared and then made his way closer to the bed. He slid onto the edge, his thigh resting against Eve's body.

"I need to give this in your bottom," he explained. "All you have to do is pull up your shirt and lower the band of your underwear. You can remain covered the rest of the way. It'll just take a minute and then you'll feel much better."

"Thank you," Eve said, barely above a whisper. "I don't think I've said it properly—or at all, for that matter. But *thank* you. I have no idea why you're going to so much trouble for people you don't even know, but I can never hope to repay your kindness, Donovan. What you've done for Cammie and Travis. And me. I don't know why—I can't even comprehend it all—but I thank God that you're here. That *we're* here."

He smiled and ran a finger down the curve of her cheek, fiercely satisfied that she seemed to finally be accepting his help. "You're more than welcome, Eve. But get used to it, because I'm not going anywhere and neither are you."

He carefully pushed up the oversized T-shirt to bare her slim waist and the gentle curve of her behind. It was pure temptation to stroke the baby-soft skin, but he focused on sliding her panties down just enough to bare the injection site.

"Just a stick," he warned, and then pushed the needle into her flesh.

She tensed a moment and then stiffened further.

"Ouch," she grumbled. "The medication hurt worse than the needle."

Donovan chuckled. "That's usually the way it goes. But you'll be feeling the effects any second now. I want you to relax and get some sleep. I'll wake you and Cammie for dinner. This time it'll be something better than grilled cheese sandwiches and soup. Swanny has volunteered his culinary expertise and I have to say, the man can cook."

She smiled, her eyes already dulling with the effects of the medication. "That sounds lovely. And Donovan? Thanks again. I'll never be able to repay your kindness."

He bent to kiss her forehead and she went utterly still beneath his lips. "You will, Eve. Trust me, you will. Just not in a manner you'd likely expect."

With that cryptic statement, he withdrew, seeing that Cammie had already drifted to sleep in Eve's arms. He checked her IV line, making sure it was secure and that the fluid was flowing correctly.

"Sleep well, Eve. And know you're safe," he murmured just before leaving the room and shutting the door behind him.

CHAPTER 17

AN hour later, Donovan stood in the living room where his brothers, Sam, Garrett, Joe and Nathan, had gathered along with the rest of Nathan and Joe's team: Swanny, Skylar and Edge. Sean Cameron was present as well. Donovan had wanted him pulled in so he could discreetly run a check on Eve and uncover any potential issues with the law. Steele and Maren had remained, though Maren had retreated to the kitchen to feed Olivia in private.

He needed information from Eve before he could make any huge decisions, but he couldn't wait until he got her to trust him enough to open up. Hopefully that would come later tonight when he and Eve were finally alone. But for now, he needed everyone on point because something or someone was after Eve. Her fear wasn't faked. The terror in her siblings' eyes wasn't an act.

"So what are we dealing with here, Van?" Sam spoke up, breaking the heavy silence in the room.

"I don't know exactly," Donovan said grimly. "But I need to find out fast. I'm going to try to get Eve to talk to me tonight. She doesn't trust easily, but I'm getting through to her. Getting her to agree to stay here was a huge step in the right direction."

He glanced over at Sean, who leaned against the wall, hands shoved into his uniform pockets. He'd just come off duty and hadn't been home yet. Donovan knew he was likely tired, but Sean hadn't hesitated to come when Donovan had asked him to.

"Sean, I need you to do some very discreet checking on Eve, and Cammie and Travis as well. I'm not positive they're using their real names, but Hanson is the name Travis gave. See what you can dig up on anyone matching their descriptions, but I do not need anyone to know about it. Anything you find, you come to me with, regardless of what it is you discover."

Sean's gaze narrowed. "What exactly are you expecting to find?"

"I don't know," Donovan said honestly. "What I know is that they're running and running hard and scared from someone. Cammie's terrified of men. She mentioned that her 'daddy' had hurt Eve. Not Eve's father, but Cammie's. So I'm wondering if maybe Cammie and Travis are Eve's half siblings and they share a mother, or perhaps Eve is an aunt or concerned relative. I just need whatever you can dig up without leaving any traces that you were looking."

Sean nodded. "I'll do what I can."

Donovan expanded his gaze to include the others. "I need you all on this. I want to tighten security around the compound. Do regular watches. I also want to keep an eye out in town for anyone out of place. Someone new or anyone asking questions who sounds anything like they're looking for Eve or Cammie and Travis."

"I can take a look at Amber Alerts," Sean said quietly. "If they ran, it's possible they would have been reported missing."

Left unsaid was the fact that Eve could very well be labeled a kidnapper and a danger to the children. Donovan knew that was bullshit, but it didn't mean it wasn't out there.

Donovan nodded his agreement. "Just make damn sure

you come to me with any information and don't breathe a word to anyone else. I know I'm asking you to work off the books on this and if you aren't comfortable doing something that could compromise your job, I understand."

Sean made a derisive sound. "If you believe in her, then so do I, Van. I trust your judgment. I'm not going to wave any red flags when I dig up what I can find. You'll be the first to receive any info I discover."

"Appreciate that, man," Donovan said quietly.

Then he turned his attention to Steele.

"Until I know precisely what I'm dealing with, you and your team are out. Nathan and Joe can take this. This is our home turf. We aren't going to allow some asshole to come in and threaten Eve and those kids. But at the same time I want to make damn certain our family is protected and we watch our sixes at all times. Which means the wives need to be aware of the potential dangers and make sure they don't go out alone."

Donovan directed the last at his brothers.

Sam and Garrett both nodded their agreement, grim expressions on their faces.

"As long as they're here, inside this compound, nothing can hurt them," Donovan said. "It happened once with Shea. We're never going to make that mistake again. And I fully intend to ensure Eve goes nowhere that places her or Cammie and Travis in danger."

The others voiced their agreement.

"Let's eat," Donovan said, ending the current topic. "Swanny threw together dinner. I'm going to let Eve sleep a while longer before I wake her to eat . . . and talk."

Even as the others filtered into the kitchen, Donovan walked down the hall to Eve's bedroom and peeked inside. His heart softened when he saw Cammie nestled into Eve's arms. Both of them were sound asleep. He stood watching a moment longer before silently retreating, the image still vibrant in his mind.

The others were in the kitchen, standing around with plates and forks scarfing Swanny's lasagna. Donovan rescued enough for Eve and her siblings to eat later, putting the plates into the oven so they'd stay warm.

Sean was the first to leave, saying he was heading home to get some sleep and that he'd do some digging the next morning and report back to Donovan. One by one, Nathan and Joe's team left as well, followed quickly by Steele and Maren, who promised to return the next day to examine Eve, Cammie and Travis again.

Donovan closed the door behind them and turned to see Sam and Garrett standing a short distance away. He knew that look both his brothers wore. He sighed and motioned toward the couch in the living room.

"If I'm going to be lectured by my older brothers, I at least want to be comfortable," Donovan said dryly.

Neither Sam nor Garrett refuted the lecture crack, so Donovan knew he'd been right.

"So what's up?" Donovan asked.

Sam rubbed a hand through his hair and exchanged glances with Garrett. Almost as though they were deciding who was going to speak up first.

"Just spit it out," Donovan said impatiently. "It's obvious you have something on your minds beyond what's already been discussed."

"I'm concerned—we're concerned," Sam amended. "I guess we're worried that this is some sort of wish fulfillment on your part."

Donovan reared back in surprise. "What the hell is that supposed to mean?"

Garrett shifted and then shoved his hands in his pockets. "Look, man, of all of us, you've always been the biggest homebody. You were always the one who wanted a wife and a large family. It surprised the hell out of us that you weren't the first to get married and have a house full of kids."

"We're just worried that you see Eve and her siblings as a shortcut," Sam interjected. "A ready-made family. We just want to make sure you know what you're getting into. You know nothing about Eve or her situation. And you know nothing about what you may be bringing to our front door or the danger you could be placing our families, our wives and children in."

Anger simmered and boiled up in Donovan's throat. He flexed his fingers, finally balling them into tight fists in an effort to rein himself in. The last thing he wanted to do was do or say something he'd regret in the heat of the moment.

"I'd never do anything to endanger any of my sisters-in-law or my nieces and nephews or any of the family and you damn well know it," Donovan seethed. "I'd give my life for them in a heartbeat. And if you know me so damn well, then you know I'd never turn a blind eye to any woman or child so desperately in need."

"That's the point we're making," Garrett said quietly. "You've always had a huge soft spot for women and children. Especially children. We don't want to see you get attached and then have them taken away. You have no idea about the mother or the father in the picture or if Eve herself is the danger to Cammie and Travis."

Donovan fought to keep his cool. He understood his brothers' concerns. He got it. But it still pissed him off, and judging by the looks on his brothers' faces, they knew he was pissed.

"You know we'll always have your back," Sam said. "We aren't immune to Eve or her siblings. We just don't want to see you get hurt. We're concerned that you're becoming too emotionally involved, and you have to turn it off. Treat it like any other mission. Help her and her brother and sister, but keep a distance and keep your heart out of it."

"Sarah was supposed to just be a mission," Donovan challenged. "Remember how quickly that became personal for you? And you, Sam. You got involved with Sophie while on a mission and the very last thing you should have been doing was fucking around with a woman when we were hot on the trail of Mouton. Do either of you regret that now? Look at what you have. Wives. Children, and children on the way. How can you know that Eve is not the one for me? Would you deny me the same shot at happiness that you received yourselves while on a 'mission'?"

Discomfort crawled across Sam's face, and Garrett flinched.

"I know Eve isn't just a goddamn mission. I *know* that. I also know that a lot has to be resolved. I have to gain her trust so that I can be prepared to face whatever she's running from. I don't believe for a minute that she's some criminal. She's just a desperate woman doing whatever it takes to protect her family. Wouldn't we all do the same? Whatever it takes. Just like you do for your own families. Your wives. Your children."

"You're already looking at Eve, Cammie and Travis as *yours*," Garrett pointed out. "We just don't want to see you get hurt, man."

"I just want what you both already have," Donovan said, his voice lowering and shaking lightly with emotion. "And maybe Eve is that person. Maybe not. But I won't ignore what I feel when I look at her just because I don't have all the pieces to the puzzle yet. Just like neither of you turned away from your wives who at that time were just a mission. Just someone in trouble."

"Point taken," Sam said in a grudging voice. "Know that we have your back and that if you have feelings for Eve, beyond that of someone in need, then we consider her family and one of us. We'll do whatever we can to help. No way we'll allow any harm to come to Cammie and Travis. Or Eve. But we want you to go into this with your eyes open. You'd be taking on a teenager and a four-year-old, and that's not going to be easy."

Donovan laughed, some of the tension easing from his shoulders. "Isn't that what Ma did with Rusty? Travis isn't the belligerent, defensive kid that Rusty was, not that she didn't have good reason to be. Travis is a good kid. Scared but determined to protect his sisters. He shouldn't have a care in the world at his age, but instead he's giving up his childhood and becoming a man long before his time. I'd be proud to consider him my son, though it's not like I'm old enough to have fathered him."

Sam and Garrett both chuckled, relaxing their rigid stances.

"Yeah, well, you would have had to have gotten one hell

of a head start if you fathered a fifteen-year-old kid when you weren't much older than him," Garrett said.

Donovan sighed. "Some days I feel a hell of a lot older. We've all seen more in our somewhat young lives than any dozen people will ever see or experience. That shit ages a person. It's time I started thinking about settling down and having a family of my own. Time is passing me by and I'm standing still. I love KGI. I wouldn't have any other job. But I don't want it to become my entire life. I want what you guys have. A wife to come home to. Children to fill my house. I want a *reason* to live and a reason to come back from every mission."

Sam and Garrett exchanged quick, worried glances. Donovan knew he sounded weary and that they weren't used to hearing this kind of heavy shit from him. But he was tired. He was ready for change. He was ready for life to stop passing him by while he stood on the fringes living for each mission with nothing to come home to afterward.

"Don't look at me like that," Donovan said dryly. "Like it's time to break out the straitjacket and haul me away. I'm a big boy. I can take care of myself and I damn sure don't need you interfering in my love life. You're getting way ahead of yourselves anyway. Contrary to what you might believe, I'm not plunging recklessly into a situation without examining every angle first. But when I say this, I know you'll understand what I mean, because it was like this for you when you met Sophie and Sarah. When I look at Eve, I see something more than a woman in danger. I see someone who's different from every other mission I've worked. I may not know where this will take me yet, but it's not going to stop me from taking the path."

"I get it," Garrett said softly. "It was like that for me with Sarah. But I'll remind you that you hounded me about getting too emotionally involved. You were worried about me at the time and you even offered to take over the mission because you thought I was getting in over my head. I'm just returning the favor here."

Donovan smiled. "I appreciate the brotherly concern, but

I got this. Okay? Now if you two will get on home to your wives, then I can get on with figuring out how to get Eve to trust me enough to share whatever trouble she's in."

Sam held up his hands in mock surrender. "Okay, okay, lecture over. We won't bring it up again. Swear. Just watch your six and know that we'll be watching it too. Goes without saying that whatever you need, we'll do."

Donovan rose from the couch and grinned at his brothers. "I know it'll be hard for Garrett to keep his mouth shut."

"Fuck you," Garrett grumbled.

"Hmm, and now I have blackmail material. You step out of line and I tell Sarah you're dropping F-bombs again."

Garrett glared back at Donovan while Sam burst into laughter. Donovan herded his brothers toward the door, anxious for them to be gone. Eve and the others had been asleep for several hours and they'd be hungry soon. He wanted a few moments alone with Eve so that maybe she'd open up to him.

CHAPTER 18

DONOVAN was warming the plates of lasagna and preparing to get a tray together so he could bring everyone food in bed when he looked up and saw Eve standing in the doorway of his kitchen.

He was ridiculously charmed by the image. His T-shirt hanging to her knees, slim legs and bare feet visible. Hair tousled and her eyes droopy with the remnants of sleep, her hand propped on the door frame as she gazed nervously in his direction. He liked her in his space. Like she belonged here. With him. He'd said as much to his brothers, but seeing her right here and now only solidified his feeling of . . . possession. Was this what his brothers had felt when they'd first met their wives? Had they known from the first moment that she was the one? He knew Garrett had been in way over his head from the moment he'd seen Sarah.

And yes, as Garrett had said, Donovan had even warned him off. For all the good it had done him. But now he understood. He got it in a way he hadn't gotten it then. And he knew, just as Garrett had known, that Eve's future was inexorably tied up with his. He accepted that. Would accept no other possibility. But he also knew it wasn't going to be easy. But then it hadn't been easy for any of his brothers or their team leaders. And well, nothing good was easy.

"Come on in," he invited, waving her toward the table. He knew she was uncomfortable dressed in only his shirt, but he was determined to act normal, as if she weren't standing there in just a thin pair of panties and his oversized T-shirt. "I was warming up food to bring you in bed, but if you're up to it, you can eat with me at the table, and then we'll wake Travis and Cammie up to eat. Unless they're awake already?"

He knew she would have gone in and checked on Travis, and he also knew she wouldn't have left Cammie alone in the bedroom if she was awake. Though he had intended to bring her dinner in bed, he now jumped at the opportunity to have dinner with her—alone—in the kitchen. They needed to get a lot out of the way. And he had to see if she trusted him enough yet to confide in him.

"No, they're still asleep," she said in a low voice as she moved toward the table.

Unease was evident in the way she held herself, the hesitance in her eyes as she watched him, standing awkwardly next to a chair still pushed underneath the table. And she was quick to hide her legs behind the table, as if the image of her bare legs weren't already burned into his memory.

He carried a plate of lasagna, just out of the microwave, and set it down in front of her.

"What would you like to drink? I have sweet tea, lemonade or a variety of sodas."

As he spoke, he pulled her chair out for her and motioned for her to sit. When she lowered herself, he caught her elbow, making sure she didn't suffer any effects of the medication he'd administered earlier. She went utterly still at his touch and then glanced up at him underneath her long lashes.

She had to feel it too. This electric connection between them. No way could she be unaware of the current. To reinforce the sensation, he caressed the skin just above her elbow with his fingers. It was a gesture meant to comfort, but the heat from her flesh bled into his hand and up his arm.

"Tea is fine," she murmured.

"I'll be right back with a glass and a fork for you to eat with."

He pushed the plate so it was directly in front of her and then went to collect her drink, forks for both of them and the plate he'd left sitting inside the microwave while he'd brought hers to the table.

A moment later he returned, sliding her glass across the table before taking the seat catty-corner to where she sat at the head.

"Feel up to eating?" he asked when she didn't dig in right away. "Did the medicine make you queasy? I have medication that will settle your stomach and ease the nausea if you need it."

She shook her head. "No. I'm fine. I was just enjoying the smell. It looks delicious."

She picked up her fork and delicately cut into the wedge of lasagna. He watched her eat, watched the fork disappear into her mouth and fantasized about kissing that mouth. Then he shook his head and dug into his own food. He wasn't the least bit subtle about his perusal of her. He wasn't scoring any points in his bid to make her trust him by leering at her like some crusty old man wanting to get into her pants.

He gave her a moment to eat, not wanting to potentially upset her and cause her not to finish her meal. By the looks of her, and from what he'd seen of their trailer, he knew she'd missed far too many meals already.

It was only when she slowed and then finally set her fork down with a sigh, only a few bites left, that he put his own fork down and reached over to slide his hand over hers.

She tensed but didn't pull from his grasp, a fact that gave him great satisfaction. But her gaze lifted, seeking information from him with that silent stare.

"Eve, we need to talk," he said gently.

She flinched, but didn't look away, instead facing him bravely, resignation written in the lines on her face. He hated that look. So defeated. Confiding in him wasn't conceding defeat, and he didn't want her to look at it as failure on her part to protect her siblings.

"I don't know how much I can tell you," she whispered.

He tightened his hold on her hand, stroking her knuckles with his thumb. "You can tell me anything. Everything. I need to know it all so I know what we're up against."

Her eyes narrowed in puzzlement and she looked at him in utter bewilderment. "You said *we*."

The confusion in her voice made him ache. Clearly it baffled her that he'd included himself in her problems. Well, she'd better get used to it, because he *was* inserting himself.

She shook her head as if to clear her senses. "*You* aren't up against anything, Donovan. *I* am. I can't involve you with my problems. It isn't fair. You don't know me. You don't know Travis or Cammie and you don't know what their father is capable of."

Well, they were getting somewhere at least. With those words, she'd confirmed Cammie's statement that it was her father who'd hurt Eve and who had likely done something to hurt those children. Something bad enough to make Eve cut and run, sacrificing everything in her bid to keep them safe. It also confirmed his suspicion that Eve, Travis and Cammie didn't share the same father. Which left her mother as the blood tie. Unless Eve had lied about Cammie and Travis being her siblings, something he didn't believe. He'd seen the love for them shining in her eyes. Had seen how fiercely protective of them she was.

"What did he do?" Donovan asked, trying to keep the anger from his tone. She needed gentleness and understanding. She didn't need his rage.

This time her gaze lowered and her head bowed as she stared down into her lap. He picked up her fingers so he could curl his around hers and he pulled gently to get her attention once more.

"Eve, you can trust me."

She stared into his eyes, hope stirring in the depths of hers. Just as quickly, she shut it down and her gaze dimmed, vanquishing the brief light that had shone just seconds before.

"Please don't take this the wrong way, Donovan. You've been very kind. But I can't afford to trust *anyone*. There's too much at stake. All it takes is *one* wrong decision on my part, one wrong move, and Travis and Cammie suffer as a result."

"And not yourself?"

She flushed, color rising rapidly up her throat and into her cheeks. "I don't matter. *They* do. They're so young. Innocent. They have their entire lives ahead of them and Travis has already sacrificed so much of his. I want them to have normal lives. I want them to be happy and secure. I just want them to be *safe*."

Her voice ached with emotion. It reflected so much need and desire that it made him ache.

There was so much wrong—and right—about her statement that he had to take a few moments to figure out which part he wanted to address first.

"You matter, Eve," he said, taking on the most important part of her declaration. "Never think you don't. Yes, your brother and sister should have all those things you mentioned. But so should *you*. You're young. You have your entire life ahead of you. Just how old are you anyway?"

"Twenty-four," she murmured.

Donovan sighed. Not much older than Rusty, and yet in other ways, probably a hell of a lot older. While Rusty had definitely had a not-so-great childhood, those days were behind her now. She had a life and a family. She could take on the world now, because no one around her would ever let her fall. He wanted that for Eve. The knowledge and confidence that came from knowing she was safe.

"I told you a little about me. My family. What my brothers and I do. You've seen where and how we live. We help people like you every single day. I could regale you with the impossible, horrible situations we've gotten people out of, but I don't want you to even contemplate some of those scenarios. Because if nothing else, you're safe *now*. And you're safe *here*."

Her breath caught in her throat and she went so still that he could see her pulse in her neck. She stared back at him, eyes wide and so full of the hope she'd extinguished earlier that it was like taking a fist to the gut. He could tell she was waging an inner war to end all wars. Her teeth sank into her bottom lip, and she gave him another look filled with consternation.

He should press his advantage right now and go hard at her. She was wavering and he could easily pull her in. But he didn't want her trust that way. He wanted it because it was what she gave freely. He wasn't sure why it mattered so much, but there it was.

"You make it sound so easy," she murmured. "And God, I wish it were. As if telling you, as if accepting your help, would make it all be okay."

His grip tightened around her hand, this time picking it up so he held it firmly in his grasp. A silent message to her that it *would* be okay. Unable to resist and praying he wasn't making a huge mistake, he brought her hand to his mouth and pressed a kiss to the softness of her palm.

Her eyes widened, the shock of the sensation registering every bit as much with her as it did with him. They both sat there, frozen in silence, staring at each other, awareness flowing like a current of electricity between them.

He'd never been seized by such a strong urge to kiss a woman before. With any other woman, if he felt this strongly, he would already have her in his arms, his mouth on hers— and every other part of her body he could get his mouth on. Restraint had never cost him as much as it was costing him right here in this moment. It was a pain he'd never experienced, and he hoped to hell he didn't have to experience it much longer.

"It *is* that easy," he said, his tone unwavering as he spoke. It was laced with conviction. The same conviction he wanted her to eat, sleep and breathe. "I know it will take time for you to trust me, Eve. All I can do is show—*prove*—to you that my words are not just that. Words said to make you feel better. I'm not being arrogant. I'm stating an absolute truth. My brothers and I—*all* of KGI—will protect you and Cammie and Travis. With or without you sharing what it is that we're up against. Granted, it will make my job, and theirs, a hell of lot easier if you tell me what I need to know—and I need to know *everything*—but regardless, I'm not about to let anything happen to you or your family."

She inhaled sharply and then held her breath as she stared at him. He could see the wheels turning furiously in her mind. Her indecision was written all over her face, but he also saw the moment she capitulated and acceptance registered. He almost squeezed her hand, but held himself in check, not wanting to let his elation or sense of victory be broadcast. He'd do nothing to damage the first strings of trust that were starting to form. Much like a spider's web taking shape. But nothing so sinister. No, the stirrings of the initial brush of her trust was a beautiful thing. Something he'd never forget and never take for granted because he knew what it cost her.

"I'm not sure you'll believe me," she said with helplessness he hated hearing.

"Try me," he said, careful not to offer blind reassurance because then she wouldn't believe him.

She sighed and closed her eyes, withdrawing her hand. He let it go, wanting her to be able to compose herself and gather the courage necessary to confide in him.

She slipped her hand into her lap, balling it with her other, and again, she took a deep, steadying breath.

"Would you feel more comfortable in the living room?" he asked.

He wanted her in a place and position where he could touch her. Offer encouragement. And so without waiting for her response, he stood and extended his hand to her.

She slid her soft fingers over his palm and then gripped his hand as he pulled her to a standing position. Perhaps she needed a few more moments to think of how she wanted to present her story. Donovan would wait as long as necessary and not pressure her to hurry.

She tugged self-consciously at his T-shirt, making sure it covered as much of her as possible as he led her into the living room. He seated her on the couch, taking the position next to her. He didn't immediately crowd into her space. She was agitated enough without him adding more intimacy. At least not yet. That would come later. He'd hold her, do whatever was necessary to comfort and reassure her.

One of her hands fluttered to her forehead and for a moment she massaged absently, her nostrils flaring from the deep breaths puffing in and out. Then she closed her eyes again, as if bolstering her flagging courage, and when she reopened them, resolve shone brightly.

She turned toward him, pulling her leg up to tuck underneath the shirt she wore. For a moment she clasped her ankle, anxiety reflected in the furrowing of her brow.

"Cammie and Travis are my half brother and sister," she began. "My mother married their father when I was young. At first I didn't spend much time with them. I mean she didn't have custody, and for a long time I wondered if she didn't want me. It wasn't until later that I realized she'd been protecting me."

Donovan's eyebrow went up, but he was careful to remain silent and not interrupt.

"She had Travis when I was nine and then Cammie several years later. I had thought . . . I had thought she wouldn't have any more children. But Walt—my stepfather—wanted a daughter and he insisted that my mother give him one. I can remember their argument," she said with a flinch, as if the memory still burned brightly in her mind.

"I was nineteen and I was visiting. I didn't get to see my mom much. Especially after Travis was born."

Donovan frowned and broke in to ask the question burning his tongue.

"I assume you were with your dad then since you weren't living with your mom. So where was he and where is he *now*?"

Eve flushed and he regretted interrupting her, something he'd promised himself he wouldn't do.

"My father left us when I was too young to remember him. My mother's sister—my aunt—took me in when Walt refused to let me live with them."

"What a piece of work," Donovan muttered.

"He did me a favor," Eve said wryly. "I didn't know it at the time, but now I'm grateful he refused to take me in and consider me a daughter."

Donovan tensed, knowing that what she still had to tell him was not going to be good. But he was already quite aware that nothing about Eve's situation was good.

"Go on," he encouraged, not wanting to shut her down with his interruption.

She sighed. "Anyway, I remember hearing them argue. My mother felt that she was too old to have another child. Travis's pregnancy had been very difficult for her and there was already such a gap between my and Travis's birth, and now she was looking at having an adult daughter and a pre-teenage son. She didn't want to start all over again, and I can't blame her for that. Walt told her she was being selfish and was only thinking of herself. She then reminded him that he already had a daughter. Me."

Eve's voice became shaky, and she gave a visible shudder that told him all too well what she thought of being considered her stepfather's daughter.

"I was visiting. One of the rare times I was allowed to see my mother. They were arguing in their bedroom, which was on the main floor of the house while all the other bedrooms were upstairs. And when she mentioned me, that he had a daughter, he told her that I wasn't his blood and that he wanted a daughter that was his. That there was no way he would consider another man's leavings as his child."

Even though it was evident that Eve had no wish to be considered the man's daughter, there was still pain in her voice at how coldly Walt had dismissed her. As though she weren't good enough. How abandoned must Eve have felt? Not wanted by her biological father. Not allowed to see or be with her own mother. Taken in by an aunt and rejected by her stepfather. It made Donovan furious that she'd suffered so much pain. And that much more determined to ensure that she suffered no more.

"I brought it up to my mother the next day when I got a few minutes with her alone. It was rare that Walt ever let me

be around her without him present. It was almost as if he
were afraid I'd try to turn her against him. I told her what I'd
overheard. Not the part about him not considering me a
daughter, but I asked her if she was going to have another
child."

Eve's lips turned downward and tears gathered in her
eyes.

"I'll never forget how resigned she looked. And you have
to understand. My mother loved me and Travis. It wasn't that
she didn't want to have children. But the doctors had advised
her not to get pregnant again after Trav. It was too difficult a
pregnancy for her and I knew Walt knew this. It pissed me
off that he could call her selfish when what he was asking
her to do was a risk to her health."

"And what did she say?" Donovan asked gently.

"She said that she didn't have a choice, that it was what he
wanted, and how could she deny him his wish for another
child? I told her that it was selfish of *him* to ask her to have
another. And she freaked out. Not that she got loud or argued
with me. But I remember the utter panic that entered her
expression. She got really quiet, like she was afraid that we
would be overheard even though Walt had taken Travis to
the grocery store. But she was like that. Always on guard, as
if she expected him to barge into the room at any moment."

Donovan nodded but kept quiet. She was into it now, and
the words were tumbling out, almost as if she were, for the
first time, unloading a fierce burden. And it likely was the
first time she'd spoken to others of this.

"Then I asked her if she was happy. Really happy. And I
asked her if she'd considered leaving Walt. That I would help
her. I would quit school. Get a job. Do whatever I could to
help her. And she *really* panicked then. I don't think I'd ever
seen her that scared. I mean, she was always reserved around
Walt. Skittish even. She was what I would call totally sub-
missive. What he said went. Always. But when I said all that,
she told me to promise her that I would *never* mention it
again. She was so emphatic. She *made* me promise never to

say anything to Walt about it. Then she said that if he knew, he'd never let me see her again.

"Now I already a good idea of how controlling he was, but I honestly thought it was an ego thing. That he didn't want any reminder of the fact my mother had been married before. But this went deeper than that, and it scared me. She grabbed me by the shoulders and told me she loved me and that she never wanted not to be able to see me and for me not to be a part of her life. She said if having another child secured that option for her, then she'd do it without any reservations. I began to realize then just *how* my stepfather had gotten her to agree to have another child. He'd threatened her. With *me*. It made me sick."

Donovan grimaced at the sadness and anger in her voice. He put his hand on her shoulder, squeezing lightly, a reminder that he was here and that she was safe. That her stepfather couldn't harm her now.

"I had to promise her, even though it sickened me to have to swear that I wouldn't stick up for her. That I wouldn't help her or ever mention Walt's treatment or unreasonable demands. But she was so upset. So terrified that I couldn't do anything else."

"So she got pregnant with Cammie," Donovan said softly.

Eve nodded, unable to speak for a moment as tears knotted in her throat. After a minute or two, she cleared her throat and continued.

"Walt was thrilled with my mother's pregnancy, and for a time, he was *nice*. Generous even. He allowed me to see my mother more. Even offered to help me through college, something he'd never offered before. I didn't want to take it. I wanted nothing from him, but again, my mother begged me to make peace. Not to rock the boat. She was happier than I'd ever seen her. She seemed to shine. Her pregnancy was progressing well and, to Walt's credit, not that he deserves any," she said fiercely, "he treated her very well. Made sure she rested, didn't lift a finger. He employed a full staff and they waited on her hand and foot. It was like Walt had a

lobotomy or something. He was a different man, or at least
that was the front he put on. So I capitulated. Allowed Walt
to basically come in and take over my life. Later I realized
that it was just his way of controlling not only my mother
and Travis but me as well. And I knew. I mean, I'm not a
complete idiot. I knew I shouldn't allow him to make any
decisions about my life or make me beholden to him in any
way. But I was willing to do *anything* for my mother. I
wanted her to be happy even if I knew in my heart that she'd
never truly be happy with a man like Walt. I couldn't tell her
no when it was obvious that any refusal of Walt would bring
down his wrath not only on me, but my mother and brother
as well. He would have cut me out of my mother's life. I
wouldn't have been allowed to see her or Travis and certainly not the new baby."

"You were very likely right," Donovan said quietly.

"A lot of good it did me," Eve choked out, tears still
straining at the corners of her eyes.

It was obvious she was holding very tightly to her control
and that she could crack at any moment. Donovan was prepared. He'd hold her. Let her cry. Whatever she needed
because it wasn't likely she'd allowed herself to show any
weakness in front of her brother and sister. She wouldn't have
wanted to make them more afraid than they already were.

Eve wiped at the corner of her eye, her jaw clenched tight
as she took a brief moment to gather her composure before
continuing her story.

"After Cammie was born, I was allowed to see them more
often than I had in the past. When Walt began paying for my
schooling—he chose the college. He chose everything. He
even scheduled my classes. I *hated* it. I hated how he controlled every aspect of my life. He bought me an apartment
closer to where he and Mom lived. All utilities were in his
name. Everything was. The car I drove. And on the surface
it looked like a stepfather being generous. Stepping up and
taking on a daughter who wasn't his responsibility. He liked
looking good when it suited his purposes. Everything he did
was carefully orchestrated.

"While I wasn't a real member of the family—and he was always certain to be very clear about my role in the 'family'—on paper it looked as though he had taken me in as his 'own.' Access to my mother and Travis and Cammie was strictly monitored. I was never to just come over. He told me when I could be there, and if I was even a minute late— he dictated the exact times I was to be there—he punished me by making it that much longer before I could see them again. My life was spiraling out of control, or rather becoming more firmly under his control, and I didn't see a way out. There was too much at stake. I knew it was all wrong, but God, I didn't know what to do! If I balked, my mother would suffer. I'd be cut out of her life and God only knew what he'd do to her or Travis and Cammie as a result."

She took a deep breath, strain evident on her brow. Donovan knew that they'd come to the point where things got worse and she was valiantly trying to keep her emotions in check.

"Until then, I truly didn't believe that Walt was physically abusive. Verbally and emotionally? Yes. I had no illusions that he wasn't a maniacal control freak and that he manipulated everyone around him. As naïve as it sounds, I'd never suspected his abuse was physical—there had never been evidence. Until Cammie was three years old. My mother changed. I mean not that she was ever the mom who'd raised me, the woman she'd been before she married Walt. She was more subdued. Her marriage to Walt had changed her. She'd lost her spark, the happiness in her eyes, and she rarely smiled like she used to.

"But then I started noticing bruises. Oh, she always had an excuse. Don't all abused women have ready excuses when they don't want people to know they're being abused? But the excuses kept mounting and I knew that he was hurting her physically. I couldn't stand by and let that happen. I tried to talk to my mother about it, but she immediately shut me down. She'd get this terrified look on her face and beg me never to speak of it again.

"And I couldn't do that," she whispered painfully.

She closed her eyes, tears finally seeping down her cheeks, leaving stark trails on her pale face. Donovan wanted to touch her. He wanted to wrap his arms around her and hold her while she grieved. But he knew she wasn't finished. Not by a long shot. There was still a hell of a lot that had happened to get them to the point where they were now. Desperate. Running. Scared out of their minds.

"I went to the police and told them that Walt was abusing my mother. I couldn't just stand by and allow that monster to hurt my mother. I realized that if he abused her, what was to say he wasn't also abusing Travis and Cammie?"

Dread took hold of Donovan. "What happened then?"

She lifted her tear-filled gaze to his. "Walt was furious. Of course the police merely came to the house and questioned both my mother and Walt. They both denied any such thing and Walt gave some ridiculous story about how the bruises got there. The police left. After all, they could hardly arrest Walt when my own mother denied he was abusing her."

Donovan let out a pent-up breath, knowing full well how things worked. He'd seen too many cases in real life. Knew exactly how unfair the justice system was sometimes. If Eve's mother had refused to press charges, the hands of the police were tied.

"Walt confronted me," Eve said. "He rarely *directly* communicated with me, unless it was to issue a dictate. I was largely ignored. Not part of the family. Travis and Cammie weren't even allowed to say my name in Walt's home. I was regarded as a servant, like someone in Walt's employ, and was treated accordingly."

"Did he hurt you?" Donovan demanded, his voice cold as rage brewed and stirred in his veins.

"He th-threatened me," she said falteringly. "He was furious. Told me that I better shut up and mind my own business or I would never see my mother again. He threatened to evict me from my apartment, take away all of his financial support. Not that I cared about any of that. One of the conditions of his support, which he basically forced upon me via my mother and her pleas for peace, was that I not work. He didn't want me to have the means to support myself. He wanted me solidly under his thumb just like my mother and his children. So he told me that not only would he put me out on the streets and withdraw all his financial support, which meant no school as well, but that he'd make certain there was no place that would hire me.

"I was numb. I didn't care about what happened to me. But it made me ill to know that he was beating my mother and I was supposed to knuckle under to his threats and go on as if I didn't know what was going on behind closed doors in that house."

She closed her eyes as more tears slipped soundlessly down her cheeks.

"He beat her to get back at me. He admitted it when I saw her next. When I saw what he'd done to her, he stood there and told me it was my fault. That *I'd* done this to her. That if I'd kept my mouth shut and minded my business that this wouldn't have happened to her. And he did and said all of this right in front of my mother. Blamed me as she stood there, bruises on her face and around her neck. Her hand was swollen and bruised. I think he'd broken several of her fingers, but of course he'd done nothing to help her. Hadn't taken her to a doctor. Hadn't put them in a cast. And I had to watch my mother stand there, eyes dull, all the life taken right out of her while he blamed me for the fact that she was in pain. I'll never forget the way she looked at me. Not with blame, but begging. She was begging me to let it go. Not to make him angry again."

"God," Donovan breathed. "I'm so sorry, honey. You know it wasn't your fault, right?"

She hesitated just long enough for Donovan to realize that no matter what she said, she *did* blame herself. It enraged him. He sucked in steadying breaths because he wanted to explode and that was the last thing she needed.

"I know whose fault it was," she said in an unconvincing tone. "It wasn't mine and it damn sure wasn't my mother's. I think he thought I'd let it go. That he'd bullied her—and me—into accepting it all. But it only made me that much

more determined. I was furious. I've never been so filled with
rage in my life. I honest to God could have killed him in that
moment. If I'd had any sort of a weapon, I would have killed
him on the spot and gladly gone to prison if it meant my
mother and Travis and Cammie would finally be safe and
free of him."

Donovan had a very good idea of where this was leading.
"You went back to the police, didn't you?"

She nodded numbly, her eyes glazing over, her gaze going
vacant and distant. So much pain crowded into those beautiful amber eyes. And guilt. That was what tore Donovan to
pieces. The guilt and sorrow in her expression.

"I went straight to the police. I told them everything that
had happened. How he controlled everyone around him. The
lengths he'd gone to subjugate everyone under his authority.
I told them he admitted to my *face* that he'd beaten her. That
he'd said it was my fault. I begged them to go immediately.
To look at my mother's bruises and to do something about it.
I told them there was no way to know if he abused Travis and
Cammie, that they were all so frightened of him that they
wouldn't dare go against his dictates."

"Did they believe you? Did they investigate?" Donovan
queried.

"I don't know if they believed me. I think they thought I
was a hysterical female. But yes, they took me with them and
went to Walt's house. What happened next . . ." She shook
her head, disbelief still evident in her features. "I had *no
idea* just how prepared he was for something like that. When
I think of all the foreplanning he had to do to mastermind it,
I'm just blown away. I mean, I knew he was a controlling
asshole. I knew he had money and power. But I never imagined just how far he'd go to discredit me. How long he had to
have planned to set into motion what he did. It sounds so
farfetched, and yet he made it happen."

"What did he do? Donovan asked, dread centering in his
chest.

She sent him a look filled with bewilderment. "When the
police showed up, Walt actually looked pained. All of a sudden

he adopted the look of a concerned 'parent.' He looked
grief-stricken, as laughable as it sounds. He told the officers
I had a history of mental illness and paranoid delusions.
That he hadn't wanted to hospitalize me because he hoped
I could lead a normal life. He told them he'd always considered me his daughter even though I wasn't his blood.
That he was paying for me to go to school. Paying my
expenses. Bought me an apartment. Which all sounds fishy
as hell and like crap, right? Only, he produced medical
records documenting a long history of mental illnesses, a list
of medications that I'd refused to take. And this was from a
reputable hospital that specialized in mental health. He had
a *letter* from a well-known psychiatrist! I was so dumb-
founded that I didn't even know what to say. Walt poured on
the charm. Said his wife was accident prone, and with a tod-
dler, who could blame her? That Cammie was an active
three-year-old who kept my mother busy and that the bruises
were from a fall down the stairs trying to prevent Cammie
from taking a tumble. He had the police eating out of his
hand, and he made me look like some deranged lunatic off
her meds. There was honest-to-God sympathy and *admiration* for Walt in the policemen's eyes. Like he was such a
good person for taking in a daughter from his wife's previous marriage and getting me the help I needed. I wanted to
vomit because he'd covered himself so well that I would
have believed him. There was an entire fake medical file on
me dating back to when I was just a child. It appeared as
though I'd been in and out of this facility for years. So of
course the police took him at his word and then were all
stern with me about filing false police reports and wasting
department resources when their police had far more important, *real* matters to attend to."

"Son of a bitch," Donovan bit out.

Yeah, the bastard certainly had covered every one of his
steps. He'd planned for everything, including discrediting
Eve in everyone else's minds. Her stepfather was a formidable opponent, but Donovan swore then and there that the
asshole was going down and Donovan was going to enjoy

every minute. He wanted Walt to suffer every bit as much as he'd made Eve suffer.

"He then made good on every single threat he'd issued," Eve said quietly. "He withdrew all financial support. Evicted me from my apartment. All I had were the clothes on my back and enough cash to eat for a few days. I quickly discovered just how far his reach extended when I tried to apply for jobs. I would have taken anything. I wasn't picky. My next plan was to hire an investigator to build a case against Walt, and I needed money for that. But no one would hire me. It was like there was this giant red flag that hovered over my name. Only when I left the immediate area to seek out a job elsewhere did I finally manage to score a waitressing job. The pay was shit. The tips were miserable. But it was enough to rent a one-room efficiency apartment in a shitty part of town.

"Walt cut me out entirely. Refused to allow me to see Mom, Travis or Cammie. He said he didn't want them influenced by my continuous bad decisions. That if in the future I proved I'd learned my lesson he would reconsider, but there would have to be a hell of a lot of changes, meaning I would have to submit to being under his thumb. A robot to act as programmed."

"Asshole," Donovan growled. "Did he hurt you, Eve? Did he ever hurt Travis and Cammie?"

"I'll get to that," she said quietly.

Donovan swore viciously under his breath.

"He kept me away from them, completely isolated for months. No calls. If I called, I wasn't allowed to speak to any of them. They weren't allowed to call me. I worked, saving every penny I could. I barely ate. Each dollar was precious and I knew I'd need money to build a case against Walt and expose the bastard for what he was. But I also knew that I was up against a powerful, wealthy man who had endless connections and that it wasn't going to be easy. But I was driven. I refused to just give up and allow my mother and my siblings to suffer any longer."

"You're a very courageous, loyal person," Donovan said, reaching to touch her cheek with the back of his knuckles.

She shook her head. "No," she whispered. "I'm not. If I were, I would have never let it go that long. I wouldn't have given up. My mother would still be alive."

Tears had thickened her voice and shone on her pale cheeks. Before he could correct her belief, she plunged forward, seemingly needing to get it done and said, like ripping off a bandage instead of peeling it slowly.

"And then she died," she said, a sob welling from her throat. "And I knew. I knew he'd killed her. It wasn't me being paranoid or delusional. I know that son of a bitch had killed her. Who knew why? Maybe she'd finally mustered her courage and had threatened to walk away. Maybe she tried to walk away. She would have never left Travis and Cammie there under his care. She would have taken them. Likely come to me for help. She knew I would. God knows I'd offered it to her enough times."

"Jesus," Donovan muttered. And yet there was more. So much more.

"I was shocked that he allowed me at her funeral. He acted . . . conciliatory. He asked me to come over after the visitation. The first time I'd been allowed in his home since that awful day I'd come with the police. He said Travis and Cammie needed me. That *he* needed me. I didn't care what he wanted or needed. I was only concerned about Travis and Cammie, and I wanted to see them with my own eyes. I wanted to see if he'd hurt them—if he'd *ever* hurt them. I had to know. I had to see them so I could promise them I'd get them out of there as soon as I could.

"Travis and Cammie were understandably quiet. In shock. Cammie was white faced and strangely tearless the entire time. It was as if she had no clue what was going on. Maybe she hadn't accepted that our mother was gone. I just remember how quiet and still the house was. How ominous it was. I was scared to even be there because it was a house filled with . . . evil. His presence was everywhere. His stamp was on every piece of furniture, artwork. Nothing of my mother. None of her personal touches. The entire house screamed Walt and his influence. And then . . ."

She shuddered and went silent, remaining so as she visibly grappled with her anger—and grief. When she kept silent, her forehead furrowed, her lips drawn into thin, white lines, he leaned forward, sensing that she needed more than the brief touches he'd offered.

Carefully, gauging her reaction for any signs of protest, he pulled her into his arms. After only a moment's hesitation, she went readily, burying her face in his chest. He anchored her against him, holding her tightly, his arms wrapped completely around her. He laid his cheek against her silky hair and breathed in her scent.

She felt so soft and warm in his arms and infinitely fragile. But so very precious. He'd give anything in the world to slay her dragons and the demons that haunted her dreams— and her reality.

"Then what, Eve?" he murmured against her hair. He needed to know the rest. And she needed to rid herself of the poison that had festered for so long.

She shuddered again in his arms and tensed, as if trying to hold back the mounting sobs. Had she ever cried? Even once? Or had she been too determined to put up a brave front for Travis and Cammie?

"He called me into his study. It was a room strictly off limits to everyone. My mother. Travis. Cammie. No one but him was ever allowed inside. Except business associates or friends he invited, but my mother had never stepped inside and neither had my brother and sister.

"I remember being so ill at ease. I was devastated by the loss of my mother. I was bitter and angry and convinced I was facing her killer. I worried what would happen to Travis and Cammie. If I would ever be allowed to see them again now that my mother—my only link to them—was gone.

"I hated the feeling that I was at his mercy. I hated . . . *him*. I've never hated anyone. I've never felt violence toward another human being, and yet if I'd had a gun in my hand in that moment I would have killed him."

"Why did he call you into his study?" Donovan prompted softly.

She shuddered in his arms and then went completely still. Dread filled Donovan at her hesitation. He made himself loosen his grip around her because his emotions were in turmoil and his anger and frustration was mounting. The last thing he wanted was to hurt her inadvertently. To mark her beautiful skin. It made him physically ill to even think that his hand had caused a woman pain.

"He wanted . . . He wanted me to . . . Oh God, Donovan, it's *sick*."

Tears soaked into his shirt, the material clinging damply to his skin. He stroked a hand over her hair, murmuring words of comfort close to her ear.

"He wanted me to, for all practical purposes, replace my mother."

Her voice was so filled with horror that each word was choked out as if it disgusted her to even say them out loud.

Donovan stilled as her statement played over and over in his mind. That could mean a lot of things, but he knew her stepfather's intent was sick and twisted.

"He t-touched me. In a way he'd never touched me before. In fact, he had always been careful to maintain his distance. I wasn't treated as family. As one of his children like Travis and Cammie. He was always so impersonal with me. And yet at times I could feel him staring at me and it made me so uncomfortable. I hated when he looked at me because I felt . . . *unclean*."

He pressed a kiss to the side of her head, over the soft strands of her hair, clenching his jaw in frustration that he had to sit here helpless, powerless to do anything but listen as she spilled the horror she'd endured for so many months.

Eve had said she wanted to kill her stepfather, but Donovan wanted the same. He'd suffer no remorse whatsoever, and he *still* didn't have the entire story. One that was going to get a lot worse.

"He told me that if I wanted to maintain contact with Travis and Cammie, I would do exactly as he wanted. That I'd move into the house, and into his bed. That I would act as his mistress because he'd never marry me. Never give me that *honor*, as if I would consider it such! And if I complied with all his wishes, he'd forgive my past sins and he'd allow me to act as mother and sister to Travis and Cammie. But if I resisted, if I denied him anything he wanted, he'd make certain that I would never see my brother and sister again and that furthermore he'd make it so I had nothing. And then . . .'"

Her voice trailed off and sobs shook her shoulders. He held her tighter, kissing her hair, stroking her back and rubbing in a circular motion, trying to offer comfort she badly needed.

"He told me to get on my knees and please him. That if he was satisfied by my effort, he would allow me into his house. But he wanted me to remember that if I disobeyed even once, he'd punish me and make me sorry I was ever born."

"Son of a bitch," Donovan swore. "Tell me you didn't do it."

Eve yanked away from him, her eyes stricken and wounded. "Of course I didn't. How could I? He killed my mother! He disgusted me. I'd rather have *nothing* than to accept what he was offering."

Donovan cupped her cheek. "Shh, darling Eve. I wasn't disgusted with you. Never with you. I'm furious at how he tried to manipulate you."

"He was f-f-furious when I told him to go to hell," she choked out. "He hit me. It was a cold, calculated strike, one I knew he'd meted out many times before. On my mother. He split my lip and then threw a tissue at me and told me I'd better not get any blood on his rug. Then he told me to get out and never to come back. That I'd never see Travis and Cammie again and that he would ruin me. What was there to ruin? I had nothing. He'd seen to that. All I had left was my pride. My sense of self. And I wouldn't allow him to take that too."

Donovan leaned forward and kissed her forehead, the closest he'd come to actually kissing her lips. She closed her eyes and leaned into his mouth, her breaths escaping in long exhales.

"How then did you escape with Travis and Cammie?" Donovan asked, finally putting the pieces together. But what she said next made him realize that there was much more.

"Travis called me," Eve said quietly. "It had been a few weeks since Walt had thrown me out of the house. I had no idea what he'd said to Travis and Cammie. I was certain that he would have poisoned them against me. But then Travis called, and he knew. He knew that I hadn't just deserted him and Cammie. He begged me to help them. He was worried about Cammie. Oh God, Donovan. Travis said Walt was acting weirdly toward Cammie. Insisting that she sleep with him at night. Touching her inappropriately. Travis was terrified that if they remained there any longer that he would hurt her. *Continue* to hurt her."

Curses exploded from Donovan's mouth as rage swelled out of control in his chest. It shouldn't have surprised him. Nothing should have surprised him after Eve had related so much about what an utter asshole Walt was. But he hadn't been prepared for the fact that her stepfather would have molested his only daughter. Had that been why he was so adamant about Eve's mother giving him a daughter?

He wanted to hunt the bastard down and kill him with his bare hands. Fury sizzled in his veins until it was all he could do to sit there, holding and comforting Eve, when he wanted to take the man apart who'd done so much harm to three innocent people. Four, counting Eve's mother. He didn't disbelieve Eve's assessment that Walt had killed his wife. Donovan could well believe it.

"I told Travis I'd do whatever I could. That we'd run. Together. That I'd never leave him and Cammie. That I wouldn't have left them but Walt had thrown me out of the house and forbidden contact. I later discovered that one of the maids had helped Travis. She'd known what Walt's intentions were toward Cammie and she'd given Travis her phone to call me, and with the maid's help, they sneaked out of the house at night after Walt had gone to bed. Her husband drove Travis and Cammie to meet me at a local grocery store. And he gave us his truck. I was stunned at his generosity, but he only told me that he and his wife, the maid in Walt's house, had a daughter and they'd never allow anyone to hurt her like Walt was trying to hurt Cammie. So we took his truck and drove. We kept on driving until I was able to trade it in on a different vehicle. I gave a false name and it was a dealership that wasn't exactly concerned with having all the i's dotted and t's crossed. I was concerned that Walt would have discovered who helped us and it would be too easy for him to find us if we continued to use the maid's husband's truck.

"So we set out in the other car and drove as far as we could. It broke down outside Dover, which is how we came to be here. I had enough money from temporary jobs I picked up along the way to rent the trailer. I knew we needed to stay long enough to build up enough cash to make our next move. But then Cammie got sick and I couldn't leave her, so Travis got the job in the hardware store."

"You were planning to run again last night," Donovan said gently.

Eve flushed, pulling away from him to stare down at her lap. "Yes. I thought we were gaining too much attention. I'm not saying we didn't appreciate all you and your sister were doing for us. But then there was the doctor you were going to bring over. The more people we were exposed to, the more likely it would be that we would be found. We were going to walk to Clarksville, where I could pawn my mother's jewelry, and then take a bus into Kentucky. To a larger city. My mistake was in stopping in such a small town. We needed to go someplace larger. Where we could blend in and not draw much attention to ourselves."

"I hope I've dissuaded you of that notion now."

She gazed up at him, confusion still bright in her eyes. "I just don't understand you, Donovan," she said helplessly. "I don't understand any of you. Why? Why would you help someone you don't even know? You act like you . . . *care*."

Donovan sucked in his breath, knowing that what he had to say could very well scare her off for good. That she might flee at the very first opportunity, not that he planned on giving her one. But he couldn't lie to her either. She'd never trust him if he wasn't completely honest with her. So he took a huge risk and laid it out.

"I do care, Eve. I care a hell of a lot."

CHAPTER 19

EVE stared in shock at Donovan. There was no deception in his expression. His eyes were earnest. Blatantly honest and . . . sincere. He definitely cared. But she got a ridiculous sense that it wasn't caring about someone in trouble. Like he'd care about a job he was doing. Hadn't he said that he and his brothers helped people like her all the time? How crazy was it for her to read further into this? To assume he had feelings that went beyond the normal? Like she somehow mattered to him? That he was attracted to her?

And was she attracted to him? Or was this some crazy savior/victim thing going on? Her falling for the first guy who expressed concern and seemed to care for her?

She needed her head examined because she was in way over her head.

She wanted to ask him how *much* he cared, but doing so would set her up for inevitable disappointment. She needed to be objective. Look at him as someone who could help her and Cammie and Travis. And they *did* need help. Desperately. Would she be a fool to turn him down?

Yes. The answer was simple. Cammie and Travis deserved

anything she could provide for them. It was obvious that she couldn't do it on her own. Not anymore. She—they—needed Donovan Kelly.

"Tell me, Eve. Do I have any chance of making you trust me? And if asking for your trust is too much, will you at least accept the help I'm offering? Can you give me your word that you'll stop running and give me—my brothers—the chance to help you?"

Slowly she nodded, though she wasn't sure which part she'd agreed to. Maybe all of it. Maybe she already did trust him. Otherwise, would she be here? Not that she'd had much choice in the matter, but she hadn't fought. Hadn't even attempted to turn down his aid.

Satisfaction burned brightly in Donovan's eyes, and his shoulders seemed to sag. In relief? He reached forward, touching her face with his fingertips, and she shivered at the warmth his touch provided. She was starved of affection. Of having someone touch her in such an intimate manner. Walt had touched her, yes, but every part of her had shriveled. She'd shrunk away from his touch, not wanting him anywhere near her. And Cammie. God. Nausea still rose in her stomach every time she imagined that precious little girl in the hands of a monster.

Thank God Travis had called her. Thank God for the maid who'd been willing to help them. If not for her, Cammie—and Travis—would still be under Walt's control. Eve herself would be under his control. She shuddered at what could have been. What might have already been.

She'd questioned Travis and even Cammie, albeit very gently and very vaguely. She hadn't wanted to traumatize Cammie, but she'd needed to know the extent of what Walt had done to her. If he'd ever touched her or, God forbid, gone even further. What kind of sick, twisted man could possibly do such a thing to his own daughter?

To make such overtures toward Eve was one thing. Sick, yes, but it wasn't the same as forcing his attentions on a four-year-old daughter. He'd never made a secret of his distaste for Eve and the fact that she was his wife's daughter from a previous marriage. Which made it hard for Eve to understand why Walt would suddenly make sexual overtures toward her. Maybe it had always been there. Maybe it was why he'd gone to such measures to control every aspect of Eve's life. Perhaps he'd always planned to get rid of his wife as soon as she gave him the daughter he wanted. Which made Eve wonder why he'd wanted another child. Was it so he'd have his own plaything? An outlet for his twisted desires?

She couldn't even dwell on it further because it made her sick to her soul.

"What are you thinking about, honey?"

Donovan's gentle voice broke through the horror of her thoughts and brought her back to reality. She blinked, finding his gaze. He was staring thoughtfully at her, his brow furrowed as if he were trying to see inside her mind and know what she was thinking.

"H-him," she stammered out, fighting back the wave of revulsion even speaking of him caused. She couldn't bring herself to say his name. As if by saying it he would be conjured up and standing in the room with her.

He stroked her cheek, cupping her chin with a tender grasp.

"I don't want you to think of him any longer. He can't hurt you here. I won't allow him near you or your brother and sister."

She nodded, but the horror had yet to fade. In retelling Donovan everything, the first she'd spoken of the chain of events to anyone, the memories burned bright in her mind. Grief over losing her mother welled in her soul and threatened to overwhelm her. Months of running, of being afraid that at any moment Walt would find them and take them back had beaten her down until weariness—bone-deep fatigue—had blanketed her, suffocating her until she could barely breathe.

"You need to rest," Donovan said gently. "And I need to get some food down Travis and Cammie. Want to help me wake them up and see if they're up to eating? I thought you could sit with Cammie while she eats, and I'll take Travis his food and give him another dose of pain medication after he eats."

She nodded, eager to focus on anything but what consumed her thoughts. She wanted to see Cammie and Travis again, to reassure herself that they were here. Safe. Taken care of. Getting the food and medicine they both so desperately needed.

Donovan stood, reaching his hand down to help Eve to her feet.

"What about you?" he asked pointedly. "Are you still hurting?

She flushed, wanting to deny it, but her expression had already given it away.

He frowned at her but said nothing as he steered her toward the kitchen. When they got there, he warmed two plates of lasagna and then prepared two glasses of tea. Just when she thought that perhaps he was going to ignore her silent admission, he turned with the tray in hand.

"After Cammie and Travis have eaten, I'm going to give you another dose of pain medication and you're going to sleep. I wonder when the last time was you got a full night's rest?"

She dropped her gaze guiltily.

"That's what I thought," he said grimly. "Come on. We'll check in on Travis and get him situated and then I'll take you to Cammie's room so you can help her eat."

Though his hands were full, he walked beside her, lending her his strength, though he didn't touch her. He didn't have to. Just being there was enough. He matched his pace to her much smaller one, and she glanced down, realizing she was still clad in only her underwear and his shirt.

When they reached Travis's room, she opened the door, eager to see how he was doing. If he was still hurting. And offer him reassurance that they were safe. She'd broadcasted her doubts to him. He'd picked up on her unease when they'd entered this place. Now she wanted to reassure him that she'd chosen wisely. She was sure of it.

Travis was still sleeping and she hated to wake him, but she knew he needed to eat and he likely needed more pain medication. His brow was creased even in sleep, his expression tense as though he were indeed in pain. She touched his forehead, running her hand gently across his brow.

He stirred beneath her touch and opened his eyes. They were cloudy with sleep and remnants of fatigue and pain.

"Hey," she whispered. "How are you feeling?"

"I'm okay," he said quickly. But when he tried to shift and sit up, he grimaced and quickly settled back against the pillows.

"Don't try to move," Donovan cautioned. "Just take it slow and easy. I've brought you something to eat. Eve and I will help you maneuver so you can eat. Then I'll give you another dose of pain medication so you can rest."

Travis glanced between Eve and Donovan and then realized she was only in a shirt. His eyes widened and Eve flushed. Donovan ignored the interchange and set the tray holding the plates down on the nightstand. Then he bent over Travis while Eve got on the other side and they helped ease him upward, Travis grimacing as they propped pillows behind him to support him.

"Hungry?" Donovan asked.

"Starving," Travis admitted. "It smells good, whatever it is."

Eve smiled. "Then eat. I'm going to go check on Cammie and try to get her to eat too."

"Is she all right?" Travis asked quickly, his eyes going dark with concern.

"She's fine," Eve assured him. "She's been sleeping. Like you. She's getting the medicine she needs. In a day or two she'll be better."

"And you, Evie?" Travis asked, lifting his gaze to hers. "Have you slept at all? Are you still hurting?"

"Don't you worry about your sister," Donovan said briskly as he set the tray in front of Travis. "She got some rest and she's about to get some more just as soon as we see to Cammie. I'm going to give you an injection for pain, and then she's getting the same and I want all of you to get a good night's sleep."

"Yes, sir," Travis said in a low voice.

Donovan smiled down at him and handed him a fork. "Dig in. I'm going to go down with Eve to check on Cammie, and when I get back I'll give you that shot. It'll give you time to eat before you crash again."

Travis lifted his gaze to Donovan, sincerity blazing in his eyes. "Thank you for what you're doing, Mr. Kelly. For my sisters. We appreciate it."

Donovan put his hand on Travis's shoulder and squeezed. "You're welcome, son. Now call me Donovan. The only Mr. Kelly around here is my dad. Hearing you call me that makes me feel like an old fart."

Travis grinned and relaxed, the tension easing from his face. He picked up his fork and dug in with gusto. Eve could hear his stomach growl and gave thanks once again that they were safe, under a roof that didn't leak, and that Travis had plenty to eat and the care he needed.

She leaned down and brushed her lips across Travis's brow. "I'll be back later to check on you, okay? I'm just down the hall if you need me. I love you."

"Love you too," Travis mumbled around a mouthful of lasagna.

She smiled and turned to follow Donovan from the room.

When they got to the bedroom she shared with Cammie, she went in, her heart softening when she saw Cammie still fast asleep, the IV bag still dripping steadily into the tube. It hurt her heart to see the little girl with an IV in her arm, taped and a tube leading away, but she also knew that this was what was necessary. That if Maren hadn't acted as quickly as she had, Cammie could have gotten a lot worse.

"I'll let you rouse her," Donovan said quietly. "I'll stand back until she's awake and oriented. Once you get her sitting up I'll set the tray up in front of her."

Eve went to Cammie's bedside and slid onto the bed beside her. She touched Cammie's fevered brow, tenderness assailing her.

"Cammie? Cammie, darling, can you wake up for me? I brought you something to eat. Are you hungry?"

Cammie roused, blinking sleepily as she stared up in confusion. Then her gaze settled on Eve and she relaxed.

"I had a bad dream," she mumbled, sliding her thumb inside her mouth.

Eve bent to kiss her forehead and stroked a hand through her tousled hair. "I'm sorry, darling. But you know nothing can hurt you here, don't you? It was just a dream."

"He was there," Cammie said in a low voice, still sucking at her thumb. "He was here. I woke up and he was standing by my bed just like he used to. It scared me, Evie. You promise he won't find us here?"

Donovan's expression had gone utterly black as he listened to Cammie. Eve exchanged helpless looks with him. Now that Donovan knew everything, he could read between the lines. Knew what Cammie referred to when she said that her father had watched her sleep. That he'd acted inappropriately toward her. Eve just didn't know the extent. Maybe she never would. And that killed her. She didn't want to remind Cammie of past fears. She didn't want to bring back those terrors. But at the same time, Cammie needed to talk to someone. She needed to get it out or the wounds would fester, and left unresolved it would cause her problems well into her adult life.

Donovan took a step forward, for the first time inserting himself into the conversation. Cammie's eyes flickered and she latched on to him, relief lighting her expression.

He seated himself on Cammie's other side, carefully positioning the tray in front of her. He picked up the hand that didn't have the IV attached and curled his fingers around her palm.

"Listen to me, sweetheart. You and Eve and Travis are safe here. I'm not going to let your father come here. Okay? Eve has told me everything that happened. Your father is a bad person and I'm not going to let him ever scare you again. Now, what I'd like for you to do right now is eat. Swanny made a special dinner just for you. Think you're up for that?"

"Did he make grilled cheeses?" Cammie mumbled around her thumb.

Donovan gave her an indulgent smile. "Not exactly. But it's *sort* of like a grilled cheese. Only better. Promise. It has lots of yummy cheese. And noodles. Make you a deal. Try the lasagna and if you don't like it, I'll make you a grilled cheese instead."

Cammie smiled. "'Kay."

He pushed the tray toward her and Eve reached for the fork, cutting into the wedge and cutting small bites. Cammie looked eagerly at the cheesy noodles and meat sauce and opened her mouth when Eve forked a bite and lifted it to her lips.

Cammie chewed, her expression thoughtful, and then she gifted Donovan with a broad smile.

"Good?" he asked.

"Yummy," Cammie replied, eager for the next bite.

Eve fed her, Cammie eating as fast as she could get the fork to Cammie's mouth. She ate more than Eve had herself, and Eve smiled as Cammie smacked her lips appreciatively when the last was gone.

"That was good, Mr. Donovan."

Donovan ruffled her hair affectionately. "How about you call me Van? That's what my family and friends call me, and I'd very much like you to consider me family."

Cammie looked delighted, and then she sobered and lowered her gaze.

"Hey, little bit. What's that look for?" Donovan asked.

"I wish you were my daddy," she said wistfully.

Eve's heart lurched, and a knot formed in her throat. Tears clogged her eyes and she looked away so no one would see.

Donovan leaned in and brushed a tender kiss over Cammie's brow. "I'd like that very much. Who knows? Maybe one day it'll happen."

Eve's jaw dropped, and she turned a disapproving frown on Donovan, not even trying to hide her displeasure over his statement. The last thing she wanted was to give Cammie false hope. But Donovan returned Eve's gaze evenly. Almost challengingly. As if to say he meant it and that it was up to Eve whether it came to pass.

Crazy. She was absolutely losing her mind. People didn't

forge connections this quickly and certainly not under the circumstances that had shoved Donovan and Eve together. She needed to remain objective and not set herself—or Cammie and Travis—up for inevitable heartbreak. They'd been through enough without adding more sorrow.

"I'm full, Van," Cammie said, her mouth stretched into a huge yawn.

Donovan smiled and then glanced up at her IV bags. "I need to switch out your piggyback. It's almost empty. And then I'm going to give your sister an injection for pain. Why don't you snuggle up to her and hold her in case the shot hurts? You can make her feel better. Then I'll leave you both to sleep. I'll make you a good breakfast in the morning and if you're a really good girl, I'll serve it up in bed."

Cammie grinned her delight. "Can I have pancakes? I love pancakes," she said wistfully. "With lots of butter and syrup."

"Is there any other way to eat them?" Donovan asked in mock horror. He kissed her brow again and ruffled her hair and then left the room only to return a moment later with another bag of IV fluid.

After setting it up and reconnecting the line to the bag, he pulled out a syringe and uncapped it.

"Climb in and get comfortable with Cammie," Donovan directed. "I'll give it on your right hip this time."

Eve climbed underneath the covers and Cammie promptly snuggled into her arms, warm and so precious against Eve's chest. She squeezed a little harder than necessary, but it felt so good to have Cammie next to her. In a safe place with no fear of discovery.

She let Donovan pull up her shirt. It wasn't as though he hadn't already seen her legs or her ass. But he was careful only to pull down the band of her panties enough to bare the injection site. She closed her eyes and Cammie reached up to pat Eve on the face.

"It'll be okay, Evie," Cammie said in a solemn voice. "Van will make it all better."

At that Eve opened her eyes and smiled. "I know he will, darling."

The needle slid into her flesh and Eve only grimaced a little as the medicine was injected. By the time Donovan adjusted her clothing and tucked the covers around her and Cammie, she was already feeling the effects of the drug. Her eyes fluttered drowsily and the pleasant hum of the medication replaced the vicious ache in her head.

Donovan leaned down, and to her surprise he kissed her softly on the lips. Nothing prolonged. But it was intimate all the same. A quick brush. He didn't leave his lips on hers for long, but she felt them there long after he'd withdrawn with a husky "Good night."

"Sleep well, my girls," he said, a note of possession in his voice. And how good it sounded when he said "my girls." It made Eve wistful. Made her think what it would be like if they were his girls. Belonging to him.

"I'll have breakfast for you in the morning, and Maren will be out to check on all of you before lunch."

"G'night, Van," Cammie said sleepily. "Love you."

Eve's eyes widened in shock, and she glanced hurriedly at Donovan to gauge his reaction. Would he be put off by the declaration? It had come out of the blue. Never would Eve have imagined those words coming from Cammie's lips. Oh, she was an affectionate, adorable little girl, but she'd been taught reserve at far too young an age. While she was openly loving with Eve and Travis, she never warmed to strangers the way she had with Donovan. And she hoped it didn't break Cammie's heart when it was time for them to move on.

But Donovan didn't seem to mind in the least. His entire face softened and a gentle smile curved his mouth upward. He ran his hand through Cammie's hair and then pressed a kiss to her forehead.

"Love you too, sweetheart. Now get some rest, okay? You'll feel better tomorrow."

"Promise?" Cammie asked around another jaw-cracking yawn.

Donovan smiled. "Promise."

CHAPTER 20

EVE'S dreams were tormented with a myriad of flashes from the past. And the present. They swirled together in one unending stream of horror.

The tornado had her in its grip again, but instead of Donovan lifting the mattress that had saved her life and protected her from further harm, Walt had been standing there, his gaze triumphant.

I have you at last, Eve. And this time you won't escape me.

She awoke with a start, sweat beading her forehead. She sat up straight in bed, her skin clammy and cold. A chill had settled deep into her body until her bones ached with it.

She glanced over at Cammie, who was still sleeping soundly. Eve didn't have a prayer of going back to sleep now. She glanced toward the window to see the faintest shade of dawn softening the sky.

With a sigh, she eased out of bed and went to the bathroom to splash water on her face. She ran the water until steam rose, wanting some way to warm herself. She wet the washcloth several times, wiping her face and neck before retreating back into the bedroom.

After a moment's hesitation she went to the closet where Donovan had put the clothes his sisters-in-law had sent over. Selecting a pair of jeans and a simple T-shirt, she dressed and slipped into the hallway, making sure she was quiet on her way to the living room.

She didn't know where she was going or why, but she didn't want to go back to bed and risk reimmersing herself in her nightmares. It was bad enough to have talked about Walt and to have relived the horror of her mother's death and Walt's subsequent behavior, but now he was invading her sleep as well.

She went to the large picture window that overlooked the lake in the distance. Dawn was beautiful over the water, painting it a soft lavender to match the sky overhead. There was not even a ripple in the water, no wind to disturb the pristine sheet of glass that spread out to the distant horizon.

This was a . . . peaceful place. It seemed incongruous to consider a veritable fortress built for the sole purpose of security—a reality of Donovan's and his family's lives— peaceful, and yet everything about the view brought her a sense of calm. Something she desperately needed right now.

Warm hands slid up her arms to her shoulders, startling her. She whirled around to see Donovan standing there in a cutoff pair of shorts and a threadbare T-shirt. He was barefooted and for some reason that image captivated her.

"Sorry if I startled you," Donovan said. "What are you doing up? Can't sleep? Everything okay?"

She sighed. "I slept. Bad dreams. Talking about it brought it all back. I dreamed of the storm, but you weren't the one who found me. Walt did. I didn't want to go back to sleep because I didn't want to have another nightmare."

He pulled her into his arms and hugged her tightly to him. His body felt so good against hers. Solid. So very steady and strong. She sighed and did nothing to resist his hold. He felt . . . right.

"I'm sorry you had bad dreams. You can come to me, you know. I don't want you to be afraid of anything, honey."

He pulled her away so he could stare down into her eyes. His gaze bore intently into hers and his head lowered. She got the strangest suspicion that he was going to *kiss* her. And suddenly it was what *she* wanted more than anything.

She wasn't wrong.

Slowly, with infinite tenderness, he pressed his mouth to hers in a warm, sweet glide that sent shivers quaking down her spine.

It was a shock to her entire system. Heat spread rapidly through her body. Every nerve ending tingled and came to life. Her breasts grew heavy and aching. Her nipples tightened and she leaned instinctively into him, wanting, needing more.

He licked over her lips, coaxing her to open them. With a gasp, she parted her lips, allowing him entrance. At once his tongue invaded, delving deep and hot over hers. He deepened the kiss, stealing her breath, holding it, savoring it before returning it so that she inhaled and swallowed up his very essence. It was a kiss unlike any she'd ever experienced.

It was pure magic.

She slid her hands up his broad chest so that her palms came to rest just below his shoulders. He tensed almost as if he were expecting her to push him away. But she leaned into him with a sigh, letting her fingertips dig into his flesh through the thin layer of his T-shirt.

He became more forceful, as if he'd waited to see if she protested. As if she could. She'd never experienced such an awakening. Couldn't imagine how she could be feeling this way when her entire life had been upended. But for the space of a few stolen moments, all her worries slid away under the reassuring stroke of his tongue.

His hands slid up her back and then down, molding the contours of her behind. Then he lifted one hand, pressed it to the small of her back before raising the other to tangle in her hair. His fingers twisted, wrapping the strands around his knuckles as he deepened the kiss, swallowing her whole.

She had no idea of the passage of time. They could have

stood there kissing for an hour or one minute. It was as if
time had stopped and the only thing that existed were the
two of them, in this room, their lips fused in a hot rush.

She gasped into his mouth, starved for air, but more
starved for his touch. She wanted more. Needed more. She
needed . . . him.

"Donovan?"

He loosened his hold on her hair, letting his hand fall
away. He tugged her away, but only the barest of inches so he
could look down into her eyes. Their bodies were still
pressed tightly together and she could feel the evidence of
his arousal, rigid and straining against her belly.

She shivered again, chill bumps racing across her skin,
every tiny hair standing on its end in the wake of the intense
sensations he evoked.

He stroked a hand lovingly over her cheek, pushing back
her tousled hair. "What is it, honey?"

"What are we doing here?" she whispered. "What's happening?"

He smiled tenderly at her, his eyes warm and flush with . . .
arousal. "What *I'm* doing is kissing you and what's happening is that I'm enjoying it a hell of a lot and I hope you are
too."

She flushed, her cheeks growing warm at the blunt statement. "This is insane," she protested. "We can't be doing . . .
this. The very last thing I should even be contemplating is
a . . . relationship."

She nearly choked as she said the word because it was
presumptuous of her to assume he wanted anything more
than sex. But he didn't act like someone who wanted a quick
lay. As she'd already noted, he acted like he cared. And if he
was so anxious for sex, wouldn't he have put the moves on
her already? Before the tornado, because of course it would
have made him an ass to come on to her when she had a head
injury and was scared out of her mind.

Her head was spinning, much like she had suffered a serious head injury. There wasn't even anything overtly sexual
or . . . desperate . . . to his kiss. It had been . . . romantic.

Tender. Exquisite even. Could a kiss be considered exquisite? Obviously so, because his definitely qualified.

"I mean, I'm a job to you, right? Shouldn't you remain objective? Surely you don't go around kissing all your female clients."

And worse was the jealousy that gripped her over the thought of him kissing another woman in distress. Did he have a white knight complex? Was his Kryptonite a woman in need?

He chuckled at that, his eyes growing even warmer as he gazed down at her. "Honey, if it weren't for mixing business with pleasure, none of my brothers would be married."

She cocked her head to the side. "What do you mean by that?"

"It means that every one of my brothers met their wives while on a mission. Bullets flying, explosions, car chases, wrecks, bad guys. You name it, they experienced it. I'd say our situation is tame in comparison."

There was laughter in his voice, and she found herself smiling despite the utter seriousness of the situation he spoke lightly of.

"None of my brothers met a nice small-town girl, dated, became engaged and got married. Well, except Ethan, and he and Rachel more than made up for their somewhat boring courtship with plenty of drama after the fact," he said in a grim voice.

Her brow furrowed at his sudden change in demeanor. "What happened?"

"Long story," Donovan said. "Rachel is a schoolteacher, and she went on a mercy mission to South America in June after school let out. Her plane crashed on the way home, and it was thought she died. There were no survivors. We thought her dead for an entire year when in fact she was being held captive by a drug cartel and they hooked her on drugs to control her."

Eve's eyes rounded in shock. "Oh my God. Are you serious? How on earth did you find out? And how did you get her back?"

"We went in and kicked some cartel ass," Donovan said bluntly. "We brought her back home, but her recovery wasn't quick. They had some rough times. She lost most of her memory from the drugs that were forced on her. She still doesn't have everything back, but enough to remember a lot of bad things that happened before she left on that trip. She and Ethan have had a rough road back together, but they're strong—she's strong. She's one hell of a survivor. She just had twins a year ago."

"Wow," Eve murmured. "You weren't kidding when you said you and your brothers kick some serious ass. Taking on a drug cartel? It sounds like something out of a movie."

Donovan's lips quirked. "That's just the icing on the cake, honey. The rest of my brothers all met their wives under less-than-ideal circumstances. So maybe now you can see that the way you and I met doesn't bother me in the least."

Eve's breath caught and she stared up at him, uncertain of what to say. What could she say? She blurted the first thing that came to her mind.

"But you don't know me. I mean, we just met. How can you possibly think you want . . . anything . . . from me? What do I possibly have to offer you except one giant head-ache? It seems to me that you're doing all the giving and I'm doing all the taking and giving nothing in return."

He nudged her chin upward with gentle fingers. "That's not true. You've given me something very precious indeed. Your trust, Eve. And I know what that cost you. So believe me when I say that I know what a gift you've given me. A woman's trust is the most priceless gift she can give to a man. Her belief in his ability to keep her safe and protect her from all harm."

He lowered his head again, not as hesitant or as slow as he'd been just moments earlier. He brushed his lips across hers but quickly fused his mouth to hers, stroking hot and wet with his tongue. This time she didn't hesitate either. She met his advance, tasting him this time instead of allowing him to do all the exploring.

She inhaled deeply, savoring the spicy masculine scent

that clung to him. It wasn't cologne or aftershave. It was just . . . him. She sighed into his mouth, enjoying the simple pleasure of being in his arms.

It was easy to forget everything but this man. Easy to forget the world around them. The danger she and her siblings faced. The very real threat of Walt and how far his reach extended. Here seemed a million miles away from reality. This was a reality she much preferred.

Was it wrong of her to want to forget? Just for a little while?

"Just to let you know," Donovan murmured against her mouth. "I'm going to take it slow with you. But *my* idea of slow and someone else's is probably very different. So consider yourself warned. When I want something, I go after it. And I play to win. I've waited a long time for this—for *you*—and I'm not going to waste a single minute in seeing where this takes us. I fully intend to have you in my bed—permanently. And soon."

Her pulse raced, fluttering wildly in her veins as she processed his solemn vow. He hadn't sounded unsure of himself at all. No, he'd uttered those words with absolute confidence. She licked her lips, her mouth suddenly dry.

"What about Travis and Cammie?" she asked in a low voice.

Donovan sent her a look of genuine puzzlement. "What about them?"

She cleared her throat. "If we . . . if you . . . if we do this thing, where does that leave Travis and Cammie? I'd never leave them, Donovan. I'd never abandon them. And there's so much unresolved. I'm for all practical purposes a *kidnapper*."

Just saying the words sent a new wave of terror coursing through her body. She trembled against Donovan, her hands shaking.

"Even if you didn't mind them being . . . here . . . with us . . . it's not like we can just pick up and play house. I'm a criminal. I could go to *jail* for what I've done."

Donovan held up his hand and then gently pressed a finger to her lips to shush her. "Listen to me, Eve. Of course you

won't abandon Travis and Cammie. I would never expect you
to do any such thing. You're a package deal. And I want the
entire package. As for you being a criminal and going to jail?
That's not going to happen. We'll find a way to take your
stepfather down. And when that happens, you—and Travis
and Cammie—and I will be a family."

She had absolutely nothing to say to that. She didn't even
know how to respond to such a statement. To such blind
acceptance. It baffled her that he would identify her as someone he wanted a *future* with when he'd known her only a few
short days. And that he'd accept baggage that most men
wouldn't ever sign up for.

And the way he said *family* instilled such a fierce wave of
longing within her that she ached with it. She wanted that.
God, she wanted that so much. For Travis and Cammie to be
safe and happy. To have all the normal things a four-year-old
and a teenager had. And children of her own. It was all she'd
ever dreamed. A large, boisterous, happy family. She wanted
to hug his solemn vow to her heart and never let go. But it
seemed so . . . impossible. All of it.

She stared at him in bewilderment because in all of this,
there was still one huge question mark. How did she feel
about *him*?

CHAPTER 21

HAVING coaxed Eve back to bed so she could rest comfortably with Cammie, Donovan retreated to the kitchen to dig up the fixings for pancakes. He wouldn't prepare them yet. He wanted to let Travis, Cammie and Eve sleep for as long as they would before disturbing them for breakfast.

He knew the moment Sean entered the main gate of the compound. An alert was triggered and the video monitors in the kitchen zoomed in on the vehicle, doing a retinal scan of the driver and confirming Sean's identity.

A few moments later, Sean tapped at the kitchen door and Donovan motioned him inside. Donovan's head came up when the alert sounded again and he saw Rusty's Jeep pulling through the gate, pausing as she stared into the camera for the retinal scan.

Sean frowned. "What's Rusty doing out so early?"

Donovan shrugged. "Guess we'll find out shortly."

Sean remained silent until Rusty came to Donovan's door. Donovan met her and pulled her into a quick hug.

"Hey, kiddo. What brings you out so early this morning?"

Her expression was troubled, which immediately put

him—and Sean—on guard. Sean looked intently at her, his gaze probing.

"Why are *you* here?" Rusty asked Sean, a note of defensiveness to her voice.

"I have information about Eve," Sean said shortly.

"So do I," Rusty said in a grim voice. "But I'd like to hear what you have to say."

"I don't think that's a good idea," Sean countered. "You need to stay out of this, Rusty. I don't want you getting involved. You could get hurt."

She rolled her eyes. "You don't spill, I don't spill. And I think you'll be interested to know that someone was nosing around the hardware store this morning."

Sean immediately came to attention, but so did Donovan. He turned to Rusty, his expression brooking no argument. "Tell me," he ordered.

Rusty sighed. "Some guy came into the hardware store this morning. Real smooth. Casual. Drives an expensive car. I got the license plate numbers so you can run them," she said to Sean.

Sean nodded his approval, grudging respect in his eyes as he stared back at Rusty.

"What did he say?" Donovan demanded. "What did you tell him?"

"I'm getting to that," Rusty said. "He looked completely out of place. Dressed in designer digs, you know? Expensive shades. Not a hair out of place. Looked styled, salon styled, I mean. And he had enough product to take a few layers off the ozone."

Donovan simmered with impatience as he waited for her to get to the point.

"He asked real casual if I'd seen a woman and two kids, one a teenager and one a four-year-old. Called her by name. Called Travis and Cammie by name. Said that he was their father and that he was deeply concerned. That Eve was unstable and a danger not only to herself but to others, and that he feared what would happen if she wasn't institutionalized and put back on her medication soon. Said he'd gotten a report that Travis had been spotted in the hardware store."

Donovan frowned. Fuck. Not what he wanted to hear. He ran a hand through his hair and grimaced.

"I couldn't very well deny that I'd seen Travis or he'd know I was lying," Rusty said. "So I told him that yeah, a kid matching Travis's description had come through several days before. Wanted to pick up a little extra cash so I hired him for a couple of days, paid him and then he split. I told him he didn't show up for work and that I hadn't seen him in days so I assumed he'd moved on. I even told the guy that he'd mentioned sisters because again, I didn't want this guy suspicious that I was hiding anything. I figured if I was honest, I wouldn't give him any reason to suspect that we were helping Eve, Travis and Cammie and that maybe he'd buy the story that they'd already left the area."

"You played it smart, Rusty," Donovan said.

Sean nodded. "You did the right thing. But I doubt I need to run the plates to figure out who he is. After what I dug up, it's pretty obvious who he is."

"What did you find?" Rusty asked, an anxious note to her voice.

Sean hesitated. "I'd rather not involve you, Rusty. I hate that you even had a run-in with this guy. You should have called me the minute he showed up. What if he'd hurt you? Or what if he hadn't bought your story? You being alone with him in the store is bullshit. You ever pull a stunt like that again and I'll tan your ass."

Rusty snorted her displeasure. "I'm not a kid, Sean. I can handle it. And I want to know what kind of trouble they're in. I like Travis a lot."

Sean glanced at Donovan, and Donovan nodded that he should spill what he'd found out in front of Rusty. She needed to know what they were dealing with, especially if this asshole had already been to the hardware store. He would speak to his dad today and make damn sure that one of his brothers was there at the store and that Sean made regular drive-bys, and under no circumstances was Rusty to work the store alone anymore.

"It's not good, Van," Sean said. "She's wanted for kidnapping. She's reported as highly unstable. A history of mental illness and she's believed to be a danger to herself and to Travis and Cammie. The father has gone public and it appears he has a lot of pull. He plays the grieving father very well. He lost his wife tragically and now he's lost his children to a deranged woman."

"What a load of bullshit," Donovan said furiously.

"You get the real story yet?" Sean asked, cocking his eyebrow up at Donovan's reaction.

"Yeah, I got it," Donovan said through gritted teeth. "Eve thinks he killed her mother and I agree with her based on everything she's told me. He's a controlling, abusive asshole, and he was making moves on Cammie before Eve got her and Travis out of his grasp."

"Son of a bitch," Sean swore. "I'd like a shot at that motherfucker."

"So would I," Rusty said darkly.

Sean pointed a finger at Rusty. "*You* stay out of it. Understand? You leave this to us, Rusty. Do *not* get involved."

"Whatever," she muttered. "I'd still like to kick him in the balls."

"So what are you going to do?" Sean asked. "What do you want *me* to do?"

Donovan sighed. "Hell if I know. Yet. I have to talk to my brothers about it. Him being here changes everything. If he knows they were here, then he's a lot closer on their trail than Eve thought. He may or may not buy that they've already left, but at least if he discovered where they'd been living, the trailer is destroyed so he can't think they would have remained here. Hell, he might even think they were killed."

"Then he might stick around longer," Sean said. "If he's worried that they were hurt or killed in the storm, he'll be scouring the local hospitals and he'll likely pull in the local and county police. You know I won't betray the fact that I know where they are, but I can't say the same for other officers. You know I won't let on to them, but if other officers discover information about Eve, then they'll likely act on it accordingly. If that happens, you've got a problem."

Donovan nodded. "Thanks, Sean. I don't like you risking your job for me."

"The day I start siding with abusive assholes and throwing innocent women under the bus in the name of *duty* is the day I hang up the badge," Sean said, his tone serious. "If my job ever requires me to hand back over a four-year-old girl to an abusive father, then it's a job I don't want anymore."

There was brief admiration in Rusty's eyes as she glanced Sean's way. But it was quickly wiped away by a look of indifference as she listened to the interchange between the two men.

"I'll go," Rusty said. "I made sure no one followed me here, just in case you worry that I ran straight here after the guy showed up. I waited a couple of hours. He showed up as soon as the store opened and I played it cool and didn't leave until later in the morning."

"I don't want you back there," Donovan said seriously. "I don't want you in this asshole's presence again. Go back to Mom and Dad's for now. I'll talk with Dad later today and let him know what's going on."

"I'm going to run too," Sean said. "I just wanted you to know what I came up with so you could be on your guard. It's going to be important to keep Eve and her siblings under tight wraps and make sure they aren't out in public."

Donovan nodded. "Thanks, Sean. And thanks, Rusty. I'll talk to you both later."

Rusty walked out of Donovan's house, Sean on her heels. She'd parked next to Sean's patrol car, and she paused in front of them both, turning to confront Sean.

He pulled up short when she turned to face him and took a step back as she stared him down.

"What's your problem with me, Sean? Why do you still see me as a stupid kid with more brass than brains?"

He blinked in surprise, and then his eyes narrowed. "I don't have a problem with you, Rusty. I just don't want you in any danger."

She rolled her eyes. "You still treat me like I'm some clueless kid. I'm not an idiot. I can handle myself. I didn't confront the guy when he came in. I played it cool and then I came right over to tell Donovan what happened."

Sean growled in frustration. "I do *not* see you as a kid."

Before she could react, before she could even think about what he was doing, he yanked her roughly into his arms. She landed against his chest at the same time his mouth crashed over hers.

It wasn't a gentle kiss. It was filled with a myriad of things she could feel. Frustration. Anger. Desire. Lust. Need.

At first she tensed, caught completely unaware by the fact that Sean Cameron—a man who'd never made secret his dislike for her—was *kissing* her. And not just kissing her, but completely ravaging her mouth.

Whoa, but the man could kiss.

She melted into his arms, opening her mouth as he deepened the kiss. His tongue lapped hungrily over her lips and then slipped into her mouth, delving deep as they tasted each other.

Holy shit! Sean Cameron was kissing her! The mind boggled. She was completely and utterly incapable of thought. Of any response. All she could do was sag there in his arms, supported by his strong hold as he laid one hell of a kiss on her.

And then just as quickly as he'd lost control, he yanked away, swearing vividly as he put her at arm's length.

"Goddamn it," he bit out. "That should not have happened. I'm sorry, Rusty. I should not have done that. I had no right. It *won't* happen again."

Before she could collect her scattered thoughts, he stalked to his patrol car, slapping that Stetson she found so sexy on his head, got in and slammed the door before roaring out of Donovan's drive. She stood there numbly, watching as he disappeared down the road toward the gate.

He'd kissed her.

She raised a trembling hand to her swollen lips, still feeling the imprint of his mouth on hers.

He'd *kissed* her. It was a thought that kept going round and round in her mind. Sean Cameron had kissed her.

Why?

And why the hell had she *let* him?

CHAPTER 22

DONOVAN surveyed the occupants of his kitchen with deep satisfaction. Travis had wanted to get out of bed, already going stir-crazy at having spent so much time lying down. Even Cammie had been eager to get up, and so he'd set her up at his dining room table with the IV pole next to her so she could sit and eat with everyone else.

Eve sat between them, her face alight with joy and relief. Donovan took it all in, loving the way they looked in his house. His family. They were his. He'd already made that decision and there was no going back for him. He just hoped like hell that Eve would be on board.

He knew she was attracted to him, that she reciprocated at least some of his feelings. He also knew that things had happened at a whirlwind pace that he hoped hadn't over-whelmed Eve. He'd been honest in that he would take it slow, but he'd been equally honest in that *slow* to someone else and *slow* to him were vastly different things.

He was exhibiting extreme patience because what his instincts screamed for him to do from the very first moment he'd laid eyes on Eve was to claim her. To take her to his bed, possess her, mark her as his, and never let her go.

Soon, though. Very soon. Tonight, if he had his way. He wanted to make love to her. To cement their growing relationship, such as it was. He wanted her to know how he felt about her, and words would only carry him so far. He wanted to *show* her.

"Okay, food's ready," he declared, carrying a stack of hot pancakes to the table.

He set it in the middle and forked up pancakes for both Travis and Cammie and then placed three on Eve's plate. When her eyes widened and she automatically shook her head, denying that she could eat so much, he ignored her and issued a stern directive.

"Eat," he said. "You need to catch up. All of you do."

But he needn't have worried that Travis and Cammie would suffer any such hesitancy. Travis dug into his pile with gusto. Donovan leaned over to help Cammie, cutting the pancakes into neat squares before drenching them in syrup. She beamed her delight back at him and then picked up her fork with the hand that wasn't attached to the IV and began stuffing bites into her mouth.

Eve seemed delighted—and inspired—by her siblings' enthusiasm and soon she followed suit, downing a good portion of her own plate. Donovan sat back, eating but mostly watching and enjoying the sight of his family enjoying a meal together.

Yeah, this was right. No matter his brothers' warning— he understood their concern—Eve was right for him. He felt it to his bones. He'd known that his brothers had known from the moment they'd met their wives that they were the one. Perhaps Sam had been longer to come around than the others, but they'd all known, and maybe Donovan had never truly appreciated the scope or depth of their feelings, the knowledge that their woman was the one. But he got it now because he felt the same exact way, and if his brothers felt even a tenth of the intensity that Donovan experienced when he looked at or thought about Eve, then he well understood their drive to possess their women. He just wasn't as stubborn as Sam and he wasn't going to waste time trying to deny what he now knew his destiny to be.

"This is really good, Mr. Van," Cammie said in a sweet voice. "Thank you for making us breakfast."

"You're welcome, sweetheart," Donovan said, grinning over her attaching *Mr.* to his name. "But this counts as lunch. The morning is all gone now. But be thinking about what you'd like for supper. I have a pretty well-stocked pantry and you know what? If I don't have the stuff on hand to make you what you want, I'll be sure to get it. Sound like a deal?"

Cammie nodded vigorously, her mouth full of pancakes.

"I'd really like some fried pork chops," Travis said wistfully. "Evie makes the best pork chops and mashed potatoes and gravy, but it's been a long time since we could afford to have it."

Then he flushed, color invading his cheeks as he realized all he'd said.

Donovan leaned forward, giving Travis a gentle, reassuring smile. "That sounds like a perfect dinner to me. But I don't think Eve should tackle the kitchen just yet. I may not make them as good as she does, but I'll do my best."

"Oh I don't mind," Eve protested. "You've done so much for us, Donovan. I don't mind cooking for us at all. It's the least I can do."

Donovan shook his head adamantly. Not that the idea of Eve in his kitchen preparing them all a meal wasn't a very appealing prospect. But they'd have plenty of time to get to that. For now he only wanted to pamper and spoil them all. "You need to rest. I can handle supper. I just want you to sit back and do nothing and recover. It's what I want all of you to do."

"He's right, Evie," Travis cut in, his tone every bit as resolved as Donovan's. "You shouldn't be cooking right now. You've taken care of us for a long time. It's time that someone took care of you."

"Bravo," Donovan softly agreed. "Very well said, Travis."

Eve flushed, but pleasure shone in her eyes as she stared back at Donovan and then over to Travis.

"Will you be taking care of us from now on?" Cammie asked.

Though the question was asked innocently enough, Donovan could see the anxiety in the little girl's eyes. As though she feared that Donovan would turn them out and send them on their way.

Even Travis glanced at Donovan, clear question in his eyes. There was a shadow there as if he feared the same, that he wondered if this was a temporary situation and that Donovan would hurt Eve.

Donovan reached for Cammie's hand, giving it a reassuring squeeze. But he included both Eve and Travis in his declaration. He wanted them all to understand exactly where he stood.

"Absolutely I'm going to take care of all of you from now on. And I'm glad you brought this up because there is something I very much wanted to discuss with you and Travis both."

Cammie's eyes widened and even Travis looked surprised. But then a guarded look entered Travis's gaze, as if he feared the worst.

"I like Eve very much and I want her to stay with me. Forever," he said, not mincing his words.

He wanted Eve to hear him say it when it wasn't just the two of them and it could be thought he was speaking in the heat of the moment and saying things he didn't really mean. By declaring his intentions in front of her brother and sister, she would realize, hopefully, that he was utterly serious and committed to making this work.

"But I want you both to stay as well. I want us to be a . . . family," he said, gauging their reaction to his statement.

Travis looked surprised—and relieved. Cammie looked delighted.

"Do you mean that?" Travis asked hoarsely. "You want us all to stay with you?"

"Yes, I do," Donovan said quietly. "I know I'm not your

real father, but I'd very much like to be a father to both of you. I'd be proud to call you my own and I'd always love and protect you."

"I don't like my real daddy," Cammie said sadly. "He scares me. He's not a good person, Van. I want *you* to be my daddy."

Donovan's heart melted a little more and if he hadn't already been solidly in love with the little girl, that would have sealed his fate.

"You don't have to worry about your real father anymore, Cammie. I'm going to take care of you and your brother and Eve. I want us to be a family. A real family. And what you don't realize is that I have a very large family and they'll all love you too. You'll have grandparents. Lots of uncles and aunts and cousins. I've already told you about Charlotte. She's your age. And there are more babies on the way," he added with a smile. "My brothers Sam and Garrett are both expecting a new baby early next year."

"I love babies!" Cammie exclaimed, clapping her hands together in delight.

Donovan turned his gaze on Eve, who'd remained silent through it all.

"And what about you, Eve?" he asked softly. "What do you want?"

At once, Travis and Cammie both turned pleading gazes on Eve as if they were afraid she would put a crashing halt to everything. It was manipulative for Donovan to have broached the subject with Travis and Cammie present, but he wasn't trying to manipulate her emotions at all. He only wanted her to know that he was utterly sincere. He hoped she knew him well enough or at least had discerned enough about his character to know that he wouldn't bring Travis and Cammie into it unless he was absolutely serious. He wouldn't risk hurting them if he wasn't certain of his feelings and intentions.

"I want you to be happy, Evie," Travis said in a quiet, grave voice. "You've given up so much for me and Cammie. He hurt you. I know that. I also know what he tried to do to you. And I know how much you've risked to get me and Cammie away from him. So if this is what you want, you have my blessing. I don't want you to give up your life because of me and Cammie."

Tears gathered in Eve's eyes. For a moment she remained silent, clearly overwhelmed by all that had been said. Cammie looked worried when Eve didn't respond right away. She got up and clambered into Eve's lap, putting her free hand to Eve's cheek.

She patted gently, wiping away the tears that slipped down Eve's face.

"Don't cry, Evie," Cammie said in a solemn voice. "Van says he's going to take care of us. Everything will be all right, won't it, Van?"

"Absolutely, sweetheart," he said gravely, but he was looking at Eve the entire time he reinforced his vow.

Eve hugged Cammie fiercely to her, and then she reached for Travis's hand, squeezing. The three of them presented a fragile image, but there was also determination. They were a unit. A solid, unbreakable family unit, one that Donovan wanted to be a part of.

Slowly, Donovan reached out for Travis's hand and then he reached for Eve's other, linking them all together.

"We're a family," Donovan said. "Going forward, you can count on me for anything. If anything ever frightens you, I expect you to come to me. If you have any concerns or just need someone to talk to, I'm always here. We have a lot to work out. There are a lot of things that have to be addressed and resolved. But we'll get there. Together."

"I'd like that," Eve said softly, for the first time openly acknowledging—and accepting—what Donovan had asked her for.

Travis looked relieved. Cammie let out a squeal of delight and then launched herself from Eve's lap into Donovan's arms, forcing him to break his hold on Travis's and Eve's hands. He laughed as she wrapped her arms around him and squeezed him tightly.

"I love you," Cammie whispered next to Donovan's ear.

For a moment he closed his eyes, a lump forming in his throat that rendered him unable to respond. He sat there, savoring the sweetness of a child's unconditional love, and he vowed then and there that he would always return it. That not even the children he and Eve would one day have would replace Cammie or Travis in his love and affection. To him they would always be his first children and have a place accordingly in his heart.

"I love you too, sweetheart. I want you to always remember that, okay?"

Cammie nodded against his neck and then burrowed more deeply into his chest. She yawned broadly and went limp against him. He shifted her in his arms so he could hold her more securely and then returned his attention to Eve and Travis.

"What are we going to do?" Travis asked in a quiet voice. "About him, I mean. He'll keep coming after Eve. He'll want to punish her for what she did. We can't let that happen, Van. He'll kill her. Just like he killed . . ."

Travis broke off and hastily looked away but not before Donovan saw the glimmer of tears in his eyes. Eve's eyes brimmed with sudden tears as well at the mention of their mother.

It made Donovan's heart ache to know that Travis was well aware of how his mother had died. That he had to come to grips with the fact that his own father had taken away the most important person in Travis's life.

"I don't want you to worry about him," Donovan said firmly. "What I want you to do is concentrate on getting better and looking out for your sisters. My brothers and I will take care of your father and ensure that he's no longer a threat to any of you. Can you trust in that?"

Slowly Travis nodded.

"Now, this little lady here is almost asleep on me, so I'm going to put her down and then perhaps you need to consider getting some rest yourself. How is your pain? Do you need more medication?"

Travis shook his head and then hesitated a moment. He

glanced at Eve and then back at Donovan before speaking again.

"Why don't you put Cammie in with me? She'll be fine there and she's used to sleeping either with me or Evie. I know Evie needs to rest too."

Donovan barely controlled his surprise. He could swear that Travis was paving the way for Donovan to have time alone with Eve by arranging for Cammie to sleep with him, and judging by the sudden rush of color in Eve's cheeks, she suspected the same.

Still, Donovan wasn't going to look a gift horse in the mouth. He and Eve did need time alone. Not just to make love—which Donovan had every intention of doing—but to be able to discuss things that would otherwise upset Cammie were she to overhear.

"If you're sure," Donovan said.

Travis nodded. "And I'm okay. For now, I mean. I may need more medication tonight. It bothers me most when I'm lying flat and it's hard to sleep."

Donovan frowned. "You should have said something last night. No reason for you to suffer needlessly. I could have given you an injection so you could rest better."

"It's okay," Travis said. "I'll be fine. I'll go lie down with Cammie now and she can sleep with me tonight after supper. I'm looking forward to those pork chops."

Donovan smiled. "Okay, then let's get you and Cammie to bed."

Before they could move, a knock sounded at the kitchen door. Since the surveillance system hadn't alerted him, he knew it had to be one of his brothers or his sisters-in-law. Glancing up, he saw Garrett through the glass window portion of the door.

Shit. Garrett could be very intimidating. The last thing he wanted was for his brother to scare Cammie and Eve shitless.

With a sigh he got up and transferred Cammie into the seat next to where he'd been sitting.

"It's just my brother Garrett," he explained to ease the look of alarm on Eve's face. "You'll be seeing a lot of him.

Well, and of everyone. Sam and Sophie will want to bring
Charlotte over to meet you, Cammie."

Cammie smiled shyly and shoved her thumb in her mouth.

Donovan went to the door, irritated with the interruption.
But he should have expected it. Garrett, being Garrett, would
have wanted to see for himself what Donovan had involved
himself in. Better to get it over and done with now so Garrett
would back off. No way Garrett wouldn't take one look at
Eve, Travis and Cammie and do a complete one-eighty about
warning Donovan off.

Garrett might be the grumpiest and the growliest of the
Kelly brothers, but he was also a complete softie when it
came to the people he loved. And Donovan had no doubt that
he'd love Eve and her siblings on sight.

To his surprise when he opened the door, Garrett was
holding a foil-covered baking pan.

Donovan's eyebrow arched. "To what do I owe the pleasure of this unexpected visit?" The emphasis on *unexpected*
wasn't lost on Garrett, but he ignored Donovan's dig and
pushed his way inside.

"I brought over a pan of caramel num-nums. I thought
Cammie would like it. They are Charlotte's favorite and
she's always begging her uncle Garrett to make her some,"
Garrett said in amusement. "Plus my wife informs me that
there isn't a woman alive who can resist chocolaty caramel
goodness."

Donovan grinned and took the pan. "Come on in. We just
finished a late breakfast. Everyone is at the table. I'll introduce you. Just, Garrett? Try not to scare the hell out of them."

Garrett adopted a look of pure innocence. "Me? I'm the
nice guy, remember?"

Donovan snorted. "Whatever. Just be on your best behavior. They're . . . they're family now, Garrett. I've told them
that. I've told Cammie and Travis that. That not only are they
my family but that my family is theirs as well. I've informed
them of how many uncles and aunts and cousins they have,
not to mention Ma and Dad."

"And how did they take that?" Garrett asked quietly.

Donovan breathed out and glanced in the direction of the dining area to make sure they weren't overheard. "They were overwhelmed, man. And if you could have seen the hope and the longing in their eyes. It damn near killed me. They were afraid I was going to let them go and that whatever help I was giving them was temporary."

Garrett scowled. "I hope you dissuaded them of that notion."

"Oh yeah, I did. I let them know in very clear terms that I wasn't going anywhere and neither were they. And that not only did they have me in their corner but all of you as well."

Garrett nodded. "Good. Now go introduce me to your family."

By those words, Garrett told Donovan that he'd accepted the situation. That Donovan had his full support. Donovan knew that Garrett wouldn't hold out, but hearing it still gave him a huge measure of relief.

Yeah, his big brothers worried about him and they even pulled the mother hen routine from time to time, but when it came down to it, they were behind him one hundred percent. Just like all the Kellys. There wasn't another family in the world like them and Donovan wasn't just saying that because they were his.

The Kellys were a loyal, loving, kick-ass bunch of people and Donovan wouldn't trade them for anything.

He and Garrett walked back to the table where the others sat and Cammie was now perched on Eve's lap, her nervousness broadcasting over the entire room. As soon as Garrett's eyes lighted on the little girl, his entire face softened.

Garrett was gruff. Grumpy and a complete hard-ass, but he was a loyal son of a bitch. Loyal to his toes and he'd sacrifice his life for any one of his loved ones. Hell, he'd taken a bullet for Sophie. And he'd do it again for any of his sisters-in-law.

"Guys, I want you to meet my older brother Garrett. Garrett, this is Eve and her sister, Cammie, and their brother, Travis."

Travis hastily rose, grimacing when he got up too fast.

But he straightened and solemnly extended his hand toward Garrett.

"It's a pleasure to meet you, sir. We've heard a lot about you."

Garrett eyed the teenager, respect gleaming in his eyes. He took Travis's extended hand and shook it.

"I'm glad to meet you too, son. I've heard a lot about you too. Donovan is very proud of you for the way you looked out for your sisters. A lot of grown men don't have the integrity you've shown."

Travis flushed, pleasure evident in his expression over Garrett's praise. Then Garrett turned his attention to Eve and Cammie, his smile warm and welcoming.

"Hey, little bit. I'm glad to meet you. I have another niece your age. Charlotte. I think you two will become great friends."

It was Eve who looked immeasurably pleased by the fact that Garrett had called Cammie his niece. She'd picked up on his acceptance and even now, a glitter of tears shone in her eyes. She looked briefly away as if to compose herself and not become too emotional. But Garrett didn't miss it.

"I brought you a special treat, Cammie," Garrett said, keeping his tone light, though he kept his gaze on Eve.

Cammie perked up, a shy smile emerging around her thumb. Her hand slipped away, allowing the tip of her thumb to rest on her lips. "What is it?"

He reached for the pan Donovan was holding and tore off the aluminum foil.

"Caramel num-nums. I don't know exactly what they're called, but they got their name from me because when you eat them all you can say is *num-num-num* because they're so good."

Cammie giggled and tentatively reached for one of the squares. Garrett lowered the pan so she could easily reach it, and then Garrett offered it to Travis before setting it in front of Eve.

"I'm very happy to meet you as well, Eve," Garrett said quietly. "And I want you to know, as I'm sure Donovan has already told you, but I want you to hear it from me. First, I and my brothers and all of our organization as well as our entire family will do everything we can to help you and make damn sure nothing ever hurts you or your brother and sister again. And second, welcome to the family."

Eve lost the battle to hold back her tears. They streamed down her face and she wiped self-consciously at them. Travis reached for Cammie, but Donovan intervened, scooping her up before Travis could hurt himself by lifting her.

Garrett then bent over and enfolded Eve in a fierce hug. She hesitated at first but then rose and returned Garrett's hug. Garrett grinned as he stepped away and then slapped Donovan on the back.

"You're a lucky son of a gun, Van. Can't say the same for them, getting stuck with a geek like you, but you certainly lucked out with them."

Donovan rolled his eyes. "How many times do I have to tell you? Geeks are hot."

Eve laughed but nodded vigorously. "Intelligence is very attractive on a man."

Garrett joined in her laughter, and then he ruffled her hair affectionately. Acting just like an older brother. And Eve soaked it up, loving every minute of it. Her eyes shone with happiness.

"I'll get out y'all's hair. I just wanted to pop in and introduce myself. Heads up, bro. I'd expect similar visits from the rest of the clan, just so you know. The wives are all champing at the bit to see the woman who landed you, and of course they'll want to give their stamp of approval. You know how protective they get of you and Joe since y'all are the only two unattached ones. And I guess now it's down to just Joe."

Donovan glanced at Eve, taking in her reaction to Garrett speaking of his and Eve's relationship like it was a done deal. A fait accompli. Her cheeks were flushed but she didn't seem embarrassed. She seemed . . . happy. A fact that made Donovan every bit as happy.

Her acceptance was the only obstacle in their relationship. As ridiculous as that sounded, given the fact that she was a wanted criminal and she and her siblings were on the run from an abusive asshole, but those things could be over-come. Her acceptance couldn't be forced. She had to give that freely and of her own accord no matter how Donovan wished that he could will it to be.

"Come on. I'll walk you out," Donovan said, eager to have his family to himself again. He wasn't ready to share them with the rest of his family. Not yet. That would come. And he most definitely wanted to introduce them to his big, boisterous, loving family. But for now he just wanted to hide them away and savor the shine of something so new and very precious.

Garrett said his good-byes and then headed toward the door, Donovan on his heels. When they got outside, Garrett turned to Donovan, his expression serious.

"She's beautiful, man. And you're right. Very fragile. Christ, I look at her and it pisses me off that some asshole had his hands on her."

"It's worse," Donovan said, anger bubbling in his chest. "He was making moves on *Cammie* when Eve intervened and got them out of there."

"*What the fuck?*" Garrett roared. "Jesus Christ, she's a baby! And her own father was trying to molest her? Did he succeed? I'll take the son of a bitch apart myself. Over my dead body will he ever get near Eve or Cammie again."

Donovan shook his head. "I don't know. Eve doesn't think he did. She's questioned Cammie, albeit vaguely and very gently. She doesn't want to upset her or plant suggestions. But Travis is the one who called Eve. It's a long story and one I'll share with you and the others when I get a chance. But he was a controlling bastard who had everyone around him under his thumb and when Eve bucked that control, he punished her and made her life miserable. And when he killed Eve's mother, he expected Eve to step in and take her place in his bed."

"The little bastard," Garrett growled. "I'd like two min-utes alone with him. I'd take off his balls and choke him on them."

"Yeah, tell me about it," Donovan said. "You'll have to wait in line for your shot. I plan to get to him first."

"I was serious about the rest of the family, Van. They all want to meet Eve and Cammie and Travis. They're worried about you, but I think once they meet her, those worries will evaporate on the spot. I know they did for me. I can't say I blame you one bit now. I don't know of anyone who could look at them and not have the reaction you did. They're good kids. Especially Travis. He acts a hell of a lot older than fifteen."

"Buy me a little time, man. Okay? Give me today at least. Maren will be over in a while to check on them all and she's bringing more IV solution for Cammie, so things will be hectic today anyway and I'd really like some time with them and let them settle in before the family descends."

Garrett nodded. "I'll call them and explain. Once I tell them I met Eve and the kids, they'll be somewhat appeased until they can check her out themselves."

"There's one other thing," Donovan said. "Eve's stepfather has already shown up at the hardware store. Rusty came out earlier to tell me he was nosing around, asking questions. He knows Travis was there, so Rusty didn't even try to lie to him. She played it good and did what she should have. She admitted he'd worked there a few days. She was up front about everything except where they are now, so he wouldn't get suspicious or suspect she was lying to him or trying to hide something. But you need to pass the word. I don't want Rusty in that store by herself anymore. Nor do I want Dad there alone either. Sean is aware of the situation and he's going to arrange drive-bys and he'll check in periodically. But until this is all resolved, I'd feel a hell of a lot better if you could get with Sam and arrange for one of us or one of Nathan and Joe's team to be at the hardware store at all times."

Garrett's expression became thunderous. "The little fucker is here already? How the hell did he find them so fast?"

"He's got a lot of money and resources, not to mention connections. Sean did some digging. Eve is wanted for kidnapping and her stepfather created medical records documenting her supposed history of mental illness. He's methodical. I have to give him that. He made it so he has proof that she's unstable and a danger not only to herself but to anyone who comes into contact with her."

"Son of a bitch. That sucks, man. Any idea what you're going to do yet?"

Donovan shook his head. "No, not yet. I'm taking it one day at a time and as bad as it may sound, right now my focus is on getting her in my bed and making her realize that this is the real deal. She has to trust me first before I can do anything to help her. I'm afraid she'll run, so I want to be damn sure she's in this with me as deep as I am."

Garrett nodded. "Makes sense. I'd do the same thing."

Donovan chuckled. "I know you would. Hell, you *did*."

"Yep. And I don't suffer one iota of remorse. It got me what I wanted. Sarah. The only thing I regret is not being up front with her a hell of a lot sooner and her finding out what she did the way she did."

"It worked out. That's all that matters. And now you're married with a baby on the way."

Garrett's face split into a goofy, idiotic grin. His entire face lit up and joy reflected in his blue eyes. He looked like a kid who'd just gotten exactly what he wanted for Christmas.

"You see now why I wanted what you and the others have?" Donovan asked softly. "Think about how you feel about the fact that the woman you love is pregnant with your child and that she's in your bed every night and she's there waiting every time you come home from a mission."

"Yeah, I get it. I just didn't want you to . . . settle. I didn't want you to jump at the first opportunity because you were afraid it would never happen for you. I—we all—just want you to be happy."

"I understand, but Garrett, I'm not settling. Eve is the one. It hasn't happened for me before now because I was waiting for her. She's it and I can't explain it any more than that. I can't explain it any more than you can explain why you took one look at Sarah and knew she was the one, why

Nathan knew from the start that Shea was it for him. Like Sam knew Sophie was his and pined his dumb ass for her for months before we pulled her out of the lake. He was a hell of a lot more stubborn than the rest of you and he resisted more, even going so far as not to trust Sophie when she showed up begging for help. I'm not going that route. Eve is it for me and I'm not going to fight it at all. Hell, I want it too much. I want . . . her."

Garrett smiled and then bumped fists with Donovan. "Oorah, man. Oorah."

Donovan grinned. "Hell yeah, oorah! None of that hooyah bullshit."

"Okay, get back to your family. I'll run now and don't worry. I'll call off the dogs and tell them to give you some space. I'll fill them in as much as I can from what little I've observed, but just know that Ma is going to be even more determined to meet Eve and her newest grandchildren the minute I tell her you're serious about Eve."

Donovan waved, feeling a ridiculous thrill over the fact that Garrett had said *get back to your family*. Hell yeah, his family. His. And he wasn't going to ever give them up without one hell of a fight. Fuck a fight. He'd breathe his last breath before ever allowing them to be taken from him.

CHAPTER 23

DONOVAN quietly looked in on Travis and Cammie, who were both sleeping soundly. He was taken with the image of the two snuggled up, Cammie cuddled into Travis's side, her arm thrown trustingly over his belly.

Her head rested over his arm and she was nestled under his shoulder. Travis's head was turned to the side so his chin was a mere inch above Cammie's tousled curls.

Maren and Steele had come by so Maren could check in on Travis, Cammie and Eve. She'd adjusted Cammie's IV medication and was satisfied that she seemed to be making good progress and was no longer running a temperature. Travis was still experiencing pain and discomfort, though he tried to mask it. Maren had insisted on giving him another injection and then told Donovan that he could switch to oral pain medication for the duration of his recovery.

She'd given Eve a clean bill of health after examining her head and questioning Eve at length about her symptoms.

Afterward, Maren and Steele had left, and Maren had said she wouldn't return unless Donovan thought she was needed.

That after the latest piggyback of antibiotics, Donovan could discontinue Cammie's IV and monitor her progress.

Once Maren and Steele had departed, Donovan, Eve, Travis and Cammie had lounged in the living room watching movies until it was evident that Travis and Cammie both were ready for bed. Garrett had evidently kept his word about having the rest of the family stand down, because no one else had stopped by, a fact Donovan was grateful for. He savored every moment of the evening alone with Eve and her siblings. He looked forward to many more evenings just like this one.

Donovan stood in the doorway, watching them a moment longer, taking pride in the sight of his family. His kids. Sure, this wasn't the way a lot of men wanted to start a relationship. With a ready-made family. Taking on a four-year-old and a teenage boy wouldn't be easy. But Donovan had fallen in love with them all and he looked forward to the day he could officially call them his and give them his name.

Cammie and Travis Kelly. He liked the sound of it. Tested it quietly on his lips.

Eve Kelly sounded even better. He was jumping the gun in a huge way. They had a long way to go before they could consider marriage. But it didn't mean he wasn't thinking about the day he made it official.

In his eyes they were already his. And in his family's eyes, they were one of them. But he wanted the world to know it. And that couldn't happen until any and all threat to them was eliminated.

He backed reluctantly through the door, closing it quietly behind him, and then he walked down the hall to where Eve was. Tonight he would make love to her. He'd make her his, and he was aching to make it happen. He ached to hold her in his arms while he made love to her. Watch her come apart underneath him, her eyes on him, them locked together in the most intimate way two people could be joined.

He wouldn't push her if she wasn't ready, but he hoped to hell she wanted him half as much as he wanted her. He'd wait forever if that was what it took, but every part of his soul prayed that she was ready.

When he reached her door, he knocked softly, listening for her summons. When he heard her call, he pushed in, his gaze automatically seeking her out.

She was perched on the bed, clad in a pair of pajamas one of his sisters-in-law had sent over with the rest of the clothing they'd gotten together for her. He'd thank them in person for their generosity and willingness to help out a total stranger, but right now his entire focus was on Eve and spending time with her alone, without outside distractions.

She found his gaze, and color flooded her cheeks. Was he that obvious? She looked adorable, sitting up against her pillows, knees drawn up and arms wrapped around her legs. But what he didn't see was any evidence that told him she wasn't open to what he planned.

He walked over to the bed and sat right next to her hip, scooting her over just enough that he could perch on the edge of the mattress. Then he reached for her hand, pulling it to his lips to press a kiss to each of her fingers.

"I want to make love to you, Eve," he said bluntly.

There were probably better ways of seducing a woman, but he was a get-to-the-point, blunt kind of guy and that wasn't ever going to change. Besides, she knew what he wanted. He'd certainly made himself clear enough, so there was no need for silly, coy games.

"Will you let me?" he asked softly.

Her pupils dilated and her color heightened further. She nervously licked her lips, and he almost groaned out loud.

"I don't have much . . . experience," she whispered. "I don't want you to be disappointed."

His heart lurched at the uncertainty written on her face.

"Honey, you disappointing me isn't *possible*. I just need to know one thing and one thing only. Do you want me as much as I want you? Do you *want* to make love with me tonight?"

Slowly she nodded, an adorably shy expression blooming

on her delicate features. She was, in a word, beautiful. And she was his. He had to quash the urge to haul her into his arms, put her on her back and plunge as deep as he could into her body. But he harnessed his inner caveman and forced himself to use restraint.

Carefully he unwrapped her arms from her legs and pulled her forward until she was in his arms, his arms wrapped around her body. They were face to face, their mouths only an inch apart. He could feel every puff of air that escaped with her breaths. They were short and jerky and her pulse was racing, fluttering like a butterfly at her neck. He was seized by the urge to kiss her right over that pulse point in her neck, and so he did just that.

She emitted a sharp gasp and then melted into his embrace, her body going slack against his. He could feel her heartbeat against his chest, felt every one of her curves, the imprint of her nipples against him.

Sweet. So incredibly sweet. She tasted soft and feminine and utterly perfect. He was holding perfection—every one of his dreams he'd ever had—here in his arms. It would never be more perfect than tonight. The first time they made love. The first expression of their growing love. Him showing her without words—what words couldn't possibly express—all she meant to him and all she was going to mean to him.

He licked over her pulse and then kissed her again, moving upward to her ear. He pulled the lobe gently between his teeth and nipped before soothing with his tongue. Then he traced the outline of her ear and the sensitive inner shell, flicking his tongue until she was squirming against him.

"I want to undress you, honey. I want to see your beautiful body. I'm going to savor every second of tonight. I want it to be perfect for you—for us. I'll never forget tonight. It means more to me than you will ever possibly know or understand that you're giving yourself to me. That you're trusting me with not only you but with Travis and Cammie as well."

"I won't forget either," Eve said huskily, her voice laced with desire.

She pulled back and lifted her hand to his face, cupping his jaw as she stared into his eyes with so much warmth that his insides did a twist-and-tumble routine.

"I want to undress you too," she said in a shy voice. "I want to see you and touch you."

He did groan this time. "You're killing me, honey. I want that too. Believe me, I want you to touch me more than I want to breathe."

She smiled and then lifted her mouth to his and kissed him. It was the first time she'd made the first move, and he savored the sensation of her exploring his mouth. Of her taking the initiative. He was a willing captive to whatever she wanted to do to him.

"How about we undress each other?" he murmured when she finally pulled back. "But I get to go first. I want you naked when you undress me so I can enjoy the sight while you do your thing."

She laughed, the sound warm and vibrant in his ears. God, but she was beautiful when she smiled. It was like a fist to his gut every time her face lit up, and he vowed that he'd do everything in his power to ensure she smiled for the rest of her life. That she would always have something to smile *about*.

He rose from the bed and reached for her hand to pull her to stand beside him. Then slowly, reverently, he began undressing her, taking his time with each piece of her clothing. When he bared her breasts, he sucked in his breath as he stared at the plump mounds. Her nipples were puckered and protruded outward as if begging for his touch. His mouth. Oh yes, he was dying to taste her.

She hesitated, lifting her arms as if to cover herself, but he caught her hands and carefully lowered them back down.

"Don't hide from me, honey. You're so beautiful. You take my breath away. Never hide from me. You're too beautiful for that."

She smiled and her arms went slack against her sides and then he reached for the waistband of her pajama bottoms, pushing them over her hips to fall to the floor. She stepped out of them and kicked them away, standing before him in just her panties.

She presented a delectable sight. So dainty and rounded in all the right places. She was thin—likely from her forced reality over the last months—but she was still curvy at her hips and breasts.

He turned her to the side as he slipped her underwear down, exposing her behind, twin globes that begged for his hands to cup them. And he would. He'd palm them as he slid inside her, angling her upward to receive him more easily. Sweat beaded his forehead as he was bombarded by the imagery of sliding into her delicate sheath.

No longer able to withstand the urge to touch her, he ran his hands down her body, caressing and petting, savoring every touch.

Chill bumps rose and dotted her flesh and she shivered as he cupped her breasts, pushing them upward for his avid gaze.

"I've been dying to taste you," he murmured just as he lowered his head to suck one puckered crest into his mouth.

She made a grab for his shoulders, her nails digging into his flesh as she strained upward, meeting his mouth. Her entire body tensed and a soft moan escaped her lips. Smiling his satisfaction, he moved to the other nipple, licking lightly in repeated swipes before sucking it between his lips, exerting more pressure than he had with the first.

She gasped again and her nails pressed harder into his skin.

"Feel good, honey?"

"Yes," she breathed out. "So good, Donovan. I feel like I've waited forever for you."

He lifted his head to look into her eyes, wanting her to know how serious he was.

"I've been waiting my whole life for you, Eve. For this. For you. For this moment. You're mine and I'm never letting you go. I hope you're prepared for that."

Her eyes went soft with answering . . . love? Could he hope for that so soon? He wasn't expecting it. Not so quickly.

But he wanted it. Wanted it with all his heart. The day she gave him those words would be a day he'd never forget. Until she gave him those words, this thing between them wasn't solid. Wasn't permanent. When she gave him the words, he would know that she would truly be his in every sense of the word.

"I want it," she said quietly, her voice thick with emotion. "I want this. I want you. I want . . . everything."

"I'll give you everything you could possibly want or need and so much more, honey. Never doubt that. I want you to go to bed at night knowing I'll always be here, and I want you to wake up in the morning with that same knowledge. I don't want a minute to pass that you don't know exactly who and what you are to me."

"Make love to me," she whispered. "Please, Donovan. I need you so much. Let me undress you so we can make love together. I've never wanted something more than I want this."

His heart was about to burst right out of his chest. His dick was straining against his jeans so hard that he'd likely wear the imprint of his zipper for days if not weeks! He'd much rather be surrounded by her velvety softness than trapped in the rough denim of his pants.

"I know you said you wanted to undress me, honey, but why don't I get it done so we can get on to more important things. Like me touching every part of your body. Me kissing every part of your body. And me inside you so deep that you feel me at the very heart of you."

Her breath hitched and her pupils flared in reaction. A full-body shiver overtook her, puckering her nipples into even tighter beads. He took her reaction as response enough and quickly divested himself of his shirt, jeans and underwear. When he turned his attention back to her, she was staring avidly at his erection.

He glanced down, following her gaze, and winced. No wonder she was so agog. He was sporting a hard-on to end all hard-ons and he was straining upward and was so tight that the head was nearly purple. He was ready to explode and he hadn't gotten anywhere near her pussy yet.

When he looked back up at her and saw her lick her lips, he damn near lost it on the spot. He reached down and pinched the head between his fingers to stave off his impending release. Jesus, it would be a miracle if he got inside her before coming everywhere.

"Just give me a minute, honey," he said in a raspy voice. "You're so damn sexy that I'm ready to come and I haven't even gotten inside you yet. I want to make this good for you, not have it be over the minute I push inside you."

She smiled, delight entering those gorgeous amber-gold eyes. The flecks of gold shone even brighter in her aroused state, making them gleam in the low light cast by the bedside lamp.

"It makes me *feel* sexy to know you react to me that way," she said shyly. "I've never had a guy look at me the way you look at me. I like it."

"I'll rip the balls off the man who ever looks at you the way I'm looking at you," he growled.

She smiled again and then crawled onto the bed, lying back against the pillows, a silent invitation in her eyes. He needed no more encouragement than that.

Thinking back on the other women he'd slept with, he could honestly say that he'd simply gotten laid. Not that his partners hadn't gotten his absolute respect and regard, but he'd gone in knowing there was no emotional involvement. Not anything close to the way he felt about Eve. This was, in essence, his very first time to *make love* to a woman.

He treated all women with utmost respect. He'd never do anything to make them feel cheap or used when he had sex with them. But they, like him, had known the score from the beginning. He'd even dated the same woman for a period of time, but they'd always been fun relationships. Nothing heavy. Nothing that involved his heart to the degree Eve had.

It wasn't that he'd had anything against a relationship or even marriage. He *wanted* those things. Had never been opposed to the idea. In fact, he'd go as far as to say that he'd actively searched for *the* one. But none of them had ever spoken to the heart of him. They hadn't stirred his soul. And he knew by seeing how his brothers were with their wives that the women he'd been with hadn't been the one. He'd waited patiently, knowing that his soul mate existed. Somewhere out there, waiting just like him. He only had to find her. And he finally had. She was here. In his house, his bed, in his arms. And he was about to make love to her for the very first time.

"Why are you staring?" she whispered, concern entering her eyes.

He kicked himself for mentally checking out for a moment. Even if it was to cement in his mind the *importance* of this night.

"I just wanted to savor this moment," he said honestly. "This is special to me, Eve. *You're* special to me. I want this to be just right. I don't want to hurry through it. I want to take it all in and remember it always. Forty years from now, I'll remember the way you looked tonight. How beautiful you are. How soft and warm and how very sweet every part of you is."

Tears glistened in her eyes and she swallowed visibly as she stared at him in almost helpless fashion.

"How can you say such beautiful things to me? You say that in forty years you'll remember how I looked and how I felt. But you know what I'll remember? I'll remember the things you said to me and I'll cherish them always."

He smiled as he crawled onto the bed to position his body over hers. Then he leaned down to kiss her, their bodies meshing, molding perfectly together.

"I guess we'll both always remember this night," he said.

"Yes," she whispered. "Now make love to me, Donovan. Don't make me wait. I want you so much. I'm burning with need. I *ache*."

He slid his mouth down her jaw, kissing a path down her body to her breasts. He licked and sucked at the taut peaks, working her into a frenzy before he moved even lower, pressing gentle kisses to the valley of her breasts and then over her flat belly to her navel.

He toyed with the sensitive area, enjoying the shivers that quaked her body as he tongued the shallow indention.

"Spread your legs for me, honey. I want to taste you."

Trembling, she parted her thighs, widening them so he could position his body between her legs. He settled down, his head just above the downy patch of hair that shielded her femininity.

Using his fingers, he parted her folds, already slick with her arousal. He inhaled deeply, taking in her scent and savoring it. Then, spreading her wider, he lowered his head even further and ran his tongue over her clit.

She bucked upward, her hands flying to his head, digging into his short hair as he circled the taut bud with his tongue. He flicked the tip over her clit repeatedly, then sucked it gently into his mouth, exerting steady pressure.

She writhed underneath him, gasping out his name as he brought her closer to the edge. She was wet, slick and hot beneath his tongue. He devoured her, losing himself in her feminine essence. This was his. She was his.

He continued to tongue her, sucking and then probing her entrance with his tongue. He wanted her crazy for him. So desperate with need and want that she'd easily accommodate his size. She was a small woman, dainty, her features and bone structure delicate. The last thing he wanted to do was hurt her.

"Donovan, please!" she begged. "I know you want it to last. I understand you want it to be good, but I want you inside me. I want to come with you inside me. I need you now. I'm so close. I can feel it! It's overwhelming. I feel like I'm about to burst into a million tiny pieces."

Her voice was almost a sob. Her pussy clenched and tightened, growing wetter as he lavished attention on her most sensitive parts. Her plea sent another surge of arousal through his body, his dick already leaking pre-cum.

Yeah, he wanted it to last, but he also knew that wasn't happening. This first time wouldn't be perfect, but they would have plenty of other times to take it as slow as they wanted. Right now he had to have her. Had to be inside her or they'd both come before he got there.

"Give me one second, honey," he rasped out. "Need to get a condom."

"Hurry," she urged.

He rolled off her and off the bed, fumbling with the nightstand drawer. He grabbed one of the foil packets and ripped it open. He rolled the condom on, nearly coming with just the pressure of his hand.

"Down, boy," he muttered. "You'll like her a hell of a lot more than you like my hand."

Eve laughed, and he looked up to see that she'd heard his muttering. Mirth shone in her eyes and she extended her hand, an invitation to come back to her. As if he needed any such thing.

"Are you sure you're ready for me?" he asked as he parted her thighs and settled comfortably between her legs.

She shifted, lifting her hips to him. "Yes!"

He lowered his body even further, reaching down to gently spread her for his entry. He positioned the head at her entrance and then removed his hand, placing both on either side of Eve's body.

Closing his eyes, he began to push forward. He gritted his teeth and sweat broke out on his forehead. No way could he take this slow and easy. He was dying to get inside her.

He thrust forward, powering into her body in one motion. She cried out, the sound freezing him. Several things registered all at once. Her cry was not of pleasure. It was a sound of pain. She was exquisitely tight around him. *Too* tight. Her body was protesting his entry with everything it had. And he registered a tearing sensation, had felt a part of her give way with his entry.

He stared down at her in shock, taking in her expression, her startled eyes and the fleeting look of pain. Then he glanced down as he slowly withdrew and took in the smear of blood on the condom.

She'd been a *virgin* and he'd plowed into her with all the finesse of a rutting bull.

CHAPTER 24

"DONOVAN?"

He looked back to see Eve staring up at him with wide, fearful eyes. His name had come out quivery and filled with apprehension. Her uncertainty nearly slayed him. She was worried that she'd done something wrong when it was he who'd fucked up royally.

Careful to remain perfectly still and not push farther inside her, he stroked a hand through her hair and then caressed her cheek.

"Ah hell, honey, why didn't you tell me?" he asked gently.

"I w-wasn't t-thinking," she stammered out. "I swear, Donovan. I was so caught up in the moment that it didn't even occur to me to tell you. I mean, I thought of it earlier, but I was nervous and didn't know *how* to tell you. I was afraid you wouldn't want me if you knew, but I swear I was going to tell you. And then I got so caught up. I wanted you so much. I wanted you to make love to me. I wasn't trying to deceive you. I promise! You have to believe me."

Her anxiety made Donovan go soft in every part of his body except the part of him that was still penetrating her, though he was extremely careful not to cause her more discomfort. He rushed to reassure her, not wanting her to take any blame for what had happened, for the way it had happened. He'd been just as caught up as her. And the fear in her eyes was undoing him. He couldn't let her think for another second that he was in any way angry with her. God, angry? How could he be when she'd just given him something immeasurably precious?

He gently hushed her with his lips, tenderly kissing her, absorbing the moment, the knowledge that he was her first lover. He was overwhelmed. Never had he placed a huge importance on virginity. He wasn't *that* much of a caveman, and he'd never been with a virgin. Never considered how humbling an experience it was for a woman to trust her first time to him. That he was Eve's first staggered him. He felt many things, indescribable, but anger? Never that.

"I'm not angry with you, Eve. Quite the opposite. I'm overwhelmed by the gift you've given me. First your trust and now your virginity. I only wish I'd known so I could have made it better for you. I would die before causing you an ounce of pain. I would have gone slower. I would have been more gentle. I would have kissed and touched and held you all night. I would have made it perfect for you."

She reached for him, framing his face in her small hands, her touch like velvet against his skin. He nuzzled into her palm, regret seeping to his very soul.

"Don't you know, Donovan? It is perfect. You made it perfect. Are making it perfect," she corrected with a gentle smile. "It will never be more perfect than with you. The first time is supposed to hurt. But it wasn't bad. It surprised me more than it hurt. Like I said, I was so caught up and you made me feel so good that when it happened, it startled me because I wasn't expecting it. I wasn't thinking that I'm a virgin and this will hurt. All I was thinking was that if I didn't have you inside me I was going to die."

"Darling Eve. So very generous and sweet."

He kissed her again, unable to resist the temptation of her passion-swollen lips. He drew away, his breaths coming in ragged spurts. He was throbbing inside her. It was taking all of the control he possessed not to thrust into her again, to lose himself in her satin heat.

"I could have made it better," he gently corrected. "It might have hurt, but I could have made it hurt *less* by not taking you so hard with that first thrust. I was overwhelmed and I wanted you so desperately. But I can make it better from here on out. And I will, Eve. Trust me to make it right."

"I do trust you," she whispered. "Please don't stop. Don't let this ruin tonight for us. I want you. Need you. It doesn't hurt anymore, Donovan. Please don't stop."

He let out a tortured groan. "I'm not stopping, honey. I don't think that's possible. But I'm going to take it nice and slow and work you back up again. Okay?"

She stirred restlessly underneath him and he clenched his teeth together, his jaw going achingly tight as he fought his release.

"I'm with you, Donovan," she said softly. "I'm okay. Really."

Still, he carefully withdrew, watching her face for any sign of discomfort. Then he slid his hand between them, stroking over her clitoris, watching when she tightened as pleasure winged its way through her body.

He leaned down, shifting his position so his head was at her breasts. Using his free hand, he caressed one breast, plumping it, teasing her nipple until it was hard once more. Then he sucked gently, coaxing each one to a rigid peak while he continued to stroke her satiny flesh with the hand between her legs.

"Donovan!" she cried out, her back arching up off the bed.

"Are you close, honey? Are you about to come?"

"Yes!"

Carefully, he fit himself back to the mouth of her pussy, probing tenderly until the head slipped just inside. Her eyes widened but no pain registered in her expression. As he pushed farther in, one agonizing inch at a time, a dreamy haze entered her eyes and she smiled. Then she closed her eyes and arched into him once more.

"Wrap your legs around me," he directed. "And hold on to me. Grab my shoulders, honey. I'm not going to last and I want to make sure you're with me."

"I am," she said breathlessly. "I'm so there."

She complied with his request, wrapping her legs around his waist and hooking her ankles just above his ass. He cupped her behind, just as he'd imagined doing, tilting her at an angle that made penetrating her easier.

Then he slid into her, all the way until his balls pressed against her ass. She gasped. He gasped. He wasn't sure which of them was the louder. Her eyes widened and her fingers dug into his shoulders, her legs squeezed his sides, clamping like vises around him.

He pulled back and paused for a brief moment before diving deep again, his gaze never leaving her so he'd know if he was hurting her.

But she gave no indication she was experiencing anything but the sweetest of pleasures. She emitted soft, feminine sounds of appreciation as he thrust into her repeatedly. She matched his rhythm and they moved in unison to a song as old as time.

He slid his hands up her body, gathering her in his arms, holding her tight so that only his hips moved, arching into and out of her. Her breasts were flat against his chest, her breaths mingling with his. He kissed her, scorching over her mouth, devouring her as his orgasm rose, threatening to blind him with lust.

"Oh!" she exclaimed, her pussy going hot and wet around him, bathing him in her sweet heat.

"That's it, honey. Come for me. I want you to get there before I let go."

"I want you with me," she said breathlessly. "I want us to go together."

"How close are you?"

"If you won't stop, I'm close!"

He sealed his mouth to hers and slid his tongue deep inside just as he planted himself just as deeply into her body.

He went hard, losing all sense of himself. Of time. Of place. There was only Eve. Beautiful, innocent Eve.

He loved her and he knew he loved her. There was no denial. No argument that she was the one. She was his. Completely his. And he'd never let her go.

She began to shake uncontrollably. Her legs trembled around his waist and her fingers fluttered over his shoulders. Her breathing sped up until she was gasping with every thrust. And then she let out a long cry, swallowed up by his mouth as they breathed the same air.

And then he followed, plummeting right over the edge, falling hard and fast, spiraling rapidly out of control. Everything blurred around him. The slap of flesh meeting flesh distantly registered and then his release boiled from his groin, pulsed up his cock and he exploded in a frenzy, jetting into the condom.

After a moment he became aware of Eve kissing him. His jaw, then his neck, then up to his ear. Murmuring sweet words against his ear. Caressing his shoulders where moments before she'd dug in with her nails, scouring his skin.

Her legs had gone slack, splayed open and resting against the mattress as he lay between them, resting deeply within her body. He was covering her completely, his full weight bearing down on her. But she seemed content to be there. She wore a dreamy expression as she continued her tender caresses.

She lifted one hand to run it over his hair and then around to cup his jaw in her soft palm. He covered her mouth with his, wanting to taste her again.

They were both breathing hard, and regretfully he shifted upward so she wouldn't bear his weight any longer. He rolled to the side and then away from her long enough to dispose of the condom. Then he rolled back and gathered her in his arms. He kissed the top of her head, holding her as close to him as he could get her.

"Are you okay?" he asked.

She nodded, bumping the top of her head against his chin. "Very okay."

He smiled. "I'll be right back, all right? I'm just going to run into the bathroom to get a washcloth to clean you up."

He could feel her blush and his smile broadened. She was so adorably shy.

Reluctantly, he extricated himself from her and hurried to the bathroom to get a warm washcloth. He returned a few moments later and gently wiped the blood from between her thighs. He tossed the cloth on the floor several feet away and climbed back into bed, immediately pulling Eve back into his arms.

She snuggled into his embrace and let out a contented sigh that he felt all the way to his toes. But it was he who was contented. He could never remember feeling as satisfied as he was right here and now, his woman in his arms, warm and soft and sated from his lovemaking. It would never be better than this.

And then he imagined them in ten years' time. With children of their own. A huge family surrounding them. More nieces, nephews. Love, good times. Laughter. Twenty years from now. Forever. Yeah, it would get better. Every single day with her would be better than the one before.

He stroked her hair, smoothing the tendrils from her face. Then he cupped her chin and tilted her head upward so she could see him. He could stare at her forever. No matter how much time passed he didn't think he would ever grow tired of seeing her in his bed, her hair tousled from lovemaking, a sleepy, contented look in her beautiful eyes.

"I don't want to ever hear from you again that I do all the giving and you do all the taking and that you aren't giving me anything. Because what you've given to me is more precious than anything I've received. I can't even describe what it means that I was your first lover. It means a lot, Eve. It means *everything*. I'll always treasure the gift of your virginity, and I'll cherish you always."

Moisture glistened in her eyes, making the gold glints vibrant and electric in the light.

"And, Eve? Just so you know. I may have been your first, but I guarantee that I'm going to be your last as well."

Her eyes widened just as he kissed her again. For several long seconds, he plundered her mouth, tasting, savoring the moment. When he pulled away, her eyes were glazed with want—and need.

She put her hand to his chest, her fingertips resting over his heart. "You can't possibly mean that, Donovan."

He arched one eyebrow and stared challengingly at her. "Can't I? I don't think you realize it, but you sealed your fate the moment you gave me your trust. And now that you've given me the gift of yourself, your virginity . . . It's something I'll always cherish. Being your first. And yes, I fully intend to be the last man who ever makes love to you."

"How can you possibly know that?" she whispered.

He kissed her nose and smiled down at her. "Because you're mine. And I'm very possessive of what I consider mine. And you are mine, Eve. You and Cammie and Travis all belong to me. We're family. You're stuck with me, and I hope to hell you're feeling half of what I'm feeling right now."

Eve sucked in her breath, not even realizing she was holding it until she became light-headed. She sucked in a deep breath, overcome by all that he'd said. He was so . . . sincere. Earnest. Could she believe him? Was she crazy to want to believe him? And should she tell him what she'd barely begun to entertain herself?

He'd been honest with her. Straightforward. No holding back. No games. She had to do the same for him.

"I think I could fall in love with you, Donovan," she said in a whisper he had to lean forward to hear. "It's crazy. I shouldn't be talking like this. I shouldn't even be thinking it. I can't be entertaining the notion of love and a relationship, the *future*, when my life is in complete turmoil."

He nudged her chin upward again until she was staring into his implacable eyes.

"You better damn well be thinking about your future— with me—because I'm already looking down the road to when we have children of our own. At the life I intend to have. With you. Travis and Cammie will always be part of our hearts and our family. I consider them my own children already. But I want children—with you—to fill our house. Lots of children, love and laughter, and I want you to give me those children. I want to see Travis and Cammie graduate high school and college, get married and have families of their own. I want to grow old with you and watch our grandchildren grow up, loved and protected just like I intend to protect you, Travis, Cammie and any children you and I have together. Our family, Eve. Our family."

She could no longer hold back the tears. They sloshed over the rims of her eyes and slid soundlessly down her cheeks, colliding with his fingers as he stroked her face.

"When you say these things, I believe you. I *want* to believe you, but I'm afraid. I'm so afraid that it will all be snatched away. I'm afraid to be happy because I couldn't bear it if it was all taken away. I don't want to *lose* you."

Donovan kissed her tears away, gently removing all traces of dampness on her cheeks. Then he smiled tenderly at her as he continued to stroke her hair and her face.

"We have all the time in the world for me to convince you that I'm not going anywhere and neither are you. We'll face your—*our*—problems head on. Together. I'll always be at your side and always at Travis's and Cammie's."

CHAPTER 25

EVE snuggled into Donovan's embrace and emitted a contented sigh. They were sitting on the couch enjoying a perfectly normal evening watching movies with Travis and Cammie.

Cammie's IV had been discontinued earlier that day when Maren had come by for her daily checkup. Travis was no longer taking pain medication, and the soreness and pain he had been experiencing was diminishing greatly.

Donovan had cooked an early dinner for them and they'd sat around the table, laughing and acting just like a . . . family.

The threat of Walt that had loomed over Eve for so long had diminished. It was easy to forget that danger existed. That it was out there lurking, just waiting for the chance to strike. But here, secluded in Donovan's home, behind the walls of the compound, Eve felt safe. Travis and Cammie felt safe. They'd smiled and relaxed for the first time since they'd run from their father.

It made Eve's heart ache for all that could be. For all she wanted. Never would she have imagined having all she now had in the palm of her hands. She'd chickened out the night before. Had been so overwhelmed by the depth of her feelings for him that she'd taken the easy way out and said she could see herself falling in love with Donovan.

It was a lie. She loved him. But it had seemed too soon. He acted as though he cared about her. Maybe even loved her. But he hadn't said the words. Neither had she. She had been afraid to say them matter-of-factly. Too worried that he wouldn't believe her, that she'd been too caught up in the moment and would have said those words without truly meaning them.

Did she? She'd examined her feelings, their making love, until her head had spun. No matter how hard she tried to talk herself out of the idea of loving Donovan so soon, her heart had stood firm and told her in no uncertain terms that she did. And yet she'd still hesitated, too afraid to give voice to the sentiment for fear that he didn't love her. That he too was carried away by the moment. By everything.

It all seemed too good to be true, and she found herself anticipating the other shoe dropping. She was just waiting for the bottom to fall out and for it all to be taken away in the blink of an eye.

Donovan's arm tightened around her and he kissed the top of her head. He touched her and kissed her often. Reassuring her, being loving and affectionate, almost as if he realized her fears of it all vanishing.

"You're quiet tonight," he murmured close to her ear.

Eve glanced down on the floor where Travis was sprawled on the rug, Cammie nestled against him as the two were absorbed in the movie.

"I'm just enjoying it," she said simply.

"Enjoying what?" Donovan asked.

She tipped her head up to him, finding his gaze. "You. Me. Us. It's going to take time for me to get used to it, Donovan. I'm so afraid that at any moment it's all going to disappear."

He smiled tenderly at her and then captured her lips in a gentle kiss. "I'm not going anywhere, Eve. I'm here for the long haul. I understand your fears, but in time they'll disappear. In time you'll know that I'm keeping you, Travis and Cammie. You all belong to me. But I also belong to you. No one else will ever have the hold on me that you do. Not my family. Not KGI. You come first."

Warmth seeped into her heart, assuaging the ache that had settled in at the thought of losing him. That it was all too good to be true.

"I don't know what I did to deserve you," she whispered. "But I thank God every day that you found me—us."

He chuckled. "And here I was wondering what I'd done to deserve you and Travis and Cammie. Guess we'll just both be grateful together."

Cammie got up from where she was lying on the floor next to Travis and crawled onto the couch, inserting herself between Donovan and Eve. She emitted a sleepy yawn and then promptly cuddled into Donovan's side.

Eve watched as his face softened and transformed as he stared down at the little girl in his arms. He stroked her curls and Eve doubted he even realized how he looked right now. His gaze so full of love. It astonished her that this man could so readily open his heart to children that weren't his own. But then he'd made it clear he did consider them his already.

She glanced over to see Travis's head propped in the palm of his hand, and he was no longer watching the movie. He was watching Eve, Cammie and Donovan. There was such hope—and contentment—in her brother's eyes that Eve knew she'd made the right decision for them all.

"How are you feeling, Travis?" Donovan asked, seeing the teenager watching them.

There was a note of fatherly concern in his tone that formed a knot in Eve's throat. Travis wasn't unaffected either.

"I'm good, sir. I appreciate your concern. What you've done for me—us. I'll never forget it."

Donovan smiled at the teenager. "You can stop calling me sir. We're family. You can call me Donovan or Van."

"Can I call you Daddy?" Cammie piped up.

Eve glanced down, surprised to see her awake. She'd been well on her way to sleeping, snuggled firmly against Donovan's side. Now she looked up at Donovan with shyness—and longing.

Donovan brushed a kiss over the top of her head. "I'd like that, pumpkin."

Cammie wrinkled her nose. "You call me lots of different names. How come?"

Donovan laughed. "That's because you're cute as a button. And they're pet names. You'll find that in my family, we call all the women we love by special pet names. You'll get used to it. It just means we love you."

"Oh," Cammie said, looking delighted.

Eve took in Cammie's obvious pleasure, and a hint of foreboding took hold. It would devastate Cammie—and Travis—if this didn't work out. She'd been right to hold off, not to get swept away and say things carelessly. She had more than herself to think about in this situation. She had Travis and Cammie and there was still the very real threat of her stepfather.

No matter Donovan's assurances that he would take care of the matter, no one was above the law, and Eve had certainly broken the law. She'd kidnapped her siblings. Oh, it wasn't kidnapping. She'd saved them. But without proof, with the solid evidence that Walt possessed detailing her mental instability, she'd committed a crime, and crime didn't go unpunished.

And if she was punished, Travis and Cammie would be punished even more. For they would go back to their father and the evil he planned to unleash on them both.

A cold chill overtook her just thinking of that sweet, innocent baby in the grasp of a sick, twisted monster.

"Eve?"

Donovan's concerned voice broke through her dark thoughts, and she turned to see him looking at her intently, worry reflected in his green eyes.

"What's wrong, honey?"

She shook her head. "I was just thinking. About . . . him. About what I've done. I'm a criminal in the eyes of the law. You and I may know—think—differently, but there it is. I could go to jail. Or to a mental institution and they'd be left at his mercy."

She trailed off, not wanting to give voice to her many fears. She didn't want Cammie and Travis to share those fears. She wanted for them the absolute knowledge that they were safe and protected from all evil in the world.

"Come here," Donovan said in a tender voice, pulling her to rest against Cammie so that Cammie was firmly sandwiched between them.

He put his arm around her, giving her a reassuring squeeze. Then he leaned over to kiss her temple, leaving his lips there a long moment.

"I don't want you to even think about him. The only thing I want you thinking about is me. Our life together. How many kids you want. Leave everything else to me. I'm not going to let him hurt you again, Eve. And I'm never going to allow Cammie within a mile of him."

"I want you to promise me something, Donovan," she said, looking earnestly up at him. She wanted him to know how utterly serious she was about this.

"What is it, honey?"

His tone was concerned, but he kept his voice low so that they were unheard over the movie Travis and Cammie were focused on once more.

"If something happens to me."

She shook her head when Donovan immediately began to protest. She brought her finger up to place over his lips, instilling firmness in her gaze.

His lips tightened underneath her fingertip, but he remained silent as he waited to hear the rest.

"If the police arrest me. If somehow he finds me and takes us, takes us all. No matter what happens to me, I want you to swear to me that you'll fight for Cammie and Travis. That you'll do whatever you have to in order to wrest them from his grasp again. If I'm not jailed and he doesn't ensure they throw away the key, he'll likely have me institutionalized. He has so much evidence supporting my so-called mental illness. It's possible. Anything is possible in his world. But swear to me that you'll protect them. They'll need you, Donovan. If they don't have me, they'll need you—and your family's protection."

Donovan wasn't happy. Indeed, he looked . . . pissed. There was anger in his eyes and he simply shook his head.

"You don't get it, do you? I'm not going to just throw up my hands were something to happen to you. I'll fight with my every breath, not only for Cammie and Travis, but for you as well, Eve. I'd never leave you to his mercy. *Never*."

"Thank you," she whispered.

"Now you're just pissing me off," he said darkly. "You don't thank me for doing what's right. For protecting what's mine. You're entitled to that. And there won't ever be a time you aren't."

She closed her eyes and laid her head on his shoulder. God, she loved this man. Didn't care if it was too soon. Didn't care if she was being foolhardy for allowing herself to become involved in a relationship when she was on the run from a killer.

She wanted this. Wanted it with everything she had. And damn anyone who said or thought differently.

They were interrupted by the ringing of the doorbell. Cammie stiffened, coming fully awake, and Travis jerked up, his eyes wide and wary.

"Hey," Donovan gently chided. "It's okay, guys. Remember the tight security we have here? If my doorbell rings and I wasn't alerted of someone coming through the gates, then whoever's at the door is someone who lives here on the grounds. No one can access this place without me knowing about it."

"Who is it?" Cammie asked anxiously.

Donovan smiled. "It's likely one of my brothers or perhaps even one or more of their wives. They very much want to meet you."

"'Kay," Cammie said.

Travis scrambled up, standing nervously as Donovan got up to go to the front door. Eve couldn't see from her angle who was there when Donovan opened the door. He stood talking a moment and then turned to walk back into the living room, a group of people following close behind.

There were four women, two holding infants, one holding the hand of a blond-haired little girl who looked to be Cammie's age. And they all wore warm, welcoming smiles.

Eve hurried to her feet, standing as she waited for Donovan

to make introductions. The affection in which he regarded the other women was evident in every aspect of his expression.

Cammie even got off the couch, looking curiously at the other little girl. Travis stood to the side, ill at ease. He wiped his hands down his pants in a gesture that told Eve he was as nervous as she was about meeting Donovan's family.

These were the sisters-in-law that Garrett had mentioned. He'd said they'd want to come over to check Eve out for themselves. Give her their stamp of approval. What was it that Garrett had said? That they were all protective of the two unmarried Kelly brothers and they would want to see firsthand if Eve was good enough for Donovan.

Ugh. No pressure! No, not at all. It was all Eve could do not to run from the living room and barricade herself in the bedroom.

Though she and Donovan had made love in the room he'd given Eve—the one she'd initially shared with Cammie— he'd made it clear the morning after that he wanted her in his bed. In his bedroom.

Tonight, she'd share his bedroom with him. They'd sleep for the first time in his bed. He'd told her very matter-of-factly that no other woman had shared his bed in his home. Not this house. He'd told her that when he built this house, he had no intention of bringing any woman here if he wasn't certain that she was the one.

What did it say about him that he'd insisted that Eve and her siblings move in with him after only meeting Eve on two occasions?

Sure, he'd said that things happened fast in his family. That he—and all his brothers—wasted no time once they met the woman they'd marry. But talking about it in the abstract and experiencing the lightning speed in which her and Donovan's relationship had progressed were two vastly different things.

"Eve?"

Once again, Donovan caught her in the middle of her wayward thoughts. A habit she had to break of drifting off during important moments. She winced and immediately focused her attention on Donovan and the group of women all staring expectantly at her.

"Hello," she said in a husky voice that she hoped didn't betray her nervousness.

"Ladies, I want you to meet a very special woman. Eve. I also want you to meet Eve's brother, Travis, and her younger sister, Cammie."

He glanced down at the little blond-haired girl holding the hand of what had to be her mother, given the strong resemblance.

"Charlotte, Cammie is your age. I'm sure she'd love to have a new friend to play with. Think you'd mind sharing some of your toys with her?"

Charlotte beamed, displaying not one ounce of shyness. Here was a confident little girl, secure in the knowledge that she was adored and spoiled beyond reason and that her family would never allow anything bad to happen to her.

Eve's heart ached because she wanted the same for Cammie. And maybe now she'd finally have the same security and innocence that Charlotte possessed. No, she'd never be as innocent as Charlotte, but hopefully she'd overcome her past and it wouldn't follow her into adulthood. If Eve had anything to do with it at all, Cammie would never again know the fear and uncertainty that had plagued the first four years of her life.

Charlotte immediately went to where Cammie stood just behind Donovan. The entire time Donovan had performed the introductions, Cammie had edged closer and closer, finally slipping her hand into Donovan's much larger one.

Her thumb automatically went to her mouth as she stared shyly back at Charlotte.

"Hi, Cammie," Charlotte chirped. "We're going to be best friends. And my mama says you'll be my cousin!"

Cammie smiled, warming instantly to the other child, and how could she not? No one could possibly look at Charlotte and not be won over instantly.

Donovan turned his attention to Eve, motioning her forward to stand beside him. He slipped an arm around her waist and looked at his sisters-in-law.

"Eve, these are my sisters-in-law Sophie—she's Charlotte's mom—and Rachel; she's married to Ethan and the twin boys are hers. You already met Garrett. This is his wife, Sarah. She's expecting their first child in eight or so months. Sophie is also pregnant with her second child and is due a little before Sarah. And last but certainly not least, there's Shea, Nathan's wife. He's the youngest of my brothers."

Eve's eyes widened as she glanced at the petite woman Donovan had introduced as Shea.

"I'm very glad to meet all of you," Eve said sincerely. "Donovan has talked so much about you that I feel like I already know you."

"We're very pleased to finally meet you, Eve," Rachel said quietly.

Of all the women, she seemed the quietest. Well, and Sarah seemed to be shyer as well. While Sophie and Shea seemed more outgoing. But after hearing of all that Rachel had endured, Eve couldn't blame her for being more subdued. How hellish to endure an entire year in captivity and not to be able to remember her family or her husband.

After hearing Donovan describe how all his brothers had met their wives—in less-than-ideal situations—Eve studied them closely now, comparing the image she'd built in her mind to the reality of them standing a few feet away.

She wasn't sure what she was expecting, but the women seemed perfectly normal. Just like average, everyday women, even if they had endured extraordinary events. It gave her hope for her own life and how normal it could be once the threat to her and her siblings was eliminated. She just prayed that Donovan's confidence that he and his brothers could handle any situation was truth.

"Donovan is very important to us all," Sophie interjected. "We'd despaired of him ever finding a woman to settle down with and have the brood of children he's always wanted. So we're very glad to meet the woman who brought him down. Next to Maren, you have our utmost admiration."

Eve cocked her head, uncertain what the last had meant.

Sarah chuckled, speaking up for the first time. "Maren

brought down the ice man. Steele. He's one of the KGI team leaders. Total and complete badass. We never thought we'd see the day he'd fall head over ass for a woman, much less be carrying around a baby!"

"Oh," Eve said, frowning a bit as she thought back to when she'd met Maren and Steele.

She hadn't paid a whole lot of attention to Steele, but she supposed she could understand where the others were coming from. He did look intimidating and daunting. It would take a special woman to bring out his tender side. Supposing he even had one. Maybe Maren was a badass in her own right and stood up to Steele.

"We also wanted to see what else you needed," Sophie said. "We gathered up some clothes, but we didn't have a lot of notice and we'd like to get what you need as well as what Travis and Cammie need. She and Charlotte are about the same size, but I don't want her to just get hand-me-downs. If Donovan will let you out of his sight for a few hours, we could take you shopping so you could get clothing for all of you."

Donovan frowned at that. "Not going to happen, sweetheart. I know you mean well, but there is no way in hell I'm letting Eve out of my sight or out from underneath my protection, and I damn sure don't want you ladies to risk yourselves by going out in public with her. Not only would my brothers kick my ass, but they'd never go for it either."

The women looked crestfallen and Donovan immediately shook his head.

"No puppy-dog eyes. Especially you, Rachel. I know you're used to batting those pretty eyes at me and I'll do damn near anything to keep you from pouting, but this is a serious matter. The risk is too great."

"But she needs stuff, Van," Sophie protested. "You can't keep her under lock and key forever!"

Eve stifled a smile at how vehement the women were in their defense of her. But she agreed with Donovan. Furthermore, she had no desire to leave the security of the compound.

The outside world couldn't touch her here and she was happy about that.

"That's why online shopping was invented," Donovan said with a grin. "I'll turn you girls loose with my credit card and y'all can go to town."

Shea brightened at that. "Oh, I'm the queen of Internet shopping. I hate going to the mall or even to the store because I never know when I'll pick up someone's random thoughts, and it can be overwhelming when I'm trying to shop and I'm hearing something someone doesn't want the world to know."

She shuddered delicately and the other women looked at her in sympathy. Eve stared at her, utterly perplexed. Shea's eyes widened as she stared back at Eve.

"You don't know, do you?" Shea asked.

"Know what?" Eve asked, feeling like she was missing a huge piece of a puzzle that everyone else had already put together.

"I hadn't told her yet," Donovan spoke up.

Shea waved her hand dismissively. "We'll fill you in tomorrow when you come over. I can steer you to some of my favorite sites. We're about the same size, so I can definitely hook you up. Just say the word and we'll commandeer one of Van's many computers."

The others snickered at the mention of computers, and Donovan rolled his eyes.

"Thank you," Eve said sincerely. "I really appreciate all that you're doing. Travis, Cammie and I . . . Well, we don't even know what to say."

"Has Travis been in school?" Rachel asked hesitantly. She rushed on before Eve could respond.

"I mean, I know you've had a hard time and you've been moving a lot. I don't know what your plans for him were, but I'm happy to help him with his studies to get him caught up so that when things settle down he can enroll in school here."

Travis's eyes brightened but he remained silent, almost as if he were afraid to voice an opinion.

"Thank you," Eve said again, emotion knotting her throat.

"He does need to get caught up. He loves school. He excels. He's always made good grades. And he's a very good athlete."

Eve glanced down, not wanting the others to see the pain she was sure was evident in her eyes.

"He should be in school with an opportunity to play sports, hang out with kids his own age. Make friends and have a normal life."

"I don't regret anything, Evie," Travis said in a quiet tone. "You did what you had to do. I'll always be grateful for the risks you've taken and for sacrificing so much for me."

"What about it, Travis?" Donovan spoke up. "Would you like Rachel to help get you caught up with your studies? Maybe this fall you can enroll here in school. Rachel teaches at the middle school and she's friends with many of the high school teachers. I know they'd be willing to work with you to get you up to speed."

"I'd like that a lot," Travis said, his voice sincere.

Rachel smiled. "Then that's settled. No hurry, though. We still have the rest of the summer, and what you need to focus most on right now is getting better. Once you're settled more and comfortable in your surroundings, then either I can come here a few days a week or you're welcome over at my house. I just live across the way."

"Thank you," Travis said.

"You're family now," Sophie said firmly. "All of you. And as I'm sure Donovan has already told you multiple times, we take family very seriously. We stick together. Because together, there isn't a force in the world that can stand up against the Kelly family and KGI."

Eve bit back the tears, determined to stop breaking down at every single thing. But for a moment she couldn't speak. Travis was similarly affected, casting his gaze downward so no one could see the emotion shining brightly in his eyes.

"Why don't you come over tomorrow afternoon, Eve?" Shea invited. "We'll get together at Sophie's. She has the biggest house. No doubt because Sam wants lots more children."

The rest of the women snickered and Sophie rolled her eyes.

"Nathan and I live in a smaller house," Shea explained. "It's really open. Apart from the bedroom, the rest is mostly one big room. He can't stand enclosed spaces ever since his captivity."

Her tone had grown more hushed, and pain briefly flooded her eyes. Then she went silent a moment before smiling.

Sophie rolled her eyes. "She's communicating with Nathan. He must have picked up on her distress and was demanding to know what the hell was wrong and if she needed him."

Shea blushed but didn't refute Sophie's statement. Eve was utterly bewildered by it all. Communicating?

"Anyway," Sarah interjected, picking up where Shea left off. "Why don't you come over and we'll hang out, have some wine. Well, you, Rachel and Shea can have the wine. Sophie and I will stick to tea. Bring Cammie—and Travis too, if he doesn't mind hanging out with the girls, that is—and Charlotte and Cammie can play. Charlotte has tons of toys that she'd be more than happy to share."

"I have Barbies," Charlotte announced.

Charlotte reached for Cammie's hand, the one she had in her mouth, and pulled it away, lacing her fingers firmly in Cammie's.

"You can play with my Barbies. I don't mind," Charlotte said solemnly. "I have lots of dolls too. And I have soldier dolls! My uncle Garrett bought them for me."

Sarah closed her eyes and shook her head. "Only Garrett would buy action figures complete with camo and assault rifles for his niece."

Everyone laughed and Donovan chuckled.

"Hey, it never hurts to start them early. Maybe Cece will grow up and run KGI when Sam hangs it up," Donovan said in amusement.

Sophie sent him a dark look. "Bite your tongue, Van. Don't plant any ideas in Charlotte's mind. The girl already wants her uncle Garrett to take her to the firing range so she can shoot his gun. God help us all. I made Sam get a gun cabinet with a combination lock so she never gets any ideas."

"You're all okay with what they do. Your husbands, I mean," Eve blurted.

The women's expressions softened. Donovan remained quiet, watching Eve.

Rachel reached over and squeezed Eve's hand. "I won't tell you that I don't live in fear when Ethan goes out on a mission, although he's cut back a lot since the twins were born. But I also know he'll do more sooner or later. But what they do . . . it's worth it. I know firsthand. If it weren't for them and what they're capable of, the resources they have, I wouldn't be here today. I wouldn't be alive."

Emotion knotted Rachel's voice and Donovan drew her into his side, kissing her temple after giving her a quick hug.

"We all fear that something could happen to our husbands," Sarah said honestly. "But as Rachel says, what they do, it's noble. They help so many people. They take down a lot of evil people. Dismantle entire operations. The world is a better place for who they are and what they do. So I can live with that. I can live with my husband risking his life because that's who he is and I wouldn't change him. He wouldn't be the same Garrett I know and love if he were a normal nine-to-five working some desk job somewhere."

Sophie and Shea both nodded their agreement.

"They've helped us," Sophie said quietly. "Each of us. It's how we met and fell in love with them. And every single one of them, not just the Kellys, but the KGI team leaders and members too would risk their lives for any of us. No questions. No hesitation. That kind of selflessness, that kind of love and loyalty, is priceless."

Eve nodded, heartened by their impassioned words. She hadn't yet experienced the full scope of Donovan's job. But he'd hinted. She'd seen the reality of the way they lived. No one lived behind a high-tech security net unless it was warranted, unless there was a very real danger to them.

Her and Donovan's relationship was so new. Still growing and deepening. They still had a long way to go. Much to discover about one another, and it made her uneasy to imagine losing him after finding such a miracle.

"You'll have us when the guys are gone," Shea said, taking her hand from Rachel's to squeeze. "We close ranks when they go off on a mission. And it's rare when they're all gone at the same time. Sam has a rule about all the brothers being on one mission. Of course over the years, there have been exceptions. But when possible, some remain behind so that we aren't left alone. And we stick together. We're not just sisters-in-law. We're friends. And we'd like to be your friend too, Eve. Donovan means a lot to all of us, and we're very happy he's found the woman who will make him happy."

Eve didn't miss the subtle warning in Shea's voice or the mirroring agreement in the other women's faces. They accepted her, but they were also warning her not to break Donovan's heart.

"Thank you," Eve said again. "I feel so fortunate to have found Donovan. All of you. It means the world to me that you're all so accepting of Travis and Cammie. They're my family. Until now, my only family. I want them to have a better life than I've been providing them. They deserve better than what I can give them."

"That's not true," Travis said fiercely.

Eve silenced him with a gentle smile. "It's true, Trav. We weren't going to be able to run forever. We needed . . . help. And now we have it."

Donovan wrapped his other arm around Eve and pulled her close, brushing a kiss over her brow. "Yes, you do, honey. You have all of us. I want you to remember that any time you get scared or worried. There are a hell of a lot of us who will be here for you. No questions. No conditions."

"So do we have a date tomorrow?" Sarah asked. "Girl time and a play date for Charlotte and Cammie?" She turned to Travis. "And what about you? Would you like to come?"

Travis looked uncertain. He looked to Eve and then Donovan for help.

Donovan laughed. "How about Travis and I have a little guy bonding time and leave you girls to do your thing."

Travis looked relieved and nodded his agreement.

Rachel rolled her eyes. "That means the husbands will likely get involved, and there's no telling what they'll plot when we're not around."

"Us?" Donovan asked innocently. "We wouldn't do any such thing."

Sophie snorted. "Whatever, Van. Okay, we're scooting on out. We just wanted to stop in and say hello to Eve and introduce ourselves. We couldn't let Garrett go on being smug that he was the only one to have met them aside from Joe."

"It was very nice meeting you," Eve said with genuine feeling. "I'm looking forward to tomorrow."

The women all said their good-byes and Charlotte gave Cammie a huge hug before running back to her mom to take her hand.

"You ladies be careful walking back," Donovan cautioned.

"Oh good Lord, Van. It's a two-minute walk across the grass," Sarah said. "I'm sure we can make it that far without any mishaps."

"Just want to make sure my girls are taken care of," Donovan said with a grin.

They all blew him kisses, said one last good-bye to Eve, Travis and Cammie and then disappeared out the front door.

When Donovan returned from seeing them out, he pulled Eve down onto the couch with him. Cammie promptly crawled back between them and resumed her position, snuggled into Donovan's side.

"Well? What do you think of the wives?" Donovan asked.

"I like them," Eve replied. "They're nice."

Donovan nodded. "They're the best. No better women anywhere. Fierce. Fighters. Loyal to their bones. They'll be good friends to you, Eve."

"I hope so," Eve said wistfully. "But Donovan, what about Shea? What was that all about? Her communicating with Nathan." She shook her head in confusion.

Donovan chuckled. "It's a long story, one I'll have to tell you sometime. The condensed version is that Shea is a telepathic empath. She and Nathan can communicate telepathically. I know it sounds crazy, but Shea—and her sister Grace—have extraordinary abilities."

"Wow," Eve murmured. "You guys certainly don't lead boring lives."

Cammie yawned and Travis walked to the couch, holding his arms down for Cammie.

"Ready for bed?" Travis asked Cammie. "I'll go tuck you in and turn in myself. I'm pretty tired."

Cammie held up her arms for Travis to pick her up, but Donovan stood, lifting her into his arms.

"You shouldn't be carrying her yet," Donovan cautioned. "I'll take her to your room and get her tucked in. You can crawl in with her afterward."

Eve watched them go, an ache blooming in her chest as she watched Donovan herd Travis and Cammie to bed. Just like a father pulling bedtime duty. The future flashed before her eyes. Donovan tucking in their own children. Nights spent snuggled on the couch watching movies and just . . . being.

She closed her eyes, savoring the wonderful sensation that hope for the future brought with it. No matter how unlikely it was that she'd enjoy such a future. It still didn't stop the instant coil of hope that warmed her veins. And she briefly considered that she could be setting herself—and Cammie and Travis—up for a far worse hurt than that wrought by her stepfather.

CHAPTER 26

EVE watched Donovan stride purposely back into the living room, a contented look fixed on his features as if he'd found pleasure in the simple task of putting Cammie to bed with Travis. It instilled a fierce wave of longing deep inside her, in places she hadn't shed light on in so very long. He gave that to her. Hope for better. For the future. *Their* future.

As he approached, he didn't sit back on the couch with her as she might have expected. Instead he stood over where she was nestled comfortably and simply extended his hand down to her, his palm up, inviting her to take hold. His eyes were warm with affection. She liked to think it was love. But she knew it was too soon for that even as she acknowledged that she herself was solidly in love with him. But she knew, or rather she hoped, that he cared for her. He'd said as much. It wasn't like she was fantasizing. It was just that the idea of assuming anything set her up for inevitable devastation.

"I don't know about you," he said as she slid her hand over his. "But I'm ready for bed."

She smiled up at him. "Tired, are you? That's too bad."

He gave her a look that sent a quiver through her belly and up to her breasts, her nipples forming taut peaks. But he also looked pleased by her playfulness. And she supposed it would please him since she hadn't exactly been a ball of laughs since they'd met. But he was changing that. He was changing her. One day at a time. One hour at a time. Each minute that she spent with him she treasured deeply.

"I said nothing about being tired. Only that I was ready to go to bed. With you. Sleep, however, is not on the agenda. At least not right away. But later?" He gave her a lazy smile, his eyes gleaming with purpose. "Yeah."

A delicate shiver danced over her skin as she let him pull her to her feet. She slid against his body, nestling herself under his arm. His strength vibrated against her, warm and reassuring. She let out a contented sigh as he turned her toward his bedroom.

"Not nervous, are you?" he asked when they entered the room. Had he sensed her hesitation? Just that tiny bit of nerves quaking over her?

He closed the door silently behind them, providing a barrier between them and the rest of the world.

She shook her head and then nodded before shaking it once more.

He chuckled. "Decisive tonight, aren't you?"

"This is new to me," she blurted.

His smile turned as warm as his eyes and he pulled her around so they were facing each other, his head lowered, his fingers tipping her chin up to meet his gaze.

"I know it is, honey. I'm not likely to forget what you gave me last night. That I was your first lover. It's a gift I'll treasure forever."

She blushed, her cheeks going warm beneath the heat of his gaze.

"Are you tender today?" he asked gently.

Her cheeks flamed with heat even more, and she ducked her head, pulling from his grasp.

He laughed softly and nudged her chin back up with a tender touch.

"I don't ask to embarrass you. I just want to know if you're up for what I have planned."

She smiled, suddenly shy as his thoughts were broadcast in his smoldering stare.

"I'll suffer through it."

"Ah, such a grand sacrifice," he said, amusement twinkling in his green eyes. "I will endeavor to not make you suffer *too* badly."

"Oh, I'm sure you will," she said breathlessly.

Then his gaze grew more serious. "Are you *too* tender, sweetheart? There are other ways of pleasuring you that doesn't require me to penetrate you."

Gah, but she had to stop this endless blushing every time they spoke intimately. But he seemed delighted with her shyness, his smile as gentle as his words.

"I'm okay, Donovan. Truly. And if it hurts too much, we can stop, can't we?"

"Absolutely. I'll not do anything that hurts you, Eve. Ever."

As he said the last, he moved in close, his body heat wrapping her in its soft cocoon. He trailed a finger down her cheek, caressing, sending shivers down her spine. Just his touch. Something as simple as the slight touch of his fingertips and she was shaking with need. Would it always be so? Would she always need him, desire him as she did in this very moment?

Perhaps it would only heighten with time. If it did, then she certainly had much to look forward to. And then she realized that for the first time she was actually thinking of the future in optimistic terms. As if she didn't have the very real fear of Walt and the police and her reality of being a wanted criminal.

Donovan did that for her. He gave her hope. He gave her the confidence that her future was not fixed. It was in fact undecided. It could be what she *wanted* it to be. And she wanted her future to be with Donovan.

A sigh escaped and he drew away, staring intently into her eyes.

"What are you thinking, honey?"

She smiled, allowing her happiness to spill onto her features. "The future."

"Ah, happy thoughts then, I hope?"

"The very best," she whispered.

His eyes gleamed in satisfaction. "Then how about we make those thoughts even happier? I want to undress you. I want to make love to you again, Eve. And tonight I want to take it nice and slow. As I should have last night. Let me make it up to you, honey. Let me give you the experience I should have given you last night."

"Oh, Donovan," she breathed out. "Don't you know? Last night was perfect. The most perfect night of my life. You can't make it any better. It's not possible. It's only your first time once, and my first time was more than I could have possibly ever imagined."

Her eyes narrowed and she glanced up at him in question. "Tell me you haven't worried about this all day."

To her surprise he looked slightly embarrassed and discomfort registered in his eyes.

"It may have occurred to me a few times," he muttered.

She laughed. "Good Lord, Donovan. You've got to stop with the virgin guilt. You didn't hurt me. I quite enjoyed our lovemaking. And if you think you're getting out of it tonight, you've got another think coming."

He relaxed, a charming grin curving his mouth upward. "Far be it for me to deny my lady anything."

"Good," she said huskily. "Now if we've gotten that out of the way, there is the matter of us both still being dressed. Think you can do something about that?"

"Last one naked is a rotten egg," he challenged.

"That's not fair," she sputtered as he started ripping at his shirt. "Women have far more to take off than men!"

"Less talking, more undressing," he said as he began peeling his jeans down his thick legs.

She hastily tore her shirt over her head, fumbling with her bra straps even as she reached for the fly of her jeans. She hadn't even stepped from the confines of the denim before he was standing in front of her, naked, arms folded over his chest in mock impatience.

She shook her head. "I guess you'll have to help me."

He gave an exaggerated sigh. "I guess I can make that sacrifice."

She rolled her eyes as he turned her to unhook her bra. But there was no impatience to his movements. His fingers worked slowly as he removed her bra, pulling it forward to slide the straps the rest of the way down her arms. Then he turned her back, reaching for her hands so she could step the rest of the way from the one leg of the jeans still remaining around her ankle. Then he reverently pulled her panties down and let the tiny scrap fall to the floor.

"That's better." His gaze raked up and down her naked body. "Much, much better," he murmured as he bent his head to kiss her.

She wrapped her arms around his neck, pulling him in close as their mouths melted together. She wasn't sure who sighed. Maybe they both did. But there was a harsh exchange of breath. She could taste him on her tongue. Inhaled his scent, holding and savoring it before finally letting it go for the briefest of moments before inhaling it all over again.

He backed her slowly toward the bed, arms wrapped as solidly around her as hers were wrapped around him. It was almost like dancing. A slow, decadent, seductive thrill. Moving sensuously, unhurried, as if they had all the time in the world.

She didn't want slow and unhurried. She wanted him with a ferocity that until now had been completely alien to her. Never had she felt such raging want. Now that her sexuality had been awakened, now that she'd been shown how very good it could be. Unspoiled by memories of Walt's depravity. She savored the coil of desire that whispered through her body, becoming more urgent with each passing second.

He started to ease her onto the bed, but she pulled him with her, surprising him with her strength as he tumbled down on top of her.

They landed with a soft bounce, him atop her, their bodies entwined, flesh on flesh. She loved the contrast between them. His hard lines to her much softer ones. He was muscled where she was soft. Her body cradled him, molded to him as if they'd always belonged. Two interlocking puzzle pieces finally put together.

She rubbed her leg up and down his thigh, nearly purring with pleasure at the simple decadence of touching him. Of being able to explore his warrior's body.

"I had every intention of taking things slow and sweet," he said in a ragged voice. "But Eve, what you do to me. You drive me crazy."

"I want you crazy," she whispered just before she sank her teeth into the lobe of his ear and nipped playfully. "I want you so crazy for me that you forget all about going slow. I want it hard and fast, Donovan. I want *you*."

He groaned and kissed his way down the side of her neck, nipping as she'd done, eliciting a gasp from her with every graze of his teeth. He went lower still, until he reached her breasts. Her nipples were painfully erect. Begging for his mouth, his tongue and yes, his teeth.

"Donovan, please!" she begged. "I'm about to crawl out of my skin! I need you inside me or I'm going to come now."

He slipped his fingers between her legs, testing and gently probing as if to reassure himself that all she said was true. She felt her slickness on his fingers, felt how easily they slid inside her body and back out again. She knew she was ready—more than ready—for him. And if she didn't have him soon, she was going to take matters into her own hands and ravish him until he begged for mercy.

It wasn't bad as ideas go, but she'd wait another night. Maybe even tomorrow. When she wasn't so on edge that the slightest touch would send her right over. Right now she just wanted it hard and fast. No other way would do.

"I've got you, honey," he soothed. "I'll take care of you."

She nodded her agreement, her jaw clenched tight as she battled back the orgasm that built and swelled inside her. He carefully parted her thighs and she nearly groaned her impatience. Deciding to prompt him, she parted her legs and circled them around his back, urging him closer.

"To hell with it," Donovan muttered. "I can't hold back any longer either."

"Finally," she breathed out.

He smiled and then positioned himself between her spread legs, guiding his erection to the mouth of her pussy. And then he groaned, dropping his forehead to hers.

"Damn it." Disgust was evident in his tone.

Her eyes flew open in alarm. "What is it?"

"Forgot the condom," he grumbled. "Shit. Give me a second, honey. Don't move an inch."

She smiled as he scrambled hastily from the bed and yanked open the nightstand drawer to get a condom. In two seconds flat, he had the condom rolled over his rigid erection and he was back on top of her.

"Wrap your legs around me again," he said. "Just like before."

She eagerly did as he instructed and then wrapped her arms around his neck, anchoring him to her as he carefully pushed inside her.

Such exquisite torture. Inch by delicious inch, he consumed her. Pushing, stretching, until he was all the way in, his body pressed tight against hers.

She lowered one arm, cupping his jaw in her palm. It was rigid beneath her touch. Teeth clenched together as sweat beaded his forehead.

"Why are you torturing us both, Donovan?" she asked softly. "I know what it's costing you. And me. Don't be afraid of hurting me. I want this. I want you."

With an agonized groan, he withdrew and then rocked forward, forcefully planting himself deeply within her. She gasped at the fullness, overwhelmed, shocked. Pleasure splintered through her body, jagged, sharp and yet so *beautiful*.

He thrust again, harder, deeper. He arched over her, thrusting again, sliding into her with ease even as her body clutched at him like a greedy fist.

Her eyes glazed over, her vision dimming as ecstasy

blazed like an inferno. Tension coiled, low and almost vicious in her belly. But it was a delicious bite. An edge of pain that led to the most mind-bending pleasure she'd ever experienced in her life.

"Am I hurting you?" Donovan demanded, his voice hoarse and thready with his own passion.

"No, yes, God no. I don't know. But please don't stop. I'm so close, Donovan. So close!"

"I'm with you, honey," he said as he pounded into her again, shaking them both, the bed rocking with their movements. "We'll go over together."

"Yes," she whispered. "Together."

She closed her eyes, arching upward, into him, closer to him. Melting against his body even as she grabbed onto him, her anchor in the sudden, violent storm. The tornado she'd survived had nothing on *this*. She lost all sense of herself. Of everything around them or even where they were. All she could do was feel. And she never wanted to lose this moment. This sensation. Knew she'd never feel it quite the same as now. It would be different. Perhaps better in the future. But never like this.

And then she broke free of her constraints. She simply floated away, weightless, a dreamy haze overtaking her. It was like being intoxicated. Drugged. All rolled into one. But if there was ever a drug that mimicked this, there'd be no hope for it. Everyone would be hooked, doing whatever they could to get their next fix. And she'd be right there in line.

After a moment, a minute, an hour, she had no idea of how long, she became aware of Donovan's weight pressing her into the mattress. His heavy breaths against her neck. The loose, sated feeling in her limbs. The blankness in her mind. And the overwhelming sense of rightness.

Peace.

How long had it been since she'd truly felt peace? Her brow furrowed as she tried to muster the mental energy to think back to when she'd ever felt so . . . safe. Cherished. Had she ever?

"What are you shaking your head at, love?"

Donovan's gentle question brought her focus back to the present and she found him staring down into her eyes, his own thoughtful as he studied her.

She smiled. "Nothing. Nothing at all. I was just being fanciful and a little silly. And who could blame me after . . . that. I don't even know what to call it. Surely there aren't enough words in the English language—or any other language, for that matter—to adequately describe what we just had."

There was a note of wistfulness even she heard. Donovan's features softened, his eyes going warm and so very tender. He stroked a finger over her cheek, his weight still blanketing her, warm and so very reassuring.

"I think what it was is wonderful," he said simply.

She nodded her agreement and then he pushed himself up and off her, pulling free of her body. She shivered the moment he left her to discard the condom. She already missed his warmth. His touch. The void left her aching, however short the distance was.

She breathed an audible sigh of relief when he rejoined her, sliding into bed next to her and arranging the covers around them as he pulled her into his arms. She snuggled into his side and pillowed her head on his shoulder.

He kissed the top of her head, an affectionate kiss that made her giddy. They just felt . . . comfortable. Like they'd been lovers for years. They . . . fit. They just fit.

She yawned broadly and let her eyelids flutter closed as he stroked his hand up and down her arm.

"Go to sleep, honey," he said. "Here in my arms and know you're safe. If you dream tonight, dream only of me."

And she did. For the first night in many long years, she slept free of the constant worry and nightmares. There, in Donovan's arms, she dreamed of the most wonderful of things.

Love.

CHAPTER 27

DONOVAN hadn't slept the night before despite the fact that he was exceedingly sated and content. Making love to Eve was satisfying on an emotional level he'd never experienced before. And yet he'd remained awake, worried and pensive. In the predawn hours, just before finally sliding into sleep, with her curled into his arms, he'd come up with a plan.

Now all he had to do was act on it. And to do so required the presence of his brothers. Nathan and Joe's team. He briefly considered calling up Steele and his team, but Steele had enough to worry over with a new wife and child. Besides, it had already been decided that Nathan and Joe's team would regularly draw missions now. Perhaps even work as the front line with Rio and Steele's team acting in more of a support role.

Neither team leader would likely be happy with that assessment, but neither would they argue because they had wives and children to focus on now. The rest of their teams? Likely not as content as their team leaders to sit back and allow another team to take up their slack.

There was also the fact that it would take longer to pull

the other teams in, and Donovan didn't have the luxury of time. Not when Eve's stepfather was already close. He trusted Nathan and Joe's team and he trusted his brothers. They were more than capable of pulling off what Donovan had in mind.

He rose early, not wanting to disturb Eve. He made his phone calls in the kitchen, quiet so the others wouldn't hear. And then he made yet another call. The most important. He'd set the bait. Now all he had to do was wait for the target to fall into his lap.

CHAPTER 28

WHEN Eve awoke, Donovan was already gone, but then she'd expected as much. He was an early riser and he didn't seem the type to lie around in bed all morning. Even if the thought was very appealing to her. A morning spent snuggling in his arms? Heaven.

She stretched, smiling at the slight twinge of discomfort that made itself known in her body. They'd made love twice, the second very much at her initiation. Well, but also the first. She'd been impatient and unwilling to let him torture her slowly as he'd planned. The second hadn't been any more slow or more patient than the first, and she was feeling the effects this morning.

Not that she'd admit a thing to him. If she so much as hinted that she was tender, as he'd put it, he'd likely not touch her tonight and she was having none of that.

She yawned broadly and lay there a moment longer before finally pushing herself out of bed and toward the shower. She glanced at the bedside clock and moved more quickly toward the bathroom. She and Cammie were supposed to go over to the sisters-in-laws' today to shop.

A perfectly ordinary occurrence. Certainly nothing to get worked up over, but she found herself looking forward to it. It signaled freedom. Normalcy. And she wanted those things above all else. She also wanted a place within the ranks of the Kelly family. She envied the wives with her every breath for what they had. What she herself wanted.

How wonderful must it be to be a part of such a family? Loyal. Tight-knit. Everyone seemed to like one another. Did they ever fight? Squabble? Get pissy and mad in the heat of the moment?

She shook her head as she stepped into the shower and let the water work its magic.

Several minutes later, she combed through her wet hair and dressed. She had no makeup and she'd never lamented that fact. Until now. She wanted to look her best for the other women. It was a female thing. No one liked to be compared to a much prettier woman. But then she hadn't noticed the other women wearing much in the way of makeup. Sarah had light makeup on. Sophie had what looked like mascara and light lip gloss. She couldn't conjure the memory of whether Shea and Rachel had worn makeup.

Then she laughed at the sheer ridiculousness of her pondering whether Donovan's sisters-in-law had worn makeup to meet her.

Ah well, perhaps she could order what she needed today. She hated the thought that she was relying on Donovan to supply her and Cammie's and Travis's needs. But she was pragmatic enough to know that she had no way of paying for anything. Donovan had insisted that she use his credit card for whatever she wanted. She wouldn't buy much. Just the necessities. There would be plenty of time later. When she had a firmer grasp of just what their relationship was and *would* be.

For now? She was happy. And that was enough. Cammie and Travis were happy. Safe. Protected. Shielded. It was all she'd ever ask for. It was enough.

She padded down the hallway, peeking into the room where Cammie and Travis had slept only to find the bed empty. Apparently Eve was the only straggler this morning. Everyone else was up and likely in the kitchen.

She went in search of the others and indeed found them in the kitchen. Cammie and Travis were sitting at the table laughing. Broad smiles were on each face, their eyes glowing with happiness. It was a sight that took Eve's breath away.

Donovan was in the kitchen. He'd donned an apron and looked frighteningly domestic for a man who was built the way he was. The apron was completely incongruous with what Eve knew him to be. A total badass.

"Ah, Sleeping Beauty awakens," Donovan said, smiling as he looked up and saw Eve standing in the doorway.

Eve smiled back and then was distracted by Cammie's squeal of "Evie!"

She walked to where her sister sat at the table, nearly bouncing in her excitement. What a difference a few days had made in her health. She was back to normal. Her face no longer carried the strain of illness. Her eyes were not as haunted. She looked and acted just as a four-year-old should. Happy and carefree.

Tears burned the edges of Eve's eyes and she hastily blinked them away, not wanting to upset Cammie or Travis. Not when there was absolutely nothing wrong. Indeed, everything was exactly . . . *right*.

She glanced up to see Donovan discreetly motioning her to come to him. After brushing a kiss over Cammie's forehead and ruffling Travis's hair on her way by, she went into the kitchen, where Donovan was plating pancakes and bacon.

"You're going to have them spoiled," Eve said in amusement.

"Nah," Donovan refuted. "Besides, I like spoiling them."

She smiled, delighted by his words—and actions.

He lowered his voice, turning so Cammie and Travis wouldn't hear.

"I know I said I'd keep Travis with me today so you and Cammie could go over to visit with my sisters-in-law and have girl time, but I need him to go with you after all."

Eve's forehead wrinkled in concern as she took in the seriousness of his tone. "Is everything okay?"

He touched her arm, squeezing lightly in reassurance. "Everything is fine. It's just that my brothers and one of the teams are meeting with me here today to go over your situation. I'd rather Travis not hear. I don't want to upset him."

Eve frowned, glancing toward her siblings and then back at Donovan. "I understand not wanting to upset Cammie and Travis, but shouldn't I be here when you discuss your plan of action? This directly involves me—and them. I want to know what you have planned."

He pulled her into his arms, cocking her head back so she could look at him. His arms were wrapped firmly around her waist, anchoring her to his body.

"I want you to put it all out of your mind. I don't want you to worry about anything. The only thing I want you to focus on is having a fun day with my sisters-in-law and getting what you and Cammie and Travis need. Leave this to me, Eve. I don't even want it on your mind. Okay?"

She wanted to argue, but knew he had a point. Though she knew his command for her to keep her mind off it was pointless. How could she be thinking about anything else? Travis and Cammie needed her to be strong. They needed her not to show fear and to display confidence in Donovan's ability to handle Walt and any other complication that arose. But at the same time, such blind faith made her uneasy. Even as she knew she could trust Donovan. She did trust him. But she was terrified of her stepfather and his control. His reach. His influence and power. And it chafed her not to somehow be a part in whatever plan Donovan had hatched. Knowledge was power. Uncertainty just bred more fear, and she'd lived with fear for far too long.

Donovan pressed a kiss to her forehead. "Trust me, Eve. Let me handle this. I won't let him hurt you or Travis or Cammie. Especially Cammie."

She sighed reluctantly but nodded her agreement.

"You'll tell me after?" she asked in a low voice. "Later?"

He stared intently into her eyes, his own blazing with

sincerity. "Of course, Eve. I won't keep anything from you. No secrets. I want you to trust me. Can you do that?"

She nodded again and his expression eased.

"Now, go back over to the table and put on a smile for your siblings. Don't give them any reason to doubt you—or me. I want you all to have a good day. You and they will love my family just as they already love you."

"Okay," she whispered as she pulled away.

"Eve," Donovan called out softly as she started to walk back to the table.

She stopped, turning back to look at him.

"It will be okay. I know I'm asking a lot, but trust me."

Again she nodded and then turned back to her brother and sister.

Breakfast was enjoyable as Cammie kept up a constant stream of chatter over her excitement of getting to go to Charlotte's house and play with her toys.

Travis didn't express disappointment over the fact that he was now accompanying his sisters. Cammie's enthusiasm was contagious, and Eve could see Travis's pleasure in her excitement. They were all so used to being alone, of relying solely on one another, that it was baffling and yet pleasing that they now had others they could trust and socialize with.

Travis seemed every bit as eager for the visit, even if he would be the only male among the women. Maybe *because* he'd be the only male. She smiled over that and realized that if things worked out, he could do all the normal things teenage boys did. Go to school. Lust after girls. She cringed at the thought, but her brother was a very handsome young man. And he'd be even more handsome when he filled back out and put on the weight he'd shed over the last several months.

After breakfast, Donovan walked them over to Sophie's house, a sprawling log cabin that butted against the lake, as did the other residences that housed his brothers and their wives. It was already hot, but the breeze from the lake was refreshing and it had the makings of a beautiful summer day. It was easy to forget that just days before a tornado had ravaged the area.

Here in the isolated bubble created by the Kellys, the outside world was a whole different universe.

The women had already gathered at Sophie's house, with the exception of Rachel, who'd called and said she was running late because she had to change both twins. Sophie laughingly informed Eve that Rachel's boys timed everything together, and as a result they ran both Rachel and Ethan ragged.

Donovan kissed Eve, making her flush with embarrassment because he did so right in front of his sisters-in-law. Then he hugged Cammie and told Travis in a grave tone to watch out for his women.

But Donovan's sisters-in-law didn't look at all bothered by the fact he'd kissed Eve. In fact they all wore delighted, smug grins.

A few moments after the women were seated in the spacious open-concept living room, two laptops out and open, Rachel burst in, looking harried as she struggled with two squirming toddlers, one on each hip. Her diaper bag was slung cross-body and bulged in front of her so it didn't get in the way of the babies, but it was evident that she was about to lose her grip on one or both.

Travis rushed forward, reaching for one of the twins. Rachel gratefully relinquished one, and Eve watched in fascination as Travis cuddled the baby in his arms. But the baby—Mason?—was having none of that. He struggled upward in Travis's grasp and reached for Travis's face, his grubby fingers pawing at Travis's laughing mouth.

"I'm sorry," Rachel said in an aggrieved tone. "He has an obsession with people's mouths."

Travis chuckled. "It's not a problem. I'm used to children."

And yes, he was, since he'd been Cammie's primary caregiver for so long. Even when Eve's mother was alive, it was often Travis who shouldered the responsibility for his younger sister. Travis was too busy worrying over his mother to burden her with Cammie, and so he shielded both as much as possible. He'd taken on far too much responsibility at far too young an age. It was a fact that grieved Eve, but there was nothing to do for it now. What was done was done. But in the future . . .

She clamped down on her wayward thoughts, determined not to give voice to the overwhelming hope that bubbled up that Travis would have a better future. One where he was able to be what he was. A teenager with no responsibilities save for making good grades and keeping out of trouble. Not that she ever expected any issues in that quarter. He was too solid. Too responsible.

He was a good kid—no, a man. He was an adult before his time, but if Eve had her way, he'd rediscover his childhood from here on out.

"You look like you're a million miles away, Eve," Shea said in a quiet voice.

Eve's gaze flickered to where Travis was now across the room helping Rachel unload her things and playing with both of the boys now that they were out of their mother's grasp.

"Sorry," she said in a low voice. "I was just thinking."

Her gaze moved from Travis to where Cammie sat across the room in a corner obviously designated as the play area. She and Charlotte were chattering like two magpies and acting like they were long-lost friends. It sent warmth through Eve's heart that her brother and sister had found acceptance in this huge, loving family.

"Whatever it was couldn't have been pleasant," Sarah ventured.

Sophie leaned forward, her expression one of concern. "Is something bothering you, Eve? You can talk to us, you know. We won't betray your confidence."

Eve smiled. Loyal, all of them. And big believers in trust. And the thing was, Eve absolutely believed they were trustworthy. There was just something about the entire family that inspired one to believe in them and their intentions.

"It's just that Donovan had Travis come with Cammie and me after all because he was meeting with his brothers and one of his teams to discuss . . . me. My situation, I mean. And while I'm grateful that complete strangers are willing to help, I wanted—needed—to know what they were planning. What they're deciding."

Sarah nodded her understanding. Shea reached over to squeeze Eve's hand.

"That's perfectly understandable," Shea said. "I'd want to be included in any conversation that dealt with my future too!"

Sophie made a sound of disgust. "Typical men. Or rather typical Kelly men. They mean well, but their motto is to surround their women in bubble wrap and take on any and all threats in their stead. If they had their way, we'd forever remain ignorant of anything that could potentially harm us. And I love them for it, but it's still aggravating."

Sarah chuckled. "That about sums up Garrett in a nutshell."

Shea rolled her eyes. "So why don't you go back over there and demand to listen in?"

Eve's eyes rounded. "Oh, I couldn't."

"Why not?" Sophie challenged, a fierce, determined glint in her eyes. "Cammie and Travis can stay with us. I know you don't want to worry them, but it's equally obvious that you're worried sick and you aren't going to feel better until you know what's going on. I get that Donovan is trying to protect you. But he doesn't understand that not knowing is worse than being confronted with whatever his plan is."

Eve slowly nodded. "Yeah. That about covers it."

"So go," Sarah quietly encouraged. "We'll hang out here with Cammie and Travis. You can let us know when we have the green light to bring them back over."

"But you guys set this up for me—for us," Eve said. "It was nice of you, and Cammie and Travis do need things. Clothing."

"As do you," Sophie gently pointed out. "But leave it to us. We're the queens of Internet shopping, remember?"

Shea elbowed her sharply. "That's *my* title, thank you very much."

Sarah laughed. "At any rate, we'll take care of the essentials. We have your sizes. Shea and Sophie have excellent tastes in clothing. And we'll make sure we get Cammie and Travis what they need."

Eve wavered on the edge of indecision. But the encouragement—and blessing—she found in the other women's eyes gave her the courage to do it.

"Okay," she breathed out, pushing herself up from her perch on the couch. "I'll head over. I just hope it doesn't make him angry with me."

Sarah put her hand on Eve's arm and squeezed lightly. "Eve, I understand that you haven't had much reason to put your faith in the male species. But trust me when I say this. Donovan may not like that you want to know what's going on. But he'll understand even as his primitive instincts scream at him to haul you back to his cave by the hair, beat his chest and mutter *my woman* and wrap you in the bubble wrap Sophie mentioned."

Shea and Sophie broke into laughter. Even Eve had to chuckle at the image Sarah painted.

"But my point is, Donovan wouldn't hurt a hair on your head, nor would he hurt you emotionally. He's just not wired that way. Of all the Kelly men, he has the biggest, softest heart when it comes to women and children. He'd cut off his right arm before ever intentionally hurting you."

Eve smiled. "Thanks. I needed to hear that I think. I feel like such a ninny. I'm not usually. I stood up to my stepfather, though in the end it did me little good. I'm not a woman who just rolls over, but the last few months have taught me a lot about self-preservation."

"So go, then," Sophie encouraged. "We'll hold the fort down here and explain everything to Rachel, if she ever gets loose from the twin devils over there. I swear I don't know how such a sweet woman gave birth to Satan's spawn. It has to be Ethan who is to blame."

That got a laugh from them all, and then came Rachel's dry rejoinder from across the room.

"I heard that."

Eve quietly thanked them and then headed for the door,

glancing quickly back to ensure that Travis and Cammie didn't notice her departure. Sophie waved her on, nodding toward Travis and Cammie to assure Eve that they would be looked after.

Taking a deep breath and squaring her shoulders, she took off across the sprawling acreage nestled behind the walls of the compound. The sun was warm on her skin, and she inhaled the sweet honeysuckle-scented air. The Kellys had carved out their own little piece of heaven. Never mind that it was a high-security compound. They'd made it home. It *looked* homey.

If she looked past the training fields, the gun range, the landing strip, the helicopter pad and the austere stone building that was called the war room, the rest looked like a quiet neighborhood of newly constructed homes. Each unique in its own way with each occupant's unique fingerprint on it.

Two of the homes were log cabins, but Nathan and Shea's house was a quaint, small cottage-looking home. More distant from the others and surrounded by thick trees and flowering bushes. It was as if they'd separated themselves from the others while still being firmly immersed in the protective barriers to the outside world.

Ironically, Donovan's home was something she would have chosen herself had she had the ability to build the house of her dreams. It wasn't as rustic looking as the cabins occupied by two of his brothers. It was very Southern looking, with shutters on the windows and a front porch that encompassed the entire front and wrapped around on both sides. There was a swing suspended from the ceiling on the right side and there were flowerpots and hanging baskets, bursting with vibrant colors.

It looked homey and inviting. It wasn't just a house. It was a *home*. The inside was still stark and bereft of things that usually dotted a home. Knickknacks. Picture frames. Mementos. Comfortable-looking furniture. But then he'd mentioned that it had only recently been completed. Perhaps he just hadn't had time to see to the more intimate details of making his house a home. Or maybe he was simply waiting for the right woman to put her own stamp on his house.

She mentally kicked herself again over the direction of her thoughts. When would she learn not to get ahead of herself? She'd known the man for a very short time and she was already planning how to decorate their—his—house.

With a shake of her head, she traipsed around to the kitchen door. Donovan and his brothers were likely in the living room and she didn't want to just barge into the middle of it all. And they were all present and accounted for, judging by the number of vehicles parked in front.

No, she'd go in through the kitchen and ease her way into the living room. And insert herself into whatever plan it was that Donovan was hatching.

Quietly she opened the kitchen door and let herself in, being careful not to make any noise when she shut it behind her. In the distance she heard the murmur of conversation and she paused a moment, mustering her courage to brazenly walk in on the planning session.

"Ninny," she muttered.

She'd certainly not had any issues marching into the police station, not once but twice, and demanding action on her mother's behalf. She'd stood up to Walt time and time again, even though the result had been swift punishment. But she hadn't allowed that to deter her. Why was she being such a wuss now?

Because she was in love with him and she didn't want to do anything to make him angry with her.

It was a ridiculous reason, and if that was the way things worked in their relationship going forward, she seriously needed a kick in the head. She wasn't going to tiptoe through life worrying that everything she did would piss him off.

Having admonished her silliness, she set off toward the living room, the murmurs growing louder as she neared.

But what she heard next stopped her cold in her tracks.

"We call and set up a meet with Walt," Donovan said, presumably to the occupants of the room. "We dangle Eve in front of him. Hopefully his need for revenge is such that he'll take her and not focus on Cammie and Travis. I love those kids and the bastard is not getting his hands on them ever again."

Eve's mouth dropped open and she shook her head, sure she hadn't heard correctly. Her heart pounded and she instantly chided herself for jumping to conclusions. Obviously she hadn't heard right. She'd march in there and get to the bottom of this at once. Then she'd put her idiocy to rest.

But still, an icy hand clutched at her heart and with Donovan's next words, a sick, oily sensation snaked its way through her veins.

"She's highly unstable. Danger to herself and those kids. Walt will satisfy himself with her. I'm positive of that. He obviously is a control freak and has an ego the size of Texas. He'll want to punish her for defying him and upending his plans."

"And what do you plan to tell Cammie and Travis about all of this?" someone else asked. She couldn't identify his voice. Perhaps it was someone she hadn't met yet.

"They won't know," Donovan clipped out. "They'll never know. There's no need. I'll take care of them. They're mine now and I'll die before ever allowing harm to come to them. Physical or mentally."

Eve stood there stunned by the conversation unfolding just a few feet away. No. *No!* It couldn't be. Nausea welled, sharp and overwhelming in her stomach. Bile rose in her throat as she hastily backed away, wanting only to be away from so much hurt. Each word, like a dull knife, hacking her into tiny pieces until there was nothing left. No heart. No soul. *Nothing.*

Hands shaking, she managed to hurry back through the kitchen door, sucking in mouthfuls of fresh air. The inside had been stifling. She'd stopped breathing the minute she'd heard Donovan's cold, ruthless words.

He couldn't mean it. He couldn't! He'd just hand her over to her stepfather after all she'd told him? After all she'd shared?

But she'd heard it. Even after denying it to herself, she'd

heard correctly. The words couldn't have been clearer. It was no wonder he hadn't wanted her, Travis or Cammie here. He wouldn't have wanted any of them to overhear what he was currently plotting with his brothers. His team. People she'd thought were so kind and generous. People she'd thought she'd found a future with. A home.

She rushed back toward Sophie's, taking the longer, less direct route so she didn't walk in front of Donovan's house. So no one inside would see her.

No tears threatened. Not yet. She was too numb. Too devastated. But soon. She knew they would come. How could they not?

Oh God. Oh God. What was she supposed to do? She felt like the worst sort of idiot for ignoring her misgivings. For not trusting her instincts when her gut screamed at her to cut and run and keep on running. She'd been such a trusting, naïve idiot. And she knew better. She knew!

And yet she'd gone against everything she felt was the right choice. She hadn't trusted her instincts, and instead she'd trusted *him.* When she'd vowed not to make the mistake of trusting the wrong people. She'd known it would only lead to disaster, and she'd been right!

His sisters-in-laws' words floated back to her. The same words she'd heard from others since coming to this place. Donovan had a soft spot for women and children. But *especially* children. The statement had always been qualified by that addition.

Especially children.

He hadn't been in love with her. He hadn't cared about her. He loved Cammie and Travis. He cared about *them.* He wanted to protect *them.* Eve was just the extra baggage.

He wanted a family. Children. But he didn't want *her.* And that hurt more than she should have allowed it to.

Tears burned where before she'd been too numb to feel, to absorb the swift shock of pain and devastation that had swept over her as Donovan had calmly plotted her downfall. How easily she'd fallen into his hands. Easy. *Too* easy. She'd given him everything. Herself. Her trust. Her virginity.

Her love.

And all he wanted from her was the children.

She closed her eyes as she reached Sophie's door, too undone to simply walk in and pretend that nothing had happened. That her world hadn't just tilted on its axis and left destruction in its wake.

She thought back over every encounter with Donovan. It was always about the children. His concern had been for them first and foremost. Eve was just collateral damage. Someone he had to deal with in order to secure Cammie and Travis's future.

What was she supposed to do?

Her first thought was to run. To take Cammie and Travis and run as far and as fast as she could and never stop again. Never trust another soul. But . . .

She bowed her head, trying to get control of her raging emotions. They couldn't see her like this. They'd know. Cammie and Travis would know. And she couldn't let them find out what she'd heard.

The *but* was that Cammie and Travis were better off here with him. No matter what kind of bastard it made him to turn on her, to sacrifice her for her siblings. Hadn't it been what she was willing to do? Whatever she had to do to secure their future, she'd been willing to do. Even if it meant sacrificing her own.

But she could not—would not—go meekly back to Walt. She would not let herself be handed over like some sacrificial lamb. Donovan would protect Cammie and Travis. He may have betrayed her trust, but she knew he wouldn't betray theirs. There was conviction in his voice when he spoke to his brothers. No reason for him to lie when she wasn't there to hear. The truth rang in his words. He *did* love Cammie and Travis. And he wouldn't allow Walt to take them away. Maybe it made her stupid to believe anything good of him, but she believed wholeheartedly that of the two choices, Walt or Donovan, Donovan was the better choice for her brother and sister.

But *she* wasn't Donovan's choice.

Grief welled in her heart, nearly choking her as a knot grew in her throat.

She couldn't stay here. She had to go. But how would she accomplish it? How soon did Donovan plan to calmly hand her over to her stepfather? How much time did she have to come up with a plan of action?

And God, how could she possibly say good-bye to her only family? To the two people she loved most in the world and the only two people who loved her? How could she leave them with a man who'd so callously lie to and manipulate a woman who was at her most vulnerable?

The lesser of the two evils. It was how she had to look at the matter. She *knew* Walt would abuse them. No matter what Donovan had done to her, no matter how badly he played her, she knew deep down that he wasn't capable of hurting Cammie or Travis.

Just her.

And that hurt. God, it hurt more than she wanted to admit to herself. She loved him. And he'd totally shit on that love. All that flowery bullshit about treasuring her gift of virginity. How he must have laughed himself silly over her naïveté. But no, even in her anger and devastation, she didn't truly believe he got any real enjoyment out of betraying her. He was ruthless, yes. Perfectly capable of doing whatever was necessary to achieve his goal. She was a mission and he'd made it clear that when he took on a mission, he won.

He'd won, all right. He'd won what he wanted. Children. His own family. He just hadn't wanted her to be a part of that family.

And now she had to walk inside this house and pretend to his family, a family she'd foolishly believed she'd be a part of, that her heart wasn't breaking into a million jagged pieces.

CHAPTER 29

"EVE! Why are you back so quickly?" Sophie asked in a startled voice when Eve entered the living room.

It had taken every bit of strength Eve possessed to compose herself enough to calmly walk into Sophie's living room and act as though nothing was wrong.

Eve sank onto the couch before her legs gave out or gave her away by shaking uncontrollably. She mustered what she hoped was an abashed, slightly rueful smile.

"I couldn't do it," she lied. "I promised to trust him. He told me he'd tell me his plan once we were alone. Later. I want to give that chance to him."

And then she wondered if he did plan to tell her anything. Or would he lie? Perhaps it had been a misunderstanding and he'd explain everything later.

Don't be stupid.

She was already trying to justify his words. She had to snap out of it and think on her feet. Fast.

"Where did you go, Evie?" Travis asked with a frown. "I looked up and you were gone."

"I just needed some fresh air," she said, her second lie.

"My head was hurting. Maybe I overdid it or perhaps I'm not as over the bump to my noggin as I thought I was."

She hated lying, but she had to set up an excuse to not share Donovan's bed tonight. She couldn't do it. She could not make love to him knowing what he had done—what he was going to do.

And it wasn't a complete lie. Her head *was* throbbing. But not from her injury.

"I understand," Sarah said quietly so Travis wouldn't hear. "He'll tell you, Eve. Donovan is a straightforward guy."

The others nodded and it was all Eve could do not to scream at them. Not to tell them that it was all a lie. That they were a lie. The family she'd thought was everything she wanted was nothing more than a lie.

"Your head really does hurt," Rachel said shrewdly. "I can see the strain in your eyes."

"Yes," Eve admitted.

Shea sat down beside Eve and gripped her hand tightly. "I know you're worried, Eve, but please don't be. Everything will be all right. Trust in that. This family has faced the worst situations you can imagine. And we always come out on top."

Oh yes, Eve could well believe that. Ruthless. Cunning. Donovan was definitely a man who was victorious when he set his mind to a goal. Look at how easily he'd manipulated her.

"I'd rather go back . . ." She'd nearly said *home*, but Donovan's house was not her home. "I'd rather go back to Donovan's and take something for the headache. Will you call ahead for me, Sophie? I don't want to interrupt. Surely they've had enough time by now. Just let him know I wasn't feeling well and that Cammie, Travis and I are heading back over."

"Perhaps it would be better if they stayed," Rachel murmured. "We'll look out for them, and you need the time to talk to Donovan so he can ease your fears."

Already shattered by what she'd discovered, it wasn't hard for Eve's imagination to shift into overdrive. Was it a setup? Were Donovan's sisters-in-law in this with him? Did they plan to separate them so Eve would be a much easier target?

Sweat beaded her forehead and her head began pounding even more viciously.

"No," she said vehemently, and then regretted her forceful outburst.

The other women looked at her with concern. Fake? Or was it real? Eve didn't know what was real anymore. And she couldn't afford to assume any longer.

"No," she said in a softer, less challenging tone. "They'll go with me. We've taken up enough of your day. Perhaps another day. When all of . . . this . . ." She nearly choked on the words. ". . . is over we can get together again."

"We'll look forward to it," Sophie said in a resolute tone. "And Eve, it won't be that long. Once they form a plan, they'll be swift in carrying it out. Donovan wants nothing more than for the four of you to be free of worry and fear. He wants a life with you."

Eve nearly begged her to stop. To end the torture she was currently enduring. Every word, every lie that crossed their lips just twisted the knife even deeper into her heart.

Instead she rose, proud of how steady she was on her feet. She went over to where Cammie was still playing with Charlotte and extended her hand down.

"It's time to go, darling. Will you help Charlotte pick up her toys?"

Cammie looked disappointed, but she didn't argue. Travis came over and began helping both girls put away the toys they'd dragged out of the wooden toy box in the corner.

"I'll call Donovan now," Sophie said.

Eve directed a forced smile in her direction. "Thank you. I'll see you all later."

After a chorus of good-byes and Cammie hugging each of the women and Charlotte—twice—Eve headed out the door with Travis and Cammie right behind her.

"Is everything all right, Evie?" Travis asked anxiously. "Is your head hurting you badly?"

This time Eve's smile was genuine and she looked up at her brother, pain slicing through her chest at the thought of being separated from him.

"Just a little ache," she said. "But I'm sure I'll be much better when we get back h—to Donovan's," she amended.

Cammie slid her hand into Eve's as they walked the path back to Donovan's house.

"I like Cece," Cammie said as she bounced along, her ponytail flopping with her motions.

Eve smiled down at her. "I'm glad."

"Will I get to play with her again?"

Cammie's eyes brimmed with anxiety as she stared up at Eve.

This time she wouldn't have to lie.

"Yes, darling. You'll get to see Charlotte a whole lot more."

"We'll be cousins," Cammie said proudly. "That's what her mama said while you were gone."

Again the twist in her chest, robbing her of breath.

As they approached the house, Eve saw several vehicles pulling out of Donovan's drive. Either they had finished or Sophie's call had halted further discussion. It wouldn't do for Eve to be present while they plotted her demise.

Donovan came out the front, concern etched on his forehead as he stared at their approach. Sophie would have told him, of course. That she had a headache and was acting "off."

Eve sighed, bolstering herself for the hours ahead. She'd have to pretend that nothing was wrong. A simple headache. And a heartache that medicine couldn't fix.

"Eve, what's wrong, honey?" Donovan asked as he strode down the steps to meet them.

Cammie promptly put her arms up for Donovan to pick her up and he complied, but he positioned her on his hip, his gaze still firmly directed at Eve as though he were trying to pry her thoughts right out of her head.

"Just a headache," she said. "I thought I was better. Maybe I overdid it."

Guilt entered his eyes and she realized he was likely

blaming himself for the two nights of lovemaking so soon after her injury.

"Come inside and get comfortable," he said, urging her toward the door, Cammie still perched on his hip. "I'll get you something for the headache. How bad is it? Any blurred vision? Nausea or dizziness?"

He was making her dizzy with all the questions and heartsick that he could pull off such a meticulous deception.

"No. I'm fine. Really," she murmured as they walked inside.

A burst of cooler air hit her and she wavered precariously for a moment, unable to help her reaction.

Beside her Donovan muttered a curse, and he let Cammie slide from his grasp to stand beside him.

"Go with Travis, sweetheart," he directed Cammie. "I need to look after Eve."

Cammie sent her a concerned look, but then Travis stepped in and took Cammie's hand. "Want a snack?" he asked cheerfully. "Let's go rustle up something in the kitchen."

Cammie quickly forgot about Eve and perked up considerably upon hearing the word *snack*.

Donovan ushered her over to the couch, sat her down and then lifted her feet, removing the canvas shoes one of his sisters-in-law had provided. He pulled the ottoman over and propped her feet up and then slid onto the couch beside her, tilting her chin up with his fingers so he could look into her eyes.

"You look tired," he said. "How bad is the headache, Eve?"

It was growing worse all the time. She didn't have to fake that much.

"Would eating help?" he queried. "You didn't eat much at breakfast."

The thought of putting anything in her roiling stomach only made the turmoil worse. She shook her head. "Just let me sit here on the couch for a while," she said. "I'll be okay."

He didn't look convinced, and indecision racked his face. But finally he conceded. He got her to lie down and positioned a pillow underneath her head before retrieving a blanket from one of the closets and tucking it around her.

"Get some rest," he murmured before kissing her forehead. "I'll take care of Travis and Cammie while you sleep."

She closed her eyes, though she knew sleep wouldn't come. She didn't want it to. She had too much to ponder and she needed to be left alone to plot her course of action. Maybe today wasn't the day he planned to dispose of her. But tomorrow? How could she know?

CHAPTER 30

DONOVAN waited and worried. Something was bothering Eve. He was sure of it. When she'd returned from Sophie's she'd been listless, and lines of pain were etched on her face. He'd wanted to call Maren, but Eve had insisted she didn't need her. He'd tried to give her an injection, but she'd refused that too.

He'd even called Sophie back, demanding to know what had happened while she'd been over there, but Sophie had told him only what she'd related when she'd first called. That Eve wasn't feeling well and had wanted to go back to Donovan's.

She'd lain on the couch for most of the afternoon and into the evening, though he hadn't known if she'd truly slept. Her features had been too tense for him to believe she'd drifted off. Either that or her sleep was fractured with bad dreams.

He'd awakened her, wanting her to eat dinner with him and Cammie and Travis, but she'd refused that too. So she'd remained on the couch while he had a quiet dinner with the others and he'd soothed Cammie when she'd asked him what was wrong with Eve.

But he couldn't soothe himself.

After dinner, he put Cammie to bed with Travis and then went back into the living room to Eve.

"It's time for bed," he said in a soft voice as he sat on the edge of the couch close to her head. "Do you think you can sleep?"

She looked . . . unhappy. And that bothered him. But she nodded and allowed him to help her to her feet. He guided her into his bedroom, and she stiffened when he started toward his bed. Did she think he'd want to make love to her? Did she think him so insensitive that he'd place his wants and needs above hers?

"Eve, you aren't feeling well," he said gently. "I just want to hold you so you'll feel better."

She relaxed a little, but he could still feel the rigidity in her body as he tucked her into bed. Taking only time to take off his shirt and jeans, he crawled into bed next to her, automatically reaching for her.

For a long time she lay there, quiet, but he knew she didn't sleep. She lay in the crook of his arm, her head pillowed on his shoulder. But she stared sightlessly up at the ceiling and she hadn't relaxed.

After two hours in which neither of them slept, he finally turned to her.

"You're not resting," he said quietly. "You aren't sleeping. Let me give you an injection, Eve. You're in pain and it's not necessary. The medicine will help you sleep and take away the pain."

He could swear that tears flashed in her eyes, but the low light streaming from the bathroom wasn't enough for him to be sure.

Without waiting a response, he got up and went into the bathroom, where he kept one of the med kits. He prepared a syringe and then returned to the bedroom, where she hadn't moved from the place he'd left her.

She obediently rolled over, presenting her hip, and once he injected the medication, she rolled back, pulling the covers up over her body in an almost defensive gesture. He discarded the syringe and then crawled back into bed, worry for her nagging relentlessly at him.

She relaxed some as the medication took hold and he pulled her closer to him, pressing his lips to her clammy forehead.

Whatever was worrying her, he'd get to the bottom of it tomorrow. But then tomorrow was also the day he'd arranged the meet-up with her stepfather. That had to be done and out of the way. Only then could he move forward with her and prove to her that she was safe. That he'd never allow anyone to harm her or her siblings, nor would anyone ever take them away.

And then it occurred to him that for all her worry earlier and for her reluctance to leave him to discuss his plan with his brothers and KGI, she hadn't asked him about it. After securing his promise that he would tell her everything, she hadn't brought up the subject even once.

He frowned in the darkness. Was that what she was fretting over? Or had she simply forgotten once the headache had taken hold? Or was the headache a result of her stress and worry?

Tomorrow. Tomorrow he'd tell her everything. Just as soon as her stepfather was out of the picture for good.

CHAPTER 31

EVE was awakened by Donovan gently shaking her from sleep. Her eyelids fluttered open and she blinked the remnants of the drug-induced fog from her vision. She hadn't wanted the injection but recognized the futility of trying to sleep when she was so wrapped up in her anguish. She needed a clear head for today.

"How are you feeling?" Donovan asked in concern.

She sent him a wan smile. "Better."

She knew he didn't believe her, and she wasn't that good an actress. He looked reluctant but also grim and determined. It was the determination that frightened her. As though despite any misgivings, he was determined to go through with his plan. Did she glimpse a gleam of conscience in those eyes? Apparently not enough for him to second-guess his intentions.

"I have to go out for a while," he said. "But I'll be back soon. Rusty is coming over to stay with you awhile. Just until I get back."

She didn't ask where he was going. She didn't have to. Fear beat a steady rhythm in her chest. Her pulse thudded violently at her temples and she could feel the headache returning and with it the heartsickness that had filled her to bursting yesterday and well into the night.

"All right," she said quietly, her heart breaking with every breath.

He leaned down and kissed her forehead, leaving his lips there for a long moment.

"This will be over soon, honey. I promise."

With that, he drew away and got up from the bed, walking toward the door.

She waited only a few moments before rising to look out the window as he drove out of the compound. Then she turned quickly away and went to her bedroom to pack a small bag. Just enough to carry in a backpack. A few changes of clothing. The little cash she had from before. Her mother's jewelry.

She then went into the kitchen, knowing Rusty would show up soon. She dug out paper and a pen and hastily wrote a note for Travis and Cammie. When she had finished, her eyes burning with tears, she folded it and went to their room, where they were still sleeping.

She didn't remain there looking at them for long. It was too painful and she didn't want them to awaken until she was away. After a silent good-bye that ripped her heart right out of her chest, she propped the note on Travis's dresser where he would see it, and then she went to find one of Donovan's guns that he kept in a drawer by his bed.

CHAPTER 32

RUSTY pulled into Donovan's drive and parked her Jeep beside Donovan's truck just as he was walking out the door. He looked grim and resolved. Her nape prickled because she knew that look. Whatever shit was going down today was heavy.

Not that Donovan had volunteered anything in the way of information. He'd only said he needed her to come and stay with Eve while he "took care of business."

Rusty pitied the poor fool Donovan intended to take care of. Though none of her brothers was ever overly descriptive in their accounts of the missions they went on, she'd gleaned enough—and hell, she had eyes—to know that a Kelly man on a mission was a very scary thing to behold.

"Thanks for coming, Rusty," Donovan said. "I hope to be only a few hours, but I'll keep in touch. I don't want Eve to worry, so if you can keep her occupied and distracted I'd appreciate it. She wasn't feeling well yesterday. I think the stress is getting to her. She had a headache and I had to give her an injection so she could sleep last night. I left her in bed, so don't disturb her. I want her to . . . rest."

Rusty could see the very real concern reflected in Dono-

van's eyes. She reached out to squeeze his shoulder. It was
odd to be offering him comfort since he was usually the one
doing the comforting and reassuring in the Kelly family. But
he looked as though he needed it, and while he'd mentioned
the fact that he had to give Eve an injection to help her sleep,
he himself didn't look as though he'd slept a wink.

"I'll take care of things here," she assured him. "Now go
kick some ass so Eve and her siblings can move forward with
their lives."

No, he hadn't volunteered any information on the who
and how of his mission today, but she wasn't an idiot. She
knew it had everything to do with Eve's stepfather and that
Donovan would be making his move in short order. She only
wished she could be there to see the ensuing ass kicking.

The corner of Donovan's mouth lifted in a semblance of
a smile, but his expression was serious and his gaze focused.
Determined. He didn't acknowledge her statement that it
was Eve's stepfather he was taking care of, but neither did he
refute it.

He ruffled her hair and then without a further word, he
strode to his truck, got in and roared down the road toward
the main entrance to the compound. Rusty watched until he
disappeared, a cloud of dust kicking up in his wake.

They really ought to consider paving the roads inside the
compound.

She waved her hand in front of her face to clear the cloud
of dust that drifted back toward the house, and then she
turned and headed to the front door, quietly letting herself in.

But when she walked inside the living room, she stopped
dead in her tracks, staring in shock at the sight before her.

Eve, her expression just as grim and determined as Donovan's had been, was standing a few feet away and she was
holding one of Donovan's pistols. And it was pointed directly
at Rusty.

"What the hell?" Rusty demanded, anger surging, her
words biting in the silence.

"You're going to get me out of this compound," Eve said
calmly.

"What the hell for?"

There was genuine bafflement in Rusty's question. What the holy hell was going on here? She felt as though she'd stepped into an alternate universe. Had the entire world gone mad on her?

"Why isn't important," Eve said, her voice like ice.

Her eyes were cold, her expression inscrutable. But the gun never wavered in her grasp, and it made Rusty damn nervous.

"Um, Eve? Just so you know, that pistol doesn't have a safety."

If she sounded nervous, it was because she was. She was bloody well terrified. And Rusty didn't scare easily. But being on the business end of a loaded, aimed gun? Yep, that would do it.

"Then you better make sure my finger has no reason to accidentally pull the trigger," Eve said in an even icier tone.

Holy fuck. The world had gone insane. Rusty shook her head, certain that this was some bizarre dream she'd walked into.

"I don't understand," Rusty said quietly, trying to stall. But how? Donovan would likely be gone for hours. Her other brothers would all be with him, as would Nathan and Joe's team in all likelihood. There was no one to help her. No one to defuse the situation. Rusty was it, and if she didn't get Eve to see reason quickly, this was going to be one FUBAR situation.

Not to mention Donovan would have her ass if she allowed Eve off the premises. With her stepfather still a wild card, it wasn't safe for Eve to leave the confines of the high-security compound. Surely she had to realize that.

"All you need to understand is that if you don't do exactly as I tell you, I'll pull the trigger," Eve said in a cold voice Rusty didn't recognize at all.

Eve was one of the most gentle, soft-spoken women Rusty had ever met. This was so out of character for her that Rusty didn't even know where to begin. But whatever she did, she had to do it quick before this resulted in death. Her death.

"I'm mentally unstable, remember?" Eve taunted. "A danger to myself and to others. Surely you know that. It's in all the news reports."

"Bullshit," Rusty snapped. "Where are Travis and Cammie?"

Her response seemed to surprise Eve.

"They're staying here," Eve said, her voice cracking with emotion for the first time since Rusty had walked through the front door.

Here was a weakness Rusty could possibly exploit.

"You'd just leave them behind?" she asked incredulously. "If you do, you aren't the person I thought you were, Eve."

Pain drifted into Eve's eyes. And grief. Honest-to-goodness devastation. It was as plain as if Eve wore a sign on her forehead.

"I can help you," Rusty said in a low voice, one she hoped was soothing and convincing. "Just tell me what's going on. You have to know I'll do anything I can to help. I can call Donovan. He'll sort this out. Whatever it is, Eve. It can be solved. It's what my brothers *do*."

"Don't lie!" Eve demanded, fury lacing the explosive outburst. "Don't lie like everyone else has. At least be honest. That would be a novelty for sure."

Rusty sent her a look of genuine confusion. She had no idea what had prompted this craziness but whatever it was, it was not good. One only had to look at Eve to know this was a woman nearing her breaking point. It was only a matter of time until she snapped. Unless Rusty was able to come up with something fast, this was all going downhill in very short order. Hell, it already *was*.

"You'd really leave Cammie and Travis?" Rusty asked again, purposely making her tone soft and unaccusing.

Pain splintered through Eve's eyes. Hell, it made Rusty hurt to see the very real agony in Eve's expression.

"Of the two, their *father* or Donovan, who would you prefer for Cammie and Travis to be with? I *know* Walt will hurt them. No matter that Donovan betrayed me, I don't think him truly capable of hurting those children. He cares for them deeply. Me, not so much, since he plans to turn me over to my stepfather. The sacrificial lamb, so to speak, so he can protect Cammie and Travis."

Rusty couldn't have been more shocked if Eve had pulled the trigger and shot her where she stood. Her mouth gaped open as she stared back at Eve. It was then she realized that Eve believed every word that had come out of her mouth. Somehow, she'd gained the belief that Donovan had betrayed her—or would. How the hell was Rusty supposed to convince her differently? For that matter, what did she really know of the situation?

Donovan hadn't shared much about Eve, or his feelings for that matter. He'd been extremely possessive of Cammie and Travis and, Rusty had thought, of Eve as well. Had she been so horribly wrong about a man she called brother?

No fucking way. Which meant Eve had some fucked-up intel. The question was, how had she arrived at such a ridiculous conclusion?

Eve took a step forward, her eyes once more gleaming with resolve. She lifted the gun higher so it was aimed directly at Rusty's chest. A cold chill snaked down Rusty's spine. She was good at reading people. It was a skill that had served her well and had saved her ass on more than one occasion.

And right now she absolutely believed that Eve meant every single word of what she was saying. This was a desperate woman, making desperate choices. She had the gun to prove it.

Shit, shit, shit. What the hell was Rusty supposed to do?

She had no choice. She had to do as Eve asked, or rather *demanded.* It was too risky. What if Eve squeezed that trigger a little too hard in her effort to convince Rusty she meant business? Even if Eve had no intention of shooting Rusty, she could well do it by accident.

"Where do you want me to take you?" Rusty asked in defeat.

There was no triumph in Eve's gaze. No sense of victory. She just looked . . . *sad.*

"To the hardware store. I'll leave you there, but I'll need your Jeep. Sorry. I don't have a choice," Eve said in a low voice.

Jesus God, she was standing there pointing a gun at Rusty and threatening to shoot unless Rusty cooperated, and in the next breath she was apologizing for the fact that she planned to steal Rusty's ride.

Eve draped a shirt over the hand holding the gun and then motioned for Rusty to walk out of the house and back to her Jeep.

When they got outside, Eve directed Rusty into the front while she climbed in back and reclined on the seat so no one would see her head. But she angled the gun so it was pointed at the side of Rusty's head. Rusty would have to be extra careful going over any bumps because she sure as hell didn't want the gun accidentally discharging.

"Make sure you don't do anything to alert anyone when we leave the gate," Eve said in a low voice that was filled with purpose. "I know retinal scans are performed upon entering but that all you have to do to get out is punch in your key code from your vehicle, so there's no need to roll down your window or even pause. If you do, I shoot. It's that simple."

That simple? Jesus. Rusty was beginning to wonder if the reports had been right and Eve *was* mentally unstable. Because normal people didn't wield a gun and make threats.

But a desperate person did.

And whatever had driven Eve to her current level of desperation had to be bad. Rusty wasn't a fool. She knew Eve had strong feelings for Donovan. But she also knew that she wasn't as confident about her acceptance in the Kelly family yet. And who could blame her? Her life had been shit. Cammie's and Travis's lives had been shit. Rusty had been quick to condemn Eve for deserting her siblings, but it was in fact a selfless gesture on Eve's part. Rusty had seen the pain that had swamped Eve's eyes at the mention of leaving them behind. That kind of grief couldn't be faked. And yet she was leaving them. With Donovan. Donovan, who she was convinced would protect them from her stepfather.

The question was, why didn't Eve trust Donovan to protect her as well? What was it she'd said? That Donovan had betrayed her?

There were so many questions Rusty wanted answers to that her head was spinning. And she had no idea how to get those answers from a desperate woman pointing a gun at Rusty's head.

This was one time when she wished Sean were actually pulling his hover routine and were around. Rusty might not be sure of the cop or his intentions. And that kiss had certainly put a different spin on things. But she did know Sean was a damn good cop with a very caring heart. How many times had he gone to the wall for the Kellys? How many times had he done things that could well jeopardize his reputation and career in law enforcement in order to do the right thing?

Yeah, she could use Sean about now. He had a level head and he was loyal to his bones. He could talk Eve around. She was sure of it. He'd certainly talked down Rachel on more than one occasion when Rachel was at her most vulnerable and precariously close to a nervous breakdown.

Eve's break from reality certainly qualified in this instance. Rusty didn't believe for a moment the woman was crazy or mentally unstable. Emotionally unstable at the moment? Hell yeah. She'd apparently been thrown one hell of a curveball. Rusty just wished she knew what the hell had gone on in that house to make Eve resort to such desperate measures.

Rusty did as Eve had demanded. She'd keyed in the code and accelerated through the gates so the cameras would only pick up on Rusty in the Jeep. She'd even murmured a caution to Eve to get as low as she could. Hell, she was practically aiding and abetting the woman. Maybe she was the one losing her damn mind.

But she wanted to help, damn it. And she wanted to buy time to figure out what the hell was going on in Eve's head.

The drive to the hardware store was short. It wouldn't be opened yet, a fact that might work in her favor because one, she was supposed to be with Eve at Donovan's house, and two, someone noticing her in this early might question it. One of the perks of living in a small town. Everyone was up in your grill and in your business, and it wouldn't surprise her one bit if a concerned citizen called Sean or one of the Kellys to let them know someone was at the hardware store before opening.

She could only hope.

"Park in the back," Eve directed, as if she'd read Rusty's thoughts about someone noticing they were in this early. "I don't want the Jeep in sight, nor do I want anyone to see me getting into it."

Rusty did as she directed and pulled around back to the loading dock, where delivery trucks backed to the entrance to unload stock.

"What exactly is your plan, Eve?" Rusty asked curiously. "I mean, you're just going to leave me here?"

The two women got out but not before Rusty saw Eve's grimace and her look of regret. She was almost apologetic as she led Rusty inside—at gunpoint—and then directed her to find rope.

"I'm going to have to tie you up and leave you behind the register. Someone will find you soon. You won't have to be there for long. But I can't have you alerting anyone before I have time to get as far away from here as possible."

Rusty took down one of the coils of rope, picking the softer kind that wasn't so damn abrasive. If she was going to have a stint tied up behind the cash register, she at least wanted to be as comfortable as possible.

She turned to Eve, casting a wary eye at the gun in her hand. She damned the fact that the surveillance cameras were capturing it all on film. Just more trouble for Eve, who was already a wanted criminal. She cringed knowing there was little to be done this time. It was all there in vivid detail.

Why the hell was she sympathizing with a woman holding a gun on her? She needed her own head examined.

"Empty the register and get the money bag from the safe," Eve said quietly. "And tell your father I'm sorry. Truly I am. I haven't met him, but he's obviously a good man and he doesn't deserve this from me. But I don't have a choice. I have to survive. I won't go back to my stepfather. I'd do anything in the world to keep Cammie and Travis safe, but Donovan will protect them. I won't be the sacrificial lamb. I wouldn't survive a day back in his power."

Rusty moved slowly toward the cash register, opening it even as she reached down and unlocked the safe that held the cash reserves. Money she would have taken to the bank this morning when she came in to open. It was telling that she had no compunction about giving it to Eve. There was something about her quiet desperation and the fact that she kept apologizing that got to Rusty.

Her brothers would say her heart was too soft and that she had no sense of self-preservation. It wasn't that at all. She saw a woman completely and utterly devastated and fighting to keep her sanity intact. And to survive. Because whatever she thought, she was convinced that she was being given up to her stepfather.

She didn't have all the pieces to the puzzle yet, but she'd heard enough from Eve to realize that Eve believed Donovan was going to turn her over to her stepfather. And keep Cammie and Travis. Jesus, but this was one twisted-up mess.

She stuffed the cash from the register into the bag holding the other cash and then carefully slid it along the counter toward Eve. And then Eve, regret simmering in her eyes, motioned for Rusty to sit so she could tie her up.

"Eve? Can I ask you what happened? What this is all about? I'm not fighting you. You can talk while you're tying me up. But I deserve that much, don't you think? I helped Travis. I like him a lot. He was me when I was that age. I'm worried about him—and you."

Eve's features tightened, anger replacing some of the regret. "Donovan has a weakness for women and children but *especially* children," she quoted. They were words Rusty had heard many times over the years. It was frequently said about Donovan. "In this case he has a weakness for Cammie and Travis. He loves them. I believe that or I wouldn't leave them with him where I know they're safer. He'll protect them."

Left unsaid was the fact that Donovan's weakness only extended to Eve's siblings and not her, and Rusty knew that was absolutely untrue. But how to get Eve to see that? What the hell had gone wrong? How could she so horribly misunderstand Rusty's brother? Couldn't she see the man was not only in love with Cammie and Travis but Eve as well?

"It's what everyone says—what everyone knows," Eve continued before Rusty could protest. "Children are his weakness. His Achilles' heel. And I was just the means—collateral damage—to get what he really wanted. Children. A family. One that doesn't include me."

She broke off, grief choking her words, and Rusty could see her fighting tears with her every breath.

"That's crazy! Donovan would damn well protect you too!" Rusty said fiercely. "If you gave him the chance. It's not just those kids he wants, Eve. He wants you too!"

Eve held up a hand after securing the knot around Rusty's ankles. "Don't! Just don't. You'll only defend him, and his actions are indefensible. You'd side with him. I'd expect you to. He's your family—your brother. I'm not. I know where your loyalty lies and it's not—and *shouldn't* be—with me."

"Bullshit!" Rusty snapped. "I'll help you. Whatever you need, Eve. We'll work this out. Let me help you if you won't let Donovan. But you taking off like this is not the answer and you know it! You're scared shitless. You don't want to hurt me. You sure as hell don't want to shoot me. You keep apologizing, for Christ's sake. Hardened criminal you aren't, and you sure as hell aren't mentally unstable. That's bullshit and I don't believe it for a minute."

Eve's expression saddened and the anger left as she gazed thoughtfully at Rusty.

"Even if I thought I could trust you, I couldn't—*wouldn't*—put you in any danger. You're right, Rusty. You were kind to Travis and I'll always appreciate that. You have a good heart, but I can't let you help me. It's too dangerous. My stepfather would kill you without thought. And as I said, your loyalty belongs to your family. Not me."

"That's bullshit!" Rusty repeated, frustration grinding

her jaw until her teeth ached from it. "No matter what you think you know, there is *no way* Donovan would throw you under the bus like you're saying he has. No fucking way! What can I say to make you believe that? If you won't believe in him, will you at least believe in me? You have to trust someone, Eve. Nobody can make it alone. We all need someone at some point. God, I learned that lesson the hard way, and thank God the Kellys were too stubborn to let me throw their kindness back in their faces."

Eve smiled faintly as she wound the rope around Rusty's wrists, tying her hands behind her back. Rusty craned her neck, staring up at Eve, looking for any sign that she was getting through to her. God, she couldn't let Eve walk out that door and into God only knew what kind of hell awaited her.

"I wish Donovan were as admirable as you in his loyalty," she said sadly. "Donovan is only loyal to *his* cause and *his* interests. And in this case, his interest is in my brother and sister. He's ruthless. Oh yes, he's utterly ruthless when it comes to protecting what he considers his. I could admire that if it weren't aimed at me and at my expense. It's the *only* reason I'm leaving Cammie and Travis with him. I can't protect them. God, I wish I could. I'd do whatever I could to ensure their safety and well-being. But I can't. You're right that everyone needs someone. And Travis and Cammie need *him*. I *do* know he cares about them and he'll protect them from Walt. Even if he sacrifices me in the process. And that hurts, but it's at least a relief that he's willing—and able—to take care of them when I can't."

She went silent a long moment as she finished securing the bonds around Rusty's hands and feet. Then she stood, reaching for the money bag on the counter.

Rusty was trying to process Eve's impassioned speech. The conviction—and resignation—in her words. She couldn't wrap her mind around what the hell Donovan had done to drive Eve to such a desperate—and selfless—act. Eve was utterly convinced that she was being handed over to her stepfather by the only person she'd allowed herself to trust. Rusty couldn't even imagine the pain Eve was experiencing.

True or not, Eve believed it wholeheartedly, and it broke Rusty's heart for this fragile woman who'd been handed far too much hurt in her life already. This was, Rusty believed, the final straw. Eve looked utterly defeated. Hopeless. And resigned to an uncertain fate.

"Do me one favor, Rusty," Eve said in a husky voice laced with tears and knotted with emotion. For a moment she remained silent, obviously grappling with the words she wanted to say. "Don't let Cammie and Travis forget how much I love them. Don't ever allow them to think I left them willingly. Make sure they're happy and loved. *That's* how you can help me."

Tears burned Rusty's eyes as Eve walked toward the back of the store. Never had she felt so helpless. Not even when she'd been a surly teenager on her own, desperate for her next meal and fearful of the lengths she'd have to go just to survive.

Eve was utterly devastated. She was broken and defeated and she left with the weight of the world on her shoulders. She believed—absolutely believed—that Donovan had betrayed her.

Had he? An uneasy sensation crawled up Rusty's spine. She knew well that Donovan could be ruthless, as Eve had just said. But how ruthless? Could he really have planned to sacrifice Eve in order to ensure Cammie and Travis's safety?

She shook herself from her thoughts and leaned back, stretching her bound legs upward toward the button that triggered a silent alarm. Now wasn't the time to ponder the what ifs. No matter what Donovan had done—or what Eve thought he'd done—Rusty had to get help and fast. She couldn't let Eve walk into the hands of a monster.

She just prayed that Donovan had already taken care of the matter and that Eve's stepfather was no longer a threat. Because now Eve was alone and vulnerable, and worse, she thought that she'd been betrayed by the man she'd put all her faith in.

CHAPTER 33

WALT Breckenridge watched with smug satisfaction as Eve ducked out the back of the hardware store and slid behind the wheel of the Jeep that she and the other woman had arrived in.

He'd known the little bitch had lied about her involvement with his children and Eve. He hadn't swallowed that bullshit story about Travis working a few days and then disappearing. And now, Donovan Kelly had arrogantly demanded a meeting with Walt in which he planned to discuss handing Eve over to him in exchange for Walt backing off Travis and Cammie.

Kelly had fed him a bullshit story about how he feared for Travis and Cammie's safety. That he was well aware of Eve's history of mental illness and that she'd gotten worse and he feared—as did Walt—that she was a danger to not only herself but others.

He played the sympathy card, commiserating with Walt about his troubles with Eve and expressing his regret over the loss of his wife, made worse when Eve went off the deep end and kidnapped his children and how desperate he must be to get them back.

And yes, it had been Eve he'd offered up, claiming he wanted her to get the help she needed from her caring step-father and that once he was assured that Eve was taken care of and he knew it was safe for the children to go back, they'd meet and arrange for Travis and Cammie to return home with Walt.

Complete and utter garbage.

Did they think him a fool? He'd researched the Kellys and their do-gooder organization, KGI.

It was a trap, no doubt inspired by Eve's lies and accusations. He wasn't falling for it and now Eve, the dumb bitch, had fallen right into his lap. She was making things far easier than he'd even imagined. But she'd never been that intelligent. Stupid. Tenacious. But not smart. Certainly no match for his superior intellect. And now he had her.

Now he'd have what he most wanted. Revenge. He'd make her pay for all she'd done. He'd put her away and ensure no one ever believed her outrageous accusations. Then, and only then, would he get his children back from the Kellys. He had far more power than they would ever dream of having. Money bought a lot of privilege. And it sure as hell bought protection.

Eve would have neither of those things, and by the time he was done with her, she'd wish she'd never crossed him. And he would hear an apology from those lips, right before he wrapped them around his dick.

Satisfied that, for now, Cammie and Travis would wait, he climbed into his car, his focus on his immediate goal. Eve. A rush invaded his veins at the thought of her at his utter mercy. He'd enjoy every single moment. Eve? Well, he doubted she'd enjoy it as much as he would. But she didn't matter. She never had.

He wanted her to suffer.

He wouldn't be as easy on her as he was on her pathetically weak mother. Her killing had been too easy. No challenge whatsoever. Eve, on the other hand, had proven to be more of a challenge than he'd imagined. He'd underestimated her once. He wouldn't make the same mistake again.

He wouldn't kill her because, as with her mother, that would be too easy. He wanted her to pay. And pay she would. He wanted him to be what she saw when she closed her eyes. What she dreamed. And know that there was no escape. That her fate was solidly in his hands.

With a satisfied smirk, he pulled out of the area that had provided cover for his vehicle—a rental that couldn't be traced back to him—and fell in behind the Jeep.

She was being careful. Not speeding. No, she wouldn't want to draw undue attention to herself or risk being pulled over by the police, and that wouldn't fit his plans at all. He had no desire to involve the law. Not here. Not where he had no influence and power.

A wreck. An abandoned vehicle. It would appear as though she wrecked and then ran. And then he'd make his meeting with Donovan Kelly and he'd play by Donovan's rules. For now. After Eve was taken care of and was in a place where she wouldn't be discovered, no record of her whatsoever, he'd return for his children.

Eve would simply disappear. Another person lost in the system. An unexplained disappearance blamed on the fact that she was on the run and mentally ill. The Kellys would likely investigate, but even they wouldn't be successful in uncovering her whereabouts.

And with her out of the picture for good, there was nothing to stop Walt from reclaiming his children.

Travis would also pay for his part in aiding Eve, but he would be brought to heel with the threat of Cammie. He wouldn't do anything that would cause her harm. In that, he and Eve were alike. A product of their weak, mindless mother. But Cammie was younger and more easily molded into what Walt wanted. And when Travis was older and less manageable, well, tragedy would strike the Breckenridge family once more. Travis would succumb to the same mental illness that Eve had been diagnosed with. An unfortunate hereditary trait passed to them from their mother. And then he and Cammie would be alone, and he'd mold her into the perfect daughter.

CHAPTER 34

RUSTY breathed a huge sigh of relief when she heard a noise from the rear of the store. The police would have responded to the alarm she triggered, though they wouldn't just waltz in the front of the store without knowing what they were walking into.

"I'm up here!" she yelled out. "It's clear. This is Rusty Kelly. My dad, Frank Kelly, owns this store. I'm tied up behind the register. I'm the only one here."

She knew they wouldn't take her at her word, because for all they knew she had a gun to her head and was being forced to call out to them. But maybe it would speed the process along a bit if they at least knew where she was.

She struggled to right herself so she could at least shove herself up to a standing position so they'd see she was alone when they entered the sales area. She could lean against the counter if she could just manage to get there!

It took considerable squirming and leg bending to achieve her goal, but she was finally able to hoist herself, nearly falling just as she gained her feet. She pitched herself sideways so the counter would break her fall and winced when the edge hit her squarely in the ribs.

Sucking in a breath to steady herself, she called out again. "I'm here and alone. I'm standing behind the register."

A few moments later, Sean appeared from the back. He cut the corner sharply, his gun raised. He quickly glanced in Rusty's direction and she saw a flash of relief in his eyes before he rapidly did a thorough sweep of the area, gun still up and grasped tightly in his hand.

Evidently satisfied that there was no danger, he strode behind the counter, fury registering in his eyes as he saw she was bound hand and foot.

"What the fuck?" he growled. "What the hell happened, Rusty? Are you hurt? Did that son of a bitch hurt you?"

"I'm fine," Rusty said in a calm voice. "But, Sean, I need you to hurry. Eve is in terrible danger."

Sean's brow furrowed even as he started yanking away the ropes that secured her wrists. As soon as her hands were free, he knelt and untied her legs as she rubbed feeling back into her numb fingers.

When he was finished he grasped her shoulders, forcing her to look squarely at him.

"What happened? I want to know everything, and don't leave a single word out."

He paused a moment and stared harder at her.

"Are you sure you're all right? Goddamn it, Rusty. You scared the ever-loving fuck out of me. I thought . . ."

He broke off with a shake of his head. As if he had said too much or was going to.

"It's a long story and we only have time for the abbreviated version, but yes, I'm all right. She didn't hurt me."

"She?" Sean asked incredulously.

"Eve," Rusty murmured, cringing in advance for the explosion that would surely follow.

Sean's eyes darkened with fury. "Are you telling me *Eve* tied you up and left you in the store? How? And why?"

Then his gaze lighted on the still-open cash register and then down to the safe that was wide open.

"No," he said, shaking his head. "No fucking way. She robbed you?"

"At gunpoint," Rusty muttered.

Sean went white. For a moment Rusty worried he might do something crazy like hit the floor. His knees buckled and then he reached out to touch her again. He feathered a hand over her face, his fingertips softly grazing her cheekbone.

Then he closed his eyes and when he reopened them, his gaze was haunted and filled with regret.

"This is going to kill Van," he said quietly.

Rusty blew out her breath. "There's a lot you don't know. Hell, that I don't know, for that matter. But we have to get in touch with Donovan like now. He's going to lose his mind when he hears this story. I know he was going to deal with Eve's stepfather today and I hope to hell he's already done whatever it is he was going to do because if not, Eve is in a lot of danger."

Sean's gaze narrowed. "You sound awfully worried about a woman who held a gun on you while she robbed the store of all its cash."

"It's complicated," Rusty said with a sigh.

"Then uncomplicate it and tell me the whole story."

She gave him a quick, condensed rundown of the morning's events, starting with when she walked into Donovan's house and found Eve pointing a gun at her. But when she got to the last, she paused and grabbed Sean's arm.

"She thinks he betrayed her, Sean. I have no idea how in the hell she got that idea, but you didn't see her. You didn't hear her. And she kept apologizing, for fuck's sake. For taking my Jeep. For stealing money from a man she hadn't even met."

"Whoa, wait. Back up a minute. Eve thinks Donovan was going to turn her in to her stepfather?"

He sounded as aghast as Rusty had felt when she'd listened to Eve's accusations.

"She believes it," Rusty said quietly. "God, Sean. I hurt for her. She was devastated. Completely defeated. She loves him and yet she thinks—she knows—he betrayed her."

"That's crazy," Sean refuted.

"To you and me, yes. But Sean, she absolutely believes it. I don't know what happened to make her think it, but I saw the conviction in her eyes. I heard it in her voice. She was destroyed, and even more destroyed that she was leaving Travis and Cammie behind. And yet she trusted that Donovan would protect them. She thinks that she was just the means of Donovan getting what he really wanted. Kids. A family. One that didn't include her. I'm telling you, Sean. If you could have seen and heard her, you wouldn't be pissed over what she did. I knew she had no intention of shooting me. I was more worried that she would do it accidentally. I offered to help her. I wanted to help her. Because I couldn't stand to look into her eyes and see so much pain that it took my breath away. And you know what she said?"

"What?" Sean asked gently.

Rusty hadn't even been aware that he'd pulled her closer to him and that even now his hand was stroking up and down her back in a gesture of comfort. She had the ridiculous thought that she'd like it if he pulled her into his arms. But she shook off that moment of insanity and refocused on the matter at hand.

"She said that she couldn't, that she wouldn't involve me because it was too dangerous and she didn't want anything to happen to me. When I asked her why she was leaving her brother and sister, she said that of the two, her stepfather or Donovan, whom would I prefer they be with? That she knew her stepfather would hurt them, but she didn't believe for a moment that Donovan would do anything but love and protect them even if she wasn't included in the picture. Damn it, Sean. She walked away because she thought Donovan was going to work a trade. Eve for the kids, and she was just collateral damage. She believes that with all her heart. And it breaks mine."

This time Sean did pull her into his arms and hugged her gently. She could feel his breath against her hair and she closed her eyes, savoring the warmth—and comfort—of his body.

"This is going to destroy Donovan," Sean said in a grim voice. "How long ago did she leave, Rusty? How much of a head start does she have?"

"I hit the alarm the minute she left. You got here in about five minutes, I'd say, so she hasn't had that much of a head start."

"Okay, then here's what I want you to do. You get in touch with Donovan. Figure out how to tell him. I'll put a BOLO out for your Jeep and Eve and get everyone I can on the case so we locate her as soon as possible."

"Thanks, Sean," she said softly.

His brow wrinkled in confusion as she pulled away.

"What for? For doing my job?"

She shook her head. "For not jumping to conclusions when you learned what Eve had done and for looking for her instead of swearing out a warrant for her arrest."

His eyes narrowed. "Do you think so little of me, Rusty?"

She shook her head even more adamantly. "No. But you're a cop, Sean. Your duty would be to arrest her for a crime that she did, in fact, commit. Kidnapping. Armed robbery. I'm sure there are a dozen other charges that I'm not even considering. Someone else wouldn't have listened to me and they wouldn't have just accepted what I said as fact. And they would have adhered to the letter of the law and arrested her as soon as she was located. You won't do that. Not until you have all the facts."

CHAPTER 35

"I don't like it," Donovan said grimly as he watched Walt Breckenridge drive away. He turned to his brothers, seeking their assessment. They didn't look any happier than he was.

It had been too fucking easy. And Walt had worn this smug, superior smile and Donovan could swear the man was laughing at them all. Was he that arrogant or was Donovan not getting a huge missing piece of the puzzle?

"I need to get home. This worries me. I want to make damn sure that Eve and Cammie and Travis are safe. Eve wasn't doing that well when I left her, and I'd hoped to bring her good news today so she wouldn't have cause to worry, and now I don't know what the hell to tell her."

"We'll get him," Garrett vowed. "He'll fuck up and we'll nail his ass to the wall."

"And until then we have to keep careful watch on Eve and her siblings because I don't trust the bastard not to make a grab for them. He's too arrogant. He's far too self-assured. He thinks he's untouchable. By us. The law. Anyone. And the asshole probably does have at least a few policemen in his pocket. Up the chain, if I had to guess. It's why Eve never got anywhere when she went to the police for help."

"The entire situation sucks balls," Joe said with a scowl.

None of his team looked as if they felt any different.

"He hates women," Skylar observed.

The others turned to her in surprise.

"I wouldn't say you were wrong, but what makes you say that?" Joe asked his teammate.

"It was pretty damn obvious," Edge growled. "He was pissed that Skylar was here. That she held a position of power. And he didn't like that she could kick his fucking ass if she chose to."

A glimmer of a smile curved Skylar's lips. "That about sums it up. He looked down his nose at me in this superior way and when I didn't cow, it pissed him off. When he figured out that I wasn't intimidated by him, it made him even angrier. He feels women are inferior. His wife. Eve. Likely Cammie as well, though he has a fixation with her that didn't extend to his wife or Eve."

"You sound like a shrink," Nathan muttered.

Donovan smiled. Yeah, Nathan would have issues with psychoanalysis. There'd been plenty of people wanting to pick his mind apart when he'd returned home after months of captivity and torture.

"I was a psychology major," Skylar said cheerfully. "Sam knows."

Nathan glowered at his brother as if it were a betrayal for him to hire a woman for Nathan's team who had a degree in psychology.

Sam chuckled. "I didn't hire her because of her psychology degree. I hired her for her ability to kick some serious ass."

"That she can," Edge defended.

Skylar sent him a sharp glance that suggested she didn't need him to defend her. The two had become close friends now that they roomed together. Donovan thought it was a prime example of the odd couple. Edge was a mountain of a man, muscled, tattooed, quiet, but like Swanny, when he spoke, others paid attention.

Skylar was his complete antithesis. Bright, cheerful. She had a sunshiny personality. If it weren't for the fact that Donovan knew firsthand her ability to kick a man's ass even if he was twice her size, he would have even called her perky. But somehow a woman who could take a man down in two seconds flat and have him begging for mercy didn't qualify as perky.

Could a cheerleader be a Rambo-ette? Because if so, Skylar deserved that moniker. Although she might be insulted to know Donovan was comparing her to a cheerleader. It wasn't an insult, but some women took it as such. Cheerleaders were actually damn good athletes. They had to be to perform the feats they pulled off.

"So what are we going to do about Breckenridge?" Sam asked, bringing the topic back to what was most important. The safety of Donovan's family.

"He was damn careful about doing anything that could be perceived as a trade. Eve for the kids," Ethan said. "I swear he knows we were trying to set him up. He didn't buy the concerned-citizen bit, but on the other hand, a legitimate father in distress would not have been so calm about agreeing that Eve needed help before the children were allowed back home. What the hell kind of parent agrees to that? If he'd been for real, he would have had the police so far up our ass we would have had the imprint of their badges for a week."

"Exactly," Donovan confirmed. "He does *not* want police involvement. But neither did he do or say anything to incriminate himself. He thanked us for our concern and then agreed that getting Eve the help she needed was the first priority. That's bullshit. As a father his first concern should have been making damn sure his children were okay. He should have demanded to see them. And then agreed to do whatever the fuck we wanted so he could get them back. Instead he leaves with this 'I'll be in touch' bullshit? Like he needs time to think about it?"

"More likely he needs time to figure out a plan to get both Eve and the children. Punish Eve. Get the children back under his thumb. Eve too, for that matter," Garrett muttered.

"The hell that's happening," Donovan growled.

"So what's the plan?" Skylar asked.

Donovan looked at Nathan and Joe and then to their teammates, Swanny, Edge and Skylar. "I want him under surveillance twenty-four-seven. I don't want him to take a piss without us knowing about it. Phone calls monitored, taps, tracking devices. The works. And I want it done yesterday. Find the son of a bitch and make sure *we're* so far up his ass he can taste what *I* had for breakfast."

"I think we should meet over at Mom's," Sam said.

"What the hell for?" Ethan demanded.

"Because the compound is safe. Ma and Dad still live outside. I want to make damn sure they know the situation and that they're protected. Until they move inside the compound, they're going to be a target for anyone wanting to strike out against us. We can meet over there and plot our next move. Not even someone as arrogant as Walt would try to make a move on a house full of cops and KGI. But you can bet your ass he's already trying to uncover our weaknesses. And Ma and Dad are big-ass weaknesses because we'd do anything it took to prevent harm from coming to them. So yeah, we're meeting there; make sure there's plenty of protection. Nathan and Joe's team can get set up on Breckenridge."

"I agree with Sam," Donovan said. "I'll go get Eve, Cammie and Travis, although, Sam, you think Soph would mind if Cammie stayed with her? Travis is old enough and he deserves to know what's going on and what we're up against. Cammie, however, is too young to understand and I don't want her frightened. We need to explain everything to Eve— and Travis. I promised Eve I'd tell her what was decided yesterday, but she wasn't feeling well. She's starting to fray at the seams. The stress and fear are getting to her, and that pisses me off."

Sam frowned as if just remembering that the wives were on the compound alone. High security or not, he wouldn't have liked the idea, and judging by the looks on Donovan's brothers' faces, they'd come to that same realization.

"I'll call Steele, Cole and P.J. Ask them to go out and stay with the wives inside the compound," Sam said. "If Dolphin, Baker and Renshaw are close, they can come as well, but I know Cole and P.J. can be there in half an hour tops."

"Good call," Garrett said in a grim voice. "I don't like leaving them alone, but I don't want them mixed up in this clusterfuck. Bad enough Mom and Dad will have to be in the middle of it all."

"As soon as we get them moved into the compound, we can all breathe easier," Ethan remarked.

The others nodded their agreement.

"You may as well let Rusty tag along," Nathan said in amusement. "She has a personal stake in this and she'll find a way in whether we let her or not. She's not going to stay put with the wives under lock and key."

Donovan chuckled. "Yeah, I'll let her come too. She likes Eve and Travis. And they like her. Today is going to be stressful enough. Rusty can provide a distraction for them if nothing else."

Joe snorted. "As if you'll have a choice."

"Let's get moving," Nathan said in his command voice.

Donovan was proud of the long way Nathan had come. He'd matured faster than he should have had to. When he was still in the army, in a lot of ways he and Joe had both been cocky kids. But then Nathan had been captured and listed as MIA, while Joe had taken a bullet that had shattered his leg.

It had been at the end of their tour, just before they were going to hang it up and go to work with their brothers at KGI. There had been times when Donovan had wondered if they'd ever get Nathan back. Truly back.

But here he was. Him and Joe both. Assuming command of their own team, and a damn good one from the looks of things. Rio and Steele were hard acts to follow, but Nathan and Joe would soon give both team leaders a run for their money.

"Doesn't anyone ever answer their goddamn phones?"

Donovan whirled around to see Sean Cameron stride into the restaurant where they'd arranged to meet Walt Breckenridge. The look on Sean's face made Donovan's blood run cold. His brothers came to attention, every single one of them tense and ready to explode into action.

"We've got big problems," Sean said tersely. "Did you take care of Breckenridge? Is he out of the picture?"

"No," Donovan said carefully, dread hitting him squarely in the gut. "Not at all. What's the problem?"

"Eve's the problem," Sean bit out. "She pulled a gun on Rusty when Rusty got to your house. She forced her to drive her from the compound to the hardware store, where she made Rusty empty the safe and cash register. She then tied Rusty up and left her behind the counter and took off in Rusty's Jeep. Oh, and she left Travis and Cammie at your place."

CHAPTER 36

TRAVIS read the letter Eve had left on the dresser in utter disbelief. His hands shook violently and he thanked God Cammie was still asleep. What were they going to do? Eve had *left* them. He didn't believe for a minute that she'd callously deserted them. Nor did he believe the lies she'd written, that they were better off with Donovan and that she didn't want him to worry about her.

It was a good-bye. The finality—and sadness—to the words on the note instilled aching grief in his heart. He was afraid for her. What if his father found her? What if he'd already found her? The thought sent a chill bone-deep through his body.

Here, she was protected. Donovan wouldn't allow anything to happen to her. What had happened to make her take off on her own?

He knew she was protecting him and Cammie—just as she'd always done. But why leave? It didn't make sense. What had driven her to this act of desperation? What did she know that he didn't? What hadn't she told him?

Rusty burst through his door just then, her glance going

toward the bed. Then she grimaced when she took in Travis's expression and the note he held in his hand.

"You know," she murmured.

"What do *you* know?" Travis demanded. "Do you know where she is, Rusty?"

Rusty sighed. "No, I'm sorry, I don't. But we'll find her, Travis. I swear to you we'll find her. Sean is letting Donovan know. Believe me when I say my brothers on a mission is a scary-as-shit sight."

"I don't understand," Travis said, allowing his frustration to leak into his tone. He was barely managing to keep it under control. He was scared. More frightened than when it had been just the three of them on the run, constantly looking over their shoulders and worried that they'd be discovered at any moment.

But they'd been together. And now Eve was God-only-knew where, and he and Cammie were just supposed to stay here with Donovan and have a happy life when Eve wasn't in the picture.

To hell with that. If this was what bought them security, then he didn't want it. He'd rather take his chances—with Eve—with his family intact, even if it meant running for the rest of their lives.

Rusty put her hand on his shoulder as if sensing the turmoil of his thoughts. "We'll find her, Travis."

He looked bleakly at her just as Cammie stirred and called out softly.

"Trav?"

Travis stared hard at Rusty, telling her without words not to tell Cammie what was going on. If Travis had his way, Cammie would never know. Eve would be found. Excuses would be made for her absence. But she would not know that their sister had left them in Donovan's care and had fled.

Travis still didn't understand any of it. He was sick to his soul and he damned Walt Breckenridge with every breath in his body. It sickened him that he was of his father's blood. That he shared that bond. How could he have come from such a monster, and what did that make himself?

No, he'd never be like him. He'd die first. Never would he hurt others as his father had.

Travis walked over to the bed just as Rusty's cell phone rang. When she answered, her eyes widened in surprise. Then she only said, "Okay, we'll be here and ready."

Travis picked Cammie up, looking at Rusty in silent question.

"Nathan and Swanny are on their way over to get us," Rusty explained quietly. "You remember them." Then her gaze shifted in Cammie's direction and then back to Travis in silent communication.

As much as it frustrated Travis not to demand information, to know what the hell was going on and if his sister had been found, he wouldn't traumatize Cammie that way.

Rusty walked over and smiled at Cammie. "What do you say I help you get dressed? Nathan and Swanny are on their way over to get us and we're going to my parents. Your grandparents," she said, emphasizing that they should be considered Travis and Cammie's grandmother and grandfather.

Tears burned Travis's eyes because they weren't his family. Eve was. Without her he had no ties. No one who loved him unconditionally and who had sacrificed everything.

Cammie looked cheered by Rusty's declaration, and then she brightened as if a sudden thought had occurred to her.

"Will Cece be there?"

Rusty shrugged, smiling. "I'm not sure, but it's entirely possible the entire family will be there."

Then, as if just realizing that Eve hadn't been mentioned, Cammie's excitement dimmed.

"Where's Evie? Won't she be there too?"

Her thumb automatically slid into her mouth as she gazed anxiously between Travis and Rusty.

"Donovan will get her," Travis said resolutely. "Now let Rusty help you get dressed so we can go see our grandparents."

"YOU want to run that by me again?" Donovan asked in a lethal tone.

He was staring holes through the young deputy, who didn't look any happier to report the news than Donovan was to receive it.

Donovan's brothers and team members had all donned serious what-the-fuck looks. And then their expressions turned to ones of sympathy. They were all looking at him like he'd just been played for the ultimate sucker.

Fuck that. No fucking way. There was no way Eve could have done what Sean just accused her of.

"You heard me," Sean said wearily. "The hell of it is, Rusty swears that Eve was convinced you betrayed her. Rusty was seriously pissed and frustrated because she wanted to help, and Eve told her that her loyalty belonged to her family. Not her. And that furthermore Eve didn't want to put Rusty in danger. Not to mention she apologized for having to take Rusty's Jeep, for tying her up and for taking money from a man she hadn't even met. Doesn't exactly sound like a hardened criminal, does it?"

Donovan's hand palmed the back of his neck and he closed his eyes. "Jesus Christ. She thinks I *betrayed* her? Where is she now, Sean? Tell me you know something. *Anything.*"

"How long ago?" Garrett bit out. "When did this all go down, Sean?"

Donovan swung around in surprise. Garrett was pissed, all right, but it didn't seem to be directed at Eve. In fact, none of his brothers or the rest of Nathan and Joe's team looked anything but . . . worried.

"Well over an hour," Sean said, his expression dark. "I responded to the alarm Rusty triggered, made damn sure she was okay and then sent her to Donovan's house so Travis and Cammie wouldn't be alone. I immediately put out a BOLO on Rusty's Jeep and Eve. I did not list her as someone to be arrested. I reported it as a suspicious disappearance."

Donovan knew exactly what Garrett was alluding to with his question. The same knowledge was reflected in every single person in the room's eyes.

The smug son of a bitch already had her. It was why he

didn't act as if he gave a damn when he'd met with Donovan and his brothers. The bastard had already nabbed her and he thought he held all the cards. He pretended innocence and, after all, he had a pretty damn good alibi. He was there with Donovan, acting in the best interests of his "family," when in fact he had Eve the entire time.

"Steady," Sam murmured, putting his hand out to Donovan.

Donovan hadn't even realized he'd bobbled. His knees went to jelly and he had to grasp Sam's extended hand to keep from dropping in his tracks.

"He has her," Donovan said hoarsely, unnecessarily. "I have to get to Travis and Cammie. This will kill them. Dear God. I did this to her? How could she think I betrayed her?"

He couldn't control the utter bewilderment in his voice. On one level he realized he should be furious. That she'd threatened Rusty. Stolen from both her and his father. That she'd put herself at such a huge risk. But he could muster nothing but horrible, aching fear. And worry that he'd lose her.

"I'd prefer to round up everyone and meet at Ma and Dad's within the hour," Sam said. "Sean, can you get every man you can spare on this? I need you to extend that BOLO to Walt Breckenridge. We can't let him leave the state. Alert the California state patrol and the city and county police where the bastard lives. I don't care what the fuck you have to tell them. Just get them on this."

Donovan nodded, still unable to form a coherent sentence. He simply couldn't comprehend it all. She thought he'd betrayed her, and yet she'd left Cammie and Travis with him. He knew only too well the lengths to which she'd go to protect her siblings. She thought the worst of him and yet she trusted him with the two people she loved most in the world.

It was incomprehensible.

"Let's roll, man. I don't think you should be driving. You head to Ma's so you can update them and be there when everyone starts rolling in. I'll get Rusty and the kids over there," Nathan said.

Then he turned to Skylar. "You're with me. Swanny, you too. Cammie's familiar with Swanny and I don't think she'd feel threatened by Skylar. Edge, you'd scare the shit out of her. You and Joe collect the wives. Try not to scare them any more than necessary and tell them everything will be explained when we all meet up at Ma's. No need in rehashing this more than once."

"Come on, Van," Ethan said quietly. "Let's go to Ma's so we can put our heads together and figure out what the fuck is going on. You'll feel marginally better once you know at least Travis and Cammie are safe."

CHAPTER 37

THE mood was grim and strained at Frank and Marlene's home. The moment Nathan and Swanny arrived with Rusty, Travis and Cammie, the children were ushered away by Marlene, who promptly sat them in the kitchen to feed them along with Charlotte, who'd arrived just moments earlier.

Sean strode in, the last to get there, and Donovan knew when he saw the deputy's face, it wasn't good.

"We found Rusty's Jeep," Sean said grimly. "Wrecked on 79 headed out of town. From the looks of it, she was rear-ended and shoved into the ditch. The passenger door was open. Air bags were not deployed. Her bag was still there with the cash from the hardware store, some jewelry and not much else."

"What the hell did you say to her, Donovan?" Rusty all but shouted.

The others stared at her in surprise. Donovan was taken aback by the anger and grief in her voice. He understood it, but he wasn't sure why it was directed at *him*. Surely she, like Eve, couldn't believe he had in any way betrayed Eve.

"You didn't see her or hear her. I did," Rusty seethed.

"She thought, no, she *knew* that you were handing her over to her stepfather. A trade of sorts. She said that she was merely the means for you to get what you truly wanted. Children. A family that didn't include her. She quoted what so many of us have said over the years. You have a weakness for women and children but *especially children*. She believes you want them and not her and that you were offering her up to her stepfather. And yet she left Travis and Cammie in your care because she believed no matter what you'd done to her that you truly loved and cared about *them* and that you'd protect them with your life."

"Where the hell would she get an idea like that?" Donovan exploded. "Goddamn it! I wouldn't have done something like that and surely you can't believe it."

"I don't know *what* to believe," Rusty said, tears clogging her voice. "All I know was that I was confronted with a desperate, terrified and devastated woman who believed to her soul that she'd been betrayed by the one person she trusted. *You.*"

Donovan couldn't even form a response. He was utterly flabbergasted. First, that Eve would ever think such a thing, and second, that a member of his own family would think, even for a moment, that he would do something so despicable.

"Donovan."

Near to his exploding point, Donovan turned at Sophie's soft call. Her eyes were red and rimmed with moisture. All the wives were present and deeply upset by the situation. But at least there was no accusation in her eyes. Just grief and worry.

"I think I may know what happened," she said in a painful voice. "Yesterday when you sent her and the kids over to my house. When we were supposed to shop and you and your brothers were getting together at your house to talk about Eve's situation."

"Yes, I remember," Donovan said, impatient for her to get to the point.

"She was worried and bothered by the fact that you hadn't let her remain behind. She thought she should be included in any decisions regarding her future. I—we—understood. We knew that if it were us in that situation that we wouldn't—couldn't—just stand to the side and let our fates be decided by others. We would have at least wanted to *know* what was going to happen, even if we weren't going to be directly involved. The uncertainty is horrible. It was horrible for Eve. She's had no control over her life in a long time. She wanted at least a semblance of control—of choice—especially when it concerned her brother and sister, whom she'd do anything at all for. Even at risk to herself. We encouraged her to go over and tell you what she was feeling. At first she didn't want to because she didn't want it to appear as though she didn't trust you. We told her you would understand. That you might not like it, but that you wouldn't be angry with her."

Donovan's gut tightened and his dread increased.

"So she decided to walk back over, only she wasn't gone that long and when she returned, she was visibly upset. She tried to play it off and when we asked her why she was back so soon, she told us she changed her mind. That she didn't want you to think she didn't trust you and that you'd promised to tell her later anyway."

"Dear God," Donovan whispered hoarsely. "She must have overheard. It's the only explanation. She must have come through the kitchen and overheard *parts* of our conversation. Out of context, some of it sounds bad. But it was a plan, goddamn it. It was supposed to be a trap. I *never* had any intention of handing Eve over to that bastard."

"Fuck," Garrett said.

It was a testament to the severity of the situation that he didn't instantly earn a reprimand from his wife for the F-bomb.

Donovan sank onto the couch, burying his face in his hands. The bastard had her. And she thought Donovan had been prepared to hand her over. She thought he didn't want her. Didn't love her. That he wanted Travis and Cammie but not her. And even after knowing—thinking—so, she'd still left them in his care because she'd known what her stepfather would do to them. God, what he would do to *her*.

Even now she was in his hands. Grief knotted his throat,

choking him when he tried to voice his fears. His fury and
helplessness. So he sat there, hands shaking as rage and sorrow vied for equal control of his emotions.

"How could she believe it?" he finally managed to get
out. "No matter what she heard, how could she *think* it? I
love her, damn it. How could she not *know*?"

"Did you tell her?" Rachel asked softly. "Donovan, you
have to understand her situation. Put aside your anger and
your grief for a moment and imagine yourself in her shoes.
She's not been able to trust anyone. She hasn't been able to
afford to. You know how hard it was for you to get through to
her. How delicately you had to handle the situation. How hard
it was to get her to agree to put herself and her siblings in
your hands. To move into your house. I can only imagine the
torture she put herself through wondering if she was making
the right decision. And now, she believes the worst. That she
did make the wrong choice. I can't even begin to imagine her
sense of betrayal. She loves you, Van. I know it. We all know
it. One only has to look at her to know that despite any fears
or reservations she's entertained, she loves you, and love will
make a person very afraid. I know from personal experience
that love can make things worse. It makes the hurt worse
when a perceived betrayal is in the mix."

Donovan was momentarily baffled as he thought back
over their many conversations about the future. Their future
together. So much of what Rachel said made sense. He saw
the discomfort and grief flicker briefly through Ethan's eyes
at Rachel's impassioned defense of Eve. Yes, he and Rachel
would both know firsthand how love could sometimes be
twisted into something ugly and black.

The idea that Eve was now feeling even a tenth of what
Rachel had described gutted him to his soul. He could put
himself in Eve's shoes and consider what she'd heard and
what she was even now experiencing, and it shredded his
heart. He never wanted that for her. He never wanted her to
experience the kind of pain she'd already experienced in her
young life. And the fact that he was currently the source of
her agony undid him. Completely and utterly undid him.

"I didn't say the words—I was afraid of coming on too strong, too quickly—but she had to know. How could she not? I've never been this way with another woman. And that bullshit about having a weakness for women and children. It doesn't mean she was a pity case for me. I wanted to spend the rest of my bloody life with her! If I never hear those goddamn words again it will be too soon. Eve isn't a mission. I damn well know the difference between wanting and needing to help a woman in a desperate situation and knowing to the bottom of my soul that she's it for me."

"Donovan, you need to put yourself in her shoes," Shea said, echoing Rachel's words. "Remember her life to now. Remember that she's never been able to trust anyone, and that over and over she's been betrayed by the very people sworn to protect her. Now imagine how devastating it was for her to hear what she heard and for her to think you would discard her so callously."

"I *saw* her," Rusty said flatly. "The rest of you can speculate on how she may have felt, but none of you saw what I saw. What I heard. She was broken, beaten down and utterly hopeless. I saw her eyes and she knew. She accepted her fate, but her being her, she wasn't going to go down without a fight. She's stood up time and time again even when she's been shut down at every turn, every time she tried to get help for her mother, for Travis and Cammie. And yet she never gave up. But now? I saw her give up right in front of me and yet she was still determined that she wouldn't be, in her words, a sacrificial lamb. That as long as Travis and Cammie were cared for, it didn't matter what happened to her, but she wasn't just going to go meekly along with Donovan's plan."

"Jesus," Donovan said, pain gripping his insides and twisting viciously. "He has her. He hurt her before. He tried to . . ." He couldn't even finish the statement, instead going silent as he tried to keep his composure.

"He'll want revenge. He'll want her to suffer. Goddamn it, he has his hands on her right *now*. She's enduring God only knows what kind of hell while we sit here and talk about the what ifs and whys. This is bullshit. It's time to dispense with the analysis and go take that son of a bitch down."

"We'll find her," Sam said firmly.

"Hell yeah, we'll get your girl back, Van," Garrett seconded.

A course of agreements circled the room.

Donovan raised his gaze, determination etched in every facet of his face. He wouldn't entertain any other option. No matter what, he had to get Eve back. Yes, he wanted children, a family, but he wanted those things with *Eve*. Without her, he had nothing. How could he ever be happy having Travis and Cammie as his own when Eve was not a member of that family unit? She was the heart and soul of their family. His family. Without her, none of them, him, Travis or Cammie, would never be whole.

"Yes, I'll get her back," he said in a tone he knew surprised his brothers. Every mission meant something to Donovan. Yes, he had a weakness for women and children, though he was sick to death of having that thrown in his face, of it being used to *hurt* the woman he loved, like somehow she'd been relegated to being just another woman in need. No one special, when she was the very air he breathed.

"And when I do I'll never let her go again. I'll never let a single day pass that she doesn't know she means the world to me. That she is my *world*, damn it!"

"Van, my God, Van!"

Everyone turned to see Marlene standing in the doorway to the living room wringing her hands. In the distance Cammie was crying and Charlotte's concerned voice was rising as she tried to comfort Cammie.

"What is it, Ma?" Ethan asked sharply.

"Travis. He's gone," Marlene said painfully. "He excused himself to go to the bathroom. He was gone a long time but he was upset before. I thought he was embarrassed and just needed time to get himself together. When I realized how much time had passed, I became concerned so I went to check on him and he was gone. He must have slipped out the back or one of the windows. I don't really know! I was paying attention to the girls and trying to keep them occupied."

Donovan closed his eyes, the nightmare only growing more horrific with every passing second. His family was being destroyed in front of his eyes and he was helpless to do anything but watch it happen.

Fuck that. Eve, Travis and Cammie belonged to him, and he sure as hell wasn't letting them go. He'd go after Walt Breckenridge and nail his ass to the wall. Legally or illegally. It didn't matter one way or another as long as the job was done.

Some things were done off the books. It was a reality of what they did. They were neither right or wrong, but some fucked-up place in between. But at the end of the day, they lived with their choices and they continued to do the job.

To save his precious family from a monster like Walt Breckenridge? He'd play dirty. He'd fight dirty. And he'd take him down by any means necessary and he'd lie, cheat and steal to get back the family he'd claimed as his own.

CHAPTER 38

"THIS situation gets more fucked by the minute," Sean said.

"What now?" Donovan demanded.

They were in down and ready mode, plotting their plan of action, and it frustrated the hell out of Donovan that they were so damn slow getting the information they desperately needed. Even his computer geek skills weren't helping at the moment, but then this wasn't a regular mission. He knew he didn't have his head on straight and he was shaking like a leaf as he went through the motions.

Nathan and Joe's team were on standby and waiting for the go command. Donovan and his brothers, after ensuring that the family was well taken care of by Steele and his team, were in load-and-go mode. But they couldn't very well act without accurate intel.

So far Sean had been a far greater source of information. Information they badly needed.

They were in the war room, where their command center and enough technology to rival a government agency was set up and going through Walt Breckenridge's entire life. His financials, residences, anything that would lead them to where he'd go now that he had Eve.

"Breckenridge flew out an hour ago from Camden on his Learjet, which means he has one hell of a jump on us, even with us using the KGI jets."

"Fuck!" Donovan exploded. "Flight plans? Destination?"

"There's more," Sean said grimly, and Donovan did not like what he saw in the deputy's eyes.

"Jesus," Sam muttered

"I just got this in from Henry County PD. I'd put out the BOLO on both Eve and Travis. Travis hijacked a plane from Henry County. We could beat him there if we hop one of the Kelly jets; however, here's the interesting part."

"Get the fuck to it," Donovan seethed. "We've wasted enough goddamn time as it is!"

"The pilot filed flight plans to Oregon."

Donovan's brow furrowed. God, but his head hurt like a son of a bitch. Oregon? What the fuck was in Oregon? Unless . . .

"He knows something we don't," Donovan said. "One of Walt's hidey-holes. Walt may have filed flight plans for California, but he would have known we'd trace that. Ten to one says the fucker is going to Oregon and that Travis knows or at least has a damn good idea of where he'll go now that he has Eve."

"Do you know where in Oregon?" Garrett asked. "Or are we flying blind here?"

Sean grimaced. "A little of both. All I know is they were flying to Wasco, Oregon. There are several small airstrips and we don't know which one, not to mention we can't fly a jet the size of the Kelly jet into one of them. It's not far out of Portland. You can get there, but from there you'd have to do the legwork, split up and cover as much territory as possible."

"Our best bet is to get in the air and figure out where the fuck Breckenridge has a place there," Donovan bit out. "We're wasting time, time that Eve doesn't have, by sitting here with our thumbs up our asses speculating. We'll do our search in the air. And goddamn it, I'm going to have to call in a favor to Resnick. I need a full background on Breckenridge. Resnick has better access to information than we do."

"I agree," Sam said firmly. "Let's get the fuck out of here. Nathan, you flying?"

Nathan shot him a look that suggested it was a dumbass question.

"Then let's get the fuck in the air," Donovan said. "We'll figure it out on the fly. The longer Eve is in that bastard's hands, the worse she'll be. I can only pray the son of a bitch hasn't hurt—or killed—her before we get to her."

"Put it away, man," Ethan said quietly. "It doesn't do you or her any good to torture yourself with the possibilities. Focus on getting her back where she belongs. If you start entertaining worst-case scenarios, you'll lose your sanity, and what she needs is for you to have a clear, level head. Those kids need you. Eve needs you. Now pull it together and let's get the fuck in the air."

"There's one more thing you should know," Sean added quietly. "One of Frank's guns is missing from his gun case. Travis must have taken it and used it to hijack the plane. How else would he have gotten the pilot to agree to take him where he's going? If and when this is all resolved, there's a shit-ton of legal issues to be resolved. Eve will go down for armed robbery, and Travis will go down for kidnapping plus a whole host of other federal charges. You've got yourself one giant clusterfuck."

Donovan closed his eyes and rubbed his forehead wearily. Desperation. All acts of desperation. He could only assume that like Eve, Travis had overheard parts of a conversation. Hell, Rusty hadn't exactly been quiet when she'd jumped down Donovan's throat. He could well believe, as Eve did, that Donovan had betrayed her. Or perhaps he'd learned that his father had Eve and he'd do anything to save her. Who knew more than Travis just what his father was capable of?

"Fuck it. We're going to have to call in a shit-ton of favors by the time this is over with. I'm going to end up owing a kidney and all of yours as well. We'll be in debt to our eyeballs and you can bet every single person we involve will call in those markers."

"I don't give a fuck," Sam said, resolve marking every word. "No price is too high to pay to save your family, Van. Just like no price is too high to pay for any of our family. We'll get it done. We always do. Now let's go get your family back."

"Christ, we're already hours behind," Donovan said in disgust. "They both have too far a head start and we're flying blind."

"All the more reason not to waste another single minute," Joe piped in.

Donovan glanced up at his brother and his team. All at the ready. Silent until now. But answering resolve was in each of their faces. He'd worried they weren't ready even though they'd proved themselves capable.

"This is the single most important mission you will ever go on," Donovan said, addressing Swanny, Skylar, Edge, Nathan and Joe. "Nothing you will ever do will be more important than what you're doing now. I need you to know that. You also need to know that I trust you—I am trusting you. With the most important things in my life. Eve and those children—my children."

Every single member of the team was instantly on alert. They recognized this important step in their progression in KGI. This wasn't just any mission. It was *the* mission. And Donovan was trusting them to pull it off. He could see their resolve. No, they wouldn't fail him.

Some of the horrific terror that had gripped him by the throat for the last hours eased. If this were anyone else, a client, Donovan would be the first to reassure them that KGI was the best and they would get the job done. And now he had to tell himself that. Place his trust in the team he'd had a hand in training from the ground up. It was time to let them go. And hope to hell that they were as capable as he believed them to be.

"We won't let you down," Skylar said softly. "We'll do this, Donovan. It's a mission, yes. But this is more than that and we all realize it. It's personal for all of us. And we'll get your family back or die trying."

Just like that. Answering determination was etched in the faces of every single member of her team. They'd all put their lives on the line for Donovan. For Eve and Travis.

"You will never know what this means to me," Donovan said quietly.

"Let's go kick some ass," Edge growled.

"That gets a hooyah from me," Ethan said.

This time there was no good-natured ribbing from his non-Navy brothers and team members. Everyone gathered up their bags, their rifles. Donovan grabbed the laptop, Hoss 2, as it was termed. A more portable version of Hoss, the mainframe computer that ran KGI. And then they all hurried from the war room and sprinted double time to the airstrip, where the jet was already fueled and ready for takeoff.

CHAPTER 39

DEFEAT tugged mercilessly at Eve. It was over with. It was done. She was done. She stared up at her stepfather, shivering at the calculated way he looked at her. There was no mistaking the lust in his eyes. The triumph. He knew he'd won and he was relishing every moment of her helplessness.

"Ready to concede defeat, Eve?" he asked mockingly. "Are you ready to give me what I want?"

"Go to hell," she bit out.

He backhanded her, dropping her in her tracks. She hit the floor as pain washed over her body. He kicked her, knocking the breath from her. Agony splintered through her ribs as he kicked again. God, he'd kill her. She knew it. Even embraced it.

Only the thought of Travis and Cammie in his hands gave her the courage to continue. Made her want to live to ensure that they'd be safe.

"Poor Eve," he murmured as he bent to haul her roughly to her feet. "Did you know your lover was prepared to hand you over to me in exchange for backing off of Cammie and Travis?"

Eve closed her eyes, hurt welling up in her soul. A hurt far more agonizing than the physical pain she endured at his hands. This was soul deep. Her heart hurt. Yes, she'd known of Donovan's plan, but hearing it from her stepfather's lips, getting confirmation of what she already knew, sent pain to the deepest recesses of her soul.

"You must have been lousy in bed if he was so willing to give you up," Walt mocked.

He walked around her in a tight circle, pacing the living room of the cabin he'd taken her to. Her knees wobbled but by sheer grit alone she managed to remain standing. Defiant.

He paused and let a finger trail down the curve of her cheek. She turned away, not wanting him to touch her, and he issued another slap.

It wasn't as hard as the last. She stumbled back but managed to regain her footing before she hit the floor again.

Her entire face ached. It was on fire from his repeated abuse. But this she could manage. It was only pain. What she couldn't face was him touching her. Him being intimate with her. Nausea curled low in her belly and her mouth watered. She swallowed, choking it back.

He wouldn't break her. He wouldn't!

"Are you prepared to give me what I want?" he asked.

Her gaze snapped to his, fire in her eyes. "Go to hell."

Rage burned a trail though his eyes, and then they turned cold.

"You don't learn," he said softly. "But you will, Eve. You'll learn that you will pay for defying me. I can be a patient man. You will agree to what I want."

"Never!"

He smiled then, and it chilled Eve's blood. "We'll see how quickly you change your mind when I make a vegetable out of you. Perhaps after a few days in the institution you'll see the error of your ways. It's an honor I'm bestowing on you. You're a fool to continue with this resistance. You won't win. I'll have you, Eve. And I'll have Travis and Cammie."

"You'll never get near them," she hissed. "He'll never allow it. He'll kill you."

Walt's eyebrows went up. "The lover who fucked you over? Your faith in him surprises me."

"Go to hell."

His eyes narrowed as fury reddened his face. "No, Eve, but you will. You're going right to hell. Before I'm finished with you, you'll welcome my attentions. You'll beg to get in my bed."

"Never."

The quiet vow fell between them. She lifted her head, staring at him through painful, swollen eyes.

His lips thinned and tightened, and then he lifted his hand, motioning for someone beyond her.

Fear and panic exploded through her veins as another man advanced on her, a syringe in his hand. She whirled, looking for an escape. Some way out of her circumstances.

Walt wrapped his hand in her hair and yanked her up short. His breath blew harshly over her face. His eyes glittered with sick arousal. The bastard was getting off on what he planned to do to her.

Realization settled over her like a suffocating fog. Once drugged, she had no power. He could do anything he wanted, even rape her, and she would be helpless to prevent it.

She fought back wildly, surprising him with her strength. Desperation lent her more than she possessed. She broke away and ran for the doorway. She was nearly there when she hit the floor, pain blistering through her.

Walt's heavy body pinned her, his chest rising and falling with exertion. And then he laughed.

"I like a good fight," he murmured. "Your mother never fought. She was too weak, too spineless. But you, Eve? Ah, I look forward to having you in my bed. I have a feeling it will always be a fight with you."

She felt the prick of a needle. Felt the surge of medication forced into her body. Tears burned her eyelids. There was no escape. He could do anything he wanted with her.

"Get her up and get her out of here," Walt bit out, the words seemingly coming from a mile away. "She'll learn soon enough that she'll do exactly as I want or suffer the consequences."

CHAPTER 40

TRAVIS paced the floor of his father's cabin, wondering for the hundredth time if he'd been wrong. What if his father didn't come here? What if he was hundreds of miles away? What if he'd been so arrogant and so sure of himself that he had taken Eve back to California?

His father didn't even know that Travis knew of this place. Or that he had the security codes to access the gate and to disarm the security system. No, his father thought him an inept idiot. At one time Travis had been bitter over that fact. Devastated at first and then bitter. And then finally resigned. He realized he no longer cared. He'd stopped craving his father's approval when he was old enough to understand what a monster he was.

He saw how his father treated Eve, who was the sweetest person Travis knew. Eve had more integrity in her little finger than Walt could ever dream of. And it appeared Donovan as well.

Grief welled in his heart, spreading until his entire chest ached. How could he have been so wrong about Donovan? How could he have done what he did to Eve? How could he have lied, said he wanted them to be family when all along he never had any intention of loving and caring for Eve? No matter that he cared for him and Cammie. How could Travis ever be happy in a family that didn't include the one person who loved him more than anyone did or ever would? Who'd sacrificed so much for him and Cammie?

The accusations Rusty had hurled at Donovan still rang in Travis's ears. He winced, hearing them over and over, the shock of them still paralyzing him. He drew in a deep breath, pushing aside his grief.

He wouldn't let Eve down. Not when she'd risked everything for him time and time again.

He froze when he heard the sound of a door opening. His grip tightened on the gun he carried and he rested it against his thigh, prepared to do whatever was necessary to defend himself but more importantly to get Eve out of his father's grasp.

His father strode into the room and blinked in surprise when he saw Travis standing there. Then his eyes gleamed and Travis could see him calculating. Coming up with an excuse, a story. Bullshit was his specialty. Travis had learned that at a very young age and he could spot it a mile away.

"Well, well, well," his father said in a dragged-out fashion. "What a surprise. I'd ask how you got here, how you even knew to get here, but it doesn't matter. It merely saves me the trouble of getting both you and Cammie back."

"What did you do with Eve?" Travis demanded. "Where is she? Did you hurt her? Did you kill her like you killed my mother?"

His father's eyebrow rose. No, he wasn't his father. He couldn't refer to him as his father. He was Walt Breckenridge. And he was a bastard of the first order.

"I didn't kill your mother. Eve did that all on her own. As for where Eve is, she's in a place where she can get the help she obviously needs. She's brainwashed you and Cammie both. What did she do, give you some sob story about me abusing your mother and then killing her?"

Travis's jaw tightened and he raised the gun to point it at

his father. It shook in his grasp and despite his efforts to settle himself, the gun still quivered. It pissed him off that Walt noticed and triumph entered his eyes. He didn't think Travis had the balls to pull the trigger.

"You killed my mother. You abused my mother. You abused *Cammie*, you sick bastard. You tried to abuse Eve. I don't need Eve to tell me those things. I have eyes. I have ears. I lived under the same roof. Do you think I'm stupid? Do you think I didn't see the bruises? Didn't hear the lame excuses? Now what did you do with Eve? Tell me or I swear to God I'll shoot you."

Walt's lips formed a lazy grin. "If you shoot me, you certainly won't find out any information on Eve, now will you? So it would seem we're at an impasse. You want information I won't give. And if you shoot, you'll never find out."

"What is *wrong* with you?" Travis shouted. "You're my father! And I'm *nothing* to you! Why do you even care? Why do you want me and Cammie so badly? Why do you want Eve?"

He broke off, the gun shaking in his hand so badly he nearly dropped it.

"I know what you want with Cammie, you sick bastard. How could you? She's a baby! And Eve! What has she ever done but care about her mother and us?"

"You all belong to me," Walt said icily. "You're mine. And I don't relinquish control over what's mine."

"That's all it is to you, isn't it? You're a psychopath. It's all about control. You don't give a damn about me or them. You don't give a damn about anything but yourself and what you can control. You're God in your own world and you think everyone is a pawn to do what you want, when you want."

Walt shrugged. "Think what you will. It doesn't change the fact that I'm holding all the cards. Now here's what I will do. You can decide which sister you want to save. You get in touch with your precious Donovan Kelly and do whatever you have to do to get Cammie here. You do that, I'll tell you where Eve is. You don't? You can kiss your precious half sister good-bye. You'll never find her. You'll never know if she's dead or alive. Cammie is your real sister. And as you said, she's a baby. So you decide, Travis. But the clock is ticking on my ultimatum. Better make up your mind fast. But know this. I'll get Cammie back one way or another. You expediting matters will make me more amenable to giving you information on that weak, spineless, utterly worthless half sister you seem to value so much."

"Weak? Spineless?" Travis's mouth gaped open. He was so furious that he couldn't even see straight. Walt's features blurred in front of him and his knees nearly buckled.

"You son of a bitch. A weak, spineless, *worthless* person wouldn't have stood up to you. She wouldn't have risked so much to try and get our mother out of your grasp. A weak person would have taken the easy road and let you control her life like you were so determined to do. She would have remained silent and let you continue your abuse. Instead she lost everything. *Everything.* And she risked it all to take me and Cammie away so we'd be safe. The only weak, spineless, worthless piece of shit in this picture is *you* and I'm horrified that we share the same blood. I can only pray to God that I never inherit a damn thing from you."

A spark of rage flashed in Walt's eyes, the first emotion other than calm smugness he'd displayed.

"You will not speak to your father in that manner," he seethed. "I own you, boy. And by God, I'll dispose of you just like I did your pathetic excuse of a mother."

Frozen by the admission, Travis stared in horror at the man who called himself his father. Yes, he'd known Walt had killed his wife, but hearing him so callously admit it stunned him.

And it was in that moment of inattention that Walt launched himself the short distance that separated the two. Travis barely had time to tighten his grip on the gun when Walt attacked.

They went sprawling, Walt on top, his hand curling around Travis's wrist, tightening until Travis was certain the bone would break. His father was strong. Much stronger than Travis would have imagined. And in this moment, he realized that Walt would kill him if he was able to wrest the gun from his hands.

They rolled and Travis struck out with his free hand, trying to knock Walt back. Walt grabbed the hand and twisted it high above his head, his other hand locked around Travis's other wrist until the hand holding the gun went numb.

Triumph gleamed in Walt's eyes as he lay atop Travis with Travis pinned to the floor.

"Such a sad story this will make," Walt said. "Overcome with grief over his mother's death and his half sister's mental illness, the son takes his own life, no doubt a result of the same mental illness that gripped his mother and half sister. Genetics, you know. It's too bad I didn't choose better in my wife. Now it will only be me and Cammie and I'll garner sympathy for the tragedy that has befallen my family."

Knowing he was now fighting for his life, Travis rammed his knee between Walt's legs. A look of agony covered Walt's face and his grip loosened. Just enough for Travis to shove the gun between them.

Realizing this, Walt recovered and reached down to once again try to wrest the gun from Travis's hand. But Travis's hand was on the trigger and when Walt squeezed, the gun went off.

Walt jerked. Travis felt the impact and for a moment he didn't know if he'd been shot or if Walt had. He was too numb, too shaken. But wouldn't it hurt?

He felt the warm, sticky sensation of blood. He smelled it. He looked down to see it blooming on both his and Walt's clothing. But when he looked back up and met Walt's stunned gaze, he saw the glaze of pain and shock. And he saw death.

Travis shoved at him, frantic to get him off. He pushed the heavy body aside and scrambled up, panicked at the blood coating his clothing. It was all over the floor. God. Walt's chest was covered with it.

Oh God. Oh God. What was he going to do? He hadn't meant to kill him! He only wanted to threaten him. Make him tell him what he'd done with Eve. He scrubbed his hands over his shirt, but all he did was smear more of the blood on his hands.

Oh God. What could he do? He was in enough trouble for what he'd already done and now he'd killed his own father! What would Eve do? And Cammie? They needed him. And now they'd be left alone. And he didn't even know if Eve was alive! If she was, he had no way of finding her now.

The front door burst open and Travis's heart sank. It would be the police. They would have heard the gunshot. There was no defense. He was covered in his father's blood. His fingerprints on the gun.

But when Donovan Kelly burst into the living room, his brothers and others he had no idea who they were on his heels, Travis burst into tears.

DONOVAN and his brothers along with Nathan and Joe's team roared up to the cabin just outside Wasco. It was their last resort. The only place they hadn't looked for Walt, and if it weren't for the fact that Resnick had come through for them, they'd still be chasing their goddamn tails.

There was a vehicle parked out front and Donovan's pulse accelerated. The arrogant bastard had driven here in his own vehicle.

Two goddamn days. Two of the longest days of his life they'd spent uncovering every rock in Walt Breckenridge's life. He'd called in every favor ever owed him. Resnick had been working around the clock, pulling every string available to him and then some. And with each passing hour, Donovan's sense of fatalism had grown until he'd resigned himself that he'd lost Eve and likely Travis as well.

They got out, guns drawn, and then they heard a gunshot.

Fear seized him and he discarded every single thing he knew about caution and he ran.

Ignoring the angry shouts of his brothers to wait until they cleared the area, Donovan burst through the front door, but nothing could have prepared him for the sight of Travis standing, pale, bloody and obviously in shock. And on the floor, lying in a pool of blood, was Walt Breckenridge.

Travis's gaze lifted to Donovan's, and then he burst into tears. He was still holding the gun and he was shaking like a leaf.

"Holy fuck," Sam breathed as he caught up to Donovan.

"Travis," Donovan said in a soothing tone. "Everything's okay, son. I need you to put down the gun before you hurt yourself. Can you do that?"

Travis looked down as if only just now realizing he was still holding the gun. Then he dropped it and Donovan's brothers and teammates scattered, afraid the gun would discharge. When nothing happened, they slowly rose and Donovan cautiously approached Travis.

"What happened, son?" he asked gently.

"I-I s-shot him," Travis stammered out. "I didn't mean to, Donovan. Oh my God, I killed him but I didn't *mean* to! I just wanted to threaten him. To make him tell me what he's done with Eve. I didn't mean to kill him! He jumped at me and we struggled. We were on the floor and he said that he was going to make it look like I'd shot myself. That I had the same mental illness Eve has and that grief-stricken over the death of my mother and the loss of Eve, I killed myself."

Donovan's blood ran cold when Travis said "the loss of Eve." But for now he had to put it aside. He had to fix this and fast.

"Listen to me," Donovan said in a harsh voice.

Travis jumped at the ferocity in Donovan's voice, but Donovan needed his full attention.

"You did not shoot your father. You understand? You did not do this. Your father was trying to kill you and we burst in and one of us shot him. Do you understand what I'm saying?"

Travis blinked and shook his head. "No. I can't let you do that. I killed him, Donovan. I killed him."

"You aren't understanding," Garrett said, coming to stand beside Donovan. "We need you to get ahold of yourself. I know you're upset. I know you're in shock. But this is important, son. Tell me you understand what I'm saying."

Slowly Travis nodded.

"Now, it went down exactly like I said," Donovan said in a gentle tone in an effort to calm Travis. "You had nothing to do with shooting him. You never saw this gun. You didn't have a gun. You never touched this gun."

"But my fingerprints," Travis said helplessly. "The blood."

Even as he spoke, he glanced sideways to see Skylar wiping down the gun and then handing it to Sam, who holstered it.

"Strip," Donovan ordered.

As he issued the command, Joe stepped up and thrust a pair of fatigues and a T-shirt toward Donovan.

"Don't move. Not even an inch. Strip where you stand. We're going to wipe you down before you put on other clothing. Now hurry. We don't have much time."

After they'd taken care of Travis and led him over to the couch to sit before he fell, Donovan sat across from him to ask what he'd been dying to know ever since Travis's words about the loss of Eve.

His tongue was thick and swollen in his mouth. The words knotted in his throat because he was afraid of what he'd hear. It took every ounce of self-control not to break down and to try to sit there calmly when every part of him was screaming that he'd lost Eve forever.

"What did he mean by the loss of Eve?" Donovan demanded. "Where is she? Did he tell you anything?"

Tears filled Travis's eyes again, and he stared accusingly up at Donovan. "How could you have done it? How could you betray her that way? She loved you. You said you wanted us all to be a family. But you traded her for us? Do you honestly think Cammie and I could ever be happy knowing we were free because you handed Eve over to that son of a bitch? I trusted you. *She* trusted you."

Donovan leaned forward and grasped Travis's shoulders, frustrated that they couldn't get to the heart of the matter. Eve. He needed to know about Eve. But he also had to reassure Travis that he'd never betrayed Eve, or Travis would likely be reluctant to hand out any information where his sister was concerned.

"Listen to me, son. I love your sister. She is my *life*. She overheard a conversation between me and my brothers about a trap we were setting for your father."

"Don't call him that," Travis choked out. "Never call him that."

Donovan nodded.

"We were setting a trap for Walt. We wanted him to think that we believed Eve was indeed mentally ill and that we were concerned she was a danger to you and Cammie. We wanted to set him up. We needed incriminating evidence. We needed something. And we had to find a way to take him out. Eve overheard the part that made it sound like I was going to give her up and that all I cared about was you and Cammie. But that's not true, Travis. I want all three of you. I want to marry Eve and I want the four of us to be family. A real family."

Hope glimmered in Travis's eyes and then they dulled again. "But Rusty said—"

Donovan grimaced. "Rusty was pissed at me because she thought I'd betrayed Eve as well. She saw Eve. She knew what Eve believed. And she knew Eve was devastated by it. Rusty cares a lot about you, Travis. Eve and Cammie too. She has a huge heart and she was taking me to task for what she thought I'd done. She was angry because she felt helpless and she knew Eve was in danger."

"You mean it?" Travis whispered. "You want to marry Eve? And you want me and Cammie?"

The hope in Travis's voice broke Donovan's heart.

"I very much want you as my son and Cammie as my daughter. One day I hope to have children with Eve, but in my heart, you and Cammie will always be my first children."

Travis slowly nodded his acceptance.

"Now, Travis, listen to me. This is important. We can't afford to waste any more time. I need to know if Walt said anything about Eve."

Travis closed his eyes and when they reopened, the grief shining nearly sent Donovan over the edge.

"He wouldn't tell me. He refused. I thought he might bring her here. He didn't know I knew about this place. But I didn't think he'd go back to his house. He tried to bargain with me. Told me I had to choose between my real sister and my half sister. He said if I'd contact you to expedite Cammie being returned to him, he'd give me information on Eve. But if I didn't, he'd get Cammie back one way or another and I'd never know what happened to Eve."

"I wish I'd been the one to kill him," Skylar said darkly from behind Donovan.

"Did Walt come here often?" Donovan asked. "We turned his home inside out and couldn't find anything that would lead us to Eve. I've investigated every angle. Except this one. A friend of mine came through for us with an in with the IRS who backtracked one of his fake organizations to this house."

"I don't know how often," Travis admitted. "I wouldn't have known about it all, but I overheard him on the phone with someone giving them the address and the key codes to disarm the security system."

"Odd that he'd go to such extreme measures for a cabin in the middle of nowhere," Joe murmured.

"Eve said that Walt had manufactured an entire medical history documenting her mental illness from an early age and that he even had a physician's statement. She said he produced them the last time she called the cops to go to your house. Did you ever see those papers after that?" Donovan asked.

Travis's eyes widened. "No. I didn't. You would have found them if you searched our house. But maybe . . ."

"They're here," Donovan finished.

He abruptly rose.

"Edge, you and Swanny clean this up. Make it look exactly as I said it went down. Sam, you have the gun, right? Give it to me so my prints are on it. For the record, I shot the bastard."

"No fucking way," Sam said emphatically. "I shot him. You've got too much of a personal stake in this."

"I can't let you do that," Donovan said just as emphatically. "You have a wife and a daughter and another child on the way. I'm not letting you take the fall for this if it gets messy."

"You have family too," Sam pointed out. "I'll get on the horn with Resnick and have him wave his magic wand. The bastard owes us big and he knows it. Besides, when I explain, he'll take care of it. There'll be a fuckload of red tape, but if I can get his ass out here, he'll have the connections to make sure this goes down as a righteous kill."

Knowing he didn't have time to argue, Donovan nodded.

"The rest of you are with me," Donovan said. "I want no stone uncovered in this house. There has to be something here. It's the only option we have left. The clock is ticking for Eve, if it hasn't expired yet. Find me something that points us in the right direction."

CHAPTER 41

"I know this slays your control-freak asses, but my team needs to take lead on this and go in and shut it down," Resnick said.

Typically, he had a cigarette dangling from his mouth, and he inhaled, then exhaled in short jerky puffs, a sign of agitation.

They were gathered outside a maximum-security private holding, a mere thirty miles from where Walt's house outside Wasco was located. Their exhaustive search of Walt's cabin had paid off. The arrogant bastard not only kept the fake medical history he'd compiled for Eve in a safe in his office, but he also had a diary where every detail of the last twenty years had been meticulously accounted for.

Donovan couldn't believe someone as careful and as cunning and intelligent as Breckenridge would be stupid enough to have written evidence of his crimes, but as Skylar had explained, he thought himself invincible. Untouchable. And he was too egotistical not to have it accounted for. He kept it hidden for his own enjoyment. His legacy, written down.

Things he took pride in. The killing of his wife and how pathetically easy it had been. How he was afforded sympathy and admiration for the way he'd taken in his stepdaughter and his smugness over the fact that he controlled his entire family.

It had disgusted him and made him even more fearful that he'd already killed Eve and disposed of her body. He'd spoken of having a cover story, but he'd left off there. Donovan had gone crazy and his brothers hadn't been able to control him. Until Skylar had uncovered financial records. Off the books under a fake corporation. And the only payments were made to a private facility outside Portland, Oregon.

Bingo.

It had to be where he had stashed Eve. And if he was paying them the sums of money and hiding it, there was something here he didn't want the world to know about.

Sam made a rude noise and Donovan just stared holes through Resnick.

"No fucking way I'm leaving Eve's fate to you and your lackeys," Donovan bit out.

Resnick's eyebrows rose, but then other than agitation smoking—which he frequently indulged in—the man didn't get worked up about much. Unless you counted the whole fiasco with Shea and Grace. It had been the first time Donovan had seen the man express any kind of emotion. It still amazed him that apparently the man had a heart underneath that give-a-fuck, good-of-the-country bullshit facade.

"Listen to me, Donovan. I've already got messes I've got to clean up for you. I'm not adding another. If my team goes in, this falls under the heading of a federal raid. You just happened to show up behind us and as such bear no responsibility in what goes down. This has to be done by the books. My lackeys, as you term them, are good and you damn well know it. They won't fuck this up."

"He has a point, Van," Garrett said in a resigned tone that told Donovan he didn't like the situation any more than Donovan did.

"Goddamn it," Donovan swore. "Okay, but let's roll. We're

wasting time. Time that Eve doesn't have. I want her out of this hellhole."

"Then let's do it," Resnick said, motioning to his team leader.

"We'll let you know when we're in and it's clear," Kyle Phillips said as he walked by Donovan. "But wait for my signal. Don't fuck this up, Kelly. Think with your head and leave your emotions out of it. It needs to go down on the level."

Leave his emotions out of it. When his heart and soul was in this goddamn hellhole enduring God only knew what. Yeah, leave his emotions out of it. Like that was going to happen.

Sam put a restraining hand on Donovan's arm as if he realized how perilously close Donovan was to saying *fuck it* and charging in ahead of Kyle Phillips and his team. He shook off Sam's hand.

"I'm cool. I'll wait."

So he stood and simmered, waiting, each second passing in agony. He listened, straining toward the building nestled in a grove of trees, isolated from the rest of the world. The entire complex was surrounded by a high stone wall with barbed wire coiled at the top. It was a goddamn prison and it gutted him that his Eve was in there. Treated like an animal. Worse than an animal.

It seemed an hour had passed, and maybe it had. He wasn't the only one simmering with impatience. His brothers and Nathan and Joe's entire team were twitchy with agitation.

"Chaps my ass that we have to take orders from that asshole," Skylar muttered. "He's not my goddamn boss."

Sam grinned beside Donovan. "I'm liking her a hell of a lot. I admit, I had doubts when I first hired her on, but I wanted to see what she was capable of. You have to admit, she's perfect. She has the delicate, harmless cheerleader look about her, but she'd remove your balls without remorse and then shove them down your throat after she broke your kneecaps."

Joe snorted, having overheard Sam's comment.

"Who would you put your money on in a bar fight? Her or P.J.?"

Donovan rolled his eyes at the juvenile comment.

Sam pretended thought, or maybe he was actually considering the ridiculous scenario. Garrett chuckled.

"My money is still on P.J. She's ruthless. And, well, she takes shit personally. Now more than ever. Not saying that's a bad thing. I've got her back and always will," Garrett added in a more serious tone. "Sky can separate her emotions and get the job done."

"She can still fight dirty," Sam added. "Which is why I like her. She's a good addition to the team. And not that this is the time or the place to discuss this, but I have someone lined up for Rio's team. He's down two men now and he can't continue operating that many short. But he gets the final say. I can recommend, but it's his team, and like Steele, they run them their way. I may sign their paychecks but I can hardly be considered their boss."

Garrett cocked an eyebrow. "Who's the guy?"

Sam smiled. "Not a guy. It's a woman. P.J. and Skylar have worked out well for us. I have a qualified candidate who came highly recommended. I think she'd be a good fit for Rio and his team. She's reclusive like they are. Doesn't say a whole lot, but she can kick ass with the best of them. She's a crack shot. She could take you down in hand to hand," he said to Garrett, ignoring his snort of disbelief. "She's also an expert in explosives. Specifically defusing bombs. She worked bomb squad for NYPD. Before that, she was in the army, a fact Nathan and Joe should appreciate. She's good and I want Rio to take a hard look at her. If I can drag him out of his fucking cave long enough."

"How long has it been?" Donovan demanded, impatient with the chitchat. He knew his brothers were only trying to distract him. Get his mind off the fact that just below, Eve's fate hung in the balance. And they were at the mercy of fucking Kyle Phillips and his black ops team.

And yeah, he had to hand it to the young Marine. He was badass in his own right. But he didn't have a personal stake in this. Donovan did.

On cue, Kyle's voice came over the com and Donovan covered his earpiece so he wouldn't miss a single word.

"It's clear. And Donovan, you need to get in here. East wing. Last room. Make it quick."

Donovan swayed, his heart nearly stopping. There was uncharacteristic concern in Kyle's voice. The man was a robot. Programmed to do the mission and only the mission. No emotion. No feelings. Just achieve the objective.

"Oh God," Donovan whispered even as he broke into a run, his brothers and the team running after him.

He burst through the doors, briefly took in the fact that the personnel were all on the floor, hands above their heads, facedown. He ignored them and got his bearings before sprinting down the hall of the east wing.

He ran through the open door and stopped dead at the sight that greeted him. Tears burned his eyes as he stared at Eve. Or what used to be Eve.

She was restrained in a straitjacket, sitting in a chair in the corner staring sightlessly out the tiny window that overlooked the back garden. Her hair was bedraggled. There was a bruise at the corner of her mouth and dried blood in a line down her chin. Her eyes were hollow and vacant and she was pale as death.

"I couldn't get her to respond," Kyle said quietly from where he stood a few feet from Eve. "She's not there. I don't know if she's checked out or if it's the meds they have her on, but something's not right. I didn't even get a flicker of response. She has no idea I'm even here. She just stares right through me."

Oh Jesus. He couldn't even muster relief over the fact she was alive. She might be breathing, but how much of her was left? Would she survive this? Would he ever get his Eve back?

"I want to know what the hell has been done to her," Donovan barked. "Get on it. I want whoever's in charge down here now, and I don't give a fuck what has to be done to make him talk."

Donovan walked quietly over to where Eve sat, still as a statue, her eyes focused on some distant point. For that matter, it didn't appear that she was seeing anything. She'd withdrawn into herself, a shield to reality.

He knelt in front of her and then saw the restraints, the fact that she was unable to move. Furious, he grabbed his knife, but Garrett was there and gripped Donovan's hand before he could flash the knife.

"Slow down, man," Garrett said quietly. "It might freak her out if you brandish a knife as pissed as you are. You talk to her. I'll cut her loose from behind."

Knowing his brother was right, Donovan shoved his knife back into the clasp on his belt, and then he reached up to gently touch Eve's face, hoping for some sign of recognition. But she didn't react to his touch. Didn't so much as flinch. Her eyes remained vacant. Empty. Lifeless.

Panic was starting to seize him and he shook uncontrollably. He wanted to weep like a baby, but he had to hold it together for Eve. She didn't need him to be a wreck. She needed him to be strong. Her rock. The only solid thing in her current existence.

Garrett quickly freed her and they unwrapped the straitjacket until she was finally free. Her arms hung limply at her sides. It was as if she were completely unaware that she was now free. Her gaze remained fixed on some distant point out the window.

"Eve," he said gently. "Eve, honey, it's me, Donovan. You're safe now. I've got you. Travis and Cammie are safe. Your stepfather is dead, honey. He can't hurt you anymore. You're free."

She didn't respond and his dread only increased. He wanted to yell at her. To shake her until she snapped out of it. But he wouldn't do any of those things because he'd never show her violence of any kind. She needed tenderness and gentleness and he'd give that to her and so much more. He'd give her his love and he'd never give her any reason to ever doubt that again.

Joe came back in, all but dragging a guy wearing a lab coat. It was obvious he was scared shitless and that Joe had put the fear of God in him. If that wasn't enough, Skylar immediately got into the man's face, and she looked damn scary. All cheerleader jokes aside, this was not a woman who looked harmless. She had death in her eyes and she flashed a wicked-looking blade in the man's face.

"You have two seconds to tell me what the fuck you did to her, or I start carving you up into tiny pieces. And it won't be quick and it won't be painless. I'll make you bleed and suffer, but you won't die. You'll only wish you had," Skylar spat.

The man went deathly white and it was obvious that whatever threat Joe had issued paled in comparison to the one Skylar just issued.

Donovan had to admit, Skylar in badass mode was pretty damn impressive. Edge just smirked, pride in his gaze as he watched Skylar in action. Swanny stood back, a half smile quirking his lips as he too watched with interest.

"She hasn't been harmed. Physically," he hastily amended. "She's been heavily sedated since her arrival. She came to us already medicated. She's been this way since she got here. We were told to keep her in lockdown mode and that she was a suicide threat and that we needed to keep her in restraints because she had violent tendencies and had injured others who cared for her in the past."

"What the fuck did you give her, and how much?" Donovan roared.

"I can give you her records," the man stammered. "Everything is documented. Her last dose was just half an hour ago and we were instructed by her physician to medicate her four times daily and to keep her in a state of sedation until he reevaluated her when he returned."

"Bullshit," Donovan growled. "Just who the hell is this physician who gave you orders? The fucker never planned to return. They wanted her kept like this."

"I'll give you every piece of information we have," the man said. "Just don't hurt my employees! They're innocent. They're just here to care for our patients."

"And yet you have so few," Skylar snarled. "This big-ass

private facility and you have, what, four patients? All undoubt-edly from wealthy families who pay you a hell of a lot of money to take care of their 'problems.' Am I right?"

Guilt flashed in his eyes, and Donovan knew Skylar was dead-on with her assessment.

"Donovan," Resnick quietly spoke up. "Take Eve and get her away from here. I'll handle things here. This will fall under federal jurisdiction. We'll shut it down and handle it through the proper channels so that this place is shut down and everyone involved will be arrested and held accountable for their actions. There's nothing for you to do here. You'll just muddy the waters. I'll make damn sure that Travis is in no way linked to Breckenridge's unfortunate death. Trust me to do this. I'll make it clean and you, Eve, Travis and KGI will not be remotely involved."

He was asking a hell of a lot, and Donovan burned with the need for revenge. For blood. He wanted to mete out pun-ishment on every fucker who'd been responsible for doing this to Eve. But Resnick was right. Eve was his first and only priority. Revenge had no place in his priorities right now.

Closing his eyes, he nodded his agreement. Then he care-fully cradled Eve in his arms, his heart breaking as she lay limply against him, her eyes never moving, her gaze never changing.

He hurried out of the facility, wishing he could burn it to the ground and take everyone in it down in flames. Ethan had slipped out, unnoticed by Donovan, and he was waiting in an SUV out front.

"Get to the airport so we can get the fuck out of here," Sam said, putting his hand on Donovan's shoulder. "The jet is fueled and ready to go. Nathan, Joe and Skylar will ride with you and Ethan. We'll be on your six. Get her on the plane and let's get the fuck home."

opposite Donovan and glanced up at his older brother, sympathy and understanding brimming in his eyes.

"Look, I know I can't say I know how you feel," Joe began. "I haven't been in love. I'm the only unattached brother, so I won't insult you by saying shit like I understand what you're going through. But I've seen it with every single one of you. I've been there when the worst has happened. She'll get through this, man. She's strong. She's a fighter."

"But she thinks I betrayed her," Donovan said painfully. "What reason does she have to snap out of it, to even respond to the man she believes in her heart and soul betrayed her, used her and lied to her? Look at her, man. She's gone. She's not here. She's checked out and I don't know if it's the meds they forced on her or if she's just checked out because her reality doesn't bear living."

"Remember how Shea was when we found her," Joe said gently. "Remember how out of it she was. How worried Nathan was that he'd lost her. That he'd never get her back. All Shea needed was time and his love. Our love. The support of her family. Our family. Eve needs that too. She'll get there, Van. She just needs you to surround her with your love. She needs to know you love her and that you'd never betray her. She'll pull out of this. Maren has already been called in and is waiting. She'll see what's to be done and if she needs more than Maren can provide. Whatever it is, we'll get it for her. With you and our family behind her, and with Cammie and Travis with her and Walt being out of the picture, she'll pull through this. She just needs time. Just like Shea needed time. But she'll get there. I believe that to my soul. I wouldn't just say shit to pacify you."

"I can't bear the thought of her thinking—knowing—that I did this to her," Donovan said hoarsely. "I'll never love another woman the way I love Eve. She's it for me, man. The one. I knew it from the first day I met her. And I should have been clearer. I should have laid it out to her, but I thought we had time. I was arrogant and convinced that I'd take Walt out, that it would be easy. That my plan to draw him out was going to be a piece of cake. I was so wrapped up in what I wanted that I didn't consider any other possibility but it going the way I wanted. And Eve paid for that. I should have been up front with her from the start. I was trying to shield her, and in doing so I made her believe that I threw her under the bus. All that shit about my weakness for women and children and especially children. Jesus, even I can see how bad that looks, how bad it sounds. I can understand why Eve thought what she thought because my entire family had recited those damning words for the world to hear. How must Eve have felt every time someone tagged on the *especially children*, as though she were some afterthought. Not as important as those kids when she's the heart and soul of it all."

"Stop torturing yourself," Joe said. "It's not doing you or her any good. Save it, man. Wrap her up in your love and support. Bring her home to Cammie and Travis. She'll pull through this. We won't entertain any other option. And you damn well know the Kellys are a stubborn, tenacious, overbearing lot and once we set our minds to something, come hell or high water, we're going to make it happen. She's family. She's one of us. And there's no way in hell any of us are giving up on her."

Donovan smiled, some of the agony easing. Just a bit.

"It's a hell of a note when my baby brother is kicking my dumb ass," Donovan muttered.

Joe grinned. "I'm savoring it. It may never happen again."

"Thanks," Donovan said sincerely. "I'm glad you and Nathan are out of the army and working with us. We weren't complete until you two joined. Now we're whole."

A shadow passed through Joe's eyes, and Donovan knew he was remembering how close they came to losing Nathan. Joe's twin.

"Just remember that I felt what Shea felt. That I had the same link to her that Nathan did. I saw what she saw, felt what she felt. And she went through hell. She was tortured and when we found her, she was a lifeless shell of her former self. But she came around, and so will Eve. Just give her time. If all they did was keep her drugged, then that's something that can be overcome."

Donovan gently thumbed the shadow of a bruise on Eve's mouth and the dried blood at her lip. "Someone hit her. And if they hit her once, who's to say they didn't hurt her in other ways? We may never know what she endured. Even if she comes around, she may never remember all that happened to her."

"Maybe that's for the best," Joe said quietly. "Some things are better left unremembered. All she needs to know is that she's loved and she's safe. The past doesn't matter any longer."

Donovan nodded. "You're right. I know you're right. But goddamn it, I want to shed the blood of every single motherfucker who had a part in doing this to her. And to leave it all to Resnick? It's the hardest thing I've ever had to do in my life."

"And the most selfless," Joe said. "You walked away because that's what Eve needed. She needs you. And so instead of getting revenge, you walked away because Eve needed you. You did the right thing, Van. Don't ever think otherwise."

Donovan gathered Eve close in his arms, closing his eyes as he pressed his lips to her forehead.

"Come back to me," he whispered. "Come back to me so I can tell you I love you. So I can tell you I love you every single day of our lives from this point forward."

CHAPTER 43

THE moment Donovan walked into his home, carrying Eve and flanked by Travis, who had hovered the moment they exited the plane, Cammie launched herself from Sophie's lap where they'd been sitting on the sofa and ran toward Donovan and Travis.

Travis immediately scooped her up, hugging her fiercely, but Cammie's gaze was on Eve, her eyes rounded in fear.

"Evie?" Cammie whispered. "What's wrong with Evie?"

She glanced at Donovan, tears filling her big eyes.

"She's okay, sweetheart," Donovan said, hoping God forgave that lie. "She's just sleeping. She's very, very tired and we must let her rest."

Maren walked forward, her forehead creased in concern.

"Not here," Donovan said in a low voice. "I'll take her in the bedroom."

As he spoke, he glanced toward Sophie, sending her a silent message to distract Cammie.

"Stay here with Cammie," Donovan said to Travis. "She needs the reassurance. I know you're worried about Eve, but

Maren will see to her and I'll let you know the moment anything changes."

Travis didn't look happy with the dictate, but he didn't
argue. Instead he turned on a bright smile for Cammie.

"I missed you, little bit. How about we go play with Cece
and her toys?"

Cammie looked doubtful, but at Donovan's urging, she
complied and slid from Travis's grasp only to grab his hand
and tug him toward the makeshift play area Sophie had constructed for the girls.

Donovan quickly carried Eve into his bedroom and gently laid her on the bed. Her eyes were closed now, where
before they'd remained open and vacant. Lifeless. Utterly
lifeless. But now she slept, and he found more comfort in
that, that perhaps she was at peace for a few moments at
least, than for her to be awake and unaware, in some private
hell that only she could feel.

He'd take it from her in a heartbeat. He'd take her pain,
her suffering, her grief and anger and he'd shoulder it all if
only he could have her back. Whole. The Eve he knew and
had grown to love more fiercely than he'd imagined ever
being able to love a woman.

He knew love existed. He knew it was a precious thing
indeed. He saw how his brothers and his team leaders were
with their wives. But did they feel the all-consuming emotion that Donovan felt? Could what he felt possibly compare
to what his brothers shared with their wives? He found it
hard to believe, but he supposed his brothers would argue
that point. They'd all take on whatever hurts their wives suffered. They'd die for them with no hesitation. There was no
sacrifice too large or too difficult to make for them.

Love was a multifaceted, painful, joyful, fulfilling and
frightening-as-hell thing.

It made a man vulnerable. It opened him up to unimagi-
nable hurts and agony. But it also gifted him with something
more powerful than anything else in the world. The love of
a woman was the most precious gift a man would ever
receive. And Donovan would never take it for granted. If he

was able to win Eve back, win her trust and her love, he'd treasure it forever. And he'd never give her cause to doubt him again. If it took the rest of his life, he would make up the hurt he'd caused her.

Maren was reading over the medical reports they had taken from the hospital, her frown deepening the more she read. Then she tossed aside the papers in disgust and went to Eve's bedside, doing a thorough examination. She gently pried open Eve's eyes and shone a penlight, checking her pupils. Then she took her vitals, listened to her respirations, counting them silently, her lips moving, the only sign that she was keeping count.

When she finished she sighed and turned to Donovan.

"They've turned her into a vegetable," she said, her eyes shiny with tears. And hatred. "Skylar told me of the journal that was found in the cabin and Walt's entry that he planned to punish Eve if she resisted his advances. If she refused his plans for her. In an odd way, he found the idea of forcing himself on her repugnant. The asshole thought Eve should feel honored that Walt wanted her in his bed, as his mistress. So if she resisted, and it's obvious that she did, he planned to institutionalize her for a time. Keep her heavily sedated and then he'd visit after she had time to come off the medication and be lucid enough to choose. Continued existence as a lifeless vegetable in restraints. Or agree to his demands to share his bed and allow him to control every aspect of her life."

"He was deranged," Donovan bit out. He was seething with fury, but at the same time he was grateful that she hadn't been sexually abused. Not that the abuse she'd endured was somehow better. But at least she hadn't been physically harmed.

"In some ways this is worse than if he'd raped her," Maren said quietly, accurately reading Donovan's thoughts. "He didn't rape her body, but he very much raped her mind. He robbed her of her choices, her sanity. He stripped her of everything. Her self-worth, her very being. I truly believe she may well have recovered sooner from a physical rape than she will from this kind of rape."

"Will she recover?" Donovan asked hoarsely. "What did

they give her, Maren? I need the truth here. Don't go easy. I need to know. Did they damage her mind permanently? Will she ever be normal again?"

"Sit down," Maren said gently, pulling at Donovan's arm until he sat in the chair by the bed.

"They kept her heavily drugged, from what I've been able to ascertain, and believe me when I say this was no legitimate medical facility so the records are spotty at best and vague. They gave her psychotropic drugs at regular intervals. Far too regular. Four times daily, and she was already heavily drugged when she arrived. Some medications like Thorazine have a longer half-life, and it could take days to fully rid her body of its effects. If we got lucky and they gave her a drug with a shorter half-life, it's possible she'll come around sooner. There's simply no way to know."

She paused as if to let her diagnosis settle in. Then she continued, her eyes filled with sympathy as she stared at Donovan. She reached for his hand, squeezing it, offering comfort.

"There's also the factor that she may not want to come back. That maybe she's retreated to a place where she feels no pain, no betrayal."

Donovan flinched, and the blood drained from his face.

"I don't say this to hurt you," she said. "But it has to be acknowledged. She thinks you betrayed her. She thinks that you don't love her and that your only concern is for Travis and Cammie. In a way, the drugs were probably a blessing to her because it numbed her. She isn't feeling anything. She doesn't know anything. She isn't cognizant of her surroundings and she likely welcomes that. Her mind is protecting her from her hurt and her very real fear of her stepfather and what he'll eventually do to her."

"What can I do?" Donovan asked helplessly.

Tears burned the edges of his eyes. He blinked and it was like rubbing sand in his eyes. His emotions were raw. His heart was shattered. It was his fault Eve was like this. It was his fault this had happened. If only he'd done things differently. If only he hadn't been so determined to shield her.

He'd made the biggest mistake of his life by not trusting in her. He didn't deserve her trust because he hadn't offered it in return. He hadn't wanted her to know anything of his plans. Stupidly, he'd thought he could fix the problem with her none the wiser and then present her with a fait accompli and they'd live happily ever after.

He, the smart one, the supposed brains of the entire operation.

He was the biggest dumbass in the world. He'd been thinking with his heart instead of using his greatest asset. Not his physical strength. Not his training. His intelligence. His mind. And Eve had paid dearly for his fuckup.

"You can't torture yourself, Van," Maren said quietly. "It does neither you nor her any good. You have to be strong for her. You have to make her want to come back. You have to convince her that you love her, that you didn't betray her. And you have to be patient and wait for as long as it takes for her to want to crawl out of the hole she's buried herself in. Because there, she's safe. Nothing can hurt her. But the real world? That can destroy her and she well knows it."

"So I just sit here and do nothing," Donovan said bitterly.

"No," Maren refuted. "You talk to her. Surround her with her family. You, Travis, and Cammie. Be persistent. Don't allow her to crawl back into that shell once the medication starts to wear off and she becomes more aware of her surroundings. Then more than ever is when you have to press. Because when the medication wears off and she doesn't have that balm, she'll retreat in other ways. The mind is a very intricate thing and it will go to great lengths to protect itself. If you allow it, she'll find a way to retreat even without the medication. So you surround her with your love. With Cammie and Travis's love. Present a united front. Show her that you're family. The four of you. And don't treat her gently, Van. I know your instinct will be to baby her. You won't want to cause her any distress. You'll back off at the first sign that she's upset. But you can't do that. You have to show her tough love and bully her if that's what it takes."

"And make her hate me more than she already does," Donovan said bleakly.

"No. You show her how very much you love her by not letting her go."

Donovan scrubbed a hand through his hair and Maren hugged him tightly.

"She'll get through this, Van. Just like Shea did. Nathan went through hell. He wondered a hundred times during the time Shea was recovering if he'd ever get her back. But love did it. His love. He didn't give up, and neither will you. And just like Shea found her way back to Nathan, so too will Eve find her way back to you and Travis and Cammie. With three people who love her as much as y'all do, how can she not? Not to mention the rest of us. We're a force to be reckoned with, as Shea can attest," she added with a laugh. Then her expression grew more serious. "I love you dearly, Van. I love you all. Even before I married Steele, you were my family even though I have a family of my own whom I love fiercely. I will be here if you need me. All you have to do is call. No matter what time, day or night. Steele and I both will be here. I hope you know that."

Donovan hugged her back, burying his face in her hair and just holding on as grief washed through him. She squeezed back hard, as if she knew just how tenuous his grip on his control was.

"I love you too," Donovan said gruffly. "And thank you, Maren. It seems you've had a hand in saving all our asses at one time or another, but this is different. This is my life. More important than any mission I've ever gone on or ever will."

She smiled and cupped his jaw as she drew away. "Be strong for her, Van. And tough. Don't baby her. Just love her and be there when she finally breaks. Because she will break. It'll get worse before it gets better. When the medication wears off and she comes back to her reality and remembers everything, she'll break and you'll have to be here to pick up the pieces and help her through it by loving her and convincing her of that love."

"Thanks," Donovan said again.

Maren walked away and Donovan turned his attention back to Eve's bedside where she slept, seemingly peaceful. But he knew that underneath it all, nightmares lurked. And sleep was the only thing keeping hell at bay.

CHAPTER 44

EVE struggled from the heavy fog that enveloped her like a blanket. It was odd. She didn't feel as . . . She struggled with what word to describe it. But she felt lighter somehow. Her veins didn't feel as though mud sludged through them, weighting her down and making her senseless and unaware. Where was she?

She grappled with her memory, trying to piece together anything that made . . . sense.

Bits and pieces came back to her like random photos flashing on a video monitor. Walt. His threats. And then nothing. She remembered staring sightlessly from a small window to a garden that badly needed tending. The sun hurting her eyes and her shutting them, only wanting to escape her reality.

But now? She opened her eyes, puzzled by how difficult a task it was, and when she did all she saw was white. It took her a moment to realize she was lying flat on her back and she was staring up at the ceiling. Then she became aware of the low murmur of voices.

Was it them? Were they coming back to put her back into the fog? She tried to summon a protest, not wanting the numbness any longer. At first it had been welcome. But why? She couldn't remember why she preferred the sense of nothingness.

"Evie? Evie, are you awake?"

Cammie! Dear God, had they taken Cammie too?

And then it all came crashing back, exploding into her mind. Everything. Donovan's betrayal. Walt forcing her vehicle off the road. The plane trip and Walt taking her to his cabin. His demands. His threats. His promise that no matter what, he'd have Travis and Cammie back with or without her cooperation. She'd left Travis and Cammie with Donovan, fully believing that no matter his feelings for her—that she didn't matter—that he at least cared for her siblings and that he would protect them. Had she been wrong about that just as she'd been wrong about so much else?

She had to break away from the hold of the fog slowly trying to envelop her once more. She had to protect Cammie. She'd do it. Whatever Walt wanted. If he'd only promise to let Cammie go.

She let out a moan of anguish and she licked her lips, trying to speak, puzzled over the raspy sound that came out in its stead.

"I'll do it," she finally managed to get out. "I'll do whatever you want. I'll do it. But you have to promise to give Cammie back. I'll be whatever you want."

Tears choked her words and she realized they were sliding endlessly down her cheeks. Everything she had done had been for nothing. All the running, the endless worry, the sacrifices she'd made and been prepared to make. It didn't matter because in the end Walt had won after all.

And then to her utter shock, Donovan appeared, his face just over hers, and even more bewildering were the tears sliding down his cheeks, grief and sorrow swamping his eyes.

He touched her face, trying to wipe the tears that ran in a never-ending river. She had no control over them. She'd lost everything that mattered. But how? Why was he here? Where was she?

"Darling Eve," he choked out. "My God, Eve. Honey, you're safe. Cammie is safe. Travis is safe. They're both here and very anxious to see you. Would you like that? They've been very worried about you. *I've* been worried about you."

She nodded eagerly, her ability to speak around the flood of tears knotting her throat utterly gone.

Cammie crawled cautiously onto the bed and then Travis pushed past Donovan, who stood back to allow Travis access to her. She stared up at her brother and sister and she wept.

Cammie hugged her on one side and Travis hugged her on the other. Her arms felt encased in lead, but she managed to lift them and wrap them solidly around her siblings, reveling in the feel of them so warm and alive. Safe. Donovan had said they were safe. They were all safe.

"Don't cry, Evie," Travis said in a tortured voice that betrayed his own tears. "Everything is okay now. You're back. You're going to be all right. Please don't cry. We're okay. All of us. Walt is dead. He can't hurt us anymore. He can't hurt *you* anymore."

She clung desperately to her brother and sister, not wanting to let go in case this was a product of the drugs that had been forced on her. Was it all just a bizarre manifestation of her heart's desire? Had she conjured them up and it was all just a hallucination? A trick of the medication?

"You're real," she choked out. "You're here. Oh my God, I was so worried. I thought . . . I thought he had you," she said tearfully.

Cammie patted her cheek and then wiped away more of the tears that Eve couldn't manage to stop.

"Don't cry, Evie," Cammie said, echoing Travis's plea. "We can be a family now. A real family. Van said so. Though he said I can call him Daddy and I want to. Can I, Evie? Can I call him Daddy and you Mama?"

"Oh, darling," Eve whispered. "I love you so very much. But . . ."

She closed her eyes unable to voice what was uppermost on her mind. She couldn't destroy Cammie's illusions. It would be cruel.

"Cammie, Travis, can you give me a moment with Eve? There's a lot I need to explain to her. Go into the living room with Rachel and Sophie. You can come back in just a bit. I promise."

Cammie kissed Eve's cheek and then smiled her sweet smile. "Van will make it all better. He promised."

And then she bounced off the bed and Travis took her hand to lead her out of what Eve now realized was Donovan's bedroom. They were in his home. In Tennessee. Miles away from where she'd been . . . She didn't even realize how long she'd been there, or how long she'd been here, for that matter.

Donovan eased onto the bed, enfolding her hand in his. He was shaking, she realized. He looked utterly undone, nothing like the calm, composed man he'd always presented. His eyes were haunted and he looked grief-stricken.

As more of the haze cleared, she took a better look at him and winced at what she saw. He looked haggard. Like he hadn't slept in days. He was unshaven, his clothing rumpled. He looked like he was hungover after going on one hell of a bender.

"I don't understand what happened," she said helplessly. "How did I get here? Why am I here? Travis said Walt was dead. How?"

Donovan stroked her cheek, almost as if reassuring himself that she was here and awake and seemingly well. For a man who professed not to care about her, he looked weak with relief to see her.

"There is so much I need to say to you," he choked out. "But I don't want to overburden you. You've been out of it for three days. Three of the longest days of my life. And if you aren't feeling up to this, if you want to rest, then it'll wait. But Eve, I cannot let you suffer the misapprehension you're under for a minute longer."

Her brow furrowed as she struggled to make sense of his impassioned words. She tried to sit up but found she lacked the strength to do so. She looked down in confusion, almost expecting to still be in restraints. But no, her arms had been free. She'd held her brother and sister in her arms, though the effort had cost her considerably.

She did want to drift back into the void. She wanted to float in the sea of nothingness where reality didn't intrude.

And now that she knew Cammie and Travis were safe, that Walt was no longer a threat, she merely wanted to be away from the truth.

But wait. He'd said he didn't want her to suffer the misapprehension she was under. What did it mean?

"What is it you want, Eve?" Donovan asked, concern burning in his eyes.

"Can you help me sit up?" she asked, shamed that she couldn't even perform this one small task.

"Of course. But be careful. I don't want you to overdo it."

He gently lifted her forward with one arm and then stuffed several pillows behind her back so she was propped up and comfortable. Then he eased her back and she nearly sighed in relief at the comfort of the feather pillows surrounding her like the softest cloud.

"I don't understand any of this," she said, still feeling as though she were in some bizarre alternate reality. "You said . . ." She broke off, tears welling again as grief hit her square in the chest.

Donovan scooted closer to her until their bodies were touching, and he gathered her hands in his, leaning forward until their foreheads touched in an intimate manner.

"I never betrayed you, Eve. You have to know that before you know anything else. I love you. I love you with every part of me. There isn't a single part of me that isn't solidly, madly in love with you. And I will live with regret for what you suffered as a result of you overhearing an out-of-context snippet of conversation for the rest of my life."

She looked at him in puzzlement, hope unfurling despite her efforts to pull it back.

"It was a setup," he explained. "A plan to draw your stepfather out. I was so arrogant. Thought I had it all planned out and he'd just fall into my lap and I'd take him down and you and I would live happily ever after with Travis and Cammie."

"But I heard you say that I was mentally unstable, that I was a danger to Travis and Cammie and that you were offering me in exchange for Travis and Cammie, that Walt wanted revenge and that he'd have it if you turned me over to him."

She could barely get the words out as pain, fresh and vivid, flashed in her mind. More and more came back to her as the fog lifted, forcing her to face reality.

He closed his eyes, his forehead still pressed to hers. She felt his sigh, the soft expulsion of breath over her mouth. It was a sound laden with sadness and regret. Had she been wrong? Had she horribly misjudged him? Had she been too quick to convict him? Should she have confronted him?

There were so many what ifs that it made her head spin.

"It was part of the plan. I was working out the details," Donovan said in an aching voice. "It was what I planned to tell Walt. To sell him on the fact that you didn't matter to me. That my only concern was for the children. I told him that I was concerned that you needed psychiatric help and would benefit from being under a doctor's care. I acted as though I didn't know what an asshole he was, and I was playing the part of a concerned citizen by turning you over to him so you'd receive the help you needed. And I told him that once I was assured that you were no longer a threat to them that I would be willing to send Travis and Cammie back to him. I had hoped that he'd incriminate himself. That he would be enraged that I was holding his children hostage for all practical purposes. But he got to you first and then met with me and agreed to every single one of my stipulations, and I knew then that something was wrong. He was too smug. Too self-assured. And completely unbothered by the fact that I was keeping his children from him. And it turns out I was right because he already had you, and he left straight from our meeting and took you away from me and straight into hell."

He went silent, and she realized he was valiantly trying to regain his composure. The words had been torn from him, choked, shaky, so filled with emotion that she couldn't possibly doubt his sincerity.

"I'll never forgive myself for that," Donovan whispered. "For what you endured. For making you doubt me even for a moment. I should have told you I loved you. I should have told you I wanted forever with you instead of being vague and talking about being a family. It's little wonder you were so willing to believe the worst because I didn't give you reason to expect anything else from me. But Eve, you're my life. My world. Yes, I love Travis and Cammie, and yes, I want us to be a family. But not without you. You are the heart and soul of this family—our family. Without you, none of us are whole. Not me, not Travis and not Cammie. I want those kids, Eve. Don't ever doubt it. But I want you. Heart and soul. Body and mind. I want to have children with you. To provide brothers and sisters for Travis and Cammie. I want us to be a family."

"Oh Donovan," she whispered, so overcome that his name was all she could say.

His mouth found hers in the most tender of kisses. So gentle and reverent. And so very loving. How could she have doubted him? How could she not have known? Had she been so insecure that she'd been just waiting for the cards to fall and for the bottom to fall out? Had she been so unwilling to believe that such goodness and love existed that she'd just bided her time, believing all the while that it couldn't possibly be real?

The answer to all of those questions was yes.

"I'm so sorry," she choked out.

He lifted his head to frame her face in his palms. His eyes were fierce, blazing with intensity.

"You will never apologize to me, Eve. Never. I won't have it. I should be on my knees begging you for forgiveness, and if you'll give me the chance, I'll spend the rest of my life proving to you that no one will ever love you more than I do. No one will ever cherish you more than I. And I will never give you cause to regret placing your trust in me."

She couldn't even form a coherent response. There was so much she wanted to say but knew she didn't have a prayer of getting it all out. Tears coursed down her cheeks, colliding with his hands.

"Please tell me those are tears of joy or even relief," Donovan begged. "Anything but sadness, Eve. You've had far too much sadness in your life and I only want you to be happy from now on. And I want to be the person who makes you happy. I'll do whatever it takes to make you smile again."

She smiled back at him, shaky, but she poured every ounce of the joy welling in her soul into her smile so he would know, so he would have no doubt.

He caressed her face with both hands, back and forth, wiping away the tears as his expression grew even more serious.

"Can you ever love me, Eve? Do I have a chance at making you love me even half as much as I love you?"

"Oh God, Donovan," she said raggedly. "I do love you. So very much. I have loved you. Almost from the start. I knew the night we made love, that very first time, but I was so very afraid to hope. I worried that it was too soon, that I was too caught up in the moment and I was afraid to tell you because I wasn't sure of your feelings. And then when I heard . . ."

"Shhh," he said, warmth and answering joy lighting his eyes. "We've already covered what you heard and I want you to forget it. I realize you won't just forget it and that it will still hurt you when you think about it, but when you do I want you to remember one thing. That I love you and that I want us to have a long life together filled with love, laughter and happiness. And that I want Travis and Cammie to be a part of that and any other children you and I have down the road. But for now, I'm perfectly content with the family we have. More children can wait until both Travis and Cammie are secure enough in our love for them and each other."

"Will you hold me?" Eve asked. "I'm so very tired, but I'm so afraid that I'll wake up and this will have all been a dream. I'm afraid to go to sleep because I don't want to lose you and Travis and Cammie."

Donovan turned sideways so he was nestled against her on the bed. He reached down and pulled the covers over both of them, and then he enfolded her tenderly in his embrace. He pressed a kiss to her forehead and then whispered something that Eve could swear was a prayer. A thank-you to God for giving him back his family.

"Sleep, my darling Eve," he said, his voice filled with love. "I'll be here when you wake and every other time you wake. You'll never be alone again."

EPILOGUE

IT was Friday night, and the entire Kelly family was gathered in the football stadium of the local high school. A cool breeze blew through the stands, and Donovan curled his arm more tightly around Eve to shield her from the chill.

A cool front had burst through, dropping the temperatures from warm to unseasonably cold. Though it was only the second weekend in September, already fall was forcing its way through, beating back the sultry temperatures of summer. A welcome relief from the hotter than normal weather this summer had brought. A summer that had changed Donovan's life forever.

"There's Trav!"

Cammie's excited squeal made the entire Kelly clan focus their attention on the field where the home team had just burst through the blow-up tunnel in the end zone. The cheerleaders lined each side of the tunnel as the football players ran for the sidelines.

Donovan smiled as Travis—*his son*—loped toward the bench and then wound up in the middle of a pile of players as they jumped on each other's backs, hooping and hollering. Eve grabbed his hand and squeezed.

He glanced down at his wife. His *wife*. He'd never get tired of those two words. *My wife*. It still gutted him to remember how close he'd come to losing her. It wasn't something he could even dwell on, because it still had the power to bring him to his knees.

He squeezed her back and savored the joy on her face. Her eyes were suspiciously wet, gleaming with tears. Happy tears. If she never shed one out of sadness again it would be too soon for him.

"He looks so grown up," Eve whispered, emotion knotting her voice.

He leaned down so he could hear her above the roar.

Travis disentangled himself from the pile of players and walked further down the sideline. Then he turned, searching the stands. The entire Kelly family stood, cheering and waving madly. Travis's face split into a broad grin and he waved back just as enthusiastically. He'd been awestruck that every single Kelly was attending his game. Their acceptance in turns bewildered and overwhelmed him. But he soaked up every bit of it. He and Cammie both.

"I want to wave at Trav!" Cammie protested.

Donovan reached down and hauled her up to his shoulders, and she nearly shook herself off her perch waving at her brother.

All of them were here. Every single Kelly was present and accounted for.

Rachel, Ethan and the twins, though both boys, wiggling bundles of pure boy excitement, were firmly held. Charlotte had wedged herself between Cammie and Eve, while Donovan sat on Cammie's other side.

Garrett and Sarah were present, as were Sam and Sophie. The women sported tiny pregnancy bumps, a fact that delighted both their husbands to no end. Nathan and Shea were smiling and enjoying the evening. Swanny and Joe were also there, as was Sean. The only one not there was Rusty. She'd hated missing Travis's first home football game, but the drive back from Knoxville was an undertaking, and she had early Monday morning classes to attend.

Even Skylar and Edge were present, all wanting to show their support for Donovan's family.

Life was good.

As they stood for the national anthem and raising of the flag, Donovan's hand found Eve's and he squeezed, his heart about to burst from his chest. When a moment of silence was asked for, Donovan whispered a prayer of thanks that his family was safe. Back where they belonged. It was all he'd ever ask for. This. Being surrounded by them. Their love.

When they retook their seats, Eve turned and smiled at Donovan, joy lighting her eyes. So much had happened in the last months. Eve's uncertain, winding road back home. The worry that he'd never fully have her back, heart and mind. But he shouldn't have worried. His wife was a resilient, kick-ass, never-give-up woman. Just like all his sisters-in-law. She fit in as naturally as all his sisters-in-law had.

"Look at my grandchild!" Marlene said, pride evident in her voice as Travis took his place on the field.

Eve's smile broadened, delight crossing her face at Marlene's words.

Things hadn't been easy. They'd had a lot to overcome. All of them. Travis had dealt—was still dealing—with guilt over killing his father, even though the bastard deserved it and far worse. Eve had her own issues to deal with. And Cammie's nightmares of her father still plagued her sleep, made worse by the fact that Travis and Eve were obviously so troubled by their own separate hells.

The little girl had soaked up all the turmoil and made it her own.

But through it all, one thing had remained constant. Donovan didn't allow a single day to pass where he didn't tell his wife how much he loved her. He never let a day go by where he didn't assure Travis and Cammie that he loved them and very much wanted them to be a permanent part of his and Eve's family.

Even now he and Eve were pursuing legal adoption of them both. He wanted his children to bear his name—their name. The Kelly name and all the love and support that name entailed. He couldn't wait for the court date. They were going to have one hell of a backyard barbecue the minute those kids were legally his. And every single Kelly would be there to celebrate the event.

Travis and Cammie already called him "Dad," a fact that made him absurdly happy. And while Cammie called Eve "Mom" half the time, Travis was too used to calling Eve "Evie." And it didn't matter to Eve. She was just glad to have her family safe. Whole.

Eve's sleep was fractured by nightmares from time to time, though they'd gotten better in the last weeks. Donovan made sure that she slept in his arms and that he was always there to gently wake her from the agony of those dreams. He made love to her, whispering his love and that he would always be there.

He'd taken much needed time away from KGI when Eve returned. He hadn't wanted to leave her, even for a night. Nathan and Joe's team had taken more of the load and he—and his brothers—were impressed by their efforts.

Even Rio and Steele were impressed, though they didn't always like taking a backseat to the new team. But KGI was a well-oiled machine. With three teams now actively taking a roll, their organization had expanded to take on more missions—righteous missions. And Donovan's sisters-in-law had begun taking part in the administration, not that he or his brothers would ever allow them to take a dangerous role. But they helped out, devoting many hours to helping other women. He was so damn proud of them all, and especially Eve for wanting to help others in need. Just as she'd once been in need. As had all his sisters-in-law.

Everything was . . . perfect. No more waiting for the other shoe to drop. No fears of it all falling apart. His family was together. KGI was flourishing, even with Donovan in a more administrative role lately.

Eventually he'd go back to full time. But he was in no

hurry, because for the first time in his life, he had something that took priority over his career.

For now? He was perfectly content to allow others to take the lead so he could spend time on what mattered to him most. Eve. And their children.

He pulled Eve to him, squishing Cammie and Charlotte between them. He hugged her into his side and pressed a kiss to her temple.

"I love you," he murmured.

She smiled, her entire face lighting up.

"I love you too, Donovan."

"Look at our boy," he said, pride reflected in his voice.

"I know," Eve said, her smile as broad as his own. "This is where he belongs. In school. Doing what other teenage boys do. Playing sports. Not worrying about anything other than making good grades. It's what I always wanted for him."

Donovan smiled at the wistfulness in her tone and squeezed her again, despite complaints from the girls that he was "squishing" them.

"Where he belongs is with us, honey. We're a family now. And though I one day hope to have more children with you, in my heart, Travis and Cammie will always be our first."

"I want that too," she whispered, her eyes shining with love. "I want a lot of children, Donovan. I hope you don't mind. I want a houseful. I want to give them everything I never had. What Travis and Cammie never had until now."

"No complaints from me," Donovan said, satisfaction gripping him. "I want as many as you're willing to have. I'm going to warn you now, the picture of you pregnant and swollen with my child? Pretty heady stuff. If I have my way, you'll be nothing *but* barefoot and pregnant for the next ten years or so."

She laughed, the sound warm and vibrant, carrying through the stands. Other members of his family glanced down, delighted smiles on their faces. Their gazes were filled with love and understanding. They knew all too well the winding road she'd traveled to where she was now. And they were all as thrilled and overjoyed as he was that she was happy. Safe. Loved.

His mom looked at him then, tears glittering in her eyes. With all the love of a mother. She told him without words, with just a look, how happy she was that he'd found the love of his life.

"I don't know about the next ten years," Eve said cautiously, her lips still turned up in a grin. "But I wouldn't say no to the next five at least. Think we could manage as many as your mom and dad did?"

"As long as you promise to give me girls," Donovan said, contentment filling his heart as he imagined a houseful of daughters with Eve's beauty and smile.

"I'm beginning to see why y'all built a compound," Eve said in amusement as she directed her gaze once more to the playing field.

The crowd erupted in cheers when Travis carried the ball into the end zone. The Kellys high-fived all around and Eve was slapped on the back by more than one of Donovan's brothers.

"That's my boy!" Donovan shouted, pride filling every corner of his heart. "Our boy," he added, hugging Eve to his side.

Eve's eyes filled with tears. She looked so happy she could burst.

As they retook their seats, Donovan glanced over. "What did you mean about the compound?"

She laughed, her eyes lighting with mischief. "With all the girls you and your brothers are producing, or plan to produce, you're going to *need* a high-security complex to protect them from all the boys!"

Donovan's scowl was instantaneous. "Damn right," he growled. "No way in hell some snot-nosed punk is going to come around my daughters."

Eve grinned and then leaned into Donovan's side, emitting a contented sigh as he wrapped his arm around her.

"I'm so happy, Donovan," she said in a low voice he almost didn't hear.

He kissed the top of her head and squeezed her a little tighter.

"I'm happy that you're happy, honey. More than I can ever tell you. You mean the world to me. You, Travis and Cammie. I hope you know that."

She turned, tilting her head up so she could stare into his eyes.

"I do know. I love you so much. I never dreamed I'd find such happiness. Such a *home*."

The yearning in her voice nearly undid him. He wanted so much to wrap her in his arms, take her home and make love to her the entire night. But for now he contented himself with being here, with his entire family, watching his son excel on the football field.

"You'll always be home with me. And home for me is wherever you are. No matter where life takes us, as long as we're together, it's all I'll ever ask for."

She leaned up and kissed him. A soft kiss that contained all the sweetness that was her. He closed his eyes, savoring this moment, one of the many to come in their lifetimes.

Everything he'd ever wished for. Had dreamed of, wanted, yearned for. It was all in his arms.

No longer did he envy his brothers all they had, because Donovan had everything he could ever hope for. A beautiful, loving wife. Children. The hope of more in the future. It was all his.

He glanced down the bleachers at all of his family gathered to support Travis. He caught Joe's gaze and grinned evilly. Joe rolled his eyes because he well knew what that look was for. With Donovan firmly ensnared, Joe was the only remaining Kelly-born brother who was still single. And that made him a wanted man. His mother had already pinned him down and pointed out that he was the only son not to give her a daughter-in-law and grandchildren.

"Never," Joe mouthed.

Donovan just smiled, because never was a damn long time.